THE
PARIS
AFFAIR

THE PARIS AFFAIR

MAUREEN MARSHALL

GRAND
CENTRAL
New York Boston

Grand Central Publishing
Hachette Book Group
1290 Avenue of the Americas, New York, NY 10104
grandcentralpublishing.com
@grandcentralpub

First Edition: May 2024

Grand Central Publishing is a division of Hachette Book Group, Inc. The Grand
Central Publishing name and logo is a registered trademark of
Hachette Book Group, Inc.

The publisher is not responsible for websites (or their content) that are not
owned by the publisher.

The Hachette Speakers Bureau provides a wide range of authors for speaking events.
To find out more, go to hachettespeakersbureau.com or
email HachetteSpeakers@hbgusa.com.

Grand Central Publishing books may be purchased in bulk for business, educational,
or promotional use. For information, please contact your local bookseller or the
Hachette Book Group Special Markets Department at special.markets@hbgusa.com.

Print book interior design by Taylor Navis

Library of Congress Cataloging-in-Publication Data

Names: Marshall, Maureen, author.
Title: The Paris affair / Maureen Marshall.
Description: First edition. | New York : Grand Central Publishing, 2024.
Identifiers: LCCN 2023040974 | ISBN 9781538757802 (trade paperback) |
ISBN 9781538757819 (ebook)
Subjects: LCGFT: Romance fiction. | Queer fiction. | Novels.
Classification: LCC PS3613.A7752 P37 2024 | DDC 813/.6—dc23/eng/20230914
LC record available at https://lccn.loc.gov/2023040974

ISBNs: 9781538757802 (trade paperback), 9781538757819 (ebook)

Printed in the United States of America

LSC-C

Printing 1, 2024

To my lovely friend Laura Floyd Deck, who gifts enormous emotional resources to abandoned boxers (dogs, not cast-aside underwear or athletes) and friends alike. You are amazing.

THE
PARIS
AFFAIR

1

I ought to be jealous of the tower. She is more famous than I am.

—Gustave Eiffel

Late August 1886
Paris

The door to my flat clicked shut behind me, and I eyed the worn green carpeting in the narrow hall with long-held resentment. Apparently, I wasn't worth the cost of refurbishment when the rest of the building had been done the previous year.

Not that I could waste energy on worrying over that at the moment. I hurried down the winding stairs to the bottom floor.

"Monsieur Tighe." The concierge, Mademoiselle Jeunesse, blocked the path to the glass-plated vestibule. She lived in a ground floor apartment, ideal to manage the comings and goings of the tenants. Perhaps it was uncharitable, but her narrow-faced glare always felt to me as though she was spying. I twisted the handkerchief in my pocket. Using it to wipe away the perspiration dotting my brow would give away my anxiety. *Not now, damn it. I'm late already.*

"Bonsoir, Mademoiselle."

She stayed firm in her spot, as though daring me to push past her. The red-papered walls of the foyer went claustrophobic. Had I—or more likely my cousin and flatmate Aurélie—committed some transgression? Mademoiselle Jeunesse's lips thinned as she took in the untied cravat that hung limply around my neck. I'd forgotten to pick up the laundry in my rush to make it home to change before the performance and was reduced to reusing a crumpled one.

Damned Eiffel, keeping us late on this evening of all evenings. I was an engineer, not a lapdog. I needed to get to the ballet to watch Aurélie's debut, and Mademoiselle Jeunesse was one of the last people with whom I'd choose to speak even when I wasn't embarking on a mad dash.

The image of how my father in all his smug superiority would behave in this situation flickered in my mind's eye, and I squared my shoulders, looking down my nose at her, recapturing my inner poise. "Is there something you wish to discuss?"

Her eyes dropped to the floor. "I merely wondered if you'd be on time with your rent this month."

My mouth dried even though it wasn't due yet. The flash of movement through the filtered glass reminded me that I had seconds to catch the omnibus. I straightened the button placket of my splendid—and egregiously expensive—new waistcoat and gave her a curt nod as though dismissing her. Then I raced through the two doors to the outside and dropped my coins into the driver's hand.

In the evening's heat, it would be more comfortable to ride on the uncovered upper deck, but I opted for the humid anonymity of the main carriage. The horses lurched forward, catching me off balance, and I nearly fell into the lap of a shopgirl who giggled as she pushed her body closer to the window so I could share her seat.

"Désolé, Mademoiselle."

She giggled some more as I deftly knotted the cravat and lifted my hat to smooth my hair.

"Allow me, monsieur." She blinked coquettishly as she adjusted my tie, her hands lingering at my throat a second too long.

I raised my brows as though affronted, and she dropped her hands immediately, staring out the window as though enraptured by the swell of humanity dotting the pavement. I did my best to calm my nerves and focus on the upcoming ballet, on my cousin's elation at being onstage at last after years of training. She was part of the corps de ballet, but it was the highest step in her career thus far.

Honestly, for me, the ballet was the last place I wanted to be after a long day of calculations at Eiffel's offices in Levallois-Perret. The mood was tense at work. Eiffel had staked much of his reputation on his beloved tower, which was now at risk. Even though Eiffel's design had been chosen by committee to represent Parisian technological marvels in the upcoming Exposition Universelle, a furor of public outrage at the audacity of his modern design had pushed the government into withholding the promised five million francs of financial support.

Monsieur Eiffel hadn't faltered. Instead, he'd devised a scheme to round up private investors to cover the costs. He'd offered full repayment of the investment plus a percentage of ticket sales for two full decades. It was an astounding offer. Even though I hardly had two sous to rub together between paychecks, I scraped up a hundred-pound bank loan to get in on the deal. I'd also racked my brain to think of anyone I knew who might be enticed into investing.

Because even if I currently clung to the edges of the bourgeoisie by my bitten-off fingernails, my youth had been spent in boarding schools with any number of men who did have the kind of bank accounts that Eiffel looked for. For once in my life, I'd set aside any sense of shame and written letters to a handful of them with what I hoped was an offer too lucrative to ignore.

I'd been sure that at least one or two would have been swayed by the romantic allure of adding a new landmark to the Parisian skyline—or their wives would be, at any rate. But after nearly two months, no one had responded.

The Opéra's flamboyant façade peeked through the windscreen one block ahead. I stood, crossing my fingers no one saw me emerging from a common omnibus. I tugged the brim of my hat low and kept to the inside of the pavement until I rounded the corner and could have been coming from anywhere, checking my pocket watch. Blast—the second act had already begun.

Under one of the pretentious arches that flanked the outside of the theater stood a dark-haired man in an absurdly tall top hat smoking a cigarette. His face hid in the shadow, but the whites of his eyes widened when he caught me looking.

Two chaps turned the opposite corner and ascended the steps quickly, apparently meeting the cigarette smoker. The shorter of the two glanced around almost furtively and hung back a few feet. He lit a pipe, and I was reminded of my father, who smoked the same brand. I recognized the other as he ignored the hand stretched out for a shake by the first man: retail entrepreneur Michel de Gênet. A valuable client of Eiffel's.

De Gênet meant money. Buckets of it. He was one of the wealthiest men in Paris, who'd taken a small chain of shops his father founded and become the largest retailer in France, with a marvelous flagship on the Rive Gauche, which Eiffel designed.

"Wasn't there a more respectable place we could have met?" The annoyance in de Gênet's loud voice was palpable.

I'd been on the receiving end of his derision a number of times when I'd worked on the design for the glass-and-iron roof of his grand magasin Qualité. It was a masterpiece of form and modernity, even if I admitted my bias.

Glancing as unobtrusively as I could over my shoulder, I gave the pair a second look. I did my best to place the man speaking with de Gênet in much more hushed tones, but there was nothing familiar about his long, slender form leaning against the stonework. He, however, narrowed his eyes at me. The hairs on the back of my neck rose, though I sweltered in the warm evening air.

Peculiar. Perhaps he mistook me for someone else?

With an internal shrug, I pushed into the lower level of the Palais Garnier, maneuvering around gaggles of patrons blocking the ornate marble staircases to get to the gilt and glamor that was the foyer du danse.

The crush of Paris's most rich and famous gentlemen—Tout-Paris, as they glowingly referred to themselves—in all its male glory waited to swoop down and choose a dancer as their evening's plaything. There was a lecherous status in being able to afford the annual subscription and to be known as an abonné. I wasn't shocked there was such a proliferation of them in the lavish long salon, rather than seated in the theater.

Love of the dance wasn't what brought them.

No. It was the petits rats, the gutter flowers, or whatever slang they used to refer to the ballet dancers.

I adjusted my sleeves from the wrist and took stock. The room was full of men whose names were in the papers daily. Some stuffy bankers who likely insisted to their wives they were there for the art. Industrialists in their heaviest wool, no matter the warmth of the evening, their sons arrayed like peacocks in silk with exotic flowers tucked in their lapels. A healthy smattering of artists not giving a damn and letting everyone know it in their corduroys and velvets, jaunty scarves instead of white ties.

And me, in a bespoke tailcoat that cost nearly a month's salary.

It was armor, allowing me to fit in, ensuring no one would question whether I'd paid the outrageous subscription fee to belong in the salon. I'd scrimped for months to buy the coat. But the coat did its job: not even the maître du danse, presiding over the entire spectacle, batted an eye over my presence.

I knocked a cigarette from the silver case I'd carried since I was at university and rolled it in my fingertips as I appraised the crowd with new eyes. These weren't just vultures from whom I had to protect my cousin.

My eyes lit on one of the servers—a dancer too young to be included in the performance—decked in a froth of black netting that contrasted badly with her poverty-sallowed skin, who slipped through the crowd toward me. Her collarbone was gaunt even for a dancer, but like the rest of them, she'd likely made the calculation that being a rich man's entertainment for a single evening would feed her family for weeks. I took a champagne flute from her tray, murmuring my thanks.

Perhaps misreading my politeness for interest, her smile blazed.

I shuttered my eyes and glanced away, stomach churning that she counted me among the beasts of prey.

From the theater, applause rang over the chatter of the foyer, and there was a visible change in the atmosphere as men shifted to face the curtains that led to the dressing rooms. Very soon, the dancers of the Paris Opéra ballet would stream out to be evaluated and haggled over before being snatched up to be taken to bed. Perhaps they'd merit a late supper first, if they were lucky.

Lucky.

I had to consciously keep the snarl from my face.

The dancers would enter the foyer in what was meant to look like an impromptu parade—an utter farce as both abonnés and dancers understood it was conducted in a strict hierarchy beginning with the shimmering étoile, the star ballerina who choreographed her performances offstage with as much care as those in the footlights. After she'd preened came the arrival of dancers who'd had solos—each of which was only earned after the dancer had paid for extra classes—and it was a rare gutter flower who could afford it on her own bank account. And then finally, the members of the lowly corps, like my lovely Aurélie.

A dancer like her—dependent on me and my meager wages—was left with one avenue to showcase her craft: selling herself to an abonné who would pay for lessons, a choice that neither of us could countenance.

And yet Aurélie would not be persuaded to consider any other vocation, no matter the risk. Ballet was her passion.

Across the room, the handsome fellow who'd been smoking outside fiddled with the buttons on his white glove. He waved away the offer of champagne with a brilliant smile that fled when his black eyes met mine through the crowd. I glanced away, unnerved by his chilliness. Who was he? Who did he think I was?

I rid myself of my empty flute as nonchalantly as I could, but stole the opportunity to look over at him again. He was neither a dandy nor slick with nouveau pretentiousness. All understated elegance and reeking of money. Had we met during my work hours? Perhaps, though he'd have to have been a customer rather than another engineer, as smart as his clothes were. Even I could tell his suit was the highest of fashion.

The intensity of his returned stare lit an uncomfortable heat that scorched my ears and cheeks. Without a hint of affability, he lifted one eyebrow like a challenge. I gritted my back teeth to keep from showing my discomfort. How easy life must be for a chap like that. Perfect clothes, perfect face. Enough money to buy a subscription to choose a dancer for however long he wished before dropping her back in the gutter and walking away as though she didn't matter.

I despised him on principle. Aurélie mattered. They all did. But the truth was my cousin was the only one I had the emotional strength to support. God knows, I had little else, unless I could persuade one of my former classmates to invest in my— Eiffel's—scheme.

The lush curtains that masked the changing rooms flicked open, and Aurélie burst out, flushed cheeks and anxiety imprinted into every feature. I moved toward her as she threw herself into my arms with a gulp of air.

This wasn't our planned inconspicuous exit from the theater through chattering self-involved crowds. Instead, every speculating eye was on her. Conversation in the foyer had paused so completely I might have had cotton wool stuffed in my ears.

The master of the stage lifted his hands in dismay, but I focused on the pale gray eyes of Aurélie, steadying her.

And me.

She took a step back as though recognizing the unwanted attention. She calmed her breathing, though the pulse in her neck throbbed. Her voice was husky with agitation. Low, though it echoed in the silence around us. "Will you escort me home at once, Fin?"

"That's why I'm here." I winked even though it wasn't a natural gesture. Still, it worked to soothe her, and her shoulders loosened. I offered her my arm as though nothing unusual had occurred and prayed to navigate to a side door as quickly as possible. Between barely parted lips I asked if she was all right.

A small shudder shimmied the ornamental rosettes on her otherwise demure muted mauve frock. "A groping hand caught me behind the draperies."

"Are you hurt?" Anger rushed through me.

"Non, but I'd wager that he won't be taking home any petit rat tonight"—the flash of her teeth with the one slightly crooked canine held no mirth—"or even perhaps for the rest of the month." Her fury was clear. I needed to get her out the door before she dissolved into a fit of blue curses, but rushing at this point would only draw more attention.

As if a young woman of just eighteen as impishly pretty as Aurélie could simply fade into the background by sheer willpower. Nor was there a clear path for escape. The smog of a hundred cigars hung over the phalanx of abonnés adding to the seeming impenetrability.

Leaving would be impossible were Aurélie on her own—which, again, was why I'd insisted on being there to act as chaperone.

The swell of curious voices faded, and I was momentarily held hostage by the dark scowl across the room. That hostile man was back to his previous position, as focused on me—or surely Aurélie—as every other man within earshot. The muscle around his eye twitched as though he couldn't contain his contempt, and for the first time in years, I remembered the wriggle of shame I'd had in my belly so often as a schoolboy.

Sod that. I'd vowed never to entertain that discomfort again. I adjusted the brim of my freshly brushed top hat and squared my shoulders as I stared back. In a moment, I memorized his face and channeled the collective generations of spoiled aristocrats whose blood coursed through me. Men who used what, and whom, they wished with no thought of the aftermath for those left behind. Confident that any obstacle would simply melt away, because that was how the unspoken laws of their world *worked*.

I might not be like my forefathers. Not in any way that could be measured and counted. But I could pretend as well as any actor who'd ever trod the boards. I didn't glower back. I merely looked through him as I led Aurélie to the side door. I dismissed him as though he didn't exist.

A man in his position would hate to be overlooked. It was harrowing.

Until one grew accustomed to it.

2

It was impossible to persuade Aurélie to give me any further details about what had happened to her in the dressing room, no matter how slyly I went about asking. She insisted that I shouldn't be overly concerned. I didn't believe her, but what could I do besides hover in the foyer de la danse every evening?

In the following two weeks, I still hadn't received any correspondence, aside from an unsettling letter from my bank regarding the loan I'd taken to insert myself into Eiffel's proposition. After covering the rent, I wasn't entirely sure how I'd manage without some outside funds. I'd been so confident that I would receive some token from my former schoolmates that I hadn't questioned what I would do if I was left empty-handed. To be sure, that one hundred pounds would be my making if everything went to plan with the tower—which it would. I'd stake my reputation on Gustave Eiffel's genius. However, I couldn't pay my current bills and rent on borrowed hope of a return, three years down the line.

I found myself bone-tired after all of my employment and the additional time it took to fetch Aurélie from the theater, but if I didn't have some respite from worry for an evening, I'd be in even worse shape. Aurélie didn't have a performance the following day, and I didn't have work, so I'd prop my eyes open for long enough to have a catch-up with my friends. I caught myself humming under my breath as I hefted the kettle off the kitchen range.

Steam shrouded Aurélie's slim shoulders as I poured the warmed water into the shallow foot bath. Moonlight cascaded through the terrace doors and lit up our white-plastered kitchen, illuminating her ivory skin and silvery-blond hair like she was a ghost. Even in daylight she was pale—as if her illustrator had used watercolors instead of oil paints to fill her in.

"Too hot?" We'd indulged in this pantomime for years now, but I always asked even though I'd gotten the exact right heat down to a science.

Her battered toes underwent a transformation not unlike boiled crustaceans. Aurélie rolled her head back and sighed. "Just right. Would you fetch my oil?" She vaguely gestured to the bottle of lavender essence I'd gotten for her birthday at the beginning of August, and I carefully added a few drops.

She pressed a cold cloth to her eyes and waved her wrist to shoo me off. "I might just fall asleep, it feels so good." Lifting the corner of the rag, she sighed. "Why are you still here?"

Glancing at my pocket watch, I shrugged, feeling guilt over my eagerness to enjoy a few hours on my own cognizance.

"I can't make you something to eat before I leave?" Her slender form brought out my protective instincts even though she was as strong as a horse.

"Go, Fin. Since I was moved up to the corps, you've been hanging around my neck so I can hardly breathe. I'm perfectly fine."

She *was* fine, and I trusted she knew how to handle the penknife she kept in her boot.

"You'd tell me if that wretch accosted you again backstage, wouldn't you?" I made an effort to be nonchalant.

She gave a slight nod that wasn't reassuring. "I haven't seen him again." She stared at her feet as though into a scrying bowl before blinking back up at me. "Will you tell me if you receive a check from your school chums?" Her accented English was particularly charming when she used slang. "Perhaps if we can afford the private lessons, the abonnés will believe I have a patron and leave me alone? I know that's a lot to ask, after everything else, but it would be such a relief."

Damn. She was being pestered, despite my efforts.

I examined the back of my hand, not wishing to lie, and equally loathe to admit that I still hadn't received a response. And every day that came and went made it unlikelier that I would. I made a few noncommittal noises, but Aurélie knew me too well.

Her breath caught. "Mon Dieu, Fin, no one sends cash? Why didn't you say so? I would never have asked for that new practice pinafore. Can we afford...?" She squeezed her eyes shut tight, her voice trailing, though the thought was audible: rent, food.

I mumbled something incomprehensible to either of us. She opened her eyes again, her brow creased. "Tomorrow night I could take my turn in the presentation—"

"Under no circumstances." I cut her off with finality and smiled in a way I hoped was convincing. "Don't fret. I have more than one iron in the fire."

After the despicable things her brother—a monster I was ashamed to share kinship with—had put her through as a

13

child, I'd be damned if I let her sell herself to any of the wolfish abonnés.

There was a slight quiver of her bottom lip. "Promise? Don't tease me. If I must—"

"No, you will not." I'd learned to fib at a young age. If I didn't know better, I'd have believed the hearty tone in my voice, too. "I promise. Cross my heart."

Settling herself back in her seat, Aurélie snorted. "I'll wager you have many fires hoping for your iron at the Green Carnation." Before I could manage an outraged gasp, she continued with a sly grin. "So why are you still here instead of there?"

Disregarding her impertinence, I assumed a detached expression. "If it doesn't bother you, I might check 'round the club." Voice uncaring, fingers crossed that my yearning for an evening of my sort of entertainment wasn't terribly obvious. "I'll just be out for a few hours."

Aurélie shrugged. "I don't know why you think I care. I'm off to bed as soon as the water cools." She yawned and didn't bother to cover her mouth. "Tell everyone I send my love."

I nodded, even though she'd replaced her eye covering and didn't see. I rubbed my palm over the cords in my neck, tight with anticipation, and strode out of the kitchen, through the cramped salon lit with a single kerosene lamp to the back of the flat where Aurélie and I each had a bedroom.

In five minutes, I'd changed from my overworked evening suit into more comfortable corduroy trousers and a fresh shirt. A whole night to myself instead of occupied as Aurélie's guard dog.

Christ, I'd earned it.

Aurélie pushed the door open without knocking and slid a

gray-blue silk tie around my bare throat, knotting it with a flour-ish. She fetched my bowler off the top of my armoire and adjusted it with a tilt after a brief survey.

"I haven't even fixed my hair yet."

She smacked my hand away from the hat. "Don't. You're more handsome with it unoiled. Like an artist. One of the successful ones."

I opened my mouth to protest that I didn't care how I looked, but she sighed, half exasperated and half amused, and I didn't dare argue.

Where I was headed, it did matter, and we both knew it.

"Don't forget your boutonnière." She took the small florist's box and retrieved the cheap green flower that signaled my pref-erences to those in the know. It gave my life the slightest edge of danger—the only sort I could tolerate. Steering me to the front door by my shoulders, Aurélie teased, "Yes, I will lock it, and if you just allowed yourself to spend the entire night out, I could even use the chain."

Mustering outrage, I tightened my spine. "Aurélie, that's—"

"The truth." She winked. "It's been much too long." She came behind me and pushed me out into the hall. "You need some release or you'll burst."

Aghast, I made a low growl of horrified effrontery. She slammed the door too loud for so late in the evening and, as a final gesture, ran the chain across the slide, ensuring I couldn't come back until morning.

Aurélie might not be the very last person with whom I wished to chat about my dearth of recent sexual adventures, but she wasn't far from the bottom of the list. Still, she had a point, and I had to fight my flicker of optimism as I saw an envelope just outside our door.

A British postmark. I was awash with the sort of bright flare of hope in which I rarely allowed myself to indulge. *Please be the funds.*

Because it was either next month's rent or the minimum payment on my loan. It would hurt to give up a percent of my future earnings by signing over some of my stake, but at least I'd keep a roof over our heads.

I left the building with renewed energy and examined the return address on the letter with a steadying breath. I slapped the envelope against my palm as if I could gauge the amount like it was a stack of gold.

Lemworth Bryant.

Good old Lem had come through.

In the nick of bloody time. I'd assumed the fat lot of social climbers might have had at least some interest in renewing a relationship with the son of an earl. That's all I'd ever been to them, after all, even though I hadn't spoken to the man in eight years. *Never would again, if I had any say.* My father would be likely to sic his lawyers on me if he had a whiff of rumor that I'd made any allusion to our blood relationship—a calculation I'd gambled. No one would be sending money based on *my* name alone.

But the concern that my father might catch wind of it was why I'd only chosen to reach out to the sons of wealthy merchants. No one likely to go back and tell tales at any social events my father or his friends would deign to attend.

Ripping the flap, I pulled out a piece of card stock loftily monogrammed with Lem's initials in gold. I poked my finger around inside to feel for the bank draft, swallowing hard when it wasn't there.

I didn't even merit a letter—merely a billet-sized card, like he was declining a damned invitation.

Tighe, old man,

I'm still shaking my head in wonder at the idea of you living in Paris. I've thought about your offer. Though intriguing, I'm unconvinced that this world's fair—or exposition, or whatever balderdash the frogs are calling it—will be attended by any more guests than the other ten or so that have failed to attract visitors in the past decade. Even so, I was going to dash off a few hundred as a gesture of good will to an old mate. Regretfully, I'm being kept tight in the purse strings at the moment. New wife, new baby. Nothing left to throw at some ghastly iron eyesore. From the tone of the papers here, it doesn't appear to be terrifically popular, in any case. You'll understand my hesitation, though I wish you a rousing success of it. Sorry to hear about your brother.

Cordially, L. B.

Bloody bloody bloody—*what?* I read it through twice more before faltering on the end.

What had Harry done now? More gambling debts? An illegitimate child—like father, like son, eh? A sour smile crept across my face. Whatever this new scandal Lem alluded to, I hoped it was ruinous. For the entire bloody lot of them.

No time to dwell on those happy thoughts, however. I crumpled the note into my fist, determined to drop it into the first pile of horse dung I came across.

3

The evening was one of those unusually warm ones that happen in September: hot and stuffy and acting like a match to light my kerosene-drenched anxiety, which rushed over me all at once like a wave.

I ought to have limited my investment to money left over after paying all our bills. But there never was much, and obviously investing in Eiffel's venture at the beginning would pay off eventually. Even the lad who sorted the mail had added his meager sum to the pile. As temperate as I normally behaved, this was a deliberate gamble on my future, and I'd caught the fever as much as the rest of my colleagues.

Applying for the loan had felt sensible at the time. Practical, even. And I'd assumed that with the percentage I'd skim off of my former schoolmates—as the disclosed finder's fee—I'd have been able to make the interest payment without missing a beat.

Hands in my pockets, I wound through two back streets before coming onto the tree-lined rue Balagny, where I slowed my brisk pace to a more casual stroll.

I could manage this crisis—I'd weathered enough of them,

after all. I just needed to work out the correct formula, and no one need ever know that I'd been so daft to borrow money to join in on Eiffel's speculation.

Foolish me for counting on Lem or any of the other fellows I'd gone through school with to come through. When had anyone ever done that for me?

I moved to one of my favorite cafés and settled into my usual table at the edge. A dish of haricots blancs au beurre with a crust of bread would fill me up for next to nothing. Which was exactly the amount I had in my pocket to pay for a meal before heading to the club.

Victoire and Jody weren't expecting me this evening after my fortnight of absence. If I needed to calm myself for a half hour, that was perfectly acceptable.

If anything could slow the racing of my heart, it was numbers. I could always be soothed by their finiteness. I could scrape up living expenses and manage to pay the bank. I'd check the newspapers to see if anyone needed a few hours of engineering labor. I'd done it before, would likely do it again after this crisis.

With a flourish, I wrote out the sum I could've done in my head at age six, let alone one-and-thirty, but I needed to see the answer in writing. To remind myself why I'd wagered money I didn't have.

Twenty percent return.

An amount that could change everything. It would justify the risk. Twenty percent on the hundred pounds would make a difference, but it wasn't nearly enough to change Aurélie's and my life the way I dreamed of.

No.

I needed ten times that amount—one hundred times, if I

indulged in the fanciful daydream that it was possible. That sort of investment wouldn't merely ease our lives; it would radically transform them for the better. It would provide Aurélie with the extra classes that would propel her into stardom, and hand me the keys to the life I'd always determined I'd lead.

I'd show my father's family that I'd make it on my own effort, which was more than any of them had done.

"Bonsoir, Fin."

My head whipped up at the unfamiliar male voice. I could count on one hand the people who called me Fin rather than Finley or Tighe, and none of them would linger around a perfectly bourgeois establishment like this tonight—or any night. They kept to their own neighborhood tucked into the dark alleys of the neuvième arrondissement.

It was the man from the foyer de la danse—the one with the cigarette who'd sneered the night Aurélie fled from an abonné's unwanted pawing.

His artfully arranged red cravat matched the rose on his lapel. A lazy smile stretched across a mouth too wide for his high, olive cheekbones. Yet, if I allowed myself to notice, the composition was worthy of center stage at l'École des Beaux-Arts.

"You are Fin, aren't you? Fin Tighe?" His voice was indolent, a deep drawl like warm, melted butter.

I nodded, wary.

"How do you do? Gilbert Duhais." He shook my hand, holding it a moment too long. He pulled out the chair opposite mine and sat before being invited. He held up a single elegant finger for the garçon, who hurried past other patrons waiting patiently for his attention.

I repeated his name aloud, unable to capture the exact trill of his pronunciation even after eight years in his city. Gilbert Duhais? It might have sounded familiar. Then again, it might not.

His smile lifted on one side, and he switched to my mother tongue, though I was more than competently conversant in his. "Bien sûr, you're English. I'd forgotten."

Forgotten? Other than the single time at the ballet, I'd swear I'd never seen this chap before in my life. The waiter licked the tip of his pencil, ready to take his order.

Whilst reeling off the name of a particular vintage of wine for the waiter—and a cup of coffee—Gilbert kept his eyes on me. Once we were alone, his words tumbled out in a rush as if rehearsed. "I hoped to find you, so what a coincidence this is."

A coincidence? Perhaps—but in a city of more than two million inhabitants, I wouldn't bet on it. Especially as he'd been at the ballet when Aurélie had accidentally showcased herself by prematurely emerging from backstage into the foyer full of abonnés. My having been back to fetch Aurélie after every performance made her connection to me noticeable. I'd prepared myself to turn away abonnés if any had managed to corner me at the Palais. It never crossed my mind someone would approach me outside its gilt chocolate-box walls.

Gilbert slid a pocket watch from his waistcoat and raised a brow as though surprised at the time. He clicked it shut and returned his gaze to me.

The watch was solid gold if I wasn't mistaken. Straightening my shoulders, I said, "I'm not much of a believer in coincidence, Monsieur Duhais. Before we waste any time, let me assure you that Mademoiselle Blancmaison is not for sale for any price."

"Your bluntness contradicts your Britishness, Mr. Tighe. Quite unexpected." High color stained his cheeks, visible even in the shadowed light of the café, but his face remained composed. "Everyone and everything in Paris can be bought if the price is high enough, I can assure you, but that's not why I'm pleased for this serendipitous encounter."

I doubted that, but I was even more curious to hear his excuse for why he was pleased to have stumbled across me, though I'd hold my questions.

He seemed equally amenable for me to speak first, and a silence nearly long enough to become awkward settled between us. It was only broken by the reappearance of the waiter uncorking a bottle of red and asking what Gilbert might wish to order to eat.

Gilbert rattled off a list of enough sweets to satisfy the whole corps de ballet from tonight's performance with a hint of laughter in his voice, as though he also noticed our overly long muteness and mocked the awkwardness of it. Where would he put all of those treats? The slender cut of his evening jacket claimed he didn't make a habit of indulging. He was fit, I'd give him that.

Not that I needed to risk exposing my preferences by staring, I had to remember. I reoriented myself in my chair and trained my focus on his face, the silence between us more comfortable this time, as though we shared a secret joke. It lingered until the server and his colleague littered the small table with a variety of trifles and parfaits in cut-glass dishes. The decadence was almost obscene, yet Gilbert didn't acknowledge the unlikelihood that we could devour the entire feast.

"You've spent many evenings in the foyer de la danse, so I've heard."

I allowed the growing friendliness to fall from my face. "Safe-guarding my cousin."

"I'm teasing you, Fin Tighe. Won't you try something?" Gilbert pushed a plate toward me with his elbow, a move that would have had me whipped as a child for its lack of manners. Something about his airy nonchalance didn't shout rudeness, just that he'd been cherished as a child, rather than being constantly reminded what a burden he was.

I picked a small dish of crème brûlée and tapped the crisp sugar with the side of my spoon.

"Vanille? I should have guessed." He leaned back and rolled his eyes. "I suppose chocolate or hazelnuts—or heaven forbid!—naughty, naughty framboises are reserved for libertines?"

I was embarrassed but couldn't really pin down why. He was the one being absurd, and yet I was the one who felt a prig.

Conciliatory, he redirected his chatter to genteel topics that could have been discussed with anyone: observations on an opera he'd heard in its original German in Newcastle-upon-Tyne, of all places, which isn't far from where I grew up. As it brought up the bad memories on why I'd left and never returned, my appetite vanished, though I ate a few bites for the sake of politeness.

Something about the way Gilbert's gaze flitted over my face, like he wished to imprint it in his mind, left me unsettled, as though I was exposed. Naked.

Moving on from inanities once more, he asked, "What do you do for a living, Fin? Or are you a gentleman of leisure?" His smile curved slightly, as though mocking me.

I cocked my head. "You've found out my name and my nationality, but not what I do for a living? Come now, Monsieur Duhais."

His eyes were as dark and warm as Turkish coffee, and Gilbert had the grace to look down. He ran a finger around the inside of his collar, fashionably high and stiff with starch with no hint of grime to show he'd worn it for more than an hour or two. And the skin above looked freshly shaven without a shadow of the beard that ought to have accompanied his black hair.

Scraping a hand over my cheek, I wished I'd taken the time to shave. Not that I could compare to Gilbert, wearing clothes that likely cost double our monthly rent.

But I was used to the inadequacies resulting from a distinct lack of cash. Lifetime experience.

"Truly, I don't know." Gilbert nodded at the basic sums scratched on the paper at my elbow. "But I see that you work with numbers? This is much too advanced for me." His lower lip pulled down in a caricature of sadness, but he was obviously teasing again.

"This is merely scribbling about a profit margin." I sat back and clasped my hands behind my head.

"Ah. Oui, I understand now." He awarded me a lopsided grin. "Money, hmm? Twenty percent of five million francs? That's an extraordinary amount." One groomed eyebrow rose. "Will you rob a bank, then?" His laugh was deep, rumbling from somewhere under his ribs. "If you split it with me, I'll supply you with an alibi."

Confronted with his smile, there was nothing I could do to restrain my own, even if I knew damned well he was charming me so he could have his way with Aurélie. "No, it's a commission rate. I mean to find investors for Gustave Eiffel."

"You work for Gustave Eiffel?" The question held a hint of disgust that put my back up. "Which means you're part of the nonsense with the tower? It'll destroy the city's skyline."

Or perhaps a monument made of perfect lines and angles will become the symbol of our modern, rational world. "I do. I'm a lead architectural engineer at Eiffel et Cie. Have you kept up with the drama in the papers?"

He rubbed his chin and gave me a thoughtful stare. "I've done my best to ignore it, because from what I can understand, it's just a very large, very ugly sculpture. The arguments about it make my head ache. Are you able to make it less boring?"

"Probably not—to you. To me, it's fascinating." And it was. My favorite thing to talk about, to the chagrin of Aurélie and my friends. But everything about it exemplified the only bulwarks in my life: numbers and their impervious consistency.

Cradling his cheek in one palm, he very nearly purred. "Then make it fascinating for me, as well."

"It isn't merely an art installation—this tower is the single most bold engineering feat the world has ever known."

His skepticism pushed me to find a way to engage him. "The mathematical precision involved—hundreds of thousands of joints and angles measured to the tenth of a millimeter—" I sat back, overwhelmed for a moment. "Not even the Romans would have dared anything close at the height of their arrogance."

He lifted a sardonic eyebrow. "So, it's a *terribly complex*, ugly, large piece of art?"

Normally, I'd have given up at that, unwilling to thrust my excitement onto an argumentative listener. But there was a challenge here. Gilbert was my first real opportunity to discuss this venture with a man of means, and I'd best be more brazen.

"You mock, monsieur, but perhaps you're the sort that can't imagine a future that doesn't look like the present?" My voice was as sugary as the table covered in half-eaten sweets, but the implication set his jaw. "Genius is too easily misunderstood by the common mind, I suppose." I lifted one shoulder, added a tinge of disappointment to my tone.

Had I gone too far? He was as still as a statue. Or a cat ready to pounce.

And then he laughed again, loud enough that passersby stopped and smiled, as though they were in on the joke. It was the sort of laugh that was impossible not to share. When he finished and the world shrank back to the breadth of our table, he folded his arms across his chest. "Bravo. You've caught my interest. Tell me about these equations of yours, hmm?"

Before I stuttered and lost my train of thought, I tapped a nail bitten to the quick on the paper. "Eiffel needs to raise five million francs to have the tower built. The government has exchanged funding the tower—which was the original plan—for allowing Monsieur Eiffel to retain ninety percent of the ticket sales once it's built. To find support, he's offered his employees a hefty commission—twenty percent—in return for each franc we bring in. From his share of the profit. On top of what the investor will earn, of course." My stomach hurtled down to the floor and back up at an alarming speed. "Eiffel has connections. The twenty percent will come from the ticket sales for the entire Exposition Universelle in '89 and for the following two decades." I sat back and expelled my breath. "That's into the damned twentieth century."

With a sizable enough investment, I absolutely could get rich. If the tower was the success the firm believed it would be. That I knew it would be.

"I'm amazed they keep you working as an engineer if you have to work out simple—one might even say *common*—equations like that on paper." His eyes glittered like the stars in the sky where I was raised back in Yorkshire.

"Obviously, we both learned to calculate percentages as children." I laughed at myself along with him—a bit forced this time, but it sounded true enough. I'd had plenty of practice faking over the years. "I only wished for the visual of what I can do if I try hard."

He reached a slender arm toward the center of the table, and I couldn't help but notice that his cuff links were diamonds nearly the size of my small fingernail. His head tilted. "Fair enough. A million francs isn't worth sneezing over."

Since his English was so perfect, the awkwardness of his idiom made me smile. "Nothing to sneeze at, you mean?" Not at all.

And because he sat next to me casually wearing enough wealth to cover my wages for the next ten years, I took a gamble. "Know anyone with a few million francs to spare?"

Gilbert didn't answer, not for a long moment. Instead, he sipped his coffee, steam swirling around his nose, which had a bump as though it had once been broken. Without meaning to, I leaned forward for his response.

"I might be able to help you. Do you know my uncle, Michel de Gênet?" He waggled a finger under my nose. "Oh, you're frowning. That must mean you've had to deal with him, non?"

Blinking, I regained my composure. "I've met him." Ah. It explained why he had been outside the Opéra—to meet with his nephew. "I worked with him on the roof for Qualité."

Gilbert looked blank for a moment before snapping his fingers. "Ah, oui. I hadn't realized that was Gustave Eiffel." A small moue of discontent ran over his face before melting back into a sly smile. "Then you've had experience with his very particular—how should I say? His attention to detail."

Unable to hide my smile, I nodded. "I ended up with at least fifteen designs before it was all said and done."

"Michel is fastidious in all he does. He demands that everyone in his life be just as uncompromising." Perhaps Gilbert sensed my disbelief, because he leaned closer as though I were sharing a secret. "You don't believe that?"

The last thing I ought to have done was cast aspersions on this man's uncle, but it was too much of a struggle to hold back. "I know he's involved in a lot of charity work—"

"The Society for Organizing Charitable Relief and Repressing Mendacity." Gilbert said it with a prim tone that wasn't matched with the twinkle in his eye.

That was the name. As chaste and self-righteous as I'd remembered. "And yet, I saw him at the Palais Garnier."

"Oui, but not for any perverse reason. He needed me to do something for him. He rarely attends performances."

After another bite of crème brûlée, I was direct. "I beg your pardon. I misunderstood the situation entirely."

Gilbert readjusted in his chair. "However, you were in the foyer."

"To bring my cousin home safely. Why were you there?"

He flashed his charming smile. "Let's just say it was for similar reasons. Please don't criticize; Michel does that enough."

"But it must be your choice who you spend time with."

"That's what I used to believe, as well. But when his son died five years ago, Michel took over my life. I'm his only nephew, so no matter if I had plans to be a journalist; I had to adjust to suit him."

Poor fellow, made heir to a fortune. No. I was incapable of mustering an ounce of sympathy. On the other hand, access to some of that fortune would certainly make my life more comfortable, especially if I could entice him to invest in Eiffel's tower.

In his face, real annoyance flashed, and then he shrugged— that quintessential Gallicism I'd never mastered. "Now I study ledgers and stocks. It's very boring to me, but I learned. I'm materialistic enough to know how to butter my bread. Am I correct?"

Finishing off my dessert—my very proper, terribly dull dessert— I shook my head. "How your bread is buttered, but I comprehended your meaning."

He pouted for a half second. "I hoped I'd impress you with my command of your language, and now that's twice I was wrong."

"I'm impressed, Monsieur Duhais, believe me. It's unusual to find someone in Paris so conversant in English." Speaking in my own language was a luxury.

Once more, that sanguine smile wreathed his face. Offering me a cigarette, which I declined, he blew out a long stream of smoke after lighting his own. "I spent nearly two years in England prowling for backers for a British branch of Qualité." He sat back and picked at a nonexistent piece of fluff on his trousers.

"You'd never imagine the dull people I had to investigate." Back teeth grinding, he raised narrowed eyes, looking vexed again. Gilbert rubbed the butcher paper with his open palm and blinked away emotion. "But it was good for me to be away from Paris, as I'd suffered a bit of a broken heart." He inhaled through his nose and smiled once again.

I swallowed, lump in my throat. Compassionate murmuring wasn't my forte. It also reminded me that for all his engaging chatter, this man hadn't run into me by accident.

"You have my sympathy on that count, but please know that Mademoiselle Blancmaison would never—"

He cut me off with a sudden fierceness that made me sit back. "I will not speak of Aurélie Blancmaison *with you*." He lifted his top hat and ran his fingers through silky hair, exhaling.

The conversation I thought we were having careened off its tracks like a runaway locomotive. My dessert caught like toffee somewhere in my ribs, leaving me the distinct sensation of heartburn.

He drummed the table with such an intense stare that the hair on the back of my neck rose in anticipation. "I met your father there. In London. What are the chances?" He studied my face for a reaction. "He's a rich man. Why don't you ask him for the money? In fact, this would be the most opportune time, wouldn't it?"

My father? Scalding shock boiled my skin. I fumbled in my waistcoat for my own case of cigarettes, needing something to steady myself.

"He said if I could find you, to tell you he was sorry for Annabeth. I hope it makes sense to you?" For a single instant, Gilbert's smile lost its charm, though I might have imagined it under the circumstances.

Pushing back my chair so it scraped against the concrete flooring, I tipped my bowler, shaking. I would not discuss my sister Annabeth or her death with anyone, hadn't said her name out loud in years, and didn't care what that cold-blooded bastard who fathered us had to say about her.

Without grace, I dug into my pockets for coins to cover my bill and dropped them on the table.

Face melting into concern, he covered his mouth, wide-eyed, and stood along with me. "Bon soirée, Monsieur Duhais." My voice cracked.

Gilbert scrambled behind me and clutched at my arm. "Wait, Mr. Tighe. I beg your pardon. Let me apologize."

Not wishing to cause a scene, I stopped, my throat tightening further.

"I thought it was nice news. You must believe me." Regret pulled his mouth down at the corner.

Biting down on the inside of my cheek to keep my emotions hidden, I waved away his concern. I needed a moment to push Annabeth back where she slept. Back down deep where I didn't have to visualize her crumpled body when they pulled her from the River Ouse. The day I left England for good.

My breathing was rough; my chest ached. From experience, I cupped my hand over my mouth and held air for five seconds, and then ten, until the dizziness passed. Damn him. It had been years since I'd felt that stifling anxiety that had plagued my youth.

But Gilbert Duhais was relentless in his apologies. His feet kept the rhythm of mine as they slapped against the road. "He seemed eager for you to reach out to him. I had no idea it would cause this sort of upset."

I stopped short. With more passion than I meant to summon, I said, "The only news I care to ever learn about him is to find

31

out that he's died—in writhing agony, if there's any justice in the world—so I can raise a glass in celebration."

A deep crevice split the skin over the concerned dark gaze. "His other son is dead, did you know?"

Pieces fell into place. That must have been what Lem Bryant referred to in his letter. Harry, dead. Not that I knew the boy. A young man he'd be now. Years ago, I'd seen him walking through town with his nanny. I'd spoken with him exactly one time. When he was thirteen or so he'd approached me, asked if the rumors about my paternity were true. I told him they were. He replied it didn't make me his brother, not really. I didn't count.

Our father had already made that very clear.

"I'm gratified to hear it." The words were unbidden, but I couldn't take them back. And they were true. Not because of Harry; he was the product of his upbringing, and I didn't care about him one way or another.

I was pleased that the Earl of Rawcliffe had lost the only child who mattered to him.

Gilbert leaned back on his heels, blinking hard. He tipped his hat as if to release me, and I hurried back into the refuge of inconspicuousness, desperate not to reopen any more wounds.

4

Usually, I meandered to the cabaret, strolling leisurely down anonymous side streets still not important enough to be lit with electric streetlamps, making circuits to ensure that there was no chance of being followed. Tonight, my heart pounding in my throat, I attempted only two diversions before heading straight to the one place I could be my true self, where I didn't have to lie about what sort of preferences I had.

The premises were nondescript by design. An establishment catering to gentlemen who preferred the company of other gentlemen might be legal due to a loophole in the Napoleonic Code but also might not hold up well to police scrutiny.

Which is why the owner, my friend Jody, paid a generous sum to the gendarmerie to keep them from conducting any raids without prior notice.

In the basement of a three-story building of flats owned by Jody, there was a dark door, which may have been brown or may have been dark red. It would take daylight to know for sure.

A woman emerged from the stairs, and I had to move out of

her way or she would have run into me. "Excusez-moi, monsieur." Her words ended on a sob.

I squinted into the darkness. "Charlotte? Are you all right?"

Jody's sister hadn't been around much lately—though I suppose I hadn't, either. But she knew me well enough to call me by my name. We'd been on the periphery of each other's lives for years now. But either she didn't hear me or ignored me, and I shrugged. There was enough on my mind.

Hurrying down the steps, I rubbed my hands together with anxiety. The ten-minute walk up toward Montmartre—to say nothing of the ghastly conversation with Gilbert Duhais—had made me break a sweat.

I slipped inside a door that led toward a row of flats that belonged to people who had given up hope for Lent twenty years prior. But down the same hall, behind the third door on the left, lay my Eden, carnally decadent and pulsing with life.

The Green Carnation.

With dark walls covered in deep green stripes, the cabaret was cavelike, the lights low. This neighborhood lost most of its gas in the evenings when more well-off neighbors were at home and using more than their share.

My fists unclenched, and my guts untangled as I inhaled the smoky maleness of the place. The cabaret was crowded, full of men from all walks of life, some in evening clothes, but most dressed more casually like me. All around was vibrant chaos; drinking, laughing, even a pale-faced man in the corner crying, poor bastard.

In front of the far wall stood a crude wooden stage transformed into something magical through clever use of papier-mâché and gold paint. It was a fitting backdrop for Victoire, whose magenta silk gown should have clashed violently with her auburn hair, but she had the charisma to pull it off—and to look like an aristocrat on an evening's lark while she was at it.

She was mid-song, one of her favorites lamenting the broken heart of a woman whose lover had left her—presumably pregnant—after a whirlwind affair. I didn't care for it. Similar scenarios were too common for the women in my life, and I knew better than most that the stark reality wasn't poetic.

Accompanying her was an accordionist, and Victoire's guitar was propped behind her. She lifted one of her long, black-gloved hands and blew me a kiss over the heads of twenty or so men dancing. It was like a mother's tender stroke across my cheek.

Or at least what I imagined that would be like. Mine had died just before my second birthday.

"Fini." Jody always called me the French word for "finished," teasing me because I did my best to live up to it, ending any attachment before it became one.

His brawny arm festooned with naval insignia from years as a sailor squeezed my shoulders. He snatched off my hat and rubbed until my hair stood straight up.

Fixing it with a sigh, I moved to the bar, waving at Laurent, the barkeep and cabaret's manager, vivacious and handsome in tight trousers and white shirt that contrasted attractively with his dark skin. I indicated four fingers instead of my usual two.

Brandy poured; he pushed it across the smooth wood into my waiting hand—a hand that trembled as it raised the rim for a swallow. I drank it neat and put it down for a refill.

"Is everything all right?" Laurent leaned his elbows on the bar. I nodded from habit.

"Aurélie's well?" Jody asked. My friends' concern warmed my belly like the brandy, hitting all at once.

"I...uh...yes. We're both managing." Even I heard the hitch in my voice.

The two of them shared a look, and Jody forced me to a stool, placing his swarthy hands on my knees, mouth so close I could smell the anise and wormwood of his worst vice. He forced my chin up and looked into my eyes, concern pouring out of his so expressly I had to shut my own.

"Where's the cocky Englishman we all adore? What's happened?"

I bristled at the intimation that I was arrogant. I was cautious, that's all.

He pulled back, bulging muscular arms folded over his chest. A gold hoop dangled from each ear, like a pirate. He leaned in as to drop a kiss on each cheek as usual, but I drew away. My emotions were too raw, too close to the surface. A smattering of well-intentioned sympathy might be my undoing. Jody smirked and went back behind the bar to pour another drink and push it my way.

I shook my head because I ought to, not because I meant it.

"Medicinal, frère. You never looked so damn pale in your life, even with that fine English rose complexion." He stroked my cheek with a rough finger. He was one of the few people whom I allowed to touch me like that.

Jody had been my first lover. Perhaps I had been old at

twenty-two to have never kissed anyone—male or female. But when I stepped off the boat from England, I was wounded and broken. I needed human comfort or else I'd have died.

He taught me how to find release. *And to give it.* And God damn, I needed it tonight. And Jody was comfortable, though I already knew I'd never allow myself to love anyone after losing Annabeth. After six months together, he woke me up one morning and told me I'd break his heart when I finally decided to leave him, so he was kicking me out before I got bored.

We remained friends, occasionally falling into bed if the timing was right. It might be tonight. I needed something to anesthetize the excruciating memories Gilbert Duhais awoke so carelessly.

Jody pushed his hand over my thick hair. His own scalp was smooth as a newborn's. "What's happened?"

By now, the third brandy did its job. *Strong.* I was strong again. And engulfed in rage toward Gilbert Duhais for reminding me of all the things I'd never had and so desperately wished for. I lifted off my seat, but calm hands pushed me back down with a soothing *shhh*.

Jody cupped my chin, and I inhaled sharply. He'd kiss me next, and I could spend an hour or more—or less—and enjoy the touch of humanity I craved. I could go back to the real world refreshed, hungover or not, and continue putting one foot in front of the other for another stretch of time until the next bloody crisis.

I hovered on the threshold of control and release. Exhaled. "Nothing to trouble yourself about." I squeezed his arm. "I just heard news about my family, and I need to digest it."

"Family?" Jody narrowed his eyes. "Did you have any family other than your sister?"

I hid my face in my glass and waved my hand. How could I go for days not remembering that I'd even had a sister and then feel Annabeth's loss so keenly, like it was a fresh wound?

One drunken evening, years before, I'd told Jody how she'd died. He'd cried with me, and then he'd promised he'd never mention her again. That he'd done it tonight was proof I must have appeared as wildly out of sorts as I felt.

"My father, actually." It scraped at my insides to call that fils de pute something so familial, but Jody didn't press.

Victoire, however, had no qualms. Hurrying over once her song was over, she squeezed my face between her two hands. "Darling, you look like someone's just ripped you open." She kissed me on the lips, no doubt leaving them nearly as rouged as her own. "Not that you don't look as edible as ever, you scoundrel. One of these days you'll realize you've loved me all along and make an honest woman out of me."

She loved to tease, did Victoire, even knowing that the frocks and powders that made her feel like her true self were the strongest reason we'd never even shared a lover's kiss. Her perfect femininity was beautiful and charming—and did nothing to raise my pulse. But she always brought the edges of my mouth into a hint of a smile.

"Fin's heard something from his father." Laurent scooted Victoire's crystal glass her way, replenished.

"I didn't know you had a father. I just assumed you rose from the waves, fully formed, clad in nothing but foam and a seashell." Victoire laughed at her own absurdity and licked

38

her tongue along the edge of her mouth for an errant drop of brandy.

"I don't. Not in any true sense." And to keep from discussing him, I launched into an explanation of Gilbert Duhais and how he'd cornered me at the café.

"And he's attractive, this Duhais?" Laurent waggled his eyebrows lasciviously.

Worrying one of my fingernails between my teeth, I shrugged. "I didn't pay much attention."

Two of my friends chuckled over the likelihood of that, but then Jody frowned. "He's interested in Aurélie?"

Was he? I'd been sure before he'd launched into discussing my father. I shrugged.

"Handsome and rich, Fin, and chasing you down all over the city. Sounds like a fairy tale. Surely, you're clever enough to exploit that? Have him invest in your plans with the tower?" Victoire's voice was flippant, but the shrewdness behind her eyes was distinct. She and Jody had heard all the details the day the offer had been made to me and the other engineers at the firm. "I'd say one of us deserves a happy ending."

"I've heard you're proficient at those, Vicky." Jody ducked before she could playfully slap his cheek. "Or, Fini, if your father wishes to reconcile, what better way could he show his affection but with a nice, fat check?" Jody clinked his glass against mine and winked again.

I summoned as much outrage as I could muster, though *a nice, fat check* would solve so many problems—if it came from anyone else. "I despise him."

Victoire rolled her kohl-rimmed eyes with a *tsk*. "Don't be a fool, cher. Honestly, I curse my father daily, but if he offered me money, I'd take it without a moment's hesitation."

Never. I'd never put myself under that man's thumb again, not for any amount.

Who would inherit now that his only legitimate child had died, though? The amount of Harry's inheritance was likely astronomical—but it wasn't for the likes of me. I was hardly worthy of that. My father had instilled that in me before I could walk.

As if reading the direction of my thoughts, Jody changed the subject. "Who's Duhais's uncle?"

"Michel de Gênet, why?"

Jody frowned. "Charlotte's a domestique at his house, remember? She put your name on the reference after you designed the grand magasin." He glanced at the empty bottle of absinthe on the bar next to his glass. "She says he pays generously but is strict. Insists the servants don't touch drink, as if we were back in *your* priggish country." He pinched my cheek.

That reminded me. "Charlotte ran into me on the steps. Didn't even say hello."

"She had too much to drink. She got weepy, and I sent her back to sleep it off." He fiddled with the absinthe spoon in the empty glass before pushing it toward Laurent for washing.

He poked a finger into my rib. "This is what I told her and I'll repeat it for you: the rich may seem charitable, kind even, but you still need to be careful. People like de Gênet—and his nephew—don't care about the likes of us. It's a show to make them feel good about themselves. If things get difficult, they walk away, no mind of the consequences."

It's the story of my bloody life.

Lifting my glass for another swallow, I nodded. I pushed the image of my father's heartless face the last time I saw him from my mind and proceeded to get drunk. Perhaps the meeting was merely a coincidence as Gilbert had said.

Except I'd never believed in coincidences.

5

It was morning when I finally dragged my carcass off of Jody's sofa. I continued to work out the cramp in my neck as I trudged up to our landing and fumbled in my pocket for the key, grateful that it was Sunday and I had nothing pressing to do. A song melted through the door into the hall, as though we didn't share the building with any number of unpleasant souls who loved to lodge complaints. I pushed through the entry with my finger over my lips.

Hand over her heart, Aurélie jumped. "Good Lord, Fin, tu m'as fait peur. I never heard you come in last night." She winked. "Perhaps I should tell you to stay out all night more often."

"You chained the door. I couldn't come home. I wondered if I'd have to knock."

"Oh, I...unlocked it. Just in case." She had the sort of pale skin that ought to have blushed easily, but she didn't. When her skin turned pink like this, I knew she was keeping a secret.

"Did you go out?" I kept my words as mild as I could. Now that she was eighteen, she insisted I couldn't treat her like a child any longer. She was correct, but it chafed.

In my mind, she was still the solemn ten-year-old I'd met when I'd finally tracked down my aunt Selena a few months after Jody had thrown me out. Too late for a happy reunion, unfortunately. I was crushed that Aunt Selena had died—she'd been the only adult I recalled giving me any affection as a child. I'd adored her for it before she'd run off to some glamorous life in France to be a singer. Aunt Glad, who raised us, implied she'd been run off by my father's family, though she never explained why.

Selena had written a dutiful letter to Aunt Glad every Christmas, full of exciting stories of her life in France. Glad never responded, but she saved the letters. Annabeth and I would sneak them to read by candlelight and imagine it was us living some fantastical life in France.

The truth my cousin Paul told me was grimmer. Selena's career never happened, and she ended up marrying a petty thief who was hanged after siring two children. When I turned up at their door, Paul and Aurélie were barely surviving. Even though I was only twenty-two, just starting to work as an engineer, I couldn't let them—my family—suffer.

I wasn't like my father in that sense.

Still, I couldn't offer much more than a roof and meals. Paul was clever enough to win a place at an école and Aurélie did . . . whatever little girls did. I was self-righteous enough to consider myself something of a savior for taking them in—when I wasn't wildly letting loose at the Green Carnation and places of that ilk.

Until one Friday night—Saturday morning, really—when I came home earlier than usual. Paul was outside the door to the flat, cleaning under his fingernails with a penknife.

I remember it as though it just happened.

He stood, flustered. I wobbled, half drunk.

But I was still aware that there was something unsettling about the situation.

Before I could catch my bearings, a well-dressed man old enough to be my father opened the door to the flat and gave Paul a handful of coins.

Confused, I tore inside the flat, not listening to whatever excuse Paul was able to come up with on the fly. There was only one bedroom, which Paul and I shared. Aurélie slept on the sofa. But she was in our bed, curled to one side and weeping.

I threw a punch to Paul's chin before even asking what had happened.

He's lucky I threw him out rather than choking him on the spot. Unfortunately, he returned the next day, letting me know he'd followed me to the Green Carnation on multiple occasions, and threatened to expose my secrets unless I paid him a monthly stipend—the same amount he'd been making off his ten-year-old sister, the monster.

Shaking the memory out of my head, I focused on the present. Aurélie was as safe as I could keep her. And Paul was dead these past two years. Good riddance.

Looking at her now, I was almost proud of myself. We'd gotten on well enough. I'd scraped together the money for ballet lessons, and gradually the shadows had left her eyes as she mastered the art she loved. She treated me as an elder brother, a role, *a connection*, I needed.

"Where are you off to? It's your day off," I asked.

She buttoned the long coat over the black pinafore dress she wore to ballet practice.

"Something marvelous has happened, so listen before you're cross with me, promise?" Aurélie's eyes flitted around the room, shoulders sagging when she met my stare. "Some of the dancers came by last night and asked me along to a restaurant." She clutched my sleeve. "They can already tell I'm going to be someone in the compagnie."

I lifted her chin so she had to listen. "You are someone already, with or without them." She'd spent long hours working for this precise opportunity.

"You always think so, but you aren't the master of stage." Aurélie followed me to the small kitchen and ate the breakfast I made her standing up, every limb moving with its own frenetic spark. "He barely notices me since I refuse to parade myself." Her mouth was sprinkled with crumbs.

I handed her a napkin, which she used haphazardly, leaving half the detritus behind.

"But Rosette—you know, l'étoile? She came along, and you should have seen the height of the feathers in her hair, Fin! It was a wonder she could go under the doorway to the restaurant without stooping." She twisted her pale blond hair into a tight chignon and thrust pins in with the grace of a battle ax. I winced in solidarity with her poor skull.

"Rosette had me sit next to her, and she told me an anonymous abonné has donated to pay for some extra classes so I can have a solo—a small one, for now. But in the next production, which is why I'm headed there now."

"A solo? From an anonymous donor? And you can trust Rosette to tell the truth?" I kept my face closed, but my breath caught. The start of her dreams. Perhaps it would give her the safety of not having to depend on any man—not even me—for her career's blossoming.

"I believe I can." She had a moment of pensive introspection before launching her arms around my neck. "A solo for me—not as an understudy." She danced around the table in a full circuit, her face beaming. "Génial, non?"

"Who do you think it is?" I collected the dishes and carried them back inside to wash up.

"I have no idea, but it hardly matters, does it?" She sniffed with studied nonchalance.

Drying a plate, I put it away, minding what I said next. "This unidentified patron is likely to be using this as an opportunity to—"

She glared, ghostly gray eyes narrowing. "I'm not a naïve little girl. I know exactly what these men are after, Fin. More than you do, I'd say."

Jesus wept, she did know.

"I can't be bought by some free classes, but I'm not going to let an opportunity to prove my talent go to waste. You mustn't worry about me." Her voice was gruff. "Je suis une fille intelligente." She leaned against the threshold and stopped vibrating for a second.

"The cleverest." Though I worried for her all the time.

"But listen to this; when Rosette announced this solo, I pretended that there was no chance I could accept." Her elfin smile flashed again. "I made it clear that I wasn't looking for an abonné. That I wouldn't consider it under any circumstance. The word will get out, and if this nameless fool rescinds the offer—well, I'll cope with that. *Then*. But for now, the classes are paid in full for two months. I checked—he can't get a refund."

Anger deflated, I pointed at the clock. "Congratulations, you deserve it. Don't miss the 'bus."

Aurélie grabbed a handful of centimes from the bowl I kept near the door, wings on her feet. I forbade her to walk alone when the omnibus stopped right outside our door and went straight to her dance lessons. I continued tidying the dishes until I noticed the satchel holding her midday meal had been left behind.

Hoping to catch her, I raced down the steps to the building's entrance, calling her name. Aurélie was backed against the brass mailboxes facing Gilbert Duhais, who stood between her and the exit.

"I remember you. And the circumstances," she said to Gilbert. Her eyes lit on her bag in my outstretched hand, and she snatched it, holding it to her chest. "You're so good to me, Fin, bless you." She squeezed around him and hurried out the door, throwing one last glance at us over her shoulder.

I remember you. What had she meant? I turned away from Gilbert, but my curiosity got the better of me. "How in the hell do you know where we live?"

Gilbert looked embarrassed, though it was likelier he knew how to fake it. "I asked one of the dancers."

"And she told you?" Aurélie and I didn't spend much time swapping gossip from our work hours, but I was under the impression that the dancers looked out for one another.

Now he did show some shame. "I paid her ten francs."

Staggered by the amount, I was at a momentary loss. Then my

anger that our privacy had been invaded rushed back. I snarled, "What a waste of ten francs, Monsieur Duhais, as Mademoiselle Blancmaison has left, and wouldn't entertain a visit from you under any circumstances. You'll excuse me." I turned to go up the stairs with my back stiff.

Gilbert followed me too closely. "Fin, wait. I came to speak to you."

Stopping on the second landing, I caught my breath and forced my features into a scowl. "What on earth about?"

He blinked and ran his hand over the back of his neck whilst taking the steps two at a time to catch up with me. "I wish to apologize." He pushed a paper sack into my arms with a dazzling smile. "And I brought breakfast."

Nonplussed, I sighed. Damn the polite manners that had been beaten into my skull. Holding my shoulders high, I walked the rest of the way back to my door and held it open for him.

He passed me and entered the salon cum study cum dining area of my flat, inspecting the room as if he'd been assigned the role of juge d'instruction at the scene of a crime.

The delicious fragrance of warm croissants filled my nose. I set them on the table, flustered. "What are you really doing here?"

But that smile of Gilbert's. Dear God, the world would crumble at his feet with a glance. "I hope you don't terribly mind the intrusion."

He made his way to the kitchen and opened cupboards until he found the plates. There were only four cupboards, so it didn't take long.

"It's beautiful weather; shall we sit outside?" He made his way without waiting for my answer. "Do you have coffee? Or tea, I suppose. I got used to drinking it the British way back in your country." His touched my arm, all cherubic innocence. "Are you still cross with me?"

I had no idea how to interpret the sensations springing up like toadstools.

But Gilbert didn't wait for my response. "I sat up late last night, thinking about your excitement over that ghastly tower, and I've concluded that I like you, Finley Tighe. I'd like us to be friends. But I began on the wrong foot, and I wish to prove it."

He grasped my shoulders to squeeze by me in the doorway. His skin held a hint of the ocean, a brand of shaving soap that I hoped to afford someday.

He paused, his mouth inches from mine, so I had to draw back. "I'll put the kettle on, hmm?" Sweeping eyes over the same clothes I'd worn when he accosted me the previous evening, he raised an eyebrow. "Late night?"

Glaring to remind him it was none of his business, I gestured to the worn cast-iron kettle. He'd do what he wanted no matter what I said. He struck a match and lit the gas, and then leaned his long body against the range.

I excused myself to put on a clean shirt.

When I returned, still tucking it in, he invited me onto the terrace to sit at my own table, cheerfully set with plates and cups for both tea and juice.

Untangling the disjointed conversation, I took a breath. "Even though you say you're here as an apology, you have nothing to make up to me."

The whistle on the kettle crowed, and he made a perfect frown. "I do. I had no idea something I'd said would affect you so deeply. Annabeth was your sister?"

Not wanting him to see my reaction a second time, I went back into the kitchen and poured the kettle water into a teapot, steeling my voice not to betray myself. "Yes. But I don't wish to speak about her. Or any of them. I left England years ago and never plan on going back."

Like a child or small dog—yes, like a dog—he followed me again, making me dizzy.

His breath was hot on the back of my neck. "One day you'll tell me about her."

I couldn't imagine any circumstance in which that would be true, but I buried the protestations and scooped tea into the strainer. My hand trembled, and I changed the subject. "How do you know my cousin?"

Gilbert fiddled with the button at his throat. "I met her years ago. We had a mutual acquaintance."

I narrowed my eyes and examined him. He wasn't much older than she was, possibly twenty-six or -seven, so it would have to have been when Aurélie lived with me. "Who?"

There was room enough for two to walk past without bumping, but he tripped on the scatter rug and dropped the bag of croissants. "Mon Dieu, forgive me, I'm not usually so clumsy. I didn't sleep well last night."

His eyes were red-rimmed and puffy, now that I could focus on them instead of his mouth, like he'd stayed up late drinking, or crying. Not that either was my business.

"Tell me why you're here, Monsieur Duhais."

"Gilbert, please. We're going to be great friends, I think."

I raised my hand to cut him off. "We have nothing in common, so that's hardly likely."

He simply smiled. "I believe you'll change your mind once you've heard me out. I'll carry the tea." He picked up the teapot. "Do you have milk?"

Exasperated, I shook my head. "I'm all out, sorry."

He lifted his eyebrow. "'S shame. I love the taste of English."

Bloody hell.

He made the four or five steps to the balcony and sat. I followed, a flush of annoyance warring with my curiosity. "You were telling me the reason you descended on me this fine Sunday morning. I've said before that even though my cousin is a dancer, she isn't looking for patrons, and I won't have you harassing her." Gilbert's skeptical face pushed me to blurt, "Before I came into her life, she was subjected to intolerable abuses as a child by one who should have taken care of her. They will never happen again as long as I am alive to protect her."

He blinked rather uncertainly and swallowed hard. "Abuses?"

Damn it all, I'd never meant to bring up anything that could cast aspersions on her reputation. "The past doesn't concern you, monsieur, but just know that Aurélie isn't available."

"I'm not looking for a mistress, so please stop warning me off. Your cousin is absolutely in no danger from me. I'm here because I have some ideas regarding our conversation last night."

"Then there is nothing for us to discuss. I find talk of my father tedious, so if you're going to blather on with—"

He ignored me and opened the bag, handed me a croissant, and arranged the rest on a plate in the center of the table. The crisp, buttery pastry melted on my tongue, pointing my humor in an upward trajectory.

"Oui, I gathered that from what you told me last night. Please hear me out before you tell me to leave."

Against my better nature I unruffled my feathers. "It's not?"

"I can be a sort of partner. Introduce you to people—friends of my uncle's mostly—who have the resources to fund the tower, even though I personally think it is a tragic thing. It will destroy the view from my apartment. But I owe you."

My irritation evaporated. Help me find investors? "Why do you feel you owe me anything? And what would you get out of such a generous offer?" It was likely too steep a price.

Eyes darting, Gilbert lifted a shoulder. "I'm not terribly greedy. Perhaps a five percent cut?"

I straightened my spine, though a flush of self-preservation set my heart racing. I'd have gone all the way to ten, because there's no way I'd ever meet these affluent speculators on my own, but—

"Or four, if that's too dear?" He frowned.

He'd let me rob him blind? There had to be a catch. No one was that generous just for the sake of it.

"All right, three percent, but no lower." He reached out for a shake.

Though tempted, I held back. "I don't understand what motivates you. Has the Earl of Rawcliffe put you up to this? Because I can promise you, I wish for nothing from him, and you're welcome to tell him that."

Dropping his hand, Gilbert flashed a sheepish smile that blew away my caution like so much dandelion fluff. "Perhaps I shouldn't admit this, but when I became my uncle's heir, I lost touch with most of my schoolmates. Last night at the café, you reminded me that it's a bit lonesome working for Michel. I'd like your friendship. I feel as though I've known you for years."

"For years? I spoke to you for the first time last night." He was mad as a March hare, though I was strangely flattered.

"Your…uh…father told me so much about you."

I tapped my foot. "I can't begin to imagine what he had to say, as he was never an important part of my life."

"But he wishes to rectify that. If I can bring you around to his way of thinking, let's just say, he'll be grateful. Perhaps even agree to be a silent partner in opening another grand magasin in London. Qualité will be mine someday, and the more prosperous the brand, the better for me."

My father—no, the earl—was that interested in me? It was unfathomable, though I suppose investing in the store wasn't a fool move. I'd read that Michel de Gênet had made more than eighty million francs in the first year Qualité was open.

Whatever else I might think about the man who sired me, he was no layabout when it came to making more money. Not that I would ever condescend to be in that wretch's life. Not after all he'd done in the past.

Still, fascinating that the earl might finally realize he'd lost an ally in me. But it would never do to allow Gilbert to see my spark of interest.

"You'll lose if you're depending on my reconciling with him."

Gilbert's black eyes were fixated on mine too intensely for comfort. "I never lose, Monsieur Tighe."

My voice chilled down to an arctic temperature, exactly like my father's when I'd done something to disappoint him—like being born. "In this matter, I will not budge, so if that's your real intention in forging a *friendship* with me, let's be done with this charade."

"It isn't my most pressing hope at this precise moment, non. I can abide by your wishes and not mention him again until you wish me to; fair enough?" He mimed buttoning his lip. "I merely hope for your companionship—if we suit one another like I feel we might. And to help you—and therefore me—make some easy money."

I didn't need any more friends. But I was helpless to say no to such an extraordinary offer of assistance to find investors of my own. It had nothing to do with his handsomeness and charm.

Holding out my hand, we shook.

"Well, now that's cleared up, we will pay a visit to my store today. You need some new suits, though I hope you don't mind my bluntness. I'm inviting you to a party tomorrow night, and all the guests must believe you aren't... how can I say this without being rude?" He tapped his chiseled chin. "You must portray yourself as a man of means, and this venture is just something you're doing for the sake of the gamble."

"I have an evening jacket." An expensive one.

The look from under thick lashes was provocative. "Oui. You wore it at the ballet. And in most situations, it would be decent enough, but we need something expensive that isn't an evening jacket."

I wanted to be offended for the sake of my clothes, but couldn't muster the will. "I don't have the funds for any new—"

"Stop." Gilbert waved as if money meant nothing. "We can say you'll pay me back, if we must, but Qualité is mine. Or will be someday. And the tailor will be happy to make alterations on the suit for tomorrow evening."

A hurricane. That's what Gilbert Duhais reminded me of.

When I'd left England, I had a decision: America or France. The terror of not knowing whether one of the tropical storms that capsized fleets and swallowed islands whole would strike my ship kept me from heading west.

He was like one of those storms.

Unexpected, terrifying, and strangely fascinating. A force of nature I had no control over.

Gilbert shoved his chair back and gulped the tea before the cup went back onto the table with a crash. "Shall we?"

6

A half hour later, we stood in the magnificent great hall of the Qualité department store. I'd been inside once since it opened, just to see how the ironwork held up the sparkling glass roof. It was as glorious now as it had been then, a prism of sunlight breaking over the rainbow-gilded heads of the shoppers.

Gilbert led me past the marble-topped counters bedecked with any sort of froufrou accoutrement a well-heeled Parisian could wish for. Saleswomen veritably swooned as my companion took the time to greet each by their name. We wove our way through the labyrinth to a small salon shut off from the rest of the store with heavy black velvet curtains. When Gilbert pulled one back and ushered me inside, I hitched my breath like Aladdin when he saw the cavern of jewels.

"We've arrived," called out Gilbert as I drank in the lushness of my surroundings. The flocked damask wall hangings in gold and cream. The rich, dark wood trim.

A gray-haired man with impeccably cut trousers appeared from behind another curtain, pushing a brass rack of jackets and trousers. "Monsieur Tighe," he said with a slight bow.

Good Lord, I'd been expected? My mouth dropped, but I snapped it shut.

Gilbert went to the floor-to-ceiling beveled mirror and adjusted his already perfectly arranged green silk cravat. He hung up his hat and combed his fingers through his silky black hair and turned sideways to make sure his creases were in the right places.

The tailor gestured for me to remove my clothes. I hesitated, standing in the open.

"We've closed down the salon for you, Fin. No need to worry that anyone will see you in your short pants." Gilbert examined me with narrowed eyes while he leaned against the mirror.

My aunt Glad would have had a heyday with all of the leaning and lounging Gilbert managed in the course of an hour. He stood abruptly and pushed through the waiting clothes. "Where's the blue?"

The small man hurried back with an evening jacket missing its tails. I held the color to the light—it was a deep blue instead of black. I rubbed the silk of the lapels, cut in a round fashion.

Gilbert's eyes lit up, and he gestured for me to put it on. "The Prince of Wales is a fan. I stitched up a prototype for—"

"You stitched it?" I could hardly reconcile that with the dandy in front of me.

"My grandfather was a tailor from Amiens. Qualité began as his store, and he was lucky enough to open a small chain of them around France. My uncle Michel expanded, and here we are." He gestured to the crystal chandelier that hung down over our heads.

"I grew up thinking I'd be a tailor, before my uncle was rich enough to send me away to school." He slid the jacket over my arms and came around to my chest, buttoning it. "And can you please take off those trousers you wore last night?" The curl in his lip said everything he didn't about the state of them.

Self-consciously, I slid them off and handed them to the tailor. He hurried into a back passage, leaving Gilbert and me alone. He hooked his thumbs under the lapels and peeled the jacket off my shoulders, his body too close to mine to be an accident.

"This is on me as an investment. I'll sell a thousand of these, once everyone sees you." His black eyes shimmered with sincerity that made my mouth dry up.

I swallowed. A simple compliment? I'd never understood how to handle them. Never had much opportunity to learn.

Gilbert gripped my chin and pushed it back up. "Terribly handsome. You look exactly like your father."

I jerked my chin back and kept my voice steady. "I don't." But I glanced at the mirror, and the likeness was uncanny. Anyone who knew the man could tell we were related.

"The faint blue in the fabric makes your eyes glow." Gilbert stepped away—all business again—and surveyed me.

The tailor emerged from behind the velvet curtain and dangled another amazing tailless evening coat on one finger, and tweed in brown and blue on the other hand.

Gilbert clapped his fingertips together as my eyebrows raised. "Qualité will make a fortune off you and those shoulders, so throw away your guilt. Try the tweed. We have a number of choices, but this will make you look like a true English gentleman. The son of an earl."

My throat sealed up, and I said with a growl, "I'm not. Not in the way that matters."

One black eyebrow arched. "This conversation is tedious, Fin.

You could be. And when I drop the name of your father with investors tomorrow night—"

"I thought I was clear that I won't link my name with his?" I stepped away from the mirror, casting about for my own trousers. "Not only do I despise him, he'd be furious with me. Not that I care about his feelings, but he could destroy my life, can't you understand? I won't do that. Not for a million francs. Didn't you listen to me earlier?"

"I can promise you that he won't ruin you. That's the furthest wish he has." His voice softened. "How about six million francs, hmm? Is that fair?"

I struggled to keep my heart from beating out of my chest, pulling my clothes back on without looking at him.

"Fin, you're a riddle. If my father's family were charter members of the Order of the Garter, I'd have it printed on all my stationery."

My shaking hands struggled with the final button of my fly.

"If I hated him, I'd be even freer with his name." Gilbert's voice dipped low, wheedling.

I couldn't help but give the point consideration. My father was apparently aware I lived in Paris and wanted to apologize for his callousness to Annabeth. Why couldn't I use his name? He'd given me nothing else.

"You're his only living child, you know?" he continued, low and seductive. "What if he wished to bring you back into his circle? Make you the next in line?"

That was a bridge too far.

"He'd rather let the name die out than make me his legal heir, even if it wasn't an impossibility." Bitter bile pooled in my stomach, and I glared at the jacket in Gilbert's hands. He shrugged.

"You're so very wrong. My uncle is less than a generation into this store and already doesn't want his name to disappear. In order to inherit, I must change my surname to his. Comme ci, comme ça. I can change my name like you can change jackets, because I'm using common sense. I urge you to follow suit."

Gilbert pushed the tweed into my hands. With a frown, I tried it on.

"Next week, I'll introduce you to my uncle and his friends. They're the ones we're shopping to impress. All of them made their own fortune, their own name. And no matter the end result of the revolution, every one of them would kill for a title. Maybe you don't have one, but you're much closer than they'll ever be."

It was hard to say no to anything he suggested. I looked at the mirror, the curtain, anywhere but his insistent face. An investment from de Gênet would be a coup.

Gilbert stood behind me, his chin over my shoulder. Our eyes met in the mirror. "I'll have one delivered before tomorrow."

I insisted I couldn't take his generosity.

"Ce n'est pas bien?" He looked as though I were a slow learner. "I can't take you to meet my friends and expect them to take you seriously unless you look the part."

I threw my hands in the air. "Which part? I'm a mid-level employee of Eiffel who has the chance to improve my career and their bank accounts. What more do they expect?"

"They wish for the entire performance, my dear Monsieur Tighe. The British aristocratic experience. You already have the accent down."

Huffing, I snarled, "No, I don't."

Gilbert lifted an eyebrow. "You mean to say you grew up in working-class Yorkshire speaking in that tone like you're ordering your servants about?" He traced his small finger across my upper lip. "And that sneer. Half the women will be begging to kiss it off you and will order their husbands to write you a large check to ensure it."

"I don't sneer."

"Maybe more than half." His mouth was so close that his breath warmed my cheeks. *"Begging to kiss it off you."*

Before I could react, he pressed his fingers through my hair. "Can you get this trimmed before tomorrow evening? Hmm. Just the sides and back, the length and that hint of curl looks rather romantic. I'll write down the name of my barber; he's a genius."

Yanking his hand from my hair, I pushed him back. "My hair is fine as it is."

Gilbert continued as though I hadn't spoken. "You'll need to bring a companion to this party. A lady friend."

A deep itch closed up my throat. And there it was: his price.

"I won't be offering Aurélie for—"

His answer was swift and severe. "I agree, completely. Under no circumstances can you bring Aurélie Blancmaison. Promise me not to even consider it."

Perversely, I asked, "Why?" Bringing Aurélie would be the easiest. It wasn't as though I had such a large group of women friends to be choosy.

Gilbert turned away, rubbing his index finger and thumb as though manifesting a cigarette. "She's too young, too inexperienced. She would give away the true state of your finances." He turned back, jaw still tight. "And besides, she's a ballet dancer. It wouldn't be seemly, not in this crowd."

My temper rose for a moment. Nothing about Aurélie was anything but decent and good, no matter her career. Regardless, I would never expose Aurélie to people who might belittle her. She had enough of that at the ballet.

But what did that make me, that I was willing to rub elbows with the selfsame people?

A man who was desperate—no, *eager*—for some well-heeled investors. Aurélie wouldn't hold that against me, not as pragmatic as she was. "I'll do my best."

Gilbert nodded, pleased, and his smile returned, forcing away the fine lines radiating around his eyes. "Looking the way you do, it won't be a problem to find a woman friend, I'm sure. Everyone will be paired up, and I can't have you throwing the numbers off at the table."

Oh. "I should go now."

With another expressive shrug, Gilbert led me to the front of the store, where piles of boxes were stacked, their ribbons curling down in a waterfall of expensive decadence. "What's all this?"

"Shirts for you. And I picked some things for pretty Mademoiselle Blancmaison," he said, not looking my way. "Send her my respects, won't you? I send them as a gift without any yarn attached."

"Without strings? Good."

"Oui, here's the address." He winked and handed me a slip of paper. "Until tomorrow night. But now you'll have to excuse me. I'm late for an appointment with my uncle."

"Yes, of course. Until tomorrow."

Gilbert took a long-legged stride into the swath of customers and disappeared, leaving me alone.

The shopgirl cleared her throat. "The receipt, monsieur," she said, handing me a small square of folded paper before shutting the door to the carriage.

I opened it, worried for a moment that Gilbert had reneged on his promise to pay.

In neat handwriting the designee for the cost—a price that made my insides churn—was marked as paid by Finley Tighe, the Viscount Carleton. My blood went cold.

That had been Harry's honorary title as the legitimate son of the Earl of Rawcliffe.

It could never be me, not legally, in any case.

Bloody Gilbert had to get in the final word, I supposed. I hoped he knew what he was about.

Besides, none of this meant I'd ever honestly make peace with my father. But he owed me, after all. And it was time to send in my own chit. Make use of the relationship he'd thrust on me whether I'd ever wanted it or not.

If I dared.

7

After spending an evening agonizing over the short list of women I was well enough acquainted with to even imagine inviting as an *and guest*, I remained empty-handed. Other than ballet dancers, the horrifying Mademoiselle Jeunesse, and the florist who dyed my boutonnières, my life was devoid of female company.

Which left me with a single choice.

I prayed that bringing Victoire along as my companion to the dinner party was a stroke of genius and not a headlong rush into lunacy. Maneuvering amongst the bon ton was always risky, and these people—assuredly Tout-Paris—were utterly unknown to me. However, I'd convinced myself around midnight the night before that Vicky's stage characterization of a down-on-her-luck aristocrat would translate just as well outside of the cabaret as she managed inside its walls.

At the very least, she was more undeniably feminine than most who'd been born physically female.

In the hired carriage to the dinner party, my fingers curled into the underside of my thighs as I did my best to retain my composure. I was an engineer—not someone used to mingling with the upper echelons.

Vicky tilted her head and gave me the sort of look that said she knew exactly what I thought. I shook myself and took her hand. She always read me far too easily.

"You'll be fine, Fin. And I can absolutely hold my own. How's this?" With a voice like vintage Cabernet, she said, "How do you do? I'm Victoire Mauvais, granddaughter of the duc de Neussy."

"What if someone does know of the duke?" I couldn't keep my nerves in check.

A glorious smile lit her face. "He was my grandfather, which is why I pull it off so well. No one will doubt it, I promise you, Fin."

How hadn't I known she had such an illustrious pedigree in reality? But to be fair, I'd never shared anything about my life in England, either. They were hardly the stories we told each other on a Saturday night at the Green Carnation.

"My father was only second son, so it's not as if I lost a title. He threw me out when he found me wearing my mother's frock and pearls." She winked, though it wasn't funny. "On my knees in front of the groom. I never knew which part was the most offensive to him."

She raised her shoulders and looked out the window. Her voice was light, but I balled up my fists and wished I could make someone pay for her pain. "I grew up with a houseful of sisters, so anyone who knows of my family can imagine I'm one of them. Stop worrying."

I'd have to, as that's when the carriage pulled up to a luxurious Haussmann apartment block bordering the Champs de Mars. Not even in my most vivid dreams could I imagine myself belonging in a place like this. I pulled the scrap of paper with the address from my pocket, though I had had it memorized all afternoon.

After I closed the gate to the lift, Victoire settled her hand on my arm with a light touch. "I won't ruin this for you, Fin. You have my word."

Throat tight, shame poured over me. "No, *you* won't. But I might. Try and catch me if I stumble too much." I smoothed one of her long curls over her shoulder. "You'll be the loveliest woman here, I guarantee it."

She preened. "You do know a way to a girl's heart, don't you?"

The bell buzzed, and I held my breath. We'd be fine. If not, we'd leave.

And I'd find another engineering firm to hire me after Eiffel fired me.

If I didn't rot to death in a debtor's prison.

A servant opened the door and took Victoire's wrap. Under the bright crystal chandelier, she outshone the other guests. My shoulders loosened.

The flat was palatial, and in between ornate plaster moldings, the walls were a bright robin's-egg blue. Cream silk sofas were scattered around a white marble fireplace. Fifteen-foot arched windows were open, gauzy silk draperies rustling in the slight breeze of the evening.

At least twenty people in evening dress were scattered around, drawling in upper-class accents with a studied boredom only the truly rich ever seem to manage. I spotted Gilbert from behind in black tails, standing with a petite Créole. She was swathed in miles of satin that matched the walls, and rose on tiptoe to whisper something in his ear. He angled down to look at her, both their handsome profiles sparkling under the enormous chandelier.

As if Gilbert sensed my presence, he turned and saw me, his smile fading for a moment before he gregariously strode my way, his arm linked with his pretty companion's. Instead of shaking my hand, he kissed each cheek like we were friends. Even after so many years in France, that sort of greeting was beyond me to reciprocate.

"I'm pleased you've made it."

His companion smiled at me. "Won't you introduce me to your friends?" Her voice held a Caribbean lilt.

Gilbert answered. "Stéphanie, this is the British gentleman I told you I invited. Viscount Carleton, this is my fiancée, Stéphanie Verger." His voice was bright, professional, nothing like the joking camaraderie from our shopping trip.

Gilbert was engaged? To be honest, that caught me off guard even more than his dropping that ridiculous title.

"Finley Tighe, please."

With a smirk, Gilbert said, "The Right Honorable Finley Tighe. Isn't that the proper address?"

My hands clenched briefly. "I wouldn't have any clue." Everything about this setup felt contrived and distastefully grasping, as though each of my flaws were under a magnifying glass, waiting to be examined.

"Aren't you every bit as personable as Gilbert told me?" Stéphanie's mouth held more than a hint of an ironic smile. "Gilbert says you're hoping to find investors for Gustave Eiffel's tower, c'est vrais? I must warn you that my neighbors are aghast that this tower will lower the property value."

"Isn't there a chance that it will raise the value, mademoiselle? The Champs du Mars will be the epicenter of attractions during l'Exposition Universelle." It was the same tone I'd used when I told my schoolmates all of the lovely things I had planned for my holidays—forced smile and enthusiasm. Lies, but no one ever cared enough to question it.

Stéphanie kept keen eyes locked on mine. "We'll have to see. After all, visitors to Paris for l'Exposition will mean more customers visiting Qualité, and we can't argue with that, can we, Gilbert?"

He tapped his chin as if weighing that argument before he grinned. "Stéphanie is by far more intelligent than I am. Michel ought to put her in charge of finances—"

"Except I'm a woman, and Michel would never dream of allowing a woman to advise him on anything." Mademoiselle Verger's delicate nostrils flared briefly before she beamed at Victoire. "We've been extremely rude. Please introduce your companion, Lord Carleton."

Next to me, I had the notion that Victoire was holding back a laugh. *Lord Carleton.* How had I forgotten to mention that to her? I introduced her without stumbling over the title.

"Granddaughter of the duc de Neussy?" Stéphanie set her empty glass on a Louis Quinze sideboard. "I went to school with your sister Catherine. We still write, but I don't remember her mentioning a sister named Victoire. I've a very keen memory." Stéphanie counted off on her fingers. "I remember Catherine, of course, and Sophie, who was in the form under ours. Virginie, Cecile, and Elisabeth."

"You forgot Alice, and me." My ears buzzed with concern,

but Victoire didn't bat a lash. "Perhaps because they all call me Coquelicot for the color of my hair?" *Ladybug.* Her hair was more auburn than poppy, but the brightness of the name suited her.

"Wasn't there a brother?" Stéphanie probed.

"He died years ago." Taking advantage of Stéphanie's murmurs of condolence, Victoire pointed at the grand piano tucked into the corner of the room where two men shared the bench. "I adore this song. Will you come and sing with me, Stéphanie? Non? Then, please excuse me."

"What will you drink, Fin? Stéphanie has everything you could ever want." Gilbert leaned away from Stéphanie, who clung to his arm though her eyes followed Victoire.

"A glass of wine. Red, if you have it." I could keep my mind clear with wine, as long as I didn't drink too much. And Gilbert was correct; Stéphanie Verger had any number of things I wanted. The sorts of belongings I'd have for myself before it was all said and done.

Gilbert stroked the bare skin between his fiancée's puffed sleeve and three-quarter gloves. "Stéphanie, will you ask when dinner will be served, or shall I?"

"I will, but don't you wander off with this elegant new friend of yours, the way you do." She rapped his arm with her fan and let him go.

"Can I offer my congratulations on your engagement?" I was at a loss of what else to say.

Gilbert wrinkled his nose. "If you must." Then he turned on his high-wattage smile, looking beyond my shoulder. "Shall I introduce you about? That's why you're here, not to make small talk with me."

Chastened, I allowed him to take the lead. A threesome of gentlemen in their early twenties ignored me, focusing on their cards through the first half of our introduction, only giving me any sort of acknowledgment when Gilbert said, "Fin is the Viscount Carleton. The son of the Earl of Rawcliffe."

I ground my teeth to keep from adding that I was also the son of a ladies' maid.

"Rawcliffe's heir, you say?" One of the gentlemen, a blond youth sporting a clay pipe, cut his eyes to mine in speculation. "I went to school with Viscount Carleton. Poor Harry's dead. Do you mean to say that you're impersonating an English peer?"

A chill coursed over me like I'd eaten an entire lemon ice in one go.

Gilbert waved his hand as though the matter was trivial. "Fin is Harry's brother, Sonny. Any other slights against my friend, and I'll have to ask you to leave."

Sonny looked down his nose even though I stood and he sat. It was the sort of look perfected at the types of schools Harry must have gone to. "Sonny Tolbert. How do you do? I never heard mention of another son. My condolences and all." He exhaled a deep puff. The same flavor tobacco my father preferred.

"It's been something of a secret Rawcliffe's kept for years. Poor Harry," said Gilbert, elbowing in and shaking his head solemnly. He sighed. Shrugged. "But as Harry has died, the earl hopes to reconcile with Fin. His only remaining child."

Even if I could believe that to be the case, I'd never agree to renewing any sort of relationship with him.

Gilbert lowered his voice conspiratorially, and the men leaned in. "Bit of a scandal when the earl made a rash marriage in his youth. But now he's in a predicament, needs to produce an heir, you see, and enough time has gone by—" The Frenchman made a sort of open-handed gesture as if to imply that everyone could fill in the rest of the story.

I clenched my jaw at Gilbert's presumption. Now he was making up stories out of thin air. My haughty father would never agree to this blackening of his reputation.

"How fascinating," one of the others simpered, and pulled a chair over for me to sit. "What are you doing in Paris, Lord Carleton?"

Gilbert cut in to answer for me, holding my shoulder in a way that was meant to be steadying and wasn't. "He's scouting for speculators. Fin's a gambling man, like myself."

Three pairs of eyes sparkled. Apparently, I wasn't the only gambler in the room.

"What's the investment?"

I hesitated, still aghast at the blatant subterfuge, but Gilbert answered for me. "Gustave Eiffel's tower."

"Er...yes." I cleared my throat. "I'm an engineer for Eiffel et Cie and—"

Sonny snorted. "The son of an earl works for a living?"

My back straightened, and Gilbert made to intervene again but I cut him off. "I do indeed, Mr. Tolbert. I was never intended to be my father's heir, and frankly it's not just about money. I can't imagine sitting around allowing my brain to liquefy for lack of meaningful occupation."

The young man's face turned a furious red.

I warmed to my subject. "I studied maths at school and found I was something of a wizard at it. Why shouldn't I use my gifts?

Not only was I part of the design team for Monsieur Eiffel's tower, now I'm personally in charge of a vast team of engineers. For two years, we've spent each day figuring where to put each bolt and truss to guarantee that it can withstand high-velocity winds as well as millions of visitors ascending its staircases."

Another of the men frowned in confusion. "What tower is this?"

Sonny diverted his scorn to his friend. "Speaking of liquefied brain boxes, Stafford, you definitely come to mind. Perhaps you ought to open a paper once in a while. It's being built for the world's fair in '90."

"Eighty-nine, Mr. Tolbert, and the French refer to it as l'Exposition Universelle." I allowed a hint of a smile.

Mr. Stafford let out a snort. "You'd think a brilliant mind like yours would have caught that after living in this city for what? Five years at least."

Lifting his chin and looking me in the eye, Sonny ignored that and inclined his head as though waiting for me to continue.

"As to your question, my company won the design contest for the centerpiece of the exposition; a latticework tower taller than any currently standing structure in the entire world. Entirely formed of iron and negative space so it will be as if it's made of lace."

All of them were focused now, and my hands gestured to keep up with the speed of my words. "But it's much more than a decorative structure. Scientists around the world are eager to use its unprecedented height to study meteorology, telegraphy, and aerodynamics. One day, gentlemen, Monsieur Eiffel's tower might help humankind figure out how to design a flying machine."

Even Gilbert had lost his faintly mocking look. All of them were rapt, looking at me as though I was worth looking at, which gave me impetus to keep going.

"I'm lucky enough to be part of the tower's creation, but there's a way for others to join as well. Eiffel has a fascinating proposal for men clever enough to recognize the opportunity." I paused so they could insert themselves into that equation. "He's offering investors the chance to earn back many times over the initial outlay." I paused again, waiting for a prod.

Sonny was quick on the uptake. "Don't hold out on us, Carleton."

I didn't allow that name—or the ease with which he bestowed it—to distract me. "The tower will stand on the Champs de Mars for twenty years, and Eiffel will receive ninety percent of each ticket sale for the entire span. Millions of visitors are expected in the *first year alone* to see this marvel of technology."

A few more of the party guests, including Vicky and Stéphanie, gathered closer, listening. Victoire's eyes glittered with encouragement.

I lowered my voice as though sharing something secret. "Eiffel is willing to split twenty percent of his profit over the twenty years based on ticket sales. Depending on the amount each investor stakes, they will receive a ratio of Eiffel's sales. After they receive their entire repayment by the winter of '89, naturally." I glanced around the speculative faces. Not even the extremely wealthy didn't want more money, it seemed.

Victoire raised her wineglass as though toasting my employer. "It's as though Eiffel's got the philosopher's stone, but instead of creating eternal life, he's creating millionaires."

I was about to close the deal when Gilbert nodded toward a man standing by the piano. "Come, Fin, Hainault will be most intrigued by this proposition. We must chat with him before dinner." Clutching my elbow, he dragged me away.

I lit into him under my breath as soon as we were a half pace away. "I told you my father was off-limits. What if you've just alerted him that I'm trading on his name with that friend of Harry's?" I pulled away from his grasp. "And even if you were callous enough to risk that, it might at least have been worth the effort when I received the offers on the tips of some of those tongues back there."

He fetched us each a fresh glass of wine from a sideboard.

"What game are you playing?"

Gilbert's lips curled into a small smile. "A more diverting one than I'd anticipated." Before I could say anything else, he added in a whisper, "Sonny's been exiled from England by his father for some transgression or other. He needn't worry you." He flicked a glance over his shoulder at the chattering group we'd walked away from. "I promise, they'll be even more eager now that you didn't ask directly for their money. Trust me, Fin."

I wasn't sure that was possible.

"Chat with Hainault. He's mechanically inclined and rich as Croesus. Even better, he's the boisterous sort whose excitement is infectious." His voice cajoled. "I must tell you that your animation—now that I've witnessed you come alive—can be distracting."

"Distracting?" That wasn't good.

His gaze drifted from my eyes down to my lips and back,

slowly enough that I couldn't discount the implication. I point-edly stared at Stéphanie, his fiancée.

Gilbert laughed once. "Non. I meant to say you will be dis-tracting to Hainault. He has a weakness for handsome faces. That doesn't upset you, does it?"

"Does what u-u-upset me?" I stammered.

There was something behind his eyes that I couldn't under-stand except that it left me unsettled. "That I count a pair of les unnaturelles amongst my friends?"

The euphemism upset me much more than the idea that Gil-bert was friends with a homosexual couple. If I'd been a braver man, I'd tell him he would need to count me as another, that is, if he considered me a friend.

I offered my blandest smile. "Not in the slightest. I'm offering an opportunity to make money—not myself."

"Édouard Hainault is devoted to his partner, even if you were interested."

Was this a trap of some kind? Had Gilbert found out more about my private life than I'd believed? I couldn't imagine how he could know. The only people who were aware of who I was when the sun went down either had nothing to gain by spilling my secrets or were dead.

The familiar unfairness that I had to lie about myself churned in my stomach. When Napoleon drafted his legal code, homo-sexual practices had been deemed legal—as long as they weren't witnessed in public. Something to do with the army losing too many soldiers when there wasn't access to prostitutes. So, though my inclinations were technically within the law in Paris, any hint of gross indecency—which could be as harmless as a wink or a too-fond handshake—could earn me a fine, if not time in prison. Certainly, I'd lose my job.

Ironically, the same behavior from one of the abonnés to a girl like Aurélie was encouraged by society. The male half, at least.

Captain Édouard Hainault was as enthusiastic as Gilbert had warned, but there wasn't a scintilla of behavior that hinted he'd be as at home at the Green Carnation as I was. Of course, that meant nothing in and of itself, as I was well aware.

The world was not harmonious for men like us. Men with secrets.

Over three courses of our supper, Édouard Hainault repeated all of my selling points better than I had, and named a generous pledge. Not to be outdone, Gilbert also casually tossed out that he, too, was good for a quarter of a million francs.

A clamor rang around the table as half the guests made their own promises.

Bloody hell, it was going to work.

Gilbert raised one brow and gave me a hard stare before speaking. "Does Eiffel even need so much money as all of this on offer? He must be inundated with petitioners to make such sums from his—*your*—tower."

I pantomimed a moment of reflection though my heart was in my throat with worry that Gilbert might be pushing too hard. These people might not be so generous in the light of day without benefit of a drink or five. "You're likely correct. I'll have to speak with him tomorrow and see how much of this money he can accept."

Other than that, Gilbert didn't give me more than cursory

attention over the meal. By the time pudding was laid, I was as adept at ignoring him. After the final plates were cleared, I checked my watch and looked to Victoire. She gave me a pleading look: it was like when I'd taken Annabeth to the town fête and she'd begged to stay for another hour.

The women rose to leave for the traditional separation for after-dinner drinks, and Stéphanie tucked her arm into Victoire's. "Come and sit with me and let's figure out all the people I know that know you."

A blush crept up Victoire's neck, but she only laughed politely, and extricated her arm from our hostess. "Next time, Stéphanie, I'd be delighted, but Fin and I promised to make an appearance at another party. I'm sure you understand."

I exhaled, relief oozing from my pores over Vicky's change of face, and shook hands all around. Gilbert dismissed me with a curt nod, and his laughter with the guests followed me down the staircase to the foyer.

Stéphanie escorted us. "I'm most anxious to go to bed and write a nice long letter to Catherine all about meeting you, Coquelicot."

Victoire gave her a rousing set of kisses, holding her hands as she did so. "Please add my love. And do tell her how I looked, won't you?" Victoire puckered her lips and gave a saucy wink.

"I will." Stéphanie turned away.

With a few more profusions of politeness and fluff, Victoire and I emerged from the flat, lives still intact. For now.

I walked in a blind panic to the waiting taxi, but shut the door before speaking. "How can I do that again?" I dropped my head into my palms, mentally exhausted by the constant need to be on guard. And then remembered I wasn't the only one who might have concerns. "Bloody hell, what's your sister going to tell Stéphanie?"

Victoire squeezed my knee. "There's nothing to worry about, darling, your performance was absolutely impeccable, and believe me, I don't hand out that compliment lightly. You'll manage to keep it up. That Duhais will help you, as will I. If you had been kind enough to tell me the details beforehand, *Viscount*, I could have been more proactive, too." She wrinkled her nose and sighed, though her smile shone through. "Catherine and I have always been tight as thieves, so don't worry on that account. She's the one member of my family who loves me as I am. Where do you think I get half of my frocks? In any case, if I remember correctly, Catherine doesn't like Mademoiselle Verger nearly as much as we were told. Something about schoolgirl crushes and heartbreak."

Relieved that Victoire had a sister who loved her, I choked out a noise that may have been a laugh. "Schoolgirl crushes?"

"Did you think only boys' schools were rife with midnight cuddles?"

"There was nothing like that at my schools." I folded my arms over my chest.

Her laugh tinkled as she unbuckled her shoes and propped her feet in my lap. "That's a shame, cher. You'd have enjoyed your youth much more if you'd had a few tumbles."

I had no reply. She was likely right.

"You're still young, Fini. There's plenty of time to enjoy yourself."

Out the window, the streets transformed from splendid mansions back to the dingy side streets where I belonged. I snorted at her comment.

"Handsome Monsieur Duhais secretly stares at you nearly as often as you pretend not to notice him."

Whipping my head around, I glared. "He's engaged."

She pressed the ball of her foot into my thigh. "You're adorably naïve sometimes."

I bit back a retort and looked out the window. If Victoire was blinded to the fact that I counted myself amongst the world's cynics, I wasn't going to enlighten her.

8

The promise of so many investors had me springing from my bed the next morning before my clock rang. Victoire was correct; I had pulled it off. I may have even whistled as I shaved and dressed for work.

The empty hat rack in the corner of the office assured me that I'd arrived before either of the men with whom I'd shared work space for the past seven years. Even after my extraordinary evening, I arrived five minutes before nine, when business began for the morning.

I unrolled the schematic drawing I was currently studying and clipped it to the edges of the drafting table.

"Tighe? Good morning. All alone, eh?" Gustave Eiffel's voice yanked me out of my reverie. His blue eyes took in my solitude, and he frowned. I glanced at the clock over the door. Five past.

Out of my seat in a second, I thrust out my hand for a shake, not answering his second question. "Good morning, sir. It's a pleasure."

Emil Rochat's Swiss-accented voice rang up the stairs. "You missed a hell of an evening, Tighe. Good Lord, we didn't get home until two in the morn—" He stilled when he saw who stood in the office with me; our third desk's owner, Sébastien Levan, ran into his back before he stiffened, too.

It wasn't the right time to mention that I'd not been invited. In any case, I'd not have traded my own productive evening for a sodden one with them.

Eiffel ran his hand over his trim beard. "There you are, finally." He glanced at the clock pointedly. "Come along upstairs, gentlemen. I have some important news."

My colleagues paused to remove their coats, but I followed my employer up to the third floor and took the seat next to his usual one around the oblong table.

Ferns hung on either side of the large window, and dust mites danced in the stream of sunlight when Eiffel pushed open the red gingham draperies. A pitcher of water sat on a sideboard, and he poured himself a glass, asking if I wished for one, too. I accepted so as not to come off as contrary. He spoke of the recently completed observatory in Nice and asked if I'd made it down to see it.

I'd worked on the opening of the project, but hadn't been back since. He suggested I ought to, and I nodded while tabulating the cost of the ticket and hotel in the back of my mind.

Within minutes, the room was filled with pipe tobacco, almost obscuring the walls plastered with blueprints of some of the buildings designed by the firm. The Budapest train station, the Ponte Dona Maria bridge in Portugal, as well as the prefabricated ironwork he'd masterminded.

Eiffel rapped his knuckle on the table to quiet everyone down. Silence was instantaneous. "Perhaps you've heard rumors that

Monsieur Vallette will retire next month? I'm here to verify that it is true."

Voices erupted around the table, soon silenced by Eiffel's raised hand. "There's a position among the partners that must be filled. I'll do it swiftly. In the next week, so Vallette can train the new man. Progress on my tower cannot be compromised because we're mired in internal politics."

I traced some incisions on the old table in front of me with a finger. It was gouged all over with divots and marks from drafting tools.

Eiffel placed his palms on the table, leaning forward on straight arms. "From what I've been told, any of you would fill his shoes competently enough, but I need more than that; I need a man who can not only cover his engineering duties, but who will also help Eiffel et Cie blaze into the future. Who can visualize what my tower can be. And who has a talent for sharing this vision in a way that inspires the rest of the world to take notice."

A short-cased clock ticked in the silence of the room.

"So." Eiffel's voice was determined. "Which of you shall it be?" A knobby finger pointed at each of us in turn. I didn't blink when it was my turn for his penetrating stare. "Rochat? I'm told you're gifted in physics, but I need someone who is dedicated to this business, and I'm unsure if you fit the bill."

Rochat reddened, but held his tongue.

"Levan, a few of your personal designs have made it across my desk, but you're notorious for giving only as much time as required, no more, no matter the urgency of a project."

There was no rebuttal; Sébastien Levan had three children and a wife who hated him working one minute longer than required, so he was out the door as soon as the second hand reached quitting time. It was a miracle he'd managed to escape with Rochat last night.

"And you, Tighe. You've been here the longest, have shown the dedication I'm looking for." My hours at the drafting table had paid off.

Eiffel pushed off the table and turned to the window, hands clasped behind his back, his somber gray morning jacket stretching tight across his shoulders. He wasn't a loud man, but my ears were trained to listen. "But I need a man who can eloquently represent Eiffel et Cie to the public, and I worry that your natural unobtrusiveness will impede that."

He spun around. I wiped my damp palms along the pinched creases of my trouser knees. I was a glutton for extra starch. This was a fortuitous moment; I had to grasp it. "If you'll pardon the interruption, Monsieur Eiffel, I've some news to share, about raising funds for the tower."

Eiffel gave me another long stare, this time curiosity shining in his clever face. The silver-gray of his curls was backlit from the window like a halo. "*You've* found investors?"

Senses heightened, I could taste the bloody promotion. I wanted it. I deserved it. So many of my day-to-day struggles would disappear with a partner's higher salary, long before the profits rolled in from the commission. "Indeed. I've already secured"—I had already tallied the amount pledged by Gilbert and Hainault. I wouldn't mention the rest until that was assured—"half of a million francs."

The rest of the occupants of the room exploded into incredulous chatter, but Eiffel kept his eyes on mine until the room stilled.

"Now we have a baseline." He snapped his fingers, and we all straightened our spines. "Levan, Rochat; you have until next Monday to raise more than your colleague Tighe, or he will become the new partner." To me, he extended a hand. "Well done, monsieur. Continue with your efforts."

Needless to say, my office was unusually quiet over the next few days.

On Thursday, a note was delivered with some interest by the boy from the mailroom.

> *Fin,*
>
> *My uncle Michel invites you for drinks with his friends on Thursday. I'll pick you up at eight. No need for a companion—you can have me.*
>
> > > > *G.*

That was intriguing. However, there was the fact that Aurélie needed to be retrieved from the ballet. But Jody would do it if I sent around a note. I'd never persuade him to go into the foyer de la danse, but he'd wait outside. The cabaret wouldn't be terrifically busy until later, and Laurent was a completely competent manager. I'd grinned when I read the note the first time, and still grinned after the fiftieth.

Because I'd get the chance to pitch to Michel de Gênet, naturally. And all of his rich friends.

Mademoiselle Jeunesse saw me coming up the street and waited for me to open the door. "I'd appreciate your telling Mademoiselle Blancmaison to ask her friends to keep quiet when they come by after dark. And she must keep the front door locked. You and she might consort with the baser elements, but I fear for my life sometimes." She slipped into her flat before I could ask what she meant.

I might throttle Aurélie's skinny little neck. The neighborhood was decent enough, but nowhere was safe, especially for someone who walked through town with her pretty head in the clouds, invincible with youth's armor.

The door to my flat was unlocked, too, and I called to Aurélie a few times before she finally came into the salon. She wore black on her lashes and color on her cheeks.

"Mademoiselle Jeunesse just gave me a chiding over your bad behavior. You must keep your voice down in the stairwell." I slid off my tie and jacket.

Her eyes opened in confusion, but she smiled. "Oh, is that all?"

"*Is that all.*" I grunted and stomped to my room, stopping cold when I saw the large black paper box tied up with a cream ribbon that waited outside my bedroom.

"It came a while ago." She sniffed and said primly, "I'm sorry I squealed when the messenger brought it. I'll do my best to behave more ladylike in the future."

I cut my eyes to her and sighed. We didn't both need to be in a fit of temper. In any case, the box screamed my name. I carried it to the sofa, which had seen better days, and pulled the ribbon off carefully.

The second evening jacket. The blue one. Another note nestled on top of the fine fabric.

You needed this one. It will make your eyes supernatural.

G.

I shook it out, and not a wrinkle showed. I cleaned myself up and shaved in record time, grateful I had a freshly starched shirt to wear with it. I hummed as I did my best to re-create the perfect cravat Gilbert always wore. Not so successful.

"What do you think?" Aurélie twirled behind me so I had to turn and see her. A new dress—obviously of the finest quality— fit her perfectly. She hugged herself. "Gilbert sent me this, too."

As happy as I was for her to have such a lovely gift, it did take some of the shine off of my jacket. *Gilbert?*

"How do you know Monsieur Duhais? Has he come to the Palais to speak with you?" I kept my voice flat and did my best to knot my cravat. Giving up, I focused on my hair, which *would* wave in the blasted humidity. She stood behind me but from the angle of the mirror I watched her twist her hands together.

"Oh." Her voice was so faint I nearly didn't catch it. "Not the Palais. I met him once, a long time ago."

I cocked my head, and her eyes met mine in the reflection. She scrubbed her knuckles across her chin. "He was at school with... Paul."

His name was like a well-placed kick in my guts with a particularly strong football boot. Gilbert was friends with—my thankfully dead cousin—Paul? I drew in a sharp breath.

Though, in fairness, I'd thought Paul a decent lad for the first six months of our acquaintance, too. Merely attending classes with him wasn't a reason to extinguish the new friendship—if I could be bold enough to name it that—between Gilbert and me. Aurélie rallied more quickly than I did. "I wish the dancers were already here and could see you now. They're all half in love with you. They'd fall all the way if they saw your ass without the tails to cover it up."

Her crudeness of speech was not a result of her bringing-up. At least, not the part I was responsible for. I shot her a look. But the knock at the door kept me from reprimanding her.

Gilbert appeared as amiable as I'd ever seen him, scattering my concern.

"I love my gifts, Monsieur Duhais; what do you think?" She thrust her hip out a little too provocatively.

Friends with her wretch of a brother or not, Aurélie didn't show the slightest bit of anxiety. Perhaps they really were mere acquaintances? Lord knows I went to school with any number of young men whom I'd never claim as friends—or, as Lem Bryant made so clear, they wouldn't claim me, which carried the same result at the end of the day.

Gilbert was magnificent in matte black silk like the deepest edges of night. I ran my finger under my rounded collar, grateful that my clothes were just as elegant.

He kissed her hand like a courtier. "How delightful to see you again, Mademoiselle Blancmaison. You look even more beautiful than onstage. And it fits very well." He made a show of looking her over.

I forced a benevolent smile on my face while she preened. A bitter tang bloomed in my mouth, as I still wasn't entirely convinced that he wasn't trying to charm his way into Aurélie's life.

"Shall we go?" He turned his face to me for the first time. "That jacket." He snapped his fingers. "You'll make me a rich man." Still, he came and retied my cravat. The familiarity of the act made me catch my breath.

I angled my neck to look at Aurélie instead of Gilbert. "Do remember what Mademoiselle Jeunesse said."

"Bonne chance." Aurélie stood on tiptoe and pecked my cheek. "And I already told you I would."

I squeezed her shoulder before following Gilbert back out. Both of us were quiet on the staircase, and that continued throughout the first part of the carriage ride. And then he laughed to himself. "I forgot this last thing—you are polished to a T aside from your lapel. I thought you might like this." He handed me a small florist's box that sat on a folded newspaper.

A green carnation. An uncomfortable tingling in my hands, urging me not to take the box. The leaves were drenched with dye. But how could I refuse?

"G-g-green?" If I could throw it out the window, I would. What could he mean by this? Was it a warning that he knew about my visits to the club? After the comments regarding his friend Hainault, and now this...But truly; how could he know about me?

My father certainly couldn't have a hint of my personal life if he truly was interested in resurrecting a relationship. It was an unmentionable in England. Convicted perpetrators had received the death penalty not too many years before. One more reason to never venture back.

Gilbert rolled his eyes and, holding a cigarette between his lips, leaned forward to fix the boutonniere. Smoke tickled my nose, but I held steady, not wishing to curtail the opportunity to have him so focused, though ill at the reason why.

"The girl at the shop told me green wasn't à la mode. Did her best to talk me into blue."

How I wished she had.

He settled back in the bench across from me, and my breathing relaxed until he said, "It's an unnatural thing, this green-colored carnation. But I knew it would set off your eyes more than the blue."

His words from the dinner party echoed in my ears: les unnaturelles. Unnatural? *Depends on whom one asks.* I waved my hand. "Who's to judge what's natural and what isn't? Besides, green's the most natural color of them all, isn't it? When I lived outside of Paris, I saw it all the time in nature."

He laughed, that champagne-fizzy giggle that emanated from somewhere under his lungs. "You're right, I suppose, and it appears to be your signature. You wore one the night we first spoke. Still, keep that answer if anyone else asks." He raised his eyebrow. "You already know Michel has the highest standards? He takes any sort of failure as a personal insult to his integrity."

"I only dealt with him briefly while working on his store, and under the circumstances, I didn't blame him. He was paying a king's ransom. And the outcome is marvelous. Qualité is marvelous."

He looked out the window. "It is. He has good taste. But you must know…" He met my gaze. "I told him about your father."

Before I could gnash my teeth in annoyance, he continued. "Underneath those vaunted morals of his, he's a bit of snob. I don't know why—he was raised in an apartment smaller than yours. He never even finished lycée, but to hear him, he has an advanced degree from the Sorbonne."

Gilbert's look was warm. Too warm. His front teeth, straight and white, were slightly off-center, giving his smile a charming lopsidedness.

"And no need to mention you never got your diploma. You did the work for it, non?"

Someone pouring ice water down my neck wouldn't have caused a more violent chill. I hadn't even come clean to Eiffel about that.

"Yes, I had two examinations left when I came to France." I frowned. "How do you know so much about me?"

Because it was uncanny. If Gilbert wasn't helping me the way he was, I'd be running the other direction like the devil was on my heels.

The carriage halted at a side street, and a lamplight shone through the window, illuminating his face like some macabre mask. The horses moved again, and it disappeared.

"I spent a week with your father in London. He had quite a lot to say about you. I'm sure you're missing an opportunity now that he's all alone." Gilbert's face was bright with disbelief. "I know how much work you must have done in your university program. It boggles my mind that you wouldn't cross the finish line." His eyes fixed on mine.

As it was an open secret in the community that Annabeth and I were his natural children, Rawcliffe had kept up the appearance that he took care of us. And monetarily, I suppose he did. He paid for Aunt Glad's house, and our food and clothing. I was even sent to a second-tier school before going on to receive a university education reserved for the well-off. All that money spent on my schooling my father would have considered wasted when I walked away before the end. It was gratifying to know that in some small way I had aggravated him.

"I'm afraid you've set me up to fail." I fiddled with the top button on the placket. "There's very little I can tell anyone about the earl. I doubt I've spoken to him fifty times in my life. You know him better than I do."

A flash of sympathy crossed his features before he soothed them back to indifference. He handed me the newspaper and pointed to a boxed message. "Could this be you, hmm?"

I skimmed the advertisement. *The Earl of R— seeks his eldest son, FT, last seen in France. Reward offered for discreet inquiries.*

I gasped, and the paper fluttered to the floor of the carriage.

"It…it can't be." Not the way that connard left things with me so many years ago.

Gilbert grinned like a wolf, his dark brows drawing together almost menacingly. "Because England is full of peers with the family name beginning with R? With sons carrying the initials FT who fled to France?" He rolled his eyes with an exaggerated smile. "Surely it must be you."

My heart hadn't restarted, and I couldn't push out any words.

"Oui, it must be you, Viscount." He leaned across our legs and feet and squeezed my shoulder. "Stop worrying. He swore to me

91

that he wished to have you back in his life in your rightful place as his son. You're not doing anything wrong."

Nothing about this scenario felt authentic, and yet Gilbert was so assured. The carriage stopped next to tall iron fencing, and the jostling of the driver jumping down alerted me that we had arrived.

"In those fifty or so times you met him, how did your father project himself?"

My mind flitted to the last time, when I demanded to come in and speak to him, even though the butler tried to keep me out. I'd screamed his name, marching through his house, desperate for his help. Heat pricked my eyes thinking of his face when I told him what happened. What he'd allowed to happen to Annabeth.

And then I slammed the memory shut. Rawcliffe had done enough to destroy my life, but perhaps he truly wished to make amends, had had a change of heart once Harry died. I could imagine that. *I could.* "Formal."

Gilbert jumped down to the street and grinned up at me. "Then pretend you're him. You're already terrifically proper, so it won't be much of a stretch."

I shuddered; I never wanted to be that man. But I wanted this money from de Gênet's friends, was desperate for the security the promotion would bring Aurélie and me.

And if, on top of it all, my father was willing to offer a reward to have me re-enter his life on a more equal footing this go-round...well, I'd be a fool not to claim it. Like Victoire and Jody kept telling me.

"Proper, d'accord. That's how we all picture the British. *Dull.*" He took a step back, examining me. "But perhaps not too dull.

It's effective when you become so enthused about the tower. You become even more—" But he didn't finish his thought. He just stared at me with an unreadable expression. "Remember, you're here to find investors, not friends."

His praise—both articulated and left hanging—hit my nerves like a swallow of aged bourbon.

The gate was open for us, electric light posts every few feet glaring off the oyster shell walkway. Each step was a hard crunch, swelling up in my chest like confidence. I could do this.

"Stéphanie is Michel's stepdaughter, did she tell you?"

Stopping short, I turned to him. "She's your cousin?"

"Non, though she is my closest friend." He sighed. "Michel married her mother perhaps ten years ago? Her money paid for the expansion of the store. But she died in a riding accident last year. Her horse threw her, and she broke her neck." He lifted his eyes. "I was in England." His fingers curled around my forearm. "Marrying Stéphanie is a promise I made to her. She deserves her inheritance. My uncle is of the generation that believes women should be taken care of by a man, and that's him until she marries. You've met her—she's as independent as they come, and chafes under his protection. I'll suit her much better, and it will get him off my back to settle down, as well."

"And what do you get out of this arrangement? Are you in love with her?"

Gilbert looked pensive for a moment. "I love her very much as a friend, though I'd never bother marrying anyone for my own sake. As I mentioned before, I'm still heartbroken and likely will be for the rest of my life, but why not make hers easier?" He ground his back teeth and turned. "Stéphanie's utterly dedicated to Qualité and doesn't bother about what I do in my own time. As long as I don't humiliate her?" He ended it on a question I struggled to make sense of, unless he meant there was another woman he was interested in having an affair with. Or did he mean Aurélie?

Was this why he'd been so cagey about discussing her? If Gilbert was seen around town with a ballet dancer, it wouldn't be kept quiet for long. Keeping a ballet dancer as a mistress, by its very design, was a delicate bite of gossip to be savored and shared. It was part of the appeal for the abonnés, the flaunting of ownership, to show that their status was strong enough to secure the fantasy woman every man wished to have in his bed.

I'd sworn that would never be Aurélie's fate. If she achieved the fame she deserved, it would be only due to her skills. Her art.

But this wasn't the venue to raise that with Gilbert.

"Yes, well, I'd rather not mention Aurélie to anyone here, either. Not after she was so betrayed by her brother *Paul*."

"Aurélie's brother betrayed her?" He stopped short as though he was lost.

"Yes, she mentioned the two of you were friends."

Gilbert looked nonplussed. "I wouldn't call Paul my friend, exactly. Anyway, I did mention the ballet to my uncle. He asked where I met you. He knows it's the sort of thing men do, even if he finds it repugnant, as do I."

Not waiting to knock, Gilbert opened the door, and I was momentarily blinded from the brightness of the foyer. A crystal chandelier, easily ten feet across, suspended twenty feet over my head, lit the space with fractured light.

"Bonne chance," he said, mimicking Aurélie. He stood so close that for half a second, I could feel his breath on my cheeks.

I followed him to the back of the hall to a room paneled in mahogany. I suppose I'd expected some tepid dinner party, something more suited to a famous moralist. Instead, a billiard table sat in the middle, flanked by four or five men. Another handful were scattered about smoking cigars and holding amber liquid in Irish crystal.

Bent over the table, black hair slicked back with macassar oil, was Michel de Gênet. He deftly clicked his stick against the cue ball, and two balls spun into their respective holes. He puffed his cigar and gave his nephew a sour look.

I'd only met Monsieur de Gênet a few times nearly three years ago, but side-by-side, I could see the family resemblance. Their faces had the same cast, though de Gênet's was craggy. Still handsome, but fierce, piercing. Able to see through façades. Lies.

A shiver crawled up my spine.

But I could do this.

"Michel, this is the speculator I mentioned at lunch? The Englishman?"

I held out my hand. Black eyes stripped me to my foundations. Channeling the Earl of Rawcliffe, I lifted my chin and my eyebrows. "Finley Tighe, Viscount Carleton." Easier to roll off my tongue than I'd ever have believed even two weeks before. "How do you do?"

Annabeth would have ribbed me mercilessly for the unabashedly supercilious timbre that had molded onto my voice.

My own grasp was equally tight, and de Gênet dropped my hand first. "Welcome." He propped the stick upright and gestured to his company. "My nephew will introduce you after he pours me a drink."

Gilbert flushed but did as his uncle bid. Behind a burled wood bar larger than at many pubs I'd frequented, the footman looked startled as well. Why have a footman if he was going to use Gilbert as a server?

All of it reminded me that Jody's sister Charlotte might have been the one behind the bar. I felt a flash of shameful gratitude that I wasn't faced with her. It might have thrown my game off. I was more aware than most that a man of my claimed status shouldn't have a personal relationship with a maid. The disparities between my parents' social status was the cornerstone of my life.

But I didn't have time to think further as I was immediately pulled into conversation with one of France's wealthiest rail owners. I spent the next ninety minutes with a smile plastered on my face as one by one, I gave a short biography—mostly false—about myself. Thanks to Gilbert's determination for me to drop the name of my father, I did so with an ever-increasing ease.

De Gênet's friends were impressed by my pedigree; even I could see it. In my elegant new suit, I played the part of the English gentleman dabbling in investments for the sake of the gamble like a duck took to water. I put those tedious years of boys' public schooling to good use for once in my life.

By the time I'd made the circuit, I had pledges for investments of an additional million francs. Commissions on these would more than triple my current salary. I wasn't sure how much they'd multiply the new salary I was sure to secure when Monsieur Eiffel heard of this newest success. I was light-headed and even finished the whiskey in my hand. Better still, I had invitations to more gatherings.

De Gênet was the last man for me to charm. "Monsieur, as a

former client of Eiffel et Cie, you already know that his designs are sublime. I imagine that the link between Qualité and the future tower could only bring even more prestige to your brand." I added an almost obsequious smile to ensure I'd caused no offense. "Your exquisite taste is internationally recognized. As is my employer's."

"Eiffel is a fool, but he produces decent work. Do you play billiards, Tighe?"

It wasn't an appropriate time to argue about my employer's reputation, so I inclined my head and smiled as innocently as I could. "Not for years, but the skill might still be there."

He handed me a stick. "You may be correct." His right eyebrow rose slightly, more amused than acerbic. "Or you may be a fool. I couldn't be bothered either way. But if you win, I'll allow you to name my pledge."

I was drunk on the change in my fortunes and winked at Gilbert. Because really, who could refuse a challenge like that?

9

At one o'clock on Monday, I found the small brass plate next to the doorbell for Monsieur Eiffel's city offices. It was an unassuming townhouse from the outside, and if I hadn't checked the address at least three times before setting out from the workshop, I'd have worried I was in the wrong place.

Inside, however, was a different story. Not that I spent much time in the salons of the aristos, but the waiting area was exactly how I'd imagine it to be: sumptuous fabrics on the furniture and a hothouse of flowers and palms. I gave my name to the assistant, who asked me to sit while he checked in with the man.

"Tighe, you're right on schedule." Eiffel welcomed me himself and held the door open.

As if I wouldn't be? As soon as his note had arrived Friday afternoon, I counted the hours until my private meeting.

I removed my hat and shook his hand like an equal for the first time. His office held two desks, though the one for his son-in-law was empty. The walls were decked with photos of some of the bridges and buildings our firm had built. A monument to his ironwork genius. And that of his engineers, of course.

Perching on the corner of his desk, he bade me sit. "I hear you found additional success."

The grin that had been bottled up for an hour broke free, and I nearly laughed with the giddiness behind it. "I haven't gotten the contracts signed—I'm waiting for your lawyers to draw them up so it is all backed by more than my word. But, I have found success, yes, sir."

His blue eyes widened, and he asked if I wanted something to drink.

Already moving up the food chain. "No, thank you."

"How much have you gotten, exactly? I'll have the papers written this afternoon and delivered. But don't leave me in suspense."

I didn't mean to drag it out, but I could hardly believe my own words. "Two-point-two million francs."

His eyes narrowed, and he leaned forward as if to hear me more clearly. "*Million*, did you say?"

Grinning, I nodded.

"So quickly? You must be joking."

But I wasn't.

He fiddled with his tie pin. "Mon Dieu. And these are men who will have their banks draft this pledge? It isn't some sort of—"

"They gave me their word." I dropped the name of the railway man friend of de Gênet's whom I was meeting for dinner later in the week.

Letting out an impressed whistle, Eiffel stood and looked at one of the pictures on the wall, his hands folded behind his back. "Have you calculated how much money that would be for you?"

Down to the last sou. "Yes, sir."

"How did this happen?" He lifted his palms. "I regret to admit, I know next to nothing about you."

And I'd like to keep it that way. "A friend of mine introduced me. Gilbert Duhais. His uncle is Michel de Gênet."

The man I smashed in billiards and got a half million francs from. I hadn't played in a while, but I hadn't lost my touch.

And the bastard had bloody well offered for me to name my own pledge.

Did I imagine Monsieur Eiffel became more alert at Gilbert's name? Or was it his uncle? "Twice I've attempted to ask de Gênet to involve himself in our tower, and twice he's denied me. We had a strong difference of opinion a few years back, and I'm shocked that he'd align himself with my company. And here you are, telling me he's pledged an enormous amount. You must have some magic that I haven't been keen enough to notice before."

I wiped my finger under my collar. "The magic was my luck in befriending Gilbert Duhais."

"He's a good friend, this Duhais?"

A hundred different answers swirled around my brain, and any of them could be correct at a given moment. "Yes. I believe so."

"He came by this morning with a check, did you know?"

Blinking, I was glad I already sat because that would have knocked me over. "Duhais came here?"

Eiffel gave a long stare that was unreadable. "He did. You didn't know?"

I shook my head wondering what Gilbert might have said.

"He spoke quite glowingly about you. Almost as though—" Monsieur Eiffel cut off his own words and turned to fiddle with something on his desk. "He wanted some guarantee that he'd get a refund if the plans for the tower fell through. Not as abrasively as his uncle would have asked, but he was insistent on a guarantee."

Nervous, I was compelled to ask, "The tower *will* be built?"

The papers had been full of arguments against it for the past six months. Notables such as the writer Guy de Maupassant and the architect of the Opéra Charles Garnier were publicly against the tower, as were dozens of others with good names and plenty of ink in their wells to draft disgusted editorials. They were horrified at the idea of the tower looming over the city like some revolting modern eyesore.

"Tighe, think of it as such; we are men of facts and figures, d'accord? We believe in the natural laws that govern all of the world, all of the universe."

He ran his thumbs under his lapels as he formulated his thoughts. "And these squawking artistes are annoyed that their opinion can't dictate the will of the people of France. They imagine they're as powerful as the winds that sweep through Paris in the winter." He snorted. "Our tower is designed to withstand all of that pressure, as balanced as though it was preordained by some benevolent hand from the Universe. It will bring together everything that the French hold dear: beauty and love, science and reason in a melody that is the nearest we'll get to magic here on earth."

He picked up a newspaper and swirled it into a cone, blowing his breath to illustrate. "We like to think that everything can be explained rationally, by science. But science is more than rationality. The laws of science, of these natural forces, always end up conforming to the secret laws of harmony."

He gave a chuckle of self-deprecation, shaking me from my

thoughts. "You'll go back to Levallois-Perret and tell them all I'm a madman, spouting nonsense."

"Absolutely not, monsieur. I'll quote you, if you don't mind? It was poetic."

He clapped me on the back and poured himself a drink from a rolling tray stacked with decanters. He raised an eyebrow my way, as if asking again, and this time I nodded.

After handing me the wineglass, he raised his to me. "These rumblings won't lead anywhere. But, still, the more money we have on hand to show the government that we mean to follow through, the smoother our path. You're doing me—our company—an enormous favor, and I assure you, it is appreciated."

Our company. I was flush with a sense of success and belonging.

My boss beamed. "I think such a good turn deserves a reward. I'd like to formally offer you Vallette's old position."

I stood. "I'll be the new partner?"

Salt-and-pepper eyebrows rose. "That's what I said last week, my good man." He glanced down at my left hand. "Are you married?"

My stomach flip-flopped. I dreaded this line of questioning. I hated to lie that someday I'd find a woman to settle down with when there was no chance in the world. "I'm not."

"Any prospective wife on the horizon?"

Flushing, I looked down. "Uh, no."

Don't ask me why. *I beg you—*

"Any particular reason why not?"

"Back in England, there was a tragedy in my life. No other woman could compare with the one I lost." Blast, I hated using my sister this way, but it wasn't a lie.

"Oh, I beg your pardon." He chewed the inside of his cheek and offered me a cigar, which I took, though I disliked them. It gave him something to do besides ask more questions. Steam practically wafted from his ears as he worked to come up with another way to question me about my personal life. That wouldn't do. I turned the conversation, spent the next twenty minutes putting him on the defensive while I asked about the timeline for the tower.

"Is there anything else?" I stood, straightening my cuffs.

He laughed once. "Continue with your magic." He walked me to the front door. "I'd say you've earned the afternoon off, and you can move into your new office tomorrow."

Thanking him, I shook his hand again, unfamiliar sensations rolling in my solar plexus. *Happiness*, I believe.

"And come by here again a week from today? Same time?" He turned and then paused. "I'll have the lawyer bring the partnership contracts to the workshop tomorrow."

I'd deliver them myself.

But for now, I decided to visit the site where this behemoth was scheduled to be built, the Champs de Mars.

Would be built, if I had anything to do with it.

Monsieur Eiffel put his hand on my shoulder and hesitated. I stilled in anticipation.

"Why didn't you ever mention you were the son of an earl, Tighe? Or should I use your title? Viscount Carleton?"

Oh, Gilbert. Was there nowhere left for me to be plain Fin Tighe? Damn it. I squeezed the handle of the door to maintain my balance. "Sir?"

He smiled. "Surely a man in your father's position can help us get the needed money for the tower?" I fixated on a small patch of stubble he'd missed in his recent shave. "See what you can do now that you're a partner, yes?"

Bloody hell. Was that the real reason I was given the partnership? Mouth drier than dust, I nodded. "I'll see what I can manage." I ran my tongue over my lips hoping to unglue them. "But, sir, I've been doing quite well on my own."

His smile was enigmatic and didn't meet his eyes. "Politically, he could make my life easier, which in turn..." Eiffel let the notion drop without mentioning it. "You know. If you wish to."

Mumbling something incomprehensible to either of us, I hurried down the stairs and plunged into the streets, hoping to still my racing heart.

As if I could just send a note and patch things up. *I heard a rumor you're looking for an heir?*

But according to Gilbert, he was. And I fit the bill...or could with some maneuvering. Aside from the fact that I'd never allow my father the satisfaction of believing he'd won me over.

Because the day was lovely and my mood was unnervingly hopeful—a feeling that I could easily get used to—I decided to corral my energy into a walk across the city.

I smiled at so many strangers, I'm lucky I wasn't hauled off in a straitjacket.

But I refused to be plagued by any concern. Not today. Today I was ready to be happy. And if I could trust Gilbert, there was an actual chance that my father finally saw me as more than the product of a youthful indiscretion. I'd never allow him into my life—his behavior when Annabeth died made sure of that—but I could dangle his name to secure more funds.

He'd likely never even know.

At the bottom of a greengrocer's window was a *To Let* sign. I ducked under a startlingly clean white awning to read the details, a small flutter of excitement expanding in my stomach. I took a few steps back and held on to my hat as I craned my neck to take in the view. *Glorious.* I'd revel in living here, occupying the best-appointed flat of a comfortingly bourgeois Haussmann building. The scrolled ironwork of the balcony was geometric rather than flowery, and the golden stonework around the ten-foot windows held an echo of ancient Greece.

Indeed, I could be very content.

I fumbled in my pockets for the pencil nub I carried everywhere and wrote the proprietor's address on the back of a matchbox. It was clearly too dear, but perhaps something I could afford soon. Thanks to Gilbert Duhais.

And my new position as partner at Eiffel et Cie.

Crossing the street with one more longing glance over my shoulder, I visualized trailing bougainvillea cascading over the railing. Drinking tea on the small, but still quite private, balcony. It wouldn't be too far for Aurélie to travel to and from the theater.

I couldn't think of the last time I'd been roaming the city on a weekday afternoon and took advantage of the novelty by splurging on a red-and-yellow-pepper quiche that I ate under the statue of the Gaul on the Pont d'Iéna, watching the barges.

I grew up on a river. I worked loading and unloading boats like these when I was home from school. It never would have entered my mind that I'd run off to France like my aunt Selena when I turned twenty-two.

Now here I was, partner in one of the most—if not *the* most—prestigious engineering firms in the world.

The future could only go up from here.

After an hour with my head in the clouds, I wandered off the bridge to the Champs de Mars. I stood in the grass and tried to imagine three hundred meters high. I was familiar with the sketches for the tower—had been working on figuring out the placement for rivets and girders for two full years. But for it to turn into more than a series of arithmetic problems—well, it boggled the mind.

To be sure, I had worked on the observatory dome Eiffel built in Nice. But, as grand as the structure was, it was covered—or at least the iron part that I had anything to do with. And bridges, as beautiful as they might be, and as necessary, too...well, they weren't the same sort of creature as this tower.

Perhaps it would be some sort of scientific research facility, or a piece of art to be consumed by the masses, or divine harmony bending the forces of nature as Eiffel said. Or even all of those things and then some. But to me, the tower was a testament to show how one man—backed by a few dozen engineers like me—could mold the world's strongest fabric into a structure as intricate and beautiful as lace, that could yet withstand wind velocities up to more miles per hour than had ever been recorded in human history.

Money aside, it was a technological marvel, and I was proud to be part of it.

I held my hat on with my hand as I tipped my head back, imagining the colossus.

"Monsieur Tighe, are we lucky enough to run into you again so soon?" A melodic voice shook me from my reverie.

Whirling around, all my grandiose daydreams ground to a halt.

Stéphanie Verger and Gilbert.

"Don't you look like you're in high spirits today, Fin?" Gilbert's eyes raked over me in a brief but skin-flushing intimacy.

"Or like a madman," pointed out his fiancée with a piercing glance. She was probably just as correct.

"Imagining the tower," I said. "It will be here." My arms made a great V in the air.

Stéphanie tapped her chin thoughtfully, looking high into the sky where I gestured as if she could visualize it, too. "I wonder," she began, letting the words dangle for a good minute before filling in the rest of her thought. "So many of my neighbors plan to sell as soon as they know for sure if the project will actually be finalized."

Perhaps a bit defensively, I said, "It's latticework. The sun should shine through much of it." She wouldn't ruin my mood.

She raised a rather pointed chin up, shading her eyes with the cover of her hand. "It will either be a monstrosity or a marvel, Lord Carleton." She cut her glance to me for a split second as she dropped the title. Did she suspect my ruse? What had Gilbert told her?

In any case, I was at a loss. But she hadn't finished. "I believe that whether people love it or hate it—and I suspect it will be split both ways rather evenly until it's built—it will never be ignored. Do you know, Gilbert? I believe I've finally decided what your wedding present to me shall be."

Stéphanie turned back to the block of luxury flats where she lived. "You shall purchase as many of those apartments as come available in the next few months. When the ground breaks to build Monsieur Eiffel's tower, I think, there will be a rush to sell. You can snatch them up cheaply, and we can sit on them until the time is ripe."

Gilbert gave her a bemused look. "But if people are divided over whether it shall be detested or adored—"

"Oh, Parisians are fickle. We adore drowning out each other's opinions by each of us screaming louder. But once the tower is here, it'll be part of us. Of the city. Of the French. And we'll be ferocious in our veneration of it. My newly purchased apartments will be ludicrously expensive. And I'll recoup at least some of Maman's fortune."

There was an awkward silence as the two shared a look that was unreadable.

"Will you sell yours, too, mademoiselle? Or will Gilbert move in with you once you're married?"

Gilbert's hollow cheeks flushed like I'd slapped him.

"I believe we'll be ridiculously modern and each keep our own home, for now, don't you think?" Stéphanie's brows pushed down as she appraised Gilbert.

Whether keeping up two homes was what the sophisticates of Paris did as a matter of course or not wasn't knowledge I possessed, but something about their lack of romantic interest in each other left me oddly pleased. I didn't dare ask myself why that might be.

"I was dropping Stéphanie off. Care to share a cab back home, Fin?"

I blinked hard after realizing I'd been watching his lips form the words.

108

Stéphanie turned that searching look back to me, though I couldn't fathom what she thought.

"No, I'll walk." I didn't need to spend any more time in his company alone. We weren't truly friends, no matter what I'd intimated to my boss.

"Don't be ridiculous. I promised Sonny dinner tonight, and your place is on the way to his apartment." Gilbert stroked Stéphanie's cheek. "You don't mind, do you?"

"By all means, you don't have to ask my permission for such a thing." She raised her gloved hand for me to kiss. "You've given me so much to think about, Lord Carleton. I thank you for it."

I took a few steps back. "You ought to escort her the rest of the way home. Take care." I lifted my hat and walked back to the path before he could argue.

I'd crossed the military exercise fields and was nearly to the river when he called my name. I rubbed the back of my neck, wondering if I could pretend not to have heard.

"Get in, Fin."

I hummed, trying to lose myself in the crowds of people on their way home for the evening. Moving to an alley that cut through—and was too narrow for a cab—I expelled my breath. Damn him for making me this unsettled. I felt like a foolish schoolgirl.

"Fin, don't you think it's interesting the way we ran into each other like that?"

My shoulders sagged, and I turned around. He'd gotten out of the carriage and followed me on foot. No one could say the man wasn't persistent.

"It would be odd"—I stared at his hat as something that was

the least dangerous part to look at—"except that your fiancée's flat is close to where the tower will be built."

Gilbert took a step closer. His undivided attention felt different than before. Intense. "I think it's fate."

Fate implied something magical. Fantastical. And though I humored Eiffel with that sort of talk, this was merely a coincidence. I cracked my knuckles, remembering I didn't believe in coincidences.

Turning away cost me, but it had to be done. The man was dangerous to my sanity. "Let's hope fate's telling us we'll be successful with the tower, eh?"

He matched his steps with mine. Long, elegant legs in form-fitting trousers. "I think we'll be a success, oui. We make a good team, hmm?" Gilbert punched my arm playfully. "I don't mean to pry, but something you said has been rattling in my brain. You implied Aurélie was let down by her brother. He seemed like he was devoted to her, so I'm confused."

I snorted. "Aurélie wasn't let down by Paul. She was victimized by that low-life. He deserved to have his throat slit, frankly."

Gilbert paled but rallied after a moment. "What are your plans tonight?"

My precise plans at that moment were unmentionable. I'd visit the Green Carnation and find someone to help me lose the discomfort that Gilbert roused in me every time I was around him. Bloody hell, I needed it.

Gilbert grinned. "And now you're smiling again. I want to join in."

I stifled my groan.

"I'm off to see a friend." I stole a glance at him.

"Victoire?"

"She'll be there."

"It's rude to not invite me."

I shrugged. "It's not the sort of place you'd enjoy. Besides, you're headed to dinner, aren't you?"

"I'd enjoy having a reason to skip my meeting with Sonny. I can send him Michel's message in a note instead, hmm?" His tongue poked out of the corner of his lips.

I stopped and turned toward l'Arc de Triomphe. "Listen, I'm appreciative of the effort you've made, but, trust me, you wouldn't like my friends. They're like me."

A shadow crossed his face as a cloud covered the sun. "Engineers?"

Blood pounding, I nodded. "Very dull lot. Take care." I walked a good ten steps before he called out.

"When will I see you again?" The plaintive voice squeezed my heart.

I called over my shoulder without turning around, "Let's leave it to fate, shall we?"

10

Aurélie was an adult. She wasn't *legally* my responsibility, just because I'd taken care of her since she was young. I couldn't insist she stay home where I could ensure her safety; I had no legitimate sway over her. When she insisted she could manage to come home from the theater on her own without me to accompany her, I'd argued, but she'd been insistent.

And now, it was half past eleven, and she ought to have been back for at least an hour.

So much for the extreme happiness of my day. It was all I could do to keep my temper in check when she pushed the front door open. Humming a popular tune, she didn't notice me.

"Late night?" I asked, keeping my voice level.

Her eyes dropped. She touched the over layer of the au courant dress sent over by Gilbert and then lifted her chin. "I went to dinner with a few of the girls."

I reminded myself that she deserved some entertainments— her life was a never-ending cycle of rehearsal and performance. And she was eighteen. Still, my voice held reproof I couldn't quite shake. "Nowhere too expensive, I hope?"

I gave her a small amount of pin money each week, as I remembered too well what it was like to never have any of my own. But small was the operative word.

"There were loads of us." She laughed, higher-pitched than usual. And her cheeks were pink. *Champagne?* "Rosette's abonné paid the bill, and you know he's too desperately dull to allow anything you wouldn't approve. Still, Rosette adores him. She's become such a wonderful friend."

I was unable to do anything but nod. Almost. "Any other men there? You know that you must be—"

She threw up her arms in exasperation. "I'm not an imbécile. I've worked too hard to throw it away for a cuddle I don't even wish for, Fin." She kept grumbling on her way to the kitchen. "Non, I didn't put myself in any position to be beholden to anyone since you insist on fussing like an old hen. I merely wanted to have a break from the constant practicing and enjoy a night out with the other dancers; is that all right with you?"

Dear Lord, I wasn't cut out to be a father figure, had only muddled through this long with a big dose of luck. I followed and touched her shoulder as she unhooked her boots, as contrite as I could. "You are owed some fun, and so am I. We both work too bloody hard. Just…take care."

She smiled when she realized I wasn't going to continue. She put her hand over mine and squeezed. "I do. Amuse-toi bien."

A half hour later, I made my way to the Green Carnation. It was my turn to relax.

The wind blew some of the day's heat away, and I whistled, hands in pocket. I'd saved my skin getting that promotion. But that wasn't all—I was damned pleased with myself for raking in all the investment money. True, it would be nearly three years before we'd see if the speculations turned into cash, but the prospect of money and the power it garnered soothed my nerves like few things could.

And for longer than a quarter of an hour at a time.

Though tonight, a quarter of an hour was all I needed to rid me of this tension that racked my body.

Jody clasped my arm as I sidled up to the bar. "You're smiling tonight, eh, Fini?"

Brandy warmed a cozy path down my throat. The first glass always felt like I was removing my shoes and tie, getting rid of all the cares I had in the world. And then I noticed he hardly paid attention, which was unlike him. A worried frown marred his forehead.

"Is anything the matter?" I wasn't accustomed to Jody acting pensive.

Before answering, Jody placed a sugar cube over the absinthe spoon and set it under the fountain of water at our end of the bar. The change of color when the sugar water hit the liquor was the only mildly intriguing thing about the drink. It was a nasty thing, absinthe, and wrecked too many lives to count.

Lucky for me, I wasn't fond of anise. Thanks, I suppose, to Aunt Glad's refusing to allow Annabeth and me sweets when we were children.

Once the drink had made its louche, the cloudiness that proclaimed it drinkable, Jody settled onto a bar stool, his feet still on the floor like he might need to jump up at a moment's notice. "Charlotte hasn't been around, and it's unlike her. Do you remember the last time you saw her?"

"Charlotte?" It was hardly the question I'd expected. "The last I saw her was a few weeks ago when I ran into her on the stairs, head down. Didn't even respond when I called to her."

My dear friend rubbed his eyes with a thumb and forefinger, head shaking. I knew him more intimately than anyone else in the world, and this sort of response was unprecedented.

"What's happened?"

He tossed the drink down his throat rather than his usual sipping and stared off into nothing. "I have no clue. She's regular as clockwork visiting twice a week. This isn't like her."

"Have you sent round a note to her employer?"

One side of his mouth lifted in a sort of smile. "She can't read much, and I wouldn't do her any favors by knocking on the door and demanding to see her."

"She'll turn up, surely."

He sighed and shrugged noncommittally. "Maybe it's just that she's finally ready to quit drinking this poison and has no need to visit." He jerked his thumb at the bottle of Pernod et Fils. "You're still friendly with de Gênet's nephew, yes?" He bit his lip, crossing his arms over his chest. "Maybe you can ask him to send Charlotte to see me?"

I'm ashamed to admit my first thought was embarrassment that Gilbert should know I was on friendly terms with a maid, a member of his uncle's staff. I gave Jody a hearty smile. "Of course. I'll let you know."

"Merci, Fini."

His shoulders eased, and he smiled as his current lover appeared at the threshold of the club. "Excuse me, cher, but he's ridiculously jealous of you. Laurent, can you manage for an hour?"

115

Laurent waved him off as Jody strode to the exit. I picked up my drink and walked around the room. Someone plonked piano keys in a variation of a waltz.

Victoire sidled up to me and stroked my cheek with the backs of her fingernails. "I had such a lovely time meeting your friends, mon cher Viscount. Will you ask me again?"

"If I'm lucky enough to receive another invitation, I'd be honored for you to accompany me. You were a marvelous date."

"If God saw fit to make me a woman from the beginning, that would have been my world, you know?" Victoire took the drink from my hand and drained it.

I sighed. All through my childhood I had wondered, if only my parents had been married. But it was a fool's game. We played the cards we were handed, even if they were shite.

"Refill?" I winked. I could do that much for her.

"Please." She leaned in, her breath warm on my neck. "I'll pay you back next time." It's what she always said.

"No bother." Which is how I habitually replied.

Back at the bar, I asked for one for both of us, and sat on a stool while Laurent poured. Glasses in hand, I turned and made out Victoire in the crowd. Her arms locked around a man's waist. She giggled as he whispered in her ear. Maybe she didn't need me to buy her a drink, after all.

But I recognized that tousled black hair. I rubbed my hand over my eyes. Dizzy. My stomach sank. It had to be too much smoke, too much alcohol, though I hadn't finished a single glass.

Holy Mother of God.

The skin crawled up my spine as it always did when I saw

Gilbert, when those black eyes nailed me to the back wall and held me hanging there, like my feet couldn't reach the floor.

I blew out the smoke I'd been holding.

Had he followed me?

Obviously, but why?

Gilbert's gaze swept the room and came back to me, mouth slack.

This was a mistake. Gilbert Duhais didn't belong at the Green Carnation, didn't belong in this part of my life. Besides Victoire, the room was packed with only men. He had to recognize that this wasn't the usual cabaret clientele, didn't he?

Long legs brought him closer. What should I do? Pretend I didn't know him? Too late; his eyes hadn't moved from mine. Shake his hand? Behave as though we were running into each other anywhere else but here? Make a dash for the door, perhaps?

Victoire pressed herself against him and touched her lips to the side of his, leaving a red mark. Her smile widened, and she pointed to me, arm locked around his waist, guiding him over. "Tu as du cul, Fini."

Gilbert took her hand. Hat off, he bowed over it like he'd never wanted to do anything in his life more.

Victoire covered her heart and turned to me, unable to suppress a smile that was wide-eyed and brilliant.

She blinked and let him go, though she didn't move from her close position.

Like I was a king and he was a petitioner, Gilbert Duhais took my hand next, and kissed it even more reverentially. His tongue touched my knuckle. On purpose? Still bowed over, his eyes rose to mine and he winked.

On purpose.

Jesus wept.

He pulled me to my feet, usually not an easy task but I was so flabbergasted, I wasn't in my usual state of mind.

"Dance with me?" Gilbert's voice was deep, commanding.

Behind me Victoire sputtered. "Fin doesn't—"

"Yes."

Normally, I didn't, but there was no way I'd give up the chance to have his body that close to mine. My arm snaked around his hips, not taking a moment to think about how wise or foolish the choice was.

Any excuse to learn if his coming here was a game or if he meant it. "Did you follow me?"

An impish grin lit up his face. "I've tried before. You're too quick for me."

My head twisted to his, startling us both. Fresh, ocean-scented cologne filled my senses.

"I'm discreet." Because I was. In this world, I had to be, even if I hated it.

His gaze dropped to my mouth, and he bit his lower lip. A rush of tingles flared across my body.

"With your father who he is, you need to be if you wish to have access to his estate."

My blood went cold. Blackmail? I put my hand out to steady myself on a stool, but Gilbert winked. "That's why you back-tracked three blocks and had me running in circles to figure out where you went. I knocked on so many doors, my knuckles are bloodied." He tucked a strand of hair off my forehead, his fingers tracing behind the curve of my ear.

"Your uncle would be just as displeased, and you have more to lose than I do. Why are you here?"

To answer, he pulled me to the packed dance floor. Some couples twirled in an actual waltz, some rocked their bodies together. I had to lift my chin slightly to look into his face. I'd assumed we were the same height, but he had me by at least two inches.

Our arms wrapped around each other. I pushed my fingers between his, our faces so close that our noses touched.

He was a good dancer, I'll give him that. Without bustles and crinolines, our hips touched, thighs moving in each other's wake. He ran his tongue over his bottom lip, a lock of hair drooping into his eyes. "I couldn't resist."

Before I could blink, I was against the wall, our legs in a pattern: mine, his, mine, his. *Who knew he was so strong?* His chest pressed against mine, and his mouth hovered.

Without intention, my fingers dug into his scalp, opening his mouth with my tongue. His was sweet and hard and I sucked it. I pulled his soft lips into my mouth, nipped at them with my teeth until he panted, his breath mingled with my breath, chest against my chest, wilting in my arms.

A small groan escaped his throat, and our mouths opened at the same time again. I didn't know how much I wanted that kiss until I was in the middle of it. I pulled back from the wall, but he used all of his body to keep me there, each inch of his hard muscles touching me all over.

"Why?" I asked again.

Foreheads pressed together so his eyelashes fluttered against my cheek, fingers tickling the short hair at my neck, he whispered, "I needed to know if you tasted as delicious as you looked."

If we could have tumbled to the floor there, I'd have been thrilled. So many unmet needs in my life, but not this time. I'd get what I wanted. At least for a short while.

My voice was as hard, demanding an answer before I was lost. "And now?"

Gilbert pulled his head back, tilted it to the side, and ran his tongue over his teeth. "Make love to me."

I laughed once to shake the depth of the emotions off. But my pinky traced that swollen mouth. "I don't believe in love."

The club disappeared as he trailed kisses down my neck until he sucked hard enough to make me open my eyes.

"Aurélie is home?" His voice was like drizzled cognac set on fire.

The skin where his chin and neck met smelled better than anything in the world, and I inhaled, fingers clutching his shoulders tight.

"She is." We couldn't go there. Not that Aurélie would care if I brought home a man, but it was a hard rule. *For me.*

"Take me to *your* apartment." I could walk home in the middle of the night and still make it to work on time.

His fingertip traced the coils of my ear, his full lips curling seductively. "We can't. My uncle...non. He'd find out, and like you said, he'd be just as horrified as your father." His eyes were huge and dark. "Possibly even more outraged..." He groaned into my neck. "We can be quiet, not wake Aurélie up. I've been thinking about you all week. About this. I need you to take me home."

It was a dreadful idea. Stupid. The last thing I wanted was a quiet grope in the dark. I liked noise. I wanted to hear him moan and yell and explode.

Yet we were in the street and on the way back within two minutes.

Not kissing him during the walk nearly killed me, but suspicious eyes might peek through curtains and call for the sergent de ville. Twice I stopped to tell him this was a bad idea, that he was engaged, for Christ's sake, to ask what were we doing?

"I told you, I have the purest intentions to marry Stéphanie. I don't want to have a physical relationship, and neither does she. It's the only way for her to get back some of the money her mother invested in Qualité, because Michel refuses to give her more than an allowance that's half the size of mine." His pout nearly did me in. "I don't like her that way, I promise, and Stéphanie, she doesn't care, as long as I don't flaunt a lover in public. I'm like you, Fin." And then that smile that tugged my heart. "Just not an engineer."

Like me. Good Lord, he had no idea what that did to me.

I was going through with this. There was no way I couldn't. And after all, I was Fini and this would only happen the one time. Just once, and then I'd have him out of my blood.

Gilbert had as much to lose as me. The words were a mantra in my head, in time to our footsteps along the pavement.

The wind picked up, a North Sea chill, and I pulled my collar up to keep it off my skin. That it helped give me anonymity was a helpful side effect.

Once inside my building, we crept up the four flights of stairs like thieves, and when I opened the lock to my flat, I blew the cold from my hands, at a loss now as to why I had made such a horrible choice.

He could ruin me.

I could ruin him.

Or this could be a simple thing. Two bodies squeezing what pleasure they could from each other. Nothing more or less.

But, my God, the flush on his cheeks from the cool evening air—or perhaps from being here with me—made him even more handsome than before.

"Can I get you anything? Tea? Brandy?" I pressed my nails into my palms to not strip him there.

"A toddy?" He peeled his coat off and slung it over the back of the sofa.

Perfect. I put water on to boil in the kitchen. Five minutes later, it whistled and still he hadn't followed me. A dash of brandy, cloves, and honey, and the cups were ready. My hands shook, carrying the tray into the living room.

Which was empty.

Had I imagined the scene at the Green Carnation? Perhaps I'd downed Jody's absinthe instead of brandy and I hallucinated? Bleak disappointment ripped through my body.

His coat was where he'd left it, but Gilbert was gone. I set the cups down and went to the back, where the iron railing surrounded the fire escape.

Gone. Had he set me up? Had he made a play to see if I'd give myself up so he could...destroy me?

Frowning, I sat, poured tea into one of the cups and stirred. The drink scalded the back of my throat but left a tingling numbness I needed, to match the feeling in my chest. But could he have kissed me so passionately if he—

"Fin?"

The saucer rattled in my hand. And Gilbert said it again. Sotto voce. Carrying the tray, I went toward the voice, seeping from the door to my bedroom.

Gilbert was there, on my bed, naked, the light turned on.

"I thought you'd left." He couldn't know how much I cared. I made sure of it.

He shook his head no.

"Toddy?" Years of pretending I was unflappable left me in good stead.

He sat up and took his.

Gilbert Duhais was on my bed without clothes, and I shook like a virgin inside.

Stop it, fool. He followed you for this.

I deposited the tray before unknotting my tie and sliding it off my neck. I watched his chest rise and fall as fast as mine. I kicked off my shoes and took a drink.

"Why are the British so much better at warm drinks?" he asked, curling his shoulders in pleasure over the flavor.

I sank into the bed, holding my drink steady, and touched a hand to his abdomen, unable to stop myself. His skin was warm, velvety soft. It quivered when I traced the lines of his muscles with my fingertip.

"We're good at many things," I said, draining my cup. Being patient was not among them.

He finished his and gave it to me. I put the tray on my bureau, then I shut the door and turned the lock. This was going to be a mistake. I shouldn't have kissed him. I shouldn't have brought him home.

But since I had, I might as well be hung for a sheep as a lamb.

I closed in for another embrace, but he drew his head back. "You're a pleasure to kiss, mon vilain garçon, but I want so much more than that."

A million things exploded in my head over that statement; sorting them was a challenge I wasn't prepared for. Not then. Tomorrow could be filled with regret. Mixing business with pleasure was foolish. This man was my entrée into high society, and he could just as easily kick me back out into the cold. Destroy me on a whim.

Yet, he was here, now, and more tempting than anyone I'd ever seen. My regrets could wait.

I loosened the top buttons of my shirt and pulled it over my head. "Am I your naughty boy?" It wasn't the adjective I'd pick to describe me.

He pulled me to the bed and straddled my hips in one fluid motion. "I certainly fucking hope so."

11

The next evening, I came home to Aurélie stretched across a sofa, a clementine disappearing into her mouth. Two peels on the side table were proof that I was in charge of my own dinner tonight.

"You're early." She didn't look up from her magazine.

I placed a bucket under the faucet. "I'm everyone's blue-eyed boy at work, so I was able to leave without extra tasks."

A loud sniff alerted me she was unhappy with my response. I came back into the great room and helped myself to a piece of her fruit, though she tried to smack my hand away. I picked up her feet and sat, placing them back on my lap.

She didn't look up.

Better to get the row over with. "Something wrong?"

Aurélie shrugged, not answering, but the scowl on her face deepened. "He left his jacket when you kicked him out this morning. His money and keys were inside."

I pressed the heels of my hands into my eye sockets hard enough to see spots. The damn jacket. He would need that. "I beg your pardon. It won't happen again."

In the nearly eight years Aurélie has lived with me, I'd never once brought home a man. Shame pounded through me.

"Non, it's not really that. I tell you all the time you must have a life, and it's nothing to me if you bring a lover here. Likely safer for you. It's just that it was him."

I blinked a few times in succession. "Because it was Gilbert? Has he done something I ought to know about? Has he insulted you in any way?" If he had, no matter our partnership—or whatever it could be termed—I'd choke the life out of him.

She made some complicated action with her leg in the air before answering. It was an old habit of hers, working through her thoughts with her dance exercises. "Non. He's more than usually polite, and I believe that it's true, and not just a pretense, even if his uncle is Michel de Gênet."

Now I was even more confused. "Has de Gênet done something to you?"

Her hands fluttered around her neck, and she shook her head. "Don't be silly, how would I have met the likes of him? It's just that Gilbert reminds me of Paul." Her voice was quiet, like when she'd been a child and scared to talk to me, cousin or not. "He was the one to identify his body." Her breath was shallow.

Too many pronouns for my brain to sort through. "Excuse me?"

She shrieked her annoyance and rammed her foot into my leg. "Paul's body, crétin. Gilbert Duhais was the one to identify him."

My hackles rose. He had been the bane of my existence for a number of years, so I shed no tears when some scruff killed my cousin at a public bathhouse in the premier arrondissement.

I'd seen him earlier that week, in fact. I met him once a month to deliver the money that kept him from destroying my reputation with my employer. So much for any familial bond. To be fair, I didn't waste a second of time in mourning when we found out he'd been killed. I assumed he finally angered someone with the means to end the annoyance, and I was glad he was finally out of our lives.

The police had come to me and Aurélie to put a definitive name to his corpse, but when I arrived at the morgue, Paul's identity was already confirmed, to my relief. As glad as I was that the connard was dead, I was squeamish to witness the body, though would have for Aurélie's sake. I hated Paul, but his sister was terrified of him.

But bloody hell—how well had he known Gilbert? Why would a casual friend be the one to identify the body?

Still in the fugue of not understanding, I went to the kitchen and poured the bucket into the bath in my room. Aurélie followed me, hands clenched when I turned around.

"I beg your pardon." It was easy to say, and I was sorry that she was upset. I was even sorrier I'd spent the night with someone who reminded her of her terrible brother, even if they were merely schoolmates.

God help me, they'd better have just been schoolmates.

But Gilbert…? What sort of friendship did they have that he could have been the one to establish his identity? I could vomit.

Paul's private life was a closed door. I didn't want to be privy to it, either. But my estimation of Gilbert Duhais shrank if they were close friends. I'd never met anyone less deserving of the word *man* than Paul Blancmaison. I hoped there was a private hell for bastards who whored out their sisters.

The taint of Gilbert even knowing Paul made me more anxious

to bathe. To rid myself of chills that wouldn't stop, I set the bucket on the stove, and set up the kettle, too.

Aurélie was a step behind, and when I turned, her face was split with a smile. I could never keep up with her mood swings.

Like a child's taunt, she sang, "You brought a man home." She plucked an apple off the table and handed it to me. Even at eighteen, she was unable to peel one successfully.

I pulled out my pocketknife, and she planted a kiss on my cheek. "What would I do without you? I'll stay with you forever, yes? We can take care of each other like we do now."

I smiled, not believing it for a moment. She was destined for more than taking care of an old bachelor for the rest of her days.

"Unless you and Monsieur Duhais fall in love." She rubbed the back of her hand across her mouth, talking while she chewed. "Do men fall in love with each other?"

"Not sensible ones like me, no." I dried the washing and put it away, but she stood behind me, thinking so hard I could hear it. I lifted the bucket from the range with a dishtowel.

"Well, he might not be so sensible. And he's rich and handsome. But you're very calm, considering."

"Considering what?"

"He'll be here any moment; didn't he tell you?" She looked at her fingernails and bit her pinky before waiting for my answer. "You're taking Gilbert and any number of people to La Maison Bleue for dinner."

"Me? How do you know that? He never mentioned anything last night." The bucket sloshed in my agitation. I had no money to do that—it would be more than I made in a month—though Monsieur Eiffel had been generous with my new raise.

"I'm sure he was too busy to remember to tell you. He said for me to tell you when he came to fetch his jacket." She raised her eyes appealingly. "I think it's unfair that I can't come along. I'd be quiet as a mouse, you know? Sit there and have soup. I'm not even hungry, but, Fin—"

"What time did you say?"

Her eyes flicked to the clock on the front console. "Nine." Her forehead scrunched up. "Please, Fin? I can wear one of the dresses he sent and pretend to be every bit a lady."

"You *are* a lady, Aurélie. But this would be very boring for you. I'm to continue pleading my case over the tower with de Gênet." And I'd promised Gilbert that I wouldn't bring her. Neither his uncle nor his fiancée would appreciate that.

She stared into nothing for a moment before flashing her smile. "Don't listen to me, I'm only teasing. I must sleep early tonight, in any case. I've had too many late evenings this week."

I carried the water to my room and dumped it in, not caring that the splash wet the floor in my haste. Fifteen minutes. Not that I was going to la Maison Bleue; I absolutely wouldn't spend the sort of money that would entail.

But de Gênet must be expecting me. I calculated what cash I had on hand while scratching the shaving brush over my cheeks. I was a fool not to grow a beard and be done with this, but though I didn't consider myself particularly vain, I did appreciate the warm looks my face garnered.

I cut my chin, as expected, and was dumping the cold bucket over my head when there was a knock on the door, and Aurélie called out she would answer. I'd just thrown a towel around my waist when Gilbert pushed my bedroom door open.

Ridiculously handsome as always, this time he was wearing a tailless evening jacket like mine.

He ran his eyes down my body. "Even better than I remembered."

He stepped inside and leaned against the door, clicking the lock from behind. His lips met mine, as hungry as I was for him.

"This is for you."

My eyes opened with reluctance, and he attempted to hand me a high-value bill. I shook my head. "I'm not taking your money."

I never traded money for sex, *not ever.*

He laughed. "For dinner. I don't expect you to pay for it, and Michel will be watching like a hawk. I understand it's absurd, but it's important to him that you're not taking advantage of him. He enjoys being wooed, and if I pay—well, he thinks of anything I have as his."

My pride walked me back where I yanked on my trousers, not looking at him. "I don't want your money."

"Don't be a fool. It's my uncle's money, anyway."

From behind me, he slid the bill into my pocket and squeezed my thigh, kissed the back of my neck once, and then bit down. "If you don't take it, I'll humiliate us both by insisting that I pay the bill, and that will ruin our plans."

Shaking him off, I put on a shirt and buttoned it, gritting my teeth. "Which plans will it ruin?"

"Fin, I don't want you to be cross with me, oui?"

Good Lord. What was he dropping on me now? I knotted the tie around my neck, but he came and undid it, tying it better somehow. Like always.

Dear Lord—we already had habits.

His lips were so close to mine it was hard to focus. I went all dizzy when he was so close.

"When I met with your father in England"—he cleared his throat and made a face of contrition—"I will call him that, even though I know you don't like it." He dropped his arms around my waist, dipping his mouth to where my jaw met my neck so my knees were weak. "We spoke about his investing in a store like Qualité in London. That's why I was there, of course." He sucked my earlobe, and I groaned, pushing him away.

Gilbert frowned with a heavy sigh. "Michel believes that you can help him get that taken care of, which was why he allowed you to name that pledge to Eiffel. He never gives away anything without expectations. Can't you pretend that you're close enough to your father that you can get in a good word for Michel—"

"What sort of expectations? I don't have anything to offer your uncle. *You're* the one who has some sort of bond with my father, not me."

"Shh, don't be overdramatic. I merely mean that Michel will be more willing to help your tower if he believes you hold some sway over your father's decisions. You only need to bluff a little bit more. Lead him on."

"Pretending in casual conversation that I have a true father-son relationship with a man who wrote me off before I was born is awful enough. But this dissembling...? I can't. I won't."

Gilbert was unfussed, as though he expected this quarrel—and honestly, probably had—and brushed it aside as he always did. "Allow me to be frank. Michel has the money to open a branch of Qualité in London, but he needs the name of someone like your father to get the right permits. He won't settle for anyone with any hint of scandal attached to his name, and your father is as respectable as your queen." He held out his palms as though showing he held no secrets. "He needs you to add oil to the wheels."

"*Grease the wheels.* And, ugh." I ran my hands through my hair to keep from throttling him.

But he picked up the comb and re-parted my hair, smoothing it down. He smiled at me in the mirror. "You can keep up the pretense until you have the money. I'm sure it's merely a matter of weeks before his lawyers track you down with an offer you won't be able to refuse. In the meantime, this is important, and it won't be too difficult. Michel's never met the man. You can say whatever you'd like and I'll back you up." Gilbert hugged me close to his chest, and I allowed myself that small comfort. But just for a brief moment before I pulled away.

I could manage. After all, I'd been dining out on my father's name for weeks now. What was a drop more subterfuge? Tonight would be the last time, and then I could send Gilbert on his way and kiss Michel de Gênet's check all the way to the bank.

12

I told Michel that your father reached out to reconcile when his legitimate son died." Gilbert wasted no time when the carriage door clicked shut.

"How did Harry die?" I asked for curiosity's sake.

Bizarre that I was asking a stranger—from France—the circumstances of my half brother's death.

"He drowned. In a boating accident." Gilbert patted my hand with a short laugh. "I'd stay away from rivers if I were you. That's a bit of a coincidence, don't you think?"

I couldn't make out his face in the darkened carriage, as he sat opposite me. But I had to squeeze my knees with my hands to stop them from shaking. The casualness of his dropping Annabeth's cause of death in my lap made me want to wriggle out of my skin. It took a moment for my heart to start beating again.

Gilbert leaned forward with a worried frown. "Mon Dieu, what have I said?" Those elegant fingers clasped my hand. "I'm so sorry, Fin. I shouldn't have been so rude. He was your brother, after all. But I didn't know mention of his name upset you."

A deep inhalation and exhale helped me loosen my spine. Ah.

He referred to Harry's death, not Annabeth's. I didn't give two figs about Harry dying, aside from it leaving the Rawcliffe title without an heir, which proved advantageous for me in pinning down investors.

"What type of expectations can your uncle have that an earl's bastard son can help him?" *There.* I'd put a stop to all of this vague nonsense and find out exactly what Gilbert was asking of me, and choose—once and for all—whether I was willing to go along with it in order to get his uncle's stamp of approval.

De Gênet was the gateway to all sorts of speculators, after all. New men with new wealth and the fucking ballocks to take the risk on me.

"I gave a different interpretation than that. I explained that your father reached out to you to make amends for his neglect. That the two of you reconciled in London and—" Gilbert stopped and one knee bounced. He fiddled with his cuff link and stared out the window.

"And we what?" My voice wasn't as sharp as my insides. Like spikes in a bed of nails.

Words tumbled from those golden lips. "That he changed his will and is in the process of naturalizing you."

I fought to breathe. I didn't dare dream of such a thing even when I was a foolish boy. That wasn't a small fib; it pushed the bounds of credulity so far, they were sure to snap in my face. The reverberations could ruin me. I'd finally learned not to expect anything from that connard. All he could promise me was disappointment.

"How dare you? It's one thing for him to wish to reconcile—even though I'd never agree to it. It's another that he might be willing to leave me some token in his will. That I wouldn't believe until I saw proof. But there's no possibility that I'd ever be his legal heir, even if you've convinced me to playact that it's true to strangers. Nor would I ever wish to be."

Gilbert tilted his head and gave me a cynical look. Bloody hell, there was a tightening in my gut as I realized what a profound lie that last comment was. Was Gilbert the devil? I never counted myself much of a believer, but his ability to know the deepest things in my soul . . . well, it was supernatural.

"Simmer down, Fin. Listen to me—why is it hard to imagine, hmm?" Gilbert leaned over, his face dripping in earnestness. "He has no children but you, no brother, no nephew even. You're his son, no matter who your mother was, and he must have liked her enough as he went back and had a second child with her, yes?"

Through the fog of pain, my ears pricked up. If I sorted through the base emotions, there was a hint of logic. But no. That was too dangerous to even dream of.

"It would take an act of Parliament for me to be legitimized, and I can guarantee that they wouldn't. If any old bastard could be made into a peer, it defeats the purpose of primogeniture, doesn't it? Means aristocrats aren't as special as they like to believe."

"Calm yourself, Fin. He's the thirteenth Earl of Rawcliffe. Do you know how many generations that stretches back? *Six hundred years.* From what you know of him, can you see him allowing his name to vanish; all those men's names disappear because he doesn't want to acknowledge you're his son?" Gilbert took a deep breath through his nose and settled back, his arms crossed over his chest, his face smug. "That he doesn't have the means to ensure it can be made to look perfectly legal and proper? It's not like you ever did anything to humiliate him, have you?"

Never. I was a model boy. From the iron grip of Aunt Glad to the strictness of St. Edmund's boys' school, I'd done whatever I was told. And by the time I was at university at Durham, it wouldn't have crossed my mind not to follow the path set out for me.

The path my father had prescribed.

Until Annabeth died, he'd never been specifically unkind to me—only monumentally uninterested.

It wasn't until Paris that I changed course to live the life I chose. To a point. I still was conservative. Reserved.

"Trust me, Fin. You must trust me."

About as far as I could throw him. I dropped his hypnotic gaze and did my best not to snort.

But Gilbert was right—unless the earl had an inkling of my secret life in France, and not even my employer did—I'd never done anything to embarrass my father or his name. I'd never have found the nerve.

For a moment, the idea blazed in my chest. I couldn't imagine it was possible that I truly could get the peerage itself. That was too far a stretch, as it included hereditary rights in the House of Lords, but there were un-entailed properties and monies: things that he might write over to me, to make me believe that I wasn't a complete mistake, that he had cared, even in some shallow way.

"He's dying."

I snapped my head around. "Pardon?" A flush of adrenaline spiked with, what?—regret?—anger?—washed over me.

"Your father. He's not well." Gilbert took my hand and rubbed over my clenched knuckles. "Impending death makes men sentimental, I've heard. Now is the time to reach out. To reconcile so he can pay you back for all the misery he's caused you." His grip tightened. "And your sister, hmm?"

On the street, socialites strolled beneath the autumn-tinged trees flanking the boulevard, enjoying every convenience this modern world had on offer for those with money and prestige.

"You could be one of them. Feel as though you truly belong." His words caressed the green-eyed demons that I always worked to keep locked away.

Bloody hell, I ached deep in my bones for it. For ease and confidence. Just once. To not have to scrimp and scrape my way through life.

But how did Gilbert know how much it meant to me?

I hadn't even asked the question before he spoke again. "I didn't grow up wealthy, remember? I know what it's like to want things, to struggle. And what about Aurélie? Think of all the ways you can help her just by going along with this one small lie."

An argument that this was no small lie was about to burst from me when he covered my lips with his forefinger. "Just remember: your father wishes to reconcile with you, and he's dying. You aren't doing anything wrong, and if you'd follow my advice, you could make it a reality."

We'd arrived at the popular restaurant, and Gilbert gave me his lopsided smile. "Now, you're prepared to be Viscount Carleton, without wavering? Because it will give some sort of respectability that matters so much to Michel."

Finley Tighe, Viscount Carleton. It was embarrassing to be so easily swayed, but I was. By some glorious twist of fate, I'd be the survivor. The last one standing, of all the generations of Carletons.

I'd be the one to give the final haughty look down on his grave before I spat on it.

We descended from the carriage, and I caught Gilbert's arm so he faced me. "I'll consider this favor, but I need one in return. I need you to find out about the whereabouts of my friend's sister. She's a housemaid for your uncle."

If I'd thought about it, I'd have expected Gilbert to show some sign of impatience, and perhaps it was the glow from the restaurant sign, but his face appeared to have lost all its color. "A domestique? Why? Is she missing?"

I nodded. "She usually comes to see her brother Jody at the Green Carnation twice a week, but she's not been around for weeks. He's terrifically worried."

A shiver tracked up Gilbert's spine, but he smiled. "I'm sure it's nothing to be concerned about, but bien sûr, I'll make sure and look into it. What's her name?"

"Charlotte Barreau. Their parents have been dead for years, and she and Jody are very close." I exhaled with relief and allowed him to open the door.

I removed my hat as the maître d'hotel led us through the packed restaurant. The menu was known to be exorbitant, and I'd never thought I'd have a chance to read it firsthand. Once inside, there was a feeling of being in a beehive—the black tuxedoed waiters with their immaculate white aprons whizzed amongst the clusters of round tables draped in white tablecloths without running into one another. Mirrors around the walls made it seem like the crowd was a multitude larger and left me dizzy with the reflected lights of so many chandeliers.

As we wound through to our table, I recognized a handful of abonnés, though as far as I could tell from the quality of the silks and satins of their companions' frocks, they were not dining with their ballet dancers. And the current fashion of exotic feathers and furs tucked in any place they could be managed left me wondering if entire species had been made extinct.

Unsurprisingly, we were led to a round table in the very center of the restaurant, where Michel de Gênet held court, Stéphanie on one side and Victoire on the other. *How had that invitation happened?* I had a niggling sense of unease over the situation, though I couldn't pinpoint why. The waiter pulled out our seats on opposite sides of the table.

Victoire held out her hand to me. "Gilbert sent round an invitation last night; wasn't that kind of him to remember me?"

When he found me at the Green Carnation, no doubt. I wouldn't have included her, as much as I adored her. Her storytelling at Stéphanie's party was risqué and funny—*there*. I hadn't caught a glimpse of a sense of humor attached to the wealthy retailer.

But tonight, Gilbert's uncle was much less reserved, and florid in his compliments to both his stepdaughter and to Victoire, who blossomed once again into a duke's granddaughter before my eyes.

I spent the first hour calculating the costs of the multiple bottles of champagne, the entrées that were hardly touched, and the main courses—works of art designed to fill the stomach of a sparrow. People paid for the atmosphere, for the privilege of being seen.

And in my case, for the license to plead my case to a man who could make or break me on a whim.

Though if that man was Gilbert or his uncle, I was unsure.

The clinking of the cutlery against the delicate china was buffered by the murmur of voices all around. It was almost like an orchestra—a high-pitched giggle here, a deep, throaty laugh there.

I'd had more tempting dishes from my aunt, who was a decent cook, if nothing else, but I forced myself through a rabbit and egg aspic, which had me ready to be sick each time I poked a fork into it.

"Tell me about your father, Monsieur Tighe. Gilbert says he plans to make you his heir, but it's difficult to trust what he has to say." De Gênet's eyebrows lowered. "Is such a thing even possible in England?"

My mouth went dry. Was de Gênet testing me? Why the hell had I done this to myself? It was worse than the aspic.

Gilbert swallowed his wine and flourished his empty goblet to make a point. "The earl referenced an indiscreet marriage in his youth. Surely that would have been to Fin's mother. Even if he was ashamed at the time to let people know, now that he's in need of an heir, it's a perfect time to come clean and introduce his son to society."

Before I could conceal my surprise, I sent Duhais a stunned face. An indiscreet marriage? Never happened. My mother's family would never have allowed people to disparage her reputation if that were the case. Not for Annabeth's or my sake, but because of how it tarnished their name.

But Gilbert's resolute jaw left me muddled. No hint of a fib.

Could it be true, and perhaps my mother kept silent? I never knew her to know if she had that sort of character.

"It's a convincing story." An unexpected ally poked her nose in. "The earl could always pay for a forged marriage certificate, couldn't he?" Stéphanie impaled her steak with her fork and blinked up at me. "It can't be too difficult, if he wanted to."

"He's got the money," I said, wishing I could thank her.

Gilbert's foot knocked against mine under the table, and I flushed under his gaze. How did he dare lick his lips like that seated next to his fiancée and across from his uncle? I laid down my fork and pushed away the plate, meeting de Gênet's hooded gaze.

"He was married to another woman when I was a child, but both his son and wife are dead. And my mother died before that wedding, so it wouldn't harm anyone if he was able to produce some proof." I sat back in my chair and ran my finger around the rim of my wineglass until it sang. I was seduced by the idea.

Good Lord. Under different circumstances, it would be possible. Faint-headed, I poured myself more champagne and lifted it without thinking. Something to wash away the unpleasantness on my tongue.

"When will you go back to England?" De Gênet emptied the bottle into Victoire's glass and snapped for another.

Chivalrous. Except I'd be footing the bill. What Gilbert had stuffed in my pocket might manage about half, if I was lucky.

"I'll wait until construction for the foundation of the tower gets underway, at least," I said, because that was reasonable, and brought the conversation back to my investment needs, where I was more comfortable.

De Gênet twisted the signet ring on his right hand fully around before raising his eyes. "That's not as certain as you led us to believe. From what I read in the papers, the government is on the verge of changing their minds, to cater to all of the voices of dissent. And besides, the ground might be too soft so close to the river."

"It's all just posturing, I promise you. Eiffel has been assured the tower will be built." I waved away his concerns, praying I was correct. It would be built if the investors were onboard. "We've been busy calculating the depth of stone and concrete we'd need to keep it balanced. It's all very precise." The way I liked things: knowing there was a solution, if I figured the correct maths.

"Clemenceau scoffs and wonders why Parisians ought to have their city marred for something real French people disdain, to get some damned foreigners on our shores?" De Gênet was able to raise a solitary eyebrow, too. Aggravating.

"The more foreigners visit the tower, the better your investment with Fin, Monsieur de Gênet. You see, Clemenceau is on Fin's side without even meaning it, isn't he?" Victoire tittered as she smiled at me. *Bless her.*

Gilbert's uncle conceded her point. *Her brilliantly made point.* Maybe I could afford to invest some money in Victoire's name for all her help.

"Michel, please, mademoiselle." De Gênet lifted Victoire's hand elegantly, kissing it.

To me, he was less charming. "I wish to hold off on signing the papers you sent around until it is settled for sure."

"He won that investment off you fairly, Michel." Gilbert frowned. Which was true. I'd won it playing billiards. And I'd be livid if he reneged. It might even be catastrophic, because there was so much public outrage over the design and I—Eiffel— needed the support of someone as prestigious as Michel de Gênet. None of his friends would be likely to sign, either, if de Gênet didn't. Eiffel might not sway the government unless he had the money in hand.

I rubbed my sweating palms over my starched thighs and plunged back into the conversation. I had to win the man back to my side. "Gilbert tells me you're hoping for my *father* to give you some kind of backing to open a branch of Qualité in London?"

It was a wonder I didn't stumble over the word *father*. His attention caught, de Gênet narrowed his eyes and then smiled again, amazing me with how similar he was to his nephew.

"Gilbert doesn't know when to mind his own business, does he?"

I actually agreed with that but didn't answer the question. "My father's involved in many business opportunities in London— trade, industry. There is a chance he might be interested in a brand as well loved as Qualité." I polished off my drink. "Next time we speak, I'll be happy to bring it up to him."

I survived the lie, most likely as I had no intention of ever speaking to the man again. I wouldn't have the chance, if Gilbert was right about his health.

But the implication was clear.

"If Gilbert manages to get something so important taken care of, I might have to change my opinion about his worth to me." De Gênet's comment was offered with a short laugh, but I didn't find it humorous. Neither did Gilbert, who narrowed his eyes, though he said nothing to defend himself. Our dishes were cleared and aperitifs drunk while Stéphanie chattered about her trousseau. I'd have been sick to my stomach listening if I weren't so thrilled not to continue having to spin falsehoods.

Gilbert was a convincing bridegroom for the first time, and I caught Victoire watching me with sad eyes. I winked at her to let her know how little I minded. Just because Gilbert and I had gone to bed one time didn't mean I expected to ever do it again.

I asked the waiter for the bill, hoping my Dutch courage would keep me from looking green when I read the price. I'd never had so much champagne in one go. My head would be shredded in the morning.

My wallet, too. Bloody hell, the cost was ... well, more than I would have chosen to pay. But I kept my face straight as pulled out the money and handed it to the man.

"Victoire, can I see you get home safely?" I offered her my arm.

"We can take her," said Stéphanie. "We're headed in the same direction."

My friend gushed, "That's lovely, Stéphanie, thank you. You know, one of these evenings, we'll need to get together, like you suggested, and share all the secrets we know about our mutual acquaintances." She looked right at Gilbert, who went all rumpled and red before she turned to his uncle and batted her eyes.

I perfunctorily shook hands with the gentlemen and walked to the door, head high.

Done. I was done with any personal relationship with Gilbert Duhais, and utterly relieved. We could maintain this sort of business friendship, and that was fine.

But as I walked home through the sprinkling rain, I imagined Gilbert and Stéphanie's future. Two nice homes. Travel. Perhaps children. A pain flared in my chest, and I rubbed it absently as I trudged up the stairs to the flat. It was a pain I was too familiar with. I'd get past it. I always did.

And it wasn't about Gilbert, per se; it was the money he had. I was sure of it.

My heart was safe, as long as my bank balance moved higher. It wasn't as though I had any feelings for him, well, beyond lust. But those were transitory.

They had to be.

13

'd been asleep when the rapping at my window woke me. *At my window?* Groggy, I listened, and there it was again. A smack followed by two more in quick succession.

My limbs soft with sleep, I moved to open the curtains. Under the streetlamp, Gilbert grinned up at me, as if it hadn't been a fortnight since I last saw him. Not that I kept count.

I glared and waved him off, but he had a handful of pebbles and threw another, which would've hit my nose if glass hadn't separated us.

"Go away," I hissed under the sash, open a few inches.

He shook his head. *Bugger all.* His arm wound for another throw, and I checked the clock on my bedside. I'd been asleep for less than an hour.

Smack. Smack.

Lifting the window higher, I spoke loud enough for him to hear, and hopefully not to wake my neighbors. "Go away. I'm working in a few hours." I dropped the curtain and stepped back toward my bed.

And I had no desire to see him anyway. Or my brain didn't. I'd finally stopped thinking of him every hour. As always, my body was of another mind, but I was used to that.

Gilbert threw another rock. Bastard. I waited until the fifth and, in a lather of annoyance, asked him what the bloody hell he wanted.

He blew me a kiss. "Just to come up there. Open the door, Fin?"

"Under no circumstances will I open the—"

This time, he threw the rock to my concierge's window. Not as hard, but Mademoiselle Jeunesse was such a light sleeper. My belly clenched in anxiety. And then another.

Christ almighty, the man rubbed me the wrong way.

I hurried down the stairs and unlocked the bolt to the street. "Some of us have to work for a living. Go home."

Somehow, he slithered past me and was in the entryway, one arm slung across my hips. He licked my earlobe. "I want to sleep with you. Only sleep. I won't keep you up."

He needed to leave, and I ought to have insisted. But the concierge's door was three inches from us, and he'd banged her window. Since she hadn't opened her door, I could assume she had her eye pressed to the peephole. My years of cultivating a reputation as a respectable tenant who never caused problems destroyed. I groaned and nodded, gesturing for him to be quiet.

Instead, he took his time, footfalls heavy. Pushing him ahead, I put my fingers over his mouth as we entered the apartment, so his lips sucked one in. Yanking it out, I wiped it on my underpants. I slid the chain across and shooed him to my room, wherein I slid back into bed and curled away from him, which was foolish because I couldn't see what he was doing. After a minute or two, I turned over. His clothes off, the crystalline light filtering from the streetlamp outlined his naked body. There was a shadow over his right eye and cheekbone. I flicked on the kerosene lamp. The bruise was angry and purple.

"Fisticuffs at your age?" I tried to keep my concern at bay.

He scraped a hand over the contusion, turning away slightly. The knuckles on his hand were swollen as well. "It's nothing. A tussle with a pickpocket." He switched the light back off.

His clothes were impeccable as usual. "Did they steal anything?"

"Nothing. I chased him off. I'm exhausted, though."

"Don't you have your own bed, likely more comfortable?"

Gilbert slipped into the bed next to me, skin touching from our thighs to ankles. "Pardon, mon vilain, but I found myself on this side of the city this evening, and was too tired to make it back to my apartment."

"Awfully late. Couldn't you find someone else to bunk with?"

"I was doing something for Michel, and now I could hardly find the strength to put one foot in front of the other."

"For Michel? What sorts of things could you be doing at"— I glanced at the clock again—"midnight?"

"Sometimes it's difficult to track down people during the day." He propped up on his elbow and held my arm so I couldn't roll away. There was a slight trickle of dried blood near his hairline.

"All day I couldn't shake the need to see you," he whispered. "Mon Dieu—I dream about you."

The anguished look on his face made me believe him for a moment.

His fingers caught, snarled in my hair.

The murmurs of excited gratitude that bubbled out of his mouth enchanted me. He hypnotized me into wanting things I shouldn't want. Desperately. My hands climbed up his back and pulled him closer. He dragged his fingers against my scalp.

He kissed down my neck, my collarbone, murmuring what sounded like a prayer under his breath. I wasn't sure which of the saints was responsible for sensuous pleasures, but his supplications were answered.

Fingers explored more softly now, traced my jaw and throat. Dangerously sweet, like a pastry. I didn't trust sweet. It left me exposed. It made me long for things that could never be.

The pale moon lit his face through the linen curtain at the window. His low-hanging lids blinked, lips parted so close to mine that I had to indulge some more.

Gilbert rolled onto his elbows, his hair hanging over his forehead, eyes wide and brilliant even in the dark. "Thank you for letting me in. Bonne nuit, Fin." He dropped one last kiss. Soft, like a butterfly. Not a long kiss, and not a deep kiss, but one that reached into my heart and tugged. Then he rolled over to his side, his back pressing against my chest.

I ground against him, and he smacked my hands away with a laugh. "Sleep."

His legs tangled inside mine in a pattern that ought to have felt wrong, but didn't. My palm smoothed down the skin of his flank, hip to knee. No reaction at all except a deepening of his breath and a loosening of his muscles. I poked his shoulder and whispered, "Have you heard anything about Charlotte Barreau?"

Because though I hadn't been to see Jody, he was probably anxious for news.

Gilbert let out a low snore for his answer. The connard was asleep. He had come and woken me up—alerted my neighbors that I might not be as rosy-cheeked and innocent as I maintained—and then... nothing.

But it was nice to have him there. This once. I breathed that ocean-scented shaving soap deeply, capturing it down in my chest and lungs until it filled me up.

I yawned, settling myself further into the downy softness of the bed, and allowed the slow but steady stream of traffic under my windows to lull me back to sleep, intertwined with a man who seduced me, perplexed me, and relaxed me.

And who disappeared again before the tinny anvil chime of my Seth Thomas clock yanked me up from one of the more restful nights I remember, short though it was. I patted the bed where Gilbert had lain. Had I dreamed his visit?

There was a note left on the pillow, torn from a notebook he must have carried with him.

"Quand on a pas ce qu'on aime, il faut aimer ce qu'on a."

When you don't have what you love, you must love what you have.

14

I was working at home, deep in numbers, reviewing my team's calculations of how to fortify the two legs of the tower that would be built on softer ground. The damned Military College had refused to give up more than a few hectares of the Champs de Mars for the structure, and this was the only way we could hope to keep it sturdy on less solid ground.

A sound like a gunshot outside my door disrupted me. Pushing back from my drafting table, I sprang to the peephole, praying there was no bloody body on the landing. My relief that it was Victoire, clutching her hand over her mouth but unable to contain her giggles, and Jody, drenched in what smelled of champagne, dissipated as Mademoiselle Jeunesse stomped up the stairs to reprimand me.

"Yes, yes. I will clean up the mess. I beg your pardon for the noise." I dragged my friends into the flat and fetched a towel to dry the tatty old carpeting of the hallway.

"Fini, cher, let me take care of that," said Victoire, thrusting the bottle into my hands and taking the linen.

"What on earth are you two doing here? What about the club?" It was a Saturday night, Jody's biggest draw.

He groaned as he removed his dampened shirt. "The lights went out."

My mind raced. Where would I be able to let my proverbial hair down if he closed the Green Carnation? Not that I'd had the energy to go for the past month, as all my waking hours were consumed with the bloody tower.

However, just knowing there was a place where I could be myself amongst friends was vital.

"Something's wrong with the gas, and they won't fix it in time to open," said Victoire. "Besides, Jody's been miserable without news from Charlotte and needs a change of scenery. Have you discovered anything?"

Damn, I ought to have followed up, but it had slipped my mind. With chagrin I shook my head. "I asked Gilbert Duhais to look into her whereabouts, but I haven't seen him to find out what he may have learned." Aside from the one evening he'd appeared under my window. Charlotte Barreau wasn't what I'd been focused on that night.

"Perhaps we'll hear something soon." Victoire masterfully changed the subject. She ran her fingernails down Jody's bare chest, and he shivered and flexed. "As much as I appreciate all these muscles, Jody must borrow a shirt, Fin."

Prodded by a guilty conscience, I handed him one of the new shirts from Qualité that I hadn't worn yet.

Jody threw an arm over my shoulder. "Since I've been forced to take a night off, Vicky thought I needed to get out and visit some other cabarets. Instead of getting extra sleep. Or finding mon chaud lapin to keep me awake." He waggled his eyebrows suggestively.

Victoire helped Jody pull on his brown corduroy jacket. "You can sleep when you're dead, mon chou. Tonight, we're toasting Fin's success so he remembers us when he becomes a millionaire." She took a lazy swig of the champagne and handed it to me, wiping her mouth with the back of her hand. It left a slash of rouge like blood.

"I'm hardly going to be a millionaire," I protested. But I took the bottle and swallowed. The trail of bubbles left a tingle down my throat that was more than pleasant.

"Certainly not if you don't believe in yourself. Fetch your coat." Victoire shooed me back to my room. "We're headed down to Boul Mich, so nothing as fancy as you wear for your new friends. Tonight, we're slumming with the students."

I stood in front of my clothes press, frowning. "I don't have clothes for slumming."

"Quit grumbling. You're much prettier when you smile." Victoire flicked through my wardrobe and pulled out a navy velveteen blazer.

Jody came into my room with a wineglass for each of us. He whipped a handkerchief out of his pocket and knotted it around my throat before stepping back and squinting at me. "You still look like a snobby bastard, just in dress-up clothes."

Victoire examined me, fingertip on her lips. "*Dress-down* clothes, you mean."

I snorted. "You're both absurd. I look like a working man because that's what I am."

Jody thumped his heart. "Did you know that peasants like

our dear Viscount Carleton are often elevated to the senior management team of internationally successful engineering firms, Vicky?"

Her face deadpan, she agreed. "All part of the revolutionary plot. My tobacconist began wearing evening tails to his shop last week."

I checked my watch and shook my head sadly at the two of them. "I'm afraid France isn't due another revolution for at least six years. Should you warn your tobacconist, or shall we let him find out on his own?"

"Joking aside, Fini, I appreciate you asking your fellow about Charlotte." Jody pinched my cheek.

"Have you contacted the gendarme? Reported that she's missing? Just in case Gilbert—who is most assuredly not my fellow—doesn't have any answer?"

Jody rolled his eyes. "Your naïveté is charming. Non—the gendarme would laugh me out of the room for asking them to track down a prole like Charlotte. But I'm glad you're not linked to this Duhais. I've heard some unsavory things about him from some fellows in my old neighborhood near Belleville when I went looking for Charlotte. Odd that such a wealthy man would be seen hanging about in slums, but what do I know about how the rich entertain themselves? Vicky, what was it you remembered Charlotte called him?"

Plucking my top hat from its perch on my clothes press, Jody plopped it on my head. He was definitely on the verge of drunkenness. "De Gênet's lackey, I believe it was. Messy stuff he sticks his fingers into, not for the likes of an incognito British peer like yourself."

Even though Gilbert truly meant nothing to me, I bristled at the implication. "He sorts his uncle's accounts, so I'm not sure what Charlotte could have meant."

Victoire linked arms with both of us and pulled us tight as in a three-person embrace. "Never mind, Fin. We're headed out for an evening of debauchery so lurid, we'll be lucky if we can remember our own names by midnight. No need to think of unpleasantness."

We took a 'bus, riding on top, across town to the Latin Quarter, discreetly passing Victoire's flask between us. The vehicle rattled over the Seine via the Pont Neuf, then onto Boulevard Saint-Michel, which was lit up like a carnival with riotous atmosphere to match. So close to the universities and art school, there was an overflowing of young people and those who wished to cling to the façade of youth.

I'd had a few meetings with investors near l'École des Beaux-Arts. It wouldn't do to have my two worlds collide. "Where are we headed? I ... er ... ought to be careful about what sort of establishment I'm seen at."

Jody growled, "What sort of place? One like mine?"

How could I explain that I felt safe enough at the Green Carnation because not only had I been going there for years, but it wasn't screaming its clientele in bright lights in one of the most highly trafficked night spots in the city? "I hate asking, you know I do. But I've spent a lot of time here lately and can't risk bumping into someone who's put a large sum of money up for the tower. It's not worth losing my career."

For a moment, Jody looked sad. "Non, Fini. Vicky's been telling me about a place called le Chien Volage, which isn't a club like mine, not exactly—there are plenty of women. Some models and some like Vicky. It's just that no one cares who is kissing who. None of your new fancy friends will suspect anything you insist you must keep quiet about." He lit a cigarette and looked toward the river as though it was the most engrossing thing he'd ever seen.

Victoire squeezed my other thigh comfortingly and started another song. Halfway through, she uncurled my white knuckles from around my knees and squeezed my hands.

We ambled down the street and off to a cut-through past a gargoyle-covered church, Saint-Séverin, which sat at odds with the liveliness of the rest of the neighborhood. Two older women, head-to-toe in black with veils, came from the heavy wooden door and made the sign of the cross over us.

I decided they would have done the same to anyone wearing smiles, and that it wasn't just because they could read our particular sins.

Le Chien Volage was tucked between two cafés, and I scoured the entrance for any sign that it was "for gentlemen only." Nothing. Feeling safe, I handed over our fees, and we were allowed behind the red velvet rope. The single large room was stuffed with men in all modes of dress, though most were decked out like Jody and me. Casual, loose. Nothing like the luxurious suits at the ballet or even the bourgeois stuffiness of my workplace. A few feminine faces were tucked around—enough to give me cover if I was spotted by one of Eiffel's investors.

Victoire flitted around the room to give and receive kisses, and I elbowed my way through to the bar, taking in the vast array of humanity by means of a long mirror framed in silver-painted wood. No one to raise my heartbeat.

Until a couple in a corner table argued loud enough to capture my attention. They sat side-by-side, a chair empty across from them, one light and the other dark. The black-haired man's back was turned three quarters away from me, and he shook the blond by his shoulders before dropping his elbows to the table and sinking his face into his hands.

I'd recognize that profile anywhere, and was glad that the brass-rimmed bar and the patrons pressing behind me held me up when my knees buckled.

Bloody Gilbert. I stared. And one of those young men from Stéphanie's party. Harry's friend from school, Sonny Tolbert. Were they... together?

If I could have caught Victoire's attention, I would have escaped, but she was nowhere to be seen. I had to brazen this situation out.

I walked with an odd sideways gait to the booth Jody had found, keeping my back to Gilbert. I didn't care that he was with another man, and staying at the cabaret would prove it.

Pulling my hat brim low, I slid into the red leather bench across from Jody. My position allowed me to watch Gilbert's and Sonny's reflections in the mirror. I couldn't look away, not even when Victoire settled across from me and held court from our table, introducing everyone as they came to pay homage.

Gilbert eventually made his own way to the bar, and I caught him in my peripheral vision. His body stiffened, and he looked at me over his shoulder before he grabbed his own drinks and skirted back to his table, head lowered, as though he, too, was hiding.

Connard.

I was moments away from making my good-nights when Sonny stumbled over, muttering curses loud enough to draw attention even in this sodden crowd. He put a hand on the edge of my table as though steadying himself. "Look at you, Viscount Carleton." His left eye twitched.

A red-faced Gilbert was half a step behind, fury scrawled in every tense muscle. But he couldn't ignore my blatant stare, and he stopped, deflated. His shoulders sagged.

"Fin."

I looked Gilbert face-front, placid as I could muster, though I felt my nostrils twitch. "Duhais, what a surprise. Been here long?" I prayed my voice projected utter nonchalance.

For a few heartbeats, our eyes were locked.

"It's not what it looks like." His voice was barely audible over the din.

I forced myself to smile halfway. I pretended to suck the last drops of brandy from my empty glass. "It's nothing to me, I assure you." Hopefully, he understood the subtext that *he* meant nothing to me.

The only testament to my response was a rush of color slashing across his neck. But still, he stood there, at the foot of our table, head bowed, knotting and unknotting his fingers.

Jody pointed toward Gilbert with a heavy scowl that would make most people tremble. "This is your friend with the uncle?" Jody nearly knocked Victoire on her bottom when he pushed her to stand so he could, too.

Before I could respond or rise to my feet, Jody had two handfuls of Gilbert's lapels. "Where the hell is my sister, Duhais?"

Gilbert readjusted his stance as if noticing Jody for the first time and plucked Jody's fingers off his jacket. "Excusez-moi? Who's your sister?"

Fucking hell. It looked as though Gilbert hadn't followed up, either.

"Charlotte Barreau. She works for your uncle and hasn't been around to see me in nearly two months. She visits me on Tuesday nights and Sundays like clockwork, but she's missed all these weeks."

Two months? I'd been so busy with investors that I'd hardly paused to think about Charlotte Barreau.

"Mon Dieu, I told Fin that I'd check, but I admit it slipped my mind. I apologize for that. You ought to ring round and ask for her. No one would be annoyed by that." Gilbert stopped with abruptness. He straightened his cuffs and looked at his fingernails.

Sonny stood between Jody and Gilbert and poked the mouthpiece end of his pipe into Jody's chest hard enough that I winced. "I'd leave off if I was you. You don't know what you're talking about."

Jody wrenched Sonny's hand when he pushed it away. "Oy, back the hell off. I don't know who you are, and you have nothing to do with this."

Victoire toyed with her necklace and cast me a despairing look. But what was I supposed to do? I cleared my throat and forced a smile. "Gentlemen, this isn't the best way to handle—"

Jody grunted and waved me off, moving into Gilbert's personal space. "I've heard rumors about who you are under that fancy suit. Things you do for your uncle who pretends to be such a saint." I'd never seen Jody so furious. "I'll ask one last time before I bloody your God-damned face. What has happened to Charlotte?"

"What makes you think Duhais would know the whereabouts

of a bloody maid?" Sonny's sneer was the most condescending I'd ever witnessed.

"That's enough, Sonny. Didn't Michel need to speak with you? This is none of your concern." Gilbert let out a small huff as he adjusted his hat and pointedly looked at the door for Sonny to leave. After a moment, he did, though he used his shoulder to physically push Jody out of his path.

After watching the door swing shut behind Sonny, Gilbert's eyes darted back to Jody. "I let everyone down by not following up on my promise." His skin had darkened, but his voice was calm. "Honestly, I have no clue about any of this, but as you're a friend of Fin's, I'll have my fiancée make some inquiries. She can smooth your way, ensure the staff you've been invited to visit with the housekeeper. If...uh, Charlotte?...wishes to leave, that is to say, she's unhappy, then I suggest she find a different post. With a decent reference, that shouldn't be a problem. Stéphanie would be happy to provide that."

A vision of all of de Gênet's francs swirling down the commode propelled me to intervene, a hand on each of their chests to push them apart before a blow was struck. "There now. That's a reasonable plan, Jody."

My old friend tossed me a contemptuous scowl. "You're not thinking with your brain, Fini. I don't know what he's doing to make you bleat like a meek animal, but I wouldn't trust this *connard* or any of his associates any further than I could throw them." Jody spat at the floor and wrenched himself free from my grip, heading out into the night.

Victoire grabbed my hand to keep me from chasing after him.

"Let him cool down, cher. He'll walk home and be able to talk calmly with you tomorrow." Leaning in to kiss my cheek, she whispered, "Watch yourself, d'accord?"

She smiled at Gilbert, who still stared at the door as though unable to understand what had just happened. "You'll manage to find your way home alone tonight?" She flicked her eyes meaningfully over to a tuxedoed man making eyes at her. "I'll do the same. Or perhaps find a different escort, if you don't mind?" She blew me a kiss and walked to the gentleman, her gloved hand extended.

Gilbert slid into the booth across from me and slumped against the back of the seat, eyes screwed shut as he retrieved a cigarette from his pocket. He opened them to light it, then shut them again.

There was a weariness to him that I'd not seen before. Even in his polished suit and tie, he came off as . . . sad, perhaps. His eyes were red, which could have been the alcohol, but his lashes were spiked together like he'd cried recently. I didn't like him this way, crumpled and vulnerable. I preferred his cocksure swagger.

He blinked his eyes open. "Take me home." It was another sort of plea, and one that cut into my chest like a knife.

My voice was light. "You've been drinking from the look of you. Even if I thought it was a good idea, I couldn't. I have a rule that I never sleep with a man twice. It makes things too complicated." *Even if I could trust you.*

That reminded me. "What was Jody implying about your work for your uncle?"

Gilbert raised one shoulder and ran the back of his nail against the grain of his silk hat. "Ask the piece of shit yourself, and make sure to let me know, because I don't know what he could be talking about. I work on accounting books. I told you."

There had to be more to it than that. Not that it mattered, as once the tower was fully funded, I'd be through with Gilbert.

"Why don't you have faith in me?" He didn't say it like it saddened him. More like he couldn't understand.

"I've gone along with all of your schemes; isn't that enough?"

One shoulder lifted a fraction. "Perhaps, though I'd prefer you to believe that I've got your best interests at heart."

I rolled my eyes. "It's not always easy, to be frank."

"Most people know that I'm as good as my word, and that's why they spend time with me." He gave an affected sniff for punctuation.

With a sour laugh, I leaned back. "Do they? That man you were with—Sonny—he didn't appear to care for you overmuch."

Gilbert raked long fingers through his hair, pushing it off his forehead. "That worm. I never did trust him. Paul was right." He growled low in his throat.

"He was friends with the likes of Paul? Public school boy Sonny Tolbert?"

Gilbert visibly bit the inside of his cheek.

I was disgusted by all of it. "From where I'm sitting, friendships with Harry Carleton and Paul Blancmaison aren't good character witness for any of you."

Gilbert inhaled sharply and turned his head away. He mumbled, "You're right, now that I've gotten more of the puzzle. Sonny told me some things I never knew about Paul."

I barreled on before I lost the courage to ask. "Why is it that every time my cousin's name is brought up, it points to a deeper friendship than you've come clean about? Would you consider him a close companion?"

Gilbert's eyes darted anywhere but on my face. "Non, it wasn't like that. We...uh...we all knew one another many years ago. We were friends of a sort, all three of us, but nothing particular." And then he looked back at me, as though something had been drained from him. "Or at least, I believed we all got along, but it appears that Sonny and Paul despised one another."

Even after being such an arse, Sonny Tolbert went up a few notches in my estimation if he was canny enough to distrust Paul.

"Fucking hell." His caught his breath. "Oh, damn. *Merde.*"

His horrified shock was almost comical. Almost. "Are you all right?"

Duhais stared down at the table, but his mind was clearly elsewhere. Under his breath he mumbled in French so quickly I could only make out the name Paul.

The hysteria-tinged laughter was unexpected. His black eyes intent on mine. "Jésus, non. I must know—what was Paul's relationship like with Aurélie? Was he negligent of her safety and something bad happened to her?"

"Negligent? That sounds as though what happened was an accident." My upper lip curled in disgust. "No. He purposefully sold her to men so he could have the equivalent of pocket money." Saying it aloud had me so suffused with anger that I banged the table with my fist.

"Non?" Gilbert's face melted into true disbelief. "That's what you meant by abuse?" The pain in his voice was unmistakable.

When he stood without warning, I couldn't catch my bearings. "That changes—"

"Changes what?"

"Mon Dieu, I must think." He leaned over the table with flexed fingers, jabbing his thumbs into his temples.

The hair at the back of my neck prickled, and my throat tightened. I needed air, immediately. And to get the hell away from memories of Paul. "Bon soirée." I gave a quick glance to confirm that Victoire didn't need me and slid from the booth. Head down, I bolted into the chilled night air, gulping.

There was more to Gilbert's relationship with Paul than he admitted to, but I'd be damned if I dared to think about it. Not in the state I was in.

But at least it was settled. I couldn't resume my friendship, or whatever it was, with Gilbert.

I was, after all, *fini*.

15

Throughout October, there were no more midnight wake-ups from Gilbert, and I was relieved.

Truly.

He'd done his part in launching me, and it was now on me to make my own way. In a calfskin journal, I dutifully recorded each investment I received after his initial patronage. One column for my share and then one for his portion. He'd never be able to say I was a cheat, and honestly, that was the end of it.

De Gênet had answered the first note I'd sent asking for the money that he had promised with polite evasions. He didn't respond to the second, and I was loathe to send off any more.

That's when running into Gilbert might have been helpful, but I'd be damned before I sought him out. And anyway, I simply hadn't the time or energy to worry over him as I had to balance my now somewhat healthier bank account with all the entertaining I was doing with investors.

Luckily for my slender wallet, most of the stodgy bankers and well-heeled merchants I spent my evenings charming were thrilled to be taken into the bohemian cabarets of Boul Mich instead of chic restaurants.

I'd become adept on staying out too late too often and still making it to work on time. Usually. And if I didn't—well, the great man himself spread the word around the office that my tardiness wasn't to be remarked upon. By anyone.

Not with all the tidy pledges I was raking in.

Eiffel did, however, call me into his office in early November asking about de Gênet's unfulfilled pledge. I did my best to convince him that it was concern that the project wouldn't ever come to fruition that caused the delay, not my ineptitude.

It might even be the truth.

The government, who'd be the final arbiter of final approval to the tower, had canceled their scheduled meeting a few weeks earlier, but I could hardly be blamed for that part of the uncertainty. De Gênet and his friends had promised the largest sums of anyone, far dwarfing the smaller pledges I'd been gathering since with my late nights. But it could be intuited that they, like the rest of Paris, were torn over whether the administration would allow the behemoth to cast its giant lacework shadow over the Champs de Mars or if the idea would be scrapped at the eleventh hour.

Monsieur Eiffel appeared to accept that—though he reminded me again that my father might be a help, all too often for my comfort.

Indeed, Rawcliffe would be a tremendous help. What a shame everything I'd promised by using his name was a complete fabrication. Advice from Gilbert on how to proceed might have been useful, but not enough to sort through my complicated feelings about him. Besides, if my father's health was as bad as Gilbert had implied, perhaps he'd die before any news of me came to his attention. One could dream, after all.

Finally, the day arrived for Aurélie's solo debut in *The Two Pigeons*, and it was a relief not to feel obligated to wine and dine investors for an evening. The allure of scantily dressed women twisting their bodies into unnatural shapes was lost on me, but I wouldn't dream of missing her opening night.

I debated taking a cab to the Opéra, but decided against it. It was a clear evening for November, no clouds in sight.

I strode along the most fashionable street in the city, Boulevard des Italiens, watching my fellow strollers. I counted the colors of the rainbow worn by high-society Parisian matrons in their bustled silks from the House of Worth, draped in feathers and furs and hats intricate enough to have wooed Marie Antoinette. Their husbands and sons in their somber dark suits were a perfect foil to the women's bright frocks, which shone like gemstones under the electric lamps.

Scattered amongst them were debutantes and rich American girls in scandalously short walking dresses. Not that I was scandalized; I'd despise maneuvering in long skirts, as well, and raised my top hat to one cheeky pair whose skirts didn't even reach the top of their boots.

Possibly for the first time ever, I didn't feel…*unworthy*, I suppose, amidst such glamor. Nor did anyone look at me as though I might be a fraud, dressed to the nines as I was in my black tailless evening jacket, *merci beaucoup, Monsieur Duhais.*

And why should they? If anyone recognized my face, they'd know me as Finley, Viscount Carleton, not middle management bastard Fin Tighe. That's what I needed to remember. Giddy with the novelty, I stopped by Café Anglais for an aperitif and a cigarette before continuing my leisurely journey. The polished mahogany of the chairs glistened under the ornate electrolier above my table, and I ran my finger down the side of the linen tablecloth.

"Monsieur—pardon, Viscount Carleton, what a pleasure it is to run into you."

I turned at the female voice behind me. Stéphanie Verger was with a handsome ginger who was noticeably not Gilbert.

Extending my hand for hers, I hovered my lips over her pristine white evening glove. "The pleasure is mine, mademoiselle. I hope you're well?"

She's been attractive every time I'd met her, but this particular evening, I was astounded by how stunning she was, all decked in turquoise sateen and diamonds. Unlike so many others around town—along the Boulevard des Italiens, for example—she limited herself to one perfect peacock feather in her elaborate hairdo. But it was more than that. There was a glow about her I'd not seen before.

Stéphanie swallowed before nodding. "This is...an old family friend, Monsieur Romuald Parry." She beamed up at him, and he blushed in the way that redheads often do as she introduced me as a friend of Gilbert's.

"Michel is so old-fashioned about my safety. Makes such a fuss if I don't have a chaperone." Her eyes were overly bright. "Romu's escorting me around town as Gilbert is away."

Was it polite to inquire where Gilbert had gone? Merely for small talk—I hadn't a concern in the world about Gilbert's whereabouts.

I had no need to bother as she continued in a rush. "Michel

sent him to England, but surely you know that." She forced a laugh as she rapped my arm with her folded fan.

"Actually, I haven't seen him around, but he promised to inquire about a young woman working for Monsieur de Gênet. My friend's sister, Charlotte Barreau. Did he mention her to you?"

The fine lines between Stéphanie's brows creased as she repeated the name. "Oui, I remember. I would have been most pleased to write her a reference, but she no longer works for Michel. Désolée. If you find her, please send her to me if she needs anything." There was a flash of tension around her mouth I didn't understand. "Anything at all. Now, you must excuse us, we have an appointment to meet."

"Lovely to see you, mademoiselle. Pleasure to meet you, Monsieur Parry. Don't let me hold you up."

They moved away rather faster than I expected, not that I paid them much heed.

Not that I cared, really, but what was Gilbert doing in England? Was he meeting with my father, giving a rundown of my activities?

Perhaps his trip was merely about the British branch of Qualité?

I'd best make an effort to speak with Jody soon. Perhaps he'd even heard from Charlotte. I'd spent so many evenings wining and dining investors that I'd hardy thought about the Green Carnation for weeks. I felt a pang of loneliness and needed to find time in my schedule to see them. My friends I could count on.

Too unsettled to finish my drink, I paid the bill and headed back into the night.

My mind whirled as I finished the walk to the Opéra. The chance meeting with Stéphanie had given me too many things to think about. I trotted up the steps to the entrance and moved toward the ticket booth rather than straight upstairs to the foyer de la danse. Tonight was Aurélie's debut solo. I'd sit as close as I could afford on the night of the premiere.

The young woman at the ticket booth asked my name, which was unusual. She blushed.

"Someone already paid for your ticket, monsieur."

My eyebrows flew up. "Who?"

Her skin darkened further. "I'm not to say." She pushed the ticket through the hole, and I shook my head.

A balcony seat? Someone wishing to ingratiate themselves with me in hope of charming Aurélie? Perhaps her anonymous donor. If so, they were welcome to press their anonymous lips to my arse because I wouldn't trade Aurélie's honor for some expensive seats, or anything else.

"Monsieur Tighe." A commanding voice halted me on the first level of the ornate marble stairs. Michel de Gênet raised an eyebrow.

I hesitated, shocked to see him there. "I hadn't realized you were a fan of the arts."

He gave me a rueful half-smile. "I'm not. Watching prancing whores is not anything I choose to do, but look around." He waved at the crowd. "We're surrounded by the cream of society for tonight's premiere. I never waste an opportunity to encourage Parisians to shop at my magasin."

I swallowed hard at the word he threw out so casually— Aurélie was the most decent young woman in the blasted city. However, arguing, let alone pointing out my relationship with

Aurélie, was no way to remain in his good graces. I searched for another thread of conversation, coming up empty.

De Gênet was not as tongue-tied. "I've heard you're doing well fleecing Paris for your damned tower."

"Not in the least, monsieur. I'm sharing a valuable investment opportunity. And I've been quite successful, yes." *Fleecing.* I did my best not to crumple under his piercing gaze. "Perhaps your lawyers have forgotten about your pledge? I'd hate for you to miss out."

He waved away the implication. "Your father? When will you see him again?"

When I die and go to hell. "Possibly over the holidays. I'm not sure if you received my notes, but the sums you promised to invest would be very useful. Shall I drop by to pick up—"

Storm clouds gathered on his face. "I'd advise you not presume to tell me how to conduct my business, Viscount Carleton. It won't end well. Feel free to ask your employer how he fared when doing the same."

His cold words sent chills coursing down my spine. Luckily, I was saved from further chatter by someone else who was eager for his attention and escaped up the stairs before he remembered to introduce me.

My ticket was for the fourth and highest rise, in the small box closest to the stage. God in heaven, these cost a small fortune. And when I made my way through the elaborate—*overwrought*, if you asked me—corridors and entered through the draperies, there was no one else there.

Half-expecting to be tossed out on my ear for presuming to sit there, I lit a cigarette and scanned the crowd. The ballet was one

I'd never heard of before. I'd heard Aurélie gossiping about it for so long that it was like watching a play within a play. It would be difficult not to look for signs of loathing during the pas de deux, or which member of the corps was off beat but was related to the maestro and impossible to fire. I waited for a sign of Aurélie's pale hair, twirling my cuff links through my fingers, bored with it all.

Behind me, a sharp intake of breath ripped my eyes off the stage. Gilbert ran his tongue over his lips. "Fin."

A solitary word, but delivered in a tone that set my skin on fire.

The weeks of convincing myself that I never wished to see him again went up in smoke as I drank him in. He took the seat next to mine, his knee brushing mine as he stretched out, eyes trained on the stage.

"The original version of this story was about two male lovers, did you know? It was Greek." Gilbert didn't move his eyes away from the dancers.

How much more entertaining that would have been, to watch the two lead characters, fighting and cooing and slipping their hands around each other, if they were men. "I had no idea."

He turned to me, and his eyes crawled down my face, my chest, and then back again. "I knew you'd get my ticket."

My head cocked. "Pardon?"

Gilbert leaned into my ear, his voice tickling so my skin rose. "I told her to give the ticket to the most handsome man who came to the booth."

"Did you?" I was an idiot for being so flattered.

"You're here, aren't you? And I bought all the seats in this box as well as the one next to us, so no one will interrupt."

I calculated the cost, stomach tumbling, and sucked in my breath. "All the seats?"

He shrugged. "I wanted to see you alone. To apologize."

"Lunch would have been easier." *Certainly less expensive.* Though that didn't matter to him as it did to me. "And you have nothing to apologize to me for."

Fingers gripped my hand. "Would you have agreed to see me again if I showed up for lunch?" He raised an eyebrow and answered himself. "Non."

My eyes shut—from pleasure to have this stolen moment with him, not shame that he was right. Because he was. And the anger rushed back. "I'm still confused about what your relationship was to Paul?"

"I told you, Fin. I knew him casually from school, and then I introduced him to Michel to do some odd jobs to make money. I had no idea that he was...a monster. I can't tell you how ashamed I am to've been duped. You must believe me." His face dripped with earnestness, and I softened.

I also lived with Paul and Aurélie and was unaware of the depths of his depravity. And he was also the last person of whom I wished to think, so I changed the subject.

"I heard you were in England."

His eyebrows flew north. "Non, I've been visiting my mother in Amiens. She's been pestering me." He fumbled in his jacket and pulled out his cigarette case. "Who told you I went abroad?"

"I ran into Stéphanie."

Gilbert lit a match, his gaze focused back on the stage. "Hmm. Non. I lied to her because I needed to get away for a moment, catch my breath. Michel has me working too hard, doesn't know when to let up."

I let the explanation hang in the air for a few moments before clearing my throat. "Did you inquire about the whereabouts of Charlotte? Jody's sister? Stéphanie didn't have any information."

Finally, Gilbert looked back my way, a smile rippling across his face. "Ah, Fin, always the good friend. Turns out there was no sinister mystery. I asked Michel's housekeeper just recently. Charlotte disappeared. Ran off with the neighbor's groom, they believe, as the two were friendly and he was also gone the next day."

"It doesn't make sense that she would have kept that from Jody. They're very close."

Lifting one shoulder, Gilbert said, "People do absurd things when they're in love. There's no reason to worry. She'll turn up."

A tightness in my chest I hadn't even noticed loosened, and I exhaled a deep breath. I'd make sure to make my way to Jody's the next day to put him out of his misery over her disappearance. This was the first piece of information that might be useful. Charlotte would return to Paris—likely pregnant, but hopefully not alone—and everything would be cleared up.

Gilbert laced his fingers with mine. "Before I came here tonight, I took a detour to the Green Carnation. To tell your friend what I found out. He was even more churlish than at our last encounter. I learned a few new phrases from him—hardly edifying." He shook his head. "He said he'd still be sending a message to Michel, though I warned him it might not be a wise move." A small shrug accompanied a frown. "I did what I could. There's nothing to stop a fool if he insists on making an ass out of himself."

Damn it. I needed to speak with Jody, though if he'd already heard—and discarded the validity of—the news about Charlotte, he'd hardly appreciate me backing up Gilbert. Still, I needed to clear the air with my old friend, and it's not as though I had to fabricate a reason to drop by.

There was something else I needed to tell Gilbert. I cleared my throat. "Maybe it's time I do reach out to my father." Eiffel was correct that he could help with foreign investors, which would, in turn, make it easier for the government planning committee to finally give us the go-ahead, even if I was left riddled with anxiety over the idea.

Gilbert tapped my knee rather sharply. "I wouldn't. You were right. That pig doesn't deserve any kindness from you."

"But if he's dying—"

"Fin, don't." Gilbert flicked his tongue over his lower lip, shaking his head, hard. "Sending a letter to him now wouldn't be a good idea. Trust me."

"Have you spoken to him? Did he change his mind about wishing to hear from me?" Not that it mattered. My feelings weren't hurt in the slightest.

But—oh, I'd dined out on his name for weeks and weeks. Nausea crept up the back of my throat. If he heard, the Lord knew what he might do about it. I wouldn't put hiring a solicitor past him.

Gilbert perhaps felt my concern because he made to cup my cheek, but I pulled back, horrified that someone might see. With a sigh, he leaned away from me.

"I haven't spoken to him. Not for months now." There was a tremble to his voice that alerted me I was missing a vital part of the conversation, but he shushed me before I could argue.

175

And then Aurélie whirled onstage all alone, greeted by generous applause. She continued her dance without pause, but I could see her grin from my seat. She was stunning, dressed in a cloud of red tarlatan with a beautifully embroidered vest and skirt in black like a fairy-tale peasant. Her long hair was loose aside from a silk kerchief. The maître du danse chose wisely—the color of her hair was otherworldly, and her natural vibrancy was apparent in every step she took. Even a non-cultured philistine like me could tell there was an added finesse to each of her moves. Her limbs were more elegant, her toes pointed with more expression, somehow, as though she'd elevated the art above all the others. A guitar strummed along with the orchestra, and when the corps entered the stage with ribboned tambourines, the audience took to their feet, clapping along.

My girl was an utter genius, and everyone here was mesmerized, even me, as though seeing her for the first time. I stood as she made a brief curtsy.

Then Gilbert used two fingers to whistle so loud, all eyes transferred to us. I sat and hoped the shadows hid my face.

"Damn you, the last thing I need is for anyone to wonder what we're doing all alone in this box, Gilbert. What are you about?"

With his usual nonchalance, he rolled his eyes. "The entire theater is filled with men. Some even brought their wives for opening night. The last place anyone would look for a pair of pédés would be at the ballet looking at women."

His casual use of the wretched word gave me a shiver, but it was a good point. I let the subject drop, and he rubbed the pad of his thumb across my palm through the rest of the act as though I needed soothing.

When he spoke again, it startled me. "I told you I've been

visiting Maman. She has no idea I came back to Paris." He laughed, deep in his throat. "I'll go back tomorrow, but tonight— I needed you. When you saw me with Sonny—he isn't—wasn't ever—my lover."

How easy it was for him to lull me into forgetting how much he annoyed me. I yanked my hand away. "I don't need your concern. We're hardly even friends, are we?"

"I do worry about you, Fin. And non, I wouldn't call us friends, either. Too many other words to choose. We're lovers. It's absurd to pretend we don't mean anything to each other."

My stomach dropped with queasiness over his implication.

I was about to argue, but Gilbert's voice was urgent. "You and me—we're tangled together like a knot, and you know it as well as I do."

My eyes were trained on the unfortunate dancer trying to keep the eyes on her after Aurélie's superlative performance. "I wish to cut the knot away."

"You're a liar, Fin."

I couldn't help myself. "I return the sentiment to you."

We shared no further conversation for the rest of the act, and when it was time for Aurélie's curtsy—clutching the enormous bouquet I'd had delivered for this moment—I stood and shouted her name. She tilted her chin up and saw me, grinning before she fluttered offstage.

But my glow of secondhand glory wafted away like smoke as I noticed that Michel de Gênet was across the auditorium, in the matching box, his eyes fastened on Aurélie. Just like every other man in the audience. I'd like to have choked them all for their audacity.

De Gênet lifted his gaze to the box where Gilbert and I were the lone audience on an opening night that was more popular than I'd have imagined. What was the likelihood those seats hadn't been sold?

I stood, trembling at the thought of what de Gênet would say if he knew about Gilbert and me—if he had any inkling about what had occurred between us. I needed his money.

"Goodbye, Gilbert."

Hurrying away, I hid myself in the washroom, splashed water on my hot skin to rid myself of the color. When I emerged ten minutes later, I hoped Gilbert would have gone.

But he leaned against the gold-painted wall, waiting.

I gave a short tug on the brim of my hat and went by him without looking.

"Take me home with you." His voice echoed off the high ceiling, and I was overcome with gratitude that we were alone.

"No."

His hand gripped my shoulder. "Do you actually mean no, or are you only saying it because I've taken so long to apologize? No other man means anything to me. Nothing."

I swung around, my voice hard as granite. "And *you* mean nothing to me. Leave off."

Gilbert's mouth dropped; his soulful black eyes grew even more mournful. "Then why are you shaking?"

Exasperated, I exhaled. "Because you rattle me more than anyone I've ever met."

As if that was a compliment, he smiled like a cat who'd had a saucer of cream. He kept pace with me as I practically flew down the steps into the chilled night air, thanking God that Aurélie had plans with her dancer friends and a crowd to keep her safe. I lifted my collar against the draft, turning away from the glittering Palais into the darkness of a side street.

"Besides you, I've only ever made love to one man, and on my life, it wasn't Sonny."

A frustrated rumble emanated from my throat. "All we did was fuck, Gilbert, and I don't go back for seconds."

He shimmied his arm into the crook of mine. "Then just let me sleep with you."

"I don't have men sleep over."

Gilbert laughed, silky and deep. "I must be very special because I've slept with you twice." He stopped as though his feet were trapped in cement, holding me tight to his side before he braced the sides of my face with his palms and kissed me with such longing that I couldn't stop myself from returning it. So dangerous, but I couldn't control myself around him.

"Just once more to get you out of my system then, hmm?" He rubbed his nose against mine. "I traveled all the way from Amiens, mon vilain. Indulge me."

It was a colossal mistake. But, for whatever reason, I found myself swayed. "Fine. But this is done after tonight. No more."

Whether either of us believed it, I had no way to ascertain.

16

Last time Gilbert had slithered away before the sun rose, I woke to solitude in my bed and didn't mind much.

But this particular morning, the emptiness of the bed was profound. I rubbed my eyes, blinking from the brightness. Sunday, so no work for me, and I'd hoped to spend another hour in bed before Gilbert left to go back to his mother's house in Amiens. Out of my life for the last time.

It was better like this. I said it a few times, once out loud, even. Neither my heart nor my body believed me.

That was it. I needed some cheering up. I'd cook a good, old-fashioned English fry-up for breakfast, even if I'd eat alone. Aurélie was surely gone already—Sunday was a long day for her with rehearsals for most of the day, all after being toasted until dawn with her friends. I heard the chain to the door at five in the morning.

Outside of my bedroom, I was greeted with the smell of coffee mingled with... bacon? A spontaneous fizzing tickled my insides. I rubbed the back of my neck as I made my way to the kitchen. *Please don't be Aurélie.*

But she didn't cook. I bit my lips from the inside not to grin.

Gilbert stood in trousers and nothing else, facing away from me.

I caught my breath at the way the V of his back disappeared into those trousers. Muscles rippled. Shoulder blades danced as he flipped something in a skillet. I sniffed—whatever it was, I wanted it. Wanted him after. And an hour might not be long enough.

I cleared my throat, alerting Gilbert to my presence.

Dark circles under his eyes left me wondering if he'd slept as well as I had.

Keeping my voice level, I said, "You were supposed to be gone." But I was foolishly tickled he wasn't. I stepped into the kitchen, and my foot slid in something wet. I lifted my sole—*red*. Blood, but from what? I shivered, and grabbed a dish towel. Definitely blood. I glanced at Gilbert to check for any wounds and registered nothing.

"I did leave for a little while." He dug into his pocket and produced a key, tossing it to me. "I hope you don't mind? Grabbed that from the little bowl on your bureau. Needed to get some food."

"Were you bleeding?" I held up the rag with a frown and scanned his face, remembering the night he arrived with bruises and swollen knuckles. Two lines ran less than an inch on the side of his throat. Were those scrapes from fingernails?

I moved to touch them, and he caught my wrist. His eyebrows moved together in the middle, and then he held his hands out, palms down. "I clipped my nails yesterday after doing this to my skin." His smile faded as he looked at the bloody towel, then pointed toward the bin. "The sack from the kidneys leaked. Sorry." He pointed to a stain on his trousers. "All over my shirt, too. I had to throw it away. Let me clean up the mess."

"I did already, no bother." Poking my nose over his shoulder, I put my arms around his waist, sinking my mouth into his neck. "Smells delicious."

Him and the food. I was hungry for both, but my stomach went to the front of the line. Ham, eggs, bacon, and kidneys? He'd read my mind. I reached around and snatched a piece of bacon, popping it into my mouth. Divine.

Gilbert pivoted in my arms and faced me, pressing against me, like paper dolls Annabeth played with when we were young. The kind that could only stand if they were joined to balance each other.

Some unnamable emotion flickered in my belly. Gilbert was too easy to kiss. To hold. To spend time with.

To fuck.

That's all this was. A *superb* fuck, to be sure. Going on longer than anticipated merely because of the investing, and his uncle. And the clothes. And the high-rolling friends.

Gilbert outlined my ear with a soft fingertip. "You're so pensive. What are you thinking, *mon vilain*, hmm?"

I gave what I hoped was an enigmatic smile.

"I'm headed back to Amiens for the week and then I'll return Friday. Tell me you'll see me? I don't want to have to hunt you down. Or beat on your window." He twirled a finger through my hair, those glorious dark eyes boring into mine. "I want you to tell me that you wish to see me, too."

My throat tightened. How could I agree to...something? Not

anything defined even, but the fact that there was some agreement? I didn't have the time. Not with all the carousing I was up to my neck in. The nights entertaining potential investors might sound like pleasure, but they were work. I said so and frowned at his amused face.

"Tell me all about it."

Annoyed that he might think me incapable of handling my affairs on my own, I sketched out what I'd been up to, as he went back to his meal preparation. I was unsure if he even listened until I changed the subject and mentioned Sonny's name. Gilbert whirled around so quickly the frying pan was in danger of falling.

He righted it and continued with his task. Lightly, he said, "I'm not so friendly with Sonny lately, mon beau."

"Why not? Because he hated Paul?"

Not answering, Gilbert used two forks to scoop the last of the food onto a plate and brought it to the table with a gesture for me to sit. I didn't. His face was placid other than a brief flare of his nostrils.

"I thought I'd satisfied you that I never had any great friendship with Paul. Forget I said anything. But my feelings about Sonny have nothing to do with him. I just don't like him."

I still didn't respond, so he took a step closer to me.

Forehead against mine, Gilbert sucked my bottom lip and then pulled back to look in my face. "And now you're tense. I apologize for mentioning anything." His fingers ground into my shoulders, down between the blades. "We need to figure out how to make you relax."

He tilted my head to the side and dove in for another intense kiss. He kissed me until I nodded, till I'd say yes to anything.

Releasing me, he shooed me back to the table and plated food high. I tucked in with relish, thrilled to have something else to discuss. He sat across from me and hitched his ankle around my chair leg to drag me closer to him. He wiped the corner of my mouth with his thumb.

"I enjoy being with you." His smile snaked up his cheek. "So much more than I planned to."

Simple. Chest seized. I did my best to bluster through, blood pounding in my ears. "I like you cooking me breakfast." I scanned the table. "You made all my favorite things."

"I hoped it would make you smile." He ran the edge of his foot up my bare calf so all the hairs on my leg stood up. "You don't smile nearly enough, but when you do"—he mimed an elaborate shiver—"you take my breath away."

I chewed my pinky. Much too emotional. "This breakfast made me smile." So did the fact that he was still there—he hadn't disappeared without saying goodbye. But that wasn't the sort of thing I could say.

Gilbert took a deep breath. "Good, because we should talk—"

But someone hammered the front door like the hounds of hell were on their heels. The hair on the back of my neck rose. Who? On a Sunday, no less?

Frowning, he followed me to the door. Victoire stood on the other side of the peephole, turned to the side, shaking her head like she was confused.

"Vicky?" I opened the door for her. Her face had the traces of last night's makeup, but I'd never seen her without a full face. The chills spread down my right arm. "Are you all right?"

Clearly not. She stumbled into my arms, clung to me like a

child. I hugged her tight, stomach souring like I might throw up my lovely breakfast.

She stepped back and blinked like her eyes burned. Each blink had me more convinced I didn't want to know why she was here.

"Fin, I need your help. I don't know what to do—but you will. You know things." She twirled a limp curl around her finger.

All the skin on my body rose up from the anguish in her voice. I recognized that sound—not from her, maybe, but from deep in my own soul. I wanted to clap my hands over my ears and not listen.

"Victoire, what's happened?" My own eyes burned, needing to hear but desperate not to.

"Jody's dead."

Woozy, I clutched the back of the sofa. No. *Not Jody.*

"How?" Gilbert squeezed my hand. "Come and sit, have hot coffee? Or tea?" His voice was sensible and I was drowning, needed to cling to it to keep my head up. He meant it for Victoire, but looked at me.

Jody was dead? A sledgehammer crushed my chest inside out.

"What was it? Was he sick? My God, I've been so busy I haven't seen either of you in a donkey's years. Was it pneumonia? Or the flu?" Jody wasn't much above forty, and was healthy as an ox. Didn't have any vices aside from the one. "Fuck. Was it from absinthe?"

Victoire's skin was green, and I led her to the sofa, gesturing to Gilbert to make her something.

"No, he wasn't sick a day in his life, he always says." She made a little gasp, and I dashed for a hanky in my bureau. She dabbed her eyes before continuing.

185

"I was out late, with a friend. Spent the night. But Jody and I had plans to eat breakfast together. When I opened the door, he was there. On the floor. Oh, Fin, what will I do without him?"

I rubbed her knee, to calm both of us. A touchstone to remind her I was here, and alive.

Gilbert handed Victoire a cup of black coffee and one to me. "I splashed some whiskey, hope that's all right. You've had a shock." He sat next to me on the sofa, so close our legs touched, and dropped a kiss on my cheek.

Wincing from the hot sip, Victoire nodded.

"And he's dead?" Gilbert pushed. He was hard. "You're sure?" Not cruel, just digging for something tangible. "Perhaps he passed out, or fell and hit his head?"

Expelling all of her breath, Victoire crumbled, buried her face in my shoulder.

"If you saw him—mon Dieu, so much blood. I'm going to be sick." She stumbled to the washroom to empty her stomach, me on her heels until Gilbert held me back and went to check on her himself.

The wall held me up, thank God, because my knees were incapable. "If he's in his flat, then it's someone he knows." I winced. "*Knew.*"

Gilbert opened his palms as he stood in the doorway between the washroom and where I stood. "Could it be an accident, Victoire? Heads bleed an extraordinary amount…"

Victoire shook her head, wiping her mouth and heading back to the sofa. She picked up the coffee, put it down, her hands shaking. "His throat—" She swiped his finger over her neck.

"You haven't alerted the gendarmerie, have you?" Gilbert

fished in his evening jacket hanging by the door and pulled out his handkerchief for her, too.

I dragged a hand through my hair. "She wouldn't be sitting here if she'd raised the alarm, Gilbert."

She raised red-rimmed eyes. "Should I have informed someone?"

Before I could respond, Gilbert did. "Let's take a breath and think before rushing into something that might be dangerous." I opened my mouth to object, but he held his hand up.

"This isn't the same as a murder in some petit bourgeois apartment building, Fin. If the damned gendarmes even bother to look for a motive, which is laughably unlikely, Victoire's the easiest to arrest. I promise you—all the locals there must know about Jody, know about the club. The authorities will say he got what he deserved for being who he was."

"I couldn't take the time to look around." The look on Victoire's face gutted me. "What if it was me they wanted to kill? I could have maybe saved Jody if I hadn't lain in bed for an extra hour or—"

"No one wants to kill you." Shaking her shoulders, I growled. "*Do not* do that to yourself. You couldn't have saved him. If you'd been there earlier, you would have ended up dead, too."

But it was pointless to say. She wasn't listening. Eight years after Annabeth died, I still blamed myself. Victoire might never get past this guilt.

I calmed my voice. "Do the neighbors know you?"

Victoire sniffed. "Not really. I'm around only at odd hours when most people aren't awake. I've not been there very long this time, just a week or so."

"Why don't Fin and I go over and see what can be done? Fetch your things." Gilbert went into my room and put on one of my shirts. Even through the haziness of my mind, I recognized it was too big for him through the chest and shoulders.

My feet were frozen in place. Immobile.

Gilbert came back, touched my face. "Get dressed, mon beau."

The words roused Victoire, who noticed I was wearing only underpants. Her eyes flitted back and forth between me and Gilbert.

She knew I didn't bring men back to my apartment. And her knowing brought it home how different Gilbert was already. We recognized it, even in the midst of this nightmare. I cleared the racing in my brain to focus.

Jody's murder meant the damned Green Carnation would be investigated. As would Victoire. The local policeman whom Jody bribed to keep his eyes averted wouldn't be able to do anything to help, and Victoire had no money to spare. Gilbert was correct; her entire life would be upended. They wouldn't see her as a woman. They'd see her as a pervert, a pervert whose life was intimately connected with Jody's, and who had the means to kill him, motive be damned.

She could end up in prison. Executed, even.

"Fin, wear your oldest trousers and no jacket, hmm? We'll take those cartons from the hall. Do you have any paper and string?"

"In the kitchen; why?" I dressed in a hurry, shaking all over. I dreaded this—seeing Jody would bring it all back, all the painful images of Annabeth the last time I saw her.

He didn't answer, just removed his own trousers before yanking open the door to my wardrobe and rummaging through. He pulled out a pair of trousers that I ought to have thrown away years before. But they'd been sewn by my sister, and I'd worn them when I ran from home. I couldn't bear to toss them in the rubbish as I had nothing else from her.

After he pulled them on and surveyed himself briefly in the mirror, I finally asked what was going on. Grabbing my two shabbiest hats, he slapped one onto my head. "The very last thing I wish for is someone noticing the cut of my trousers, n'est-ce pas?"

17

The morning was heavy with smog, and not a soul looked at two men in scrubby clothes carrying boxes. I'd never have thought of this plan. Especially not this morning. If someone asked what was said on the way to Jody's flat, I couldn't have told them. Gilbert spoke of inanities about the weather and the streets, and I moved, one foot in front of the other, numb and doing my best not to show my abject terror.

I didn't want to see Jody. I could imagine well enough what he looked like. I didn't know if I could survive it, not intact. With all of the lies and stories I'd been trying to keep straight, it sometimes felt as though I held myself together in bits and pieces with brown paper and string as it was.

But ten minutes later, I stood behind Gilbert as he swung the door to the building wide. I hoped no one noticed us enter the run-down building in the bright morning, even dressed the way we were and carrying a load of boxes. The street was empty, but one could never know for sure who might be watching.

Light filtered through windows that could have used a good wash ten years ago. I understood why Jody kept this place looking like it was on its last legs, the anonymity it gave, but I saw through the eyes of the police and wondered if it would be amiss to request a rag and a bucket of suds.

My eyes darted to the door of the club. Damn it. It was my home. Where my family lived. And now where one of my family members had died.

Gilbert took the lead, going straight to Jody's door. I followed, my stomach turning over.

Peeling wallpaper hung like the tarlatan skirts of ballerinas around the tops of the walls, and the ceiling was dotted with water leaks. The air was rancid with the strong scent of urine—both feline and the masculine variety, if I wasn't mistaken.

How did Gilbert know the way? Gilbert had spoken with Jody before meeting me at the ballet. He'd not mentioned coming to the flat, but the cabaret was just downstairs.

I unlocked Jody's door but couldn't push it open. Gilbert gently shouldered me out of the way and went inside. I stayed put where I stood on the landing. My feet refused to move forward.

Please let it have been a mistake. Maybe Victoire was drunk on something. Or dreaming some squalid nightmare that—

Gilbert came back to the doorway, green around the gills. How hadn't I imagined that he might be affected by Jody's body, too? He'd usually shown a calm face when I was feeling out of sorts. But I didn't truly know him, even if it felt as though we'd been tangled up in each other's lives for years. He swallowed, his Adam's apple bobbing in his neck, stuck halfway. He held his hand to me, and I shook my head like a petulant child. I couldn't.

"I don't know what's hers," he said, his fingers gripping mine

191

tight in solidarity, or kindness, or to force me. "Shut your eyes, and I'll lead you by."

Balking, I pulled back, but even though I was stronger, he was more determined.

One of the few things I was grateful to Aunt Glad for was her lack of religious fervor. Not even the fearsome old priest at my preparatory school could persuade me that there was something more sinister than the world we lived in.

In this dank hallway, led by the handsome man I'd allowed into my life—to enjoy what comforts I could whether I deserved them or not—*I wondered*. For a half second, I could believe I was descending into the pits of hell. One hand-carved for me, with my personal demons.

He stood behind me, hands on my shoulders, voice in my ear, hot. "Close them, mon vilain." Gilbert placed his fingers over my eyes to hide them, and led me to the small bedroom off the nearly as small room where Jody had lived and died.

I'd only been here a handful of times since I'd moved out.

Why didn't I come and spend an afternoon? Let him know how much I treasured his friendship? And now I never could. With my eyes shut, my other senses heightened. Over the horrid stench of blood was the echo of a familiar pipe tobacco. Astley's: the same brand my father smoked.

"Do you smell that?"

"Smell what?" The door shut behind me, and Gilbert removed his hands from my eyes. His mouth was tight, pinched.

"Jody didn't smoke, nor does Victoire. Can you smell it?"

A flicker of worry crossed his eyes as he cast about the room. "Non. It's your imagination, or perhaps it was someone smoking in the hall outside." He ran his hands down my biceps, squeezed. "You don't want to see your friend, trust me. But look closely in here, check if there's anything that might tell who did this."

A haphazard arrangement of unguents and powders trailed across the available surfaces, shirts mingled with frocks half hanging on a broom handle supported by two rickety chairs, half drooping like a ghoulish curtsy. On the bureau there was a dress shirt with bloodstains down the front. I picked it up. The satin tag inside the collar read Qualité. I'd loaned this one to him.

Jody must have recently washed because socks were draped across anything they could be—lampshade, curtain rod, headboard of his bed. A week's worth of underthings he'd never get to wear.

"When does the last train go to Amiens?"

"Amiens?" Gilbert shook his head in disbelief. "I'm not going back to Maman's—how could you think it? You're in no condition to handle this on your own, hmm?"

Bloody hell, I wanted to argue with him. But there were no words.

Mechanically, we scoured the room for anything that was likely to be Victoire's, though I suppose Jody wouldn't mind us taking anything of his. My knees buckled. Jody—my very closest friend in the entire world—was on the floor in the other room, and never going to muss my hair and call me Fini again.

Gilbert caught me and, with a tenderness I never believed I'd receive, kissed my forehead, his hands meeting behind my back. "I'm so sorry, Fin. Sickened. We're going to figure out who did this to him."

I'd experienced more than my share of male chests pressed

against me, but never in comfort, not this sort, anyway. But a chill took root at the base of my spine and made its way up to my neck in agonizing slowness. I nodded into his shoulder. "We should alert the gendarmerie. They'll look into it and figure out who could—"

"Don't be simple, hmm? We can't afford to allow the police to sniff around this."

Blinking, I shook my head as though I'd misheard him. "Not tell the police? Even after we've cleared it out?"

Gilbert sighed from the depths of his belly. He touched my cheek gently. "You cannot call the police, Fin. Do you think that anyone will send your Monsieur Eiffel money if it becomes known who your friends are? To say nothing of your father. If he learns, you'll never touch a shilling of his money."

I balled one of Victoire's black stockings into my pocket.

Gilbert settled his stance on his back foot and searched my face. "And who shall inherit this building now that Jody is gone, hmm?"

I narrowed my eyes. "I'd assume his sister will come back to town sometime. There's no reason for her to disappear forever."

"Bien sûr. I'm sure she will return sooner or later. Did Jody leave behind a will? Just in case?"

"I don't know. Possibly. Laurent is a secondary owner of the club, but I wouldn't be surprised if Jody put something aside for Victoire. They were friends for ages before I even came to Paris. What exactly are you asking?"

Gilbert's face held a look of skepticism that infuriated me. "But what if he didn't? How would Victoire manage to take care of herself if—"

My back teeth ground together so hard they squeaked, refusing to allow my mind to drift in that direction. "I would swear on my life and those of everyone I care about that under no circumstances could *Victoire*"—I jabbed my finger at the closed door in Jody's direction—"ever hurt Jody."

He rubbed at the black stubble speckling his jaw. "You know they'll be looking at her because she is who she is. People at the club know they were close. Someone will tell the police, if only to turn attention from themselves. Will you make it easier to have her executed?"

The entire sordid conversation left me clammy with perspiration. "But we must tell the police. His...body...can't stay here, surely you understand that?"

There was a grim set to Gilbert's jaw. "Fin, perhaps I ought to be clearer about what I do for my uncle."

Taken aback by the new direction, I stumbled backward. "What do you mean? You do accounting."

His nostrils flared like a bull's, but he took a deep breath. "Mostly, like I said." He lifted one shoulder and yanked the coverlet off the bed for some reason. "But other times, I help Michel deal with situations that benefit no one if they were to be made public, tu comprends?"

"Pardon? No, I don't comprehend."

Gilbert ran his tongue over his lips, then rubbed them together. Stalling for time to gather his thoughts, I realized through the haze of my mind. "Most of the time it's just research. Look into people who might oppose him." He rubbed the back of his neck and abruptly turned away. His voice sounded miles off. "But sometimes, I tidy up...problems."

195

"Problems?" For the love of Christ, I couldn't stop repeating his words, as if it might make them make sense.

"Nothing for you to worry about, I promise. It just means that I know how to take care of Jody." He turned away. "Come now. I'll cover his body with this blanket, and you help me scan the other room for any clues."

Incredulous, I folded my hands over my chest. "And if with these clues we find the killer, then what do men like us do about it?"

He made a fist with his hands, and then held them behind his back. "When we figure it out, we'll punish the bastard." A tick in his cheek twitched.

"Punish how?" Nothing about the word felt comfortable leaving my mouth.

"Come, Fin, this is no time to be so damned bloody-minded. You can grill me later when we are not in any danger. We need to finish and go quickly." With his hand on the door, I touched his shoulder.

"How would *we* be able to punish the killer?"

His face turned in profile over his shoulder; he didn't look into my eyes. "We'll either get them in jail, or we kill them."

The hair on my neck stood up, but I snorted. "Like it's that easy?"

Black eyes cut to mine, and a smile that didn't reach his eyes. "When revenge is your only thought, I promise that you can figure out how to make it happen."

18

Nothing else in the apartment appeared out of place—though Victoire would have been a better judge than I was if she hadn't been incapacitated back in my own flat. In shock. Trauma that would scream guilt to anyone who didn't know her.

It was my duty to protect her by allowing Gilbert to handle this on his own. It wasn't because of the blasted tower or anything to do with my father. For Victoire. To keep her safe.

A loud sob wrenched from my throat, and Gilbert clamped his hand over my mouth.

"Shh. We don't need the neighbors to look out and see us. Be able to describe us if anyone comes looking for Jody. We could face la guillotine, too, non?"

My skin went clammy, cold at the idea. School lessons about the French Revolution and the mass slaughter by guillotine felt so long ago, but it was still considered the most humane way of execution in France. I touched my throat and took a deep breath because I still could.

"I say we go back to your apartment and discuss our options with Victoire." He flicked his eyes to Jody's prone body, now covered. "There's nothing we can do for him now, anyway. And we both know the police won't give a damn about the truth— only about finding someone to pin this on and be done with it."

Every fiber of my being revolted at the idea of walking away, but he was right.

"We leave here, quiet as mouses and do not breathe a word, all right, mon vilain?"

How he could continue to call me the cheeky endearment in the midst of this touched me and made me queasy, all at once.

I took a deep breath—a mistake, since I inhaled the already souring smell of the body of my friend. I gagged and then shook, hyperventilating.

Gilbert clutched my arms. "Stop it."

That calm voice roused me. I nodded and covered my mouth with my hands, breathing through them to calm myself down.

Placing his finger over his lips to warn me again, he cracked open the door, and we hurried out as unsuspiciously as possible.

Neither of us spoke. Not until we were back in my flat with Victoire, who had regained a touch of color in her cheeks.

"I'll have the body removed," said Gilbert, like it had already been decided. Though I guess he had.

"And what?" I had the wherewithal to ask.

"I'll bury him. Or pay to have it done. And if it's important, I can find a priest."

"Jody wouldn't give a fuck about a priest. Not unless he was getting his cock sucked by one." Victoire tilted her chin up to look at me. "I feel like an absolute wretch, but I suppose it's better for us not to be tied to anything unsavory, d'accord?"

I slumped onto the sofa and took her hands in mine. "Jody wouldn't blame us, you know he wouldn't."

Gilbert pulled the cork out of the gin and handed it to Victoire. Then he took me by the hand back to the kitchen. "Will you be all right? You must promise me that you will always carry a knife, to protect yourself."

He was leaving me to cope on my own.

My breath came hard, sharp, hurt. "I always carry a pocketknife." My father had insisted.

His face cleared. "Non—I'm staying. I meant, in the long haul? Will you be all right?"

Would I? I shrugged. I'd never had a choice. And no one had ever cared.

"Thank you." I moved past him to turn on the gas for the kettle to hide my discomfort at the reliance I'd had on him for the past hours. He latched on to my shoulder and turned me back to him.

"I'll get the tea for you." He guided me to a chair, and I sat, knees shaking, hands twisting.

"I've never seen you so distraught. I'm so sorry. Death is never a pretty sight, but it's enough to drive you to madness when it's the body of someone you love. I wish no one had to go through that." He looked over his shoulder as he poured water to fill the kettle.

"It's harrowing. I've never recovered from seeing...my sister."

"If you talk to me, it might help." The kettle scratched against the grate. The greasy food was rancid. I glanced at the bacon and eggs, congealed grease blanketing them. The kidneys were dark with blood, and I did what Victoire had done earlier, making it to the wash closet before losing my breakfast.

Gilbert rubbed my back, pushed my hair from my forehead. "I'm going to take care of this. I promise."

He drifted back to the kitchen, and I listened to the plates being scraped, grateful that he understood. His footsteps receded and then came back.

"Victoire passed out. Which is good. She needs to not think. But come, mon vilain. Telling me about it all might help." He held out his hand.

Fingers entwined, we walked to my room, where he bade me sit. Crouching, he removed my shoes, as if I were a child. Not that I remembered anyone ever doing it for me, but I did for Annabeth, before she could button her boots.

Then, he undid my shirt, steady-handed, efficient, and pulled back the corner of the coverlet. He nodded for me to lie down, and I dropped my trousers.

He stripped himself, too, and got in the other side. The decadence of being in bed midday wasn't lost on me. Gilbert lay on his back and curled his arm around me, pulling my cheek to his shoulder.

"Tell me about her." He pulled me closer. "Tell me about the two of you growing up."

Why did I want to? I'd never told anyone, but today, I couldn't bottle it up inside anymore. My fingers folded around the edge of the India cotton coverlet, well worn and soft.

The light through the curtains was gray, as if it might rain, which was appropriate. It would be too much for the sun to shine when Jody lay in his flat, alone and cold.

Gilbert's thumb stroked my arm, gentle enough to almost not notice, though I did. I wasn't used to being touched tenderly. He pressed his lips against my forehead, reminding me that, for some reason, he cared.

"My mother died having Annabeth, when I was close to my second birthday. I don't remember anything about her."

I wished I did. So many lonely times it would have helped *to have one memory*, one thing to cling to. To know I'd been loved. Wanted, even.

"We were sent to live with her sister, Gladys. She was a particularly cheerless woman. Spiteful." I sighed, uninterested in thinking about Aunt Glad. I cleared my throat. "We lived a few miles from the big house where the earl lived. He was married to someone *good enough* when I was a child. My aunt told me. It was around when I was first sent to school."

My smile was faint. I'd been so happy to escape Aunt Glad, but miserable to leave Annabeth behind to cope without me.

"How old were you?" His voice was a soft rumble in my ear.

I traced the contours of his abdomen with my fingers. We were both equally dark, but I had more hair than he did.

"Six. Or seven. It's all a blur." I never revisited my childhood if I could help it. "I only came home between terms and met the earl once a year. He came to give Annabeth and me each a guinea at Christmas." I scowled into his shoulder. Dreadful Aunt Glad took those guineas until eight-year-old Annabeth told the earl to keep his money since we didn't get to have it.

We always kept them after that, which was one of the only decent things he ever did for us.

I kept going, talked about my loneliness in school. Everyone knew who my father was—and how he wasn't in my life as a true parent, not in any meaningful way. But I worked my arse off, because when my marks were near perfect, I received letters of congratulations—notes, really; a line dashed off and posted without any thought, in all likelihood.

But to me, they meant the world.

I kept them in a box under my bed. Collected them. One each term for years. The only correspondence I could have received until Annabeth learned to write at the local grammar school.

Lucky for me, I was athletic and not terribly abused by the older boys, no matter my status as the known-but-never-acknowledged son of an earl. I rowed and played cricket with enough skill to be on the school teams and had friends of a sort. But I was never invited home with anyone between terms because no one was sure how to treat me. Was I owed deference as the son of a peer, or treated with contempt because I was equally the son of his family's servant?

But when I was home, I spent as much time as I could with my sister, who existed in the same sort of limbo, only more depressing because she had no outlet to excel and earn even a meager acceptance with her classmates. And worse, she was very pretty. Even as a brother, I was aware.

"Worse?" Gilbert interrupted for the first time. Then he chuckled. "I love my sister, but she'd give up half her wardrobe to be beautiful, I promise. There's no virtue in plainness." He kissed each of the fingers on one of my hands in turn.

"But your sister has a dowry, no doubt a good one with your uncle's money, and we had no idea if Annabeth would get a penny." I lifted my head.

Gilbert's eyes were more mournful than ever. "Show her to me."

"I don't have a picture." I left England without anything, to my long-lasting regret.

"Tell me. Paint her so I can see."

"I'm not good at this." Wistful, Annabeth was. She could have described anything under the sun in a way you could smell it, taste it. "Her hair was shiny, hung in curls. So black it was blue. And blue eyes, too."

"She looked like you, hmm?" He wrapped a lock of hair around his finger, rubbing it so it tugged my scalp like a kiss.

Another shrug. "Much prettier."

His voice was more succulent than brandied cherries. "I promise, you're the loveliest man I ever saw."

Warmth spread through my insides like rivers and canals of hot chocolate.

"Pretty girls don't need a dowry, do they?"

Gilbert had no idea. "They do if they aspire to be a rich man's wife, especially with the taint of our birth. All the poor fellows were too cowed to call on her. But once I finished university, we decided we'd set up a house together and see what we could do for her."

It was our favorite thing to talk about from the time we were children. Perhaps it was the circumstances of our parentage, or our dreadful childhood with Aunt Glad, but we were unusually devoted to each other.

"She was the dearest person in the world to me." Even I could hear my voice was hollow.

His lips lingered against mine. Soothing. Our bodies resettled, facing each other, sharing a pillow. "Tell me what happened to her."

My eyes dropped to his mouth, wishing we could spend the time kissing, but he was insistent, lifting my chin so I had to look back up.

"You have the most beautiful eyes I ever saw, Fin," he said, "and the saddest. Tell me why."

I blinked. "Just before I sat for my examinations, a friend of the earl's called Andrew Hessle came to take me to lunch. I was flattered because he'd told Hessle that I was a genius."

My father's praise still mattered. How dreadful was that? I expelled a lifetime of air. "He wanted to invest in my future. To help me open a firm in York. Something like what Eiffel has. Hessle owned a handful of mines scattered over England, and my degree was in mining—the engineering behind making mines safer."

Rolling over, I covered my face with my inner arm. "But there was a catch. He wanted me to introduce him to Annabeth. He'd seen her in town when he visited my father. Wanted to get to know her." I bit back the angry bile in the back of my throat. "I wrote to her, asked her if she would do me this favor. I went home on the train to push her into it when she hesitated."

All I could see were the pound signs—the beautiful notion that I might be respectable after all. Maybe I'd be good enough for my father to care for. After all those desperate years of trying to force him to recognize my desire to please him.

His voice was a whisper. "Why did she hesitate?"

I couldn't look in his eyes, focused on the window. I watched a cloud pass over the sun. "She didn't like Hessle. He'd orchestrated a meeting on the street, made her anxious with his solicitude. But I pooh-poohed it all and begged."

And she'd given in. Annabeth always said yes to me. Perhaps, if our father had insisted she, too, carry a knife, she'd have had a different fate.

Rolling over, I drew my legs up like an infant. The words tumbled out in a rush. "Hessle raped her. And when she fell pregnant, he refused to accept blame. She went to our father, who said she—of all people—ought to have known better. He washed his hands, said there was nothing he could or would do for her."

She'd written the entire traumatic episode to me in a letter dotted with teardrops. I'd caught the next train to Goole to take care of her. "That's why I missed my final exams. I was so terrified, but she wasn't home. Even our aunt was worried—which I'd never seen from her. I went to the big house. *Demanded to speak to Miles Carleton himself.* And he'd said he wouldn't ruin a business relationship for our sake, not when my sister had no proof of her accusations. He had his fucking butler escort me out, bodily. He couldn't be bothered to even do that himself."

"Oh, Fin, my heart breaks for you. I'm so sorry." He squeezed my hand tight.

"A fisherman dragged her up a week later. He had to cut her body out of his net." Bloated, grotesque. Her eyes still open. I'd have thrown up again if there were anything in my stomach. But I was empty.

I had been empty for years.

Gilbert's sharp breath clawed me from the inside out. "She killed herself?"

I nodded once. "Our aunt Glad cried. The only time I ever saw her do that. But she said that, as a suicide, Annabeth couldn't be buried in a churchyard." I needed to spit. Punch something. *Scream.*

I swallowed it all back down. I was good at it by now. Instead, I stomped across the room to the window, peeking out at the world, going on with its business, like Jody wasn't in a pool of his own blood. Like Annabeth hadn't been destroyed because of my greed.

"And you left?" Gilbert moved behind me, his body so close the warmth seeped from his skin to mine.

A slow nod. "That day." I turned and raised my eyes to his, surprised to see sympathy instead of disdain.

He drew me into his arms, his cheek pressed to mine. "I'll get help to move Jody tonight. You won't need to be involved."

Gratitude surged up my being. "From who?"

Caressing my face, he looked infinitely weary. "Don't worry. Money can buy anything."

I wouldn't know. But I trusted him, whether that was foolish or because I was too scared to see my friend and it was easier to believe.

He rumpled my hair, lightly scratching my scalp so I shivered. "Come back to bed, mon vilain." I must have blanched, because he shook his head. "Not for that. But you're drained. Come and rest. Let me take care of you."

Still, I recoiled.

"Please." He held out his hand, and I took it. "It makes me happy."

No one ever took care of me before. And if only for today, I needed to allow myself that small comfort.

19

Gilbert and Victoire spoke in hushed voices in the salon, but I didn't sleep during the day often enough for it not to rouse me. I was still rubbing away the sleep when I interrupted them.

Vicky's eyes were red-rimmed and flat, like she'd died, too. "I'm going to the Carnation. I've got a show tonight, and it might cause talk if I'm not there." She straightened her shoulders. "It should be a normal evening. The gendarmes did their monthly raid last weekend, so it's unlikely they'll turn up." She rubbed the tassel of her evening scarf between her fingers. "What will we do next month without Jody to pay them off?"

"Laurent can take over, and he probably knows whom to bribe." A chill passed over me. "What will you tell him? The truth or…?"

Victoire gave a solemn shake of her head. "I think it's best to say Jody went looking for Charlotte. Everyone knows he is—was—worried." The frown in her forehead deepened. "And I feel we ought to try harder to track her down, too. Though I don't even know where to begin." She clenched her fist and muttered a stream of curses that I couldn't keep up with.

I folded her into my arms again. "We'll come up with some-thing. Gilbert, can I ask you to...I don't know...ask some of your uncle's staff besides the housekeeper?" Both Aunt Glad and Aunt Selena had been in service at my father's house before he and my mother formed a tryst. I knew enough that the maids were unlikely to confide in the housekeeper, who would have held herself to be a higher rank. "Charlotte must have been friends with some of the other maids. Perhaps they're holding a secret for her?"

"I'm not sure that they would confess anything to me, but I can ask Stéphanie to dig deeper. They know she's willing to help them when there are any problems—" Gilbert snapped his mouth shut and inhaled, forcing a smile. "After his body is gone. That's the first priority." Gilbert probably had no intention of hurting us, but that stung. The finality of it was like lead in my stomach. But this was the only choice we could make.

Gilbert pinched my chin in his thumb and forefinger. "Stay here, Fin. In the worst case, I might need someone to post bail for me."

He said it with a sharp laugh, but it wasn't funny. And then they were gone.

I threw myself into mundane tasks to occupy myself. My shoes had never shone so brightly, and the kitchen floor wasn't so clean when we moved in. But I ran out of things as the sun went down and I found myself at loose ends.

I stared at a bottle of gin, contemplating. Alcohol would dull my mind. But even if I wasn't seeing the horrible deed through to the end—I could at least stay sober.

"Gracious, the smell of ammonia is awful, I might choke. Can I open the window?" Aurélie pushed open a sash, and a cold gust of wind made the kerosene lamp flicker. Wearily, she removed her boots before she even looked at me. She leaned back into the sofa and wiggled her toes, eyes shut.

And then they snapped open. "Why are you sitting here in the dark?" An edge of worry crept into her voice as she glanced around. "Are you hurt?" She leaned toward me and grasped my hand.

Why was it so difficult to speak of death? It was inevitable and would happen to all of us. Yet the words stuck in my throat. Her concern brought her to her feet.

Eyes wide, she trembled. "What is it? Tell me."

"Jody died."

She took a deep breath through her nose. "Jody? What do you mean, he died? How did he die?" Aurélie's voice rose an octave with each question.

In a few words, I sketched out what had happened.

She frowned. "A pickpocket? Or did he owe someone money?"

"It was in his flat."

She grabbed a glass from the kitchen and poured herself some of the gin. I moved to stop her, and she rolled her eyes. "You pretend that I'm a little girl, Fin, but you know I'm not." She drank down the entire glass and settled back in her seat. "Was he a prostitute?"

"No. He wasn't." I clenched my jaw.

Aurélie clucked her tongue at me. "As if I judge what people do to fucking survive. Don't be a fool. I wonder who killed him, is all." She tossed her hair and reached for the bottle, but I drew it away from her.

"The last thing you need is a bellyful of liquor. Have you eaten anything?"

There was a tightness around her eyes. "Non. Have you?"

I shook my head.

"You look like death. Let me make us something."

Any other time, I'd insist on being the one to cook for her, but I was too numb to do anything. She banged through cupboards as if she didn't know where to find anything, but twenty minutes later, she set a plate of runny eggs and burnt toast in front of me. Grateful, I shoveled the food in.

"Did anyone call for the authorities?" she asked like she wanted to know the next day's weather.

My mouth dried up like the Sahara. "No."

Dragging an arm across her eyes, I realized she was on the verge of tears. "Fait chier. I've spent the past minutes wondering if the police were going to take you away." She broke down and threw her arms around my neck.

"Take me away?" Bewildered, I shook my head, though she couldn't see as her face was buried in my shoulder.

"I'm so sorry. But it's what happened to my father. The police took him. And then Maman died, and I was left with Paul, and my life was so awful. I can't bear for someone to take you away, Fin. Please don't go anywhere."

"I won't. Not till you don't need me anymore." A day that was coming faster than I wished.

She squeezed me tight enough that I fought to breathe. Then

she gulped some air and stood back up. "It's hard to imagine you not with me."

Her eyes still shimmered, and she had to blow her nose. I handed her a handkerchief.

"Who's taking Jody's corpse?"

"Pardon?" I might need a drop of the gin after all.

"Jody. If no one called the gendarmes, then someone else must take him away." She said it as though I were a child. "If they sold him to medical students, someone would want to know about the throat, so that's out. But maybe the river? But he'd probably come back up—"

I slapped my hand over my mouth and opened my eyes in horror.

"Merde, pardon. I forget you had a life before I was in it. You know I didn't mean to bring up Annabeth—"

Waving away her concern, I poured a small glass of gin. Just to restart my heart.

"Well, it would cost a lot to get his body somewhere he wouldn't be tracked down. And Victoire's broke, isn't she?"

To be honest, I had no idea what Victoire had or didn't have in the bank. "And how do you know about men getting rid of murdered bodies?"

Aurélie wrinkled her nose like she was deciding if she would tell me or not. "You're very innocent sometimes, you know? You saw where I grew up."

She rubbed her chin across her shoulder like she did when she was a little girl and I got her the first new dress she'd ever had for herself. The fabric was soft, and she darkened the collar with the oil from her skin.

"C'est le bordel ici." Aurélie pointed to Gilbert's tie flung over the back of the sofa. Her mouth made an O. "He's taking care of it? Thank God, then I don't have to worry. He's the sort that will pay men who won't get caught."

It was the echo of what Gilbert had said back in Jody's flat. "How do you know?"

"Everyone knows." She wrinkled her nose.

The skin rose on the back of my neck. "Do they? How come I didn't?"

With a wave of her hand as though it was immaterial, she picked up the gin and swallowed it down in one. "Gossip with the dancers. You know the neighborhoods most of them come from. They've all seen him around. But don't fret. No one would think of putting Gilbert's name with Jody's."

Even in my gloom I had the wherewithal to ask what sorts of things Gilbert was known for in the seedier streets of the poorer arrondissements.

"Oh, mostly finding out information. It's not like he's dangerous to you, surely. All you need to concentrate on is that Gilbert will have the resources to take care of this."

She glided across to her room and came back minutes later in a pink silk robe over an old cotton nightgown, a glass in her hand. "Tomorrow is Monday. I don't have to go to rehearsal until afternoon. Fill it up. If I'm old enough for abonnés to harass me, I'm old enough to join you."

Her bitterness nipped at my senses.

"What's happened?" Damn it, I should be taking better care of her.

"An old piece of shit came backstage." She twisted her arm

around so I could see bruises. Her skin was so pale; the marks were easy to make out as fingers and a thumb.

Jesus wept.

"He called my name, and I pretended I didn't hear, so he grabbed me, trying to stick his tongue down my throat. Maybe the same from last time, I don't know. I didn't look at his face. I looked where to aim my kick, so I got away."

This time.

"What can I do?" There had to be something. All of this time spent scrounging for pledges for Eiffel when I ought to be taking care of her. I was letting her down when she needed me.

She twisted her white-blond hair around her fingers. "It's so unfair. I want to dance, not any of this other stuff."

Rubbing the spot between my eyes, I sighed. "I wish there was something I could do when you're backstage—"

"You're too good to me as it is, Fin. And I love you. I just wanted to complain—I can't do it at school, but this isn't a nice night to do it to you, either."

There was a slight knock at the door, and then the doorknob twisted. Gilbert gave me a short nod.

Raising her glass in the air, Aurélie said, "Grab one for your gin, Gibby."

Gilbert smiled faintly at the nickname, raising that eyebrow at me on his way to get himself a glass. I winked, relieved to do something besides frown for a moment or two.

He settled on the couch in the middle of us, and we both scooted over to make space. "Aurélie, I brought some chocolates. They're in the kitchen. Why don't you fetch them?" Gilbert didn't turn from my face.

She snorted. "Then why didn't you—" She threw her hands up. "I don't care if you kiss Fin, or hug Fin, or go to bed with Fin, Gibby. But I won't be sent away like a child."

"There are chocolates. I forgot them, and I've had a complete shit day." He gave me a smacking kiss. "Is that better?"

It was for me. She rolled her eyes and stomped into the kitchen.

Murmuring before she came back, I said, "I told her that Jody died...but not much else. She'll keep it quiet." I kissed him again, this time slower. He blinked his eyes when I moved away, and tried to pull me back. "Did you...take care of him?"

"Non, not me. But his apartment will be emptied before dawn. All his clothes, all his belongings. It will be as though neither of them was ever there."

I couldn't fathom the amount of money that would cost. "I appreciate your help, but I'm confused. How do you have these connections? What is it that you actually do for your uncle?"

"Let's not talk about it tonight. It's nothing too sordid, I promise."

My face must have registered how unsatisfactory that answer was. He shifted his weight to his back leg, nostrils flaring. "Michel is a businessman, not a criminal. Nor am I. He mostly likes me to check references—you know, to ensure the men he makes deals with won't damage his reputation."

There were too many questions but, frankly, I didn't have my wits to formulate them.

"Tell me, what were you doing before I got here? Because, to be honest, I might take a nap." He thumbed toward my room.

A frisson of pleasure that Gilbert wasn't going back to his own flat lit me up inside warmer than the gin.

"I was complaining to Fin that I'm tired of men expecting something from me when all I wish to do is dance." Aurélie reached for another two chocolates. I bit back the urge to tell her she'd be sick if she indulged in too many.

Gilbert rubbed the stubble that dotted his chin and cheeks. "But isn't that the game you're playing?"

Fair eyebrows rose on her forehead. "No."

"Fin's holding them off until you choose, non?"

Aurélie snorted and bit at one of her pinkies. "Over his dead body." And then she winced. "Non. I want to dance and dance and then when I am too old, I want to teach dancing."

She reached for another chocolate, and I waved her hand away. "It's chocolate or gin, Fin. And your bottle is running low."

I didn't want a drink, but she didn't need it, either. "Fine. One more, and then put them away for God's sake."

Gilbert smacked his fist into his palm. "All this time I wondered how a decent man like Fin was going to sell you off."

Holy hell. I'd never explained, had I? I winced, hating that that was what he'd believed.

Aurélie scoffed. "He won't even let me speak to the men. But they're getting restless." She showed Gilbert her bruises and snuck another chocolate, which I pretended I didn't see.

Gilbert ran his hand through his hair until it stood straight up. I tamped it down, wanting to touch him in any capacity. He caught my hand and rubbed it to his cheek, a grin spreading across his face. "I have a plan. Écoutez, we could pretend I'm your lover, just to protect you. It gives me a good reason to be here, and I'll happily pay for your lessons. It's nothing to me, you know it isn't. But—mon Dieu—how amazing to have an excuse to spend the night here when I wanted to." He wrinkled his nose and looked at me under his lashes. "When you want me to, bien sûr."

Aurélie touched her throat, frowning. "Aren't you engaged?"

"Yes, what about Stéphanie?" I schooled my face to look serious.

Gilbert waved a hand. "Inasmuch as Stéphanie even thinks about what I do in my spare time, a ballerina is better to complain about to her friends than you, Fin. And my uncle, too. He'd probably be relieved, to be honest."

He winked at me. "And I promise you, when you get bored with me, I can end my make-believe affair with Aurélie." He tapped her knee. "But I'll still pay for those damn lessons until you're the étoile, hmm?"

She pressed her mouth tight and shook her head. "Non, that's a good plan. The old pieces of shit will leave me alone if they think I settled on you."

Then she sighed. "I only want to focus on my art. Oui. It's clever. *The right plan.*" She threw her arms around his neck so his glass tilted and dribbled gin in my lap.

But I wasn't sure I was ready to take that sort of step. I enjoyed Gilbert in my bed, but was it more than that? I got caught up in the beauty of the flush high on his cheeks. *Damn if I didn't enjoy Gilbert Duhais in my bed.*

The man who saved my fortunes.

And Victoire from the guillotine, of course.

Who offered to spare my cousin humiliation and degradation.

The disadvantages were invisible at that moment—which I recognized might be because of the gin. But might not be.

"So are we in agreement? Is it a fair compromise?"

More than fair. No one had ever been kinder than he'd been to me since we woke up so many hours before.

And I couldn't imagine ever getting tired of Gilbert. *I'm sure I will.* Just couldn't imagine it.

He stood, gave me his hand, and pulled me to stand, nearly tumbling into his arms.

"Mademoiselle—I recommend no more than two more chocolates or you might see them sooner than later, mixed with all that gin. But I'm going to bed, and taking this beautiful man with me."

20

The next day at the office was even more dismal than I'd anticipated, and it was all I could do to keep my eyes off the clock on my wall. I organized the reams of calculations I had no real intention of scanning that evening, but still slid into the oxblood leather attaché case I'd gifted myself upon my promotion. The physical drain from keeping up appearances when all I wished to do was indulge in my grief over Jody was taking a heavy toll.

"Tighe—er, Carleton, why aren't you upstairs?" Monsieur Eiffel met me at the door and glared at the leather case. "I sent word that we had an emergency meeting."

Biting my bottom lip to keep from rolling my eyes, I held back a sigh. Word had not reached me, which had happened more than once lately.

Eiffel squinted at my face. "Mon Dieu, you're quite peaked. Are you ill?"

But before I could come up with anything reasonable to admit to, he waved me out of the office and up the stairs. I'd never seen Eiffel so agitated, and I had to strain to catch up to the news that apparently everyone else but me was already apprised of.

Luckily, even through the fog of my sadness over Jody, I was able to gather the details. A certain Comtesse du Poix—and an accomplice whose name I wasn't able to ascertain—had thrown one more obstacle into the unrelenting drama of whether or not our tower would be constructed.

As soon as the government ministers had finally agreed to allow it to proceed, the comtesse filed a suit claiming that the structure—which, coincidentally, would be squarely in the spot of her favorite morning constitutional—would prove to be a catastrophic safety hazard.

Her play was well staged. She'd held an interview with more than one journalist, listing some of the direr risks she could contemplate. Wind or rain might topple the tower into her apartment building on the Champs de Mars. Its menacing height looming over the well-heeled residential addresses was destined to retain the threat for an entire twenty years, increasing the chance of calamity. And the most difficult argument to counter: it could serve as a giant lightning rod likely to commit God only knew what sort of carnage to the vulnerable Parisians.

The meeting with Eiffel dragged on three quarters of an hour longer than it needed, as the collective indignation of the employees overrode any chance of a plan to logically refute the comtesse's quarrels. My relief at the conclusion of the meeting was short-lived, as Eiffel held me back by the fabric of my jacket sleeve.

"Viscount Carleton, a word."

That small niggling of anxiety over the title never went away, and it probably showed. Though, under the circumstances, my concern was expected, no matter its cause.

"Sir?"

Eiffel pursed his lips as if framing words before he spoke them. "I need your help. The entire success or defeat of this project might be upon your shoulders."

I was momentarily speechless. Was he speaking hyperbolically? Had there been some message from England about my fraud? I blinked hard to combat the queasiness threatening to knock me down.

He clapped his hand on my shoulder and gave a grave shake of his curly head. "We simply must get our side of this quarrel— the logical side, *the scientific side*—in front of the public before this horrible woman destroys our chances to have our tower built."

Parisians were still of two minds regarding the project, which would entirely dominate the skyline for the next two decades. The absurd fears propagated by the comtesse might be a compelling reason for many undecided to turn irrevocably anti-tower exactly when we needed the final government approval.

"I agree—most certainly—but I'm not sure how I—"

"Michel de Gênet." Eiffel's smile was small and grim. "He must be brought round to support us, very publicly, very quickly. And I'm relying on your relationship with him and his nephew. You're the only one who can do it, and you must do it tonight, or tomorrow at the latest."

My mouth dropped for a moment before I managed to bluster out, "But, monsieur, de Gênet isn't someone I'd call a friend. To even say that he's an acquaintance that I could easily drop by for a tête-à-tête might be pushing the boundaries."

De Gênet hadn't even handed over his investment, though this was hardly the best time to remind Eiffel of that.

"Use that brain of yours and think of something you can offer him, something you can do for him that no one else can."

I realized I was pinching the skin between my thumb and forefinger so hard that it hurt. "Something *I* could offer him? Monsieur, I beg your pardon, but that's absurd. De Gênet's a millionaire, and I'm just—"

A quick pound of Eiffel's fist into his open palm stopped me cold. "*You* are merely a British aristocrat whose father rubs elbows with the damned Prince of Wales, Viscount Carleton. Send your father a telegram, see what he can do? For God's sake, he'd surely be willing to help. I must exhaust any possible avenue to get out of this nightmare, and you seem to be holding more cards than the rest of the office put together."

A rush of adrenaline coursed through me, leaving me with a sheen of sweat and heart palpitations. My mouth was too dry to respond. A telegram to the Earl of Rawcliffe? Even if I possessed one tenth of the daring to do it, Gilbert had cautioned me not to.

Eiffel shook his finger at me once, twice, and then his shoulders slumped. "I'm not being fair. I don't wish to add to your burdens; but I have few choices, and you've been so adept until now charming the high rollers. And you have more of a chance with de Gênet than I would. He and I are not on friendly terms." He cracked a weak smile. "Whatever it is that you've been doing, go at it a hundred times harder, and get us out of this situation."

Blessedly, he walked out before I collapsed back into a chair, head in hands.

How…? And then, like a beam of light breaking through a storm, a possible lifeline.

Gilbert.

He would think of a plan—or at least help me strategize. I pushed back out of the chair and scrabbled together enough coins to pay for a cab rather than waste an extra second on the bus journey.

Gilbert popped off the sofa when I flung open the door to my flat. The relief that I wouldn't need to track down his whereabouts overrode my curiosity that he'd made himself so comfortable at our flat. "Gilbert, you've got to get me to see your uncle this evening. It's urgent."

As if we were in a stage play of tranquil domesticity, Gilbert removed my hat and ran his fingers through the waves falling over my brow. "Un moment, Fin. I've got a surprise first, and then you can tell me all about it, hmm?"

Tucked into the waist of his trousers was a dishcloth, which he removed, waving it like a cheeky toreador until I followed him to the kitchen. The scent of a home-cooked meal drew me like a moth to the cooking range. I lifted the lid of the unfamiliar cast iron pot simmering away and was greeted by an appetizing medley of vegetables and bobbing chicken that nearly had me lose my train of thought.

Nearly. I dropped the lid with a dull clang back onto the pot. "No, this is an emergency. Michel—can you get me a way to speak with him immediately? Tonight, if possible?"

"Michel?" A flicker of confusion...or perhaps anxiety...crossed his face before he went back to the smile he'd worn when I came in. "That's an easy request. He's expecting you."

The uncertainty I'd clung to for the past hour was unwilling to dissipate. In fact, it transformed into a new concern; why was Michel expecting to see me? I asked as much.

"C'est simple, Stéphanie is having a party, and he assumed you'd be there."

Relief swept over me as Gilbert went on to urge me to get ready to eat. It was all logical.

Following at my heels as I washed my hands and neck in the basin, Gilbert told me he'd met Mademoiselle Jeunesse on the stairs with Aurélie that morning—when he walked her to the dance school.

Gilbert stood behind me and massaged my shoulder blades with his thumbs. "When I dropped her off at the ballet tonight, I kissed Aurélie on the cheek; I hope you aren't too jealous."

It took a moment to comprehend what he meant. I wasn't jealous; that wasn't the right emotion, because it was a decent plan and should keep back most of the abonnés once the rumor flew that Aurélie had chosen a patron. Especially if it was well known throughout the foyer de la danse that Gilbert wasn't a man to be trifled with.

I splashed more water on my face, willing my heart to slow its rapid beating. I followed him back out to the salon, where he plumped the sofa cushions before sitting.

"There's an open bottle of wine left from my dish; why don't you pour us each a glass?"

Grateful for something else to occupy me, I complied. I filled both glasses with equal amounts and then added more to my own to still my shaking hands.

Back in the salon, I handed him his drink. "I don't get the feeling that your uncle likes me much."

I downed half my glass, and Gilbert raised his eyebrow. "He

doesn't like anyone much. Don't drink so quickly. You need to keep your wits."

Chastened, I followed him to the table and watched as he deftly portioned the fricassee.

I waved the steam into my nose to keep my nerves steady. "Did you make this?"

"Do you think it'll be nice?" He gave that half smile that implied he knew exactly how delicious it smelled.

"Of course, but I'm not sure that I'm comfortable with you making yourself at home when no one is here." It sounded grumbling to me, too, but my tension knew no bounds.

He raised an eyebrow. "Don't tell me you've had second thoughts about us?"

A million of them, but I was being unfair. The notion of whether this arrangement was going to kill me or, well . . . *save me* had managed to plague me even with so many other thoughts chasing themselves through my mind all day.

The coziness plucked at my heartstrings. I raised my eyes to his, which were troubled, and so I clutched his closest hand in mine for a long moment. "What do you think?"

That sunshine smile crept up his cheek in the way that pierced my heart. "I think I'll be staying the night."

My stomach lurched with pleasure until I remembered all that would have to happen first. "What's the occasion for tonight's party?"

Gilbert resumed eating. In between bites, his voice was light-hearted. "Ah, one of Stéphanie's artistic soirées; artists and writers, those sorts of people. She asked me to bring you and Victoire, though I said I believed she was unwell. Stéphanie has a passion for cultivating fascinating women."

"Did you explain to her about pretending that Aurélie is your mistress?"

He grinned. "I did, and she thinks it's a good idea, for Aurélie's sake. She knows full well that that's the only reason. Says she'd enjoy meeting her. I'll have to sort that out sometime. She's fascinated by the world of ballet dancers." The tone of his voice turned even jollier. "Michel will be waiting for you."

It was close to eight already, and though it was convenient for my workday career for the party to begin sooner than later, it was unfashionably early for the smart set. "Michel hardly seems the type to enjoy bohemians. Especially of the *wicked woman* variety."

"He can pretend that he's there to offer them a way off of their path of sin. I asked him once why he's most compelled to save the prettiest ones." Gilbert gave an easy nod, but I wasn't won over.

"Gilbert, this is more than just a soirée for me. I'm tasked by Eiffel to recruit your uncle to publicly back the tower. I've no idea how I'm to manage that and can't imagine that a brief chat over canapés is going to be the best tack. I'd prefer to meet with him on his own. There's a possible hitch with the tower, and I need to explain before Michel gets wind of it."

"Too late, I'm afraid. And impossible to get him on his own, because he's headed out of town." Gilbert fumbled with his cigarette box and a match. "Even if he wasn't, it would be exceedingly foolish to try and force him to do anything. Not if you ever want to get your hands on his money."

Possibly noting the annoyance wafting off of me, Gilbert

changed his tone. Wheedled, even. "A party is the perfect time, Fin. You can be diplomatic. Charming. Soothe Michel's concerns. He's a monster when—" Gilbert paused and looked away, as if searching for the best answer. "When Michel forms an opinion against something, he won't change his mind."

"Monster? Are you warning me that your uncle is likely to physically threaten me? Truly?"

Gilbert threw his hands up, exasperated. "Non. That isn't what I'm saying. I'm pointing out that I know Michel best. You should follow my advice, or it will have disastrous consequences." His jaw tightened, showing that temper might run in his family.

For Eiffel and the company, surely. But the notion that this was even more directed at me, personally, sent a chill up my spine.

Blast it all. A short conversation, easy rather than pleading...or arguing...was a better choice. "Will you help me?"

"I won't abandon you at the last minute. I've already paid your Monsieur Eiffel, and I might need that investment someday." Gilbert chucked me under the chin, bringing my eyes to his. "My uncle particularly likes the hors d'oeuvres with capers, hmm? I'll ensure there is a plate of them near where you should approach him. And a glass of champagne. You know what he wants in return from you, mon beau. Just promise to deliver."

Mesmerized by that lopsided grin, I nodded without thinking. Then reality slapped me across the face. "Fucking hell, I can't promise anything in my father's name. I have no right to, and it's too dangerous." I dragged my hand through my hair and turned to pace the rug. "It's one thing to dine out on his name— and granted, I *have* gone further than I ever ought to have with dropping that blasted Viscount Carleton nonsense like so many pencil shavings under my drafting desk. But this...this notion that I can get away with swindling a man as powerful as your uncle...Gilbert, I can't possibly."

He nodded sagely, and then gave his customary shrug. "You must. Michel hates public controversy. To have him help you in this...you must offer him something."

"Why can't he woo some other British notable? One who is willing and eager to be his partner?"

Gilbert ran his tongue over his back molars. "I should have said before, but I did go to London briefly a while back. Just for a quick visit. I was scouting appropriate space to build our grand magasin. I've found the perfect plot"—he kissed his fingertips in excitement—"right on Jermyn Street across from Fortnum and Mason's. The agent said another retailer was hoping to raise the capital, so we must secure it at once. Michel has the funds, of course, but there's some rigmarole about needing to have a British citizen on the deed, and Michel knows you, and you need his money. It makes sense for it to be you. And you're the earl's son."

"*But you're misunderstanding my point.* I'm not in a legal position to help Michel, nor will I ever be. I'll admit that you've sparked the hope that my father might leave me a small sum for an inheritance, but not the actual earldom, even if you pretend there is a chance. Gilbert, this is a giant ruse. A lie. *A sham.* And one I'll be caught out at as soon as I dare to go that far. I simply can't do it."

Without pausing to allow that to sink in, he shrugged. "Then you will lose. You will lose Michel's backing, his investment in your tower. You will lose his friends, very likely. And then, I hope I'm wrong, but I'll wager you'll lose your job."

I was at a complete loss as to how to keep the first domino from tipping over. "There must be something else I can dangle...?"

"Non. This is the least dangerous course. The only other thing—" He cut himself off.

Bewildered, I stared at him.

"Please, Fin. Just one more night of lies." He stroked my cheek and softened his voice. "Your father could even be dead already. The lawyers might be searching for you to be the next earl, and I believe that it can be you, even if you think it's impossible. Don't look so stubborn. I'm on your side, and if you just stop arguing and let me tell you how to manage this, there will be nothing to fret over. You'll come to the party, Michel will agree to back you, and as soon as this moves forward, we can be done with all of these pretenses, I swear."

Try as I might, I was unable to puzzle together all the seeming layers of subtext. I was desperate to believe Gilbert that everything would be resolved, that my anxiety was overly extreme.

When he finished hypnotizing me with his rationality, he stood by my side, close but not touching. "If you see me hold Stéphanie's arm, or laugh at her jokes, or do anything that looks like I have tenderness toward her, remember that it's you I wish I was touching, or laughing with, or looking at like a lover should."

The sweetness of the sentiment collided with the horror of the reality of what we were doing to ourselves and to Stéphanie Verger. The tightness around Gilbert's eyes told me he agreed. I was helpless to say no. If that was all I could get from Gilbert, then by God, that's what I would take.

"You will trust me, mon beau?" he asked, moving to the door.

As if there were an alternative.

"Don't sulk." He rubbed his hands over his eyes. "Fin, I know you feel as though I'm asking you to be less than the man you are, and if there was another way…" The plaintive tone of his voice broke my resolve.

"We'll manage." I gave him a smile I didn't feel, and his shoulders loosened.

Still, he hesitated, gripping the door handle, but I ignored him. I went to shave and dress and otherwise to prepare to simultaneously beg and charm de Gênet, which was horrid enough. But the worry that this would be my new normal, sharing Gilbert with someone else, and always having to hide my relationship with him, was toxic, as well. After a minute, Gilbert left, the front door banging behind him.

A woman's voice called out his name, and I went to the window to see who it was. Aurélie's face was wreathed in confusion as she watched Gilbert hurry down the street, hand on his hat as if to keep it from flying off in his speed.

21

The door opened to Aurélie, her mouth running quicker than her feet.

"Was Gilbert here? I could have sworn I saw him, but when I called out, he ignored me." Her eyes widened. "What's that divine smell?" She nearly fell into my chair and shoveled a forkful of cold fricassee into her mouth.

"He was, but he just left. He probably wasn't expecting to hear you. You're never home this early—is everything all right?" I removed the plate, replacing it with a fresh one heaped with warm food.

"Bien sûr. I landed badly from a leap during practice and they sent me home. I wasn't hurt, not much, and it's already feeling much better. Did I tell you we all think the piano player is the maître du danse's lover? They probably decided to send me home so they could indulge, even though they're both married—what's wrong with you?"

When she glanced at me, she catapulted back to her feet and threw her arms around my neck. "Oh, forgive me, I wasn't thinking about Jody. How are you managing?"

I shook my head, unable to allow myself to succumb to my sadness.

Taking a step back, she eyed me suspiciously. "Why are you so dressed up? There's no performance tonight."

I sketched out the dilemma with the comtesse and de Gênet quickly as I carried the cooking pot back to the kitchen. When I returned, Aurélie was working on pliés holding the back of the sofa. "Didn't do enough of them today?"

She wrinkled her nose. "Indeed. But since I'm not going to practice, I believe I'm going to spend the evening on the town with Rosette."

I knew better than to warn her to give her body a rest. "I'll give you money for the taxi. And for your ride home, because I assume it will be late, and you have no business out on the streets alone."

Aurélie hadn't listened as she'd flown back to her room, presumably to change.

One of the benefits of being a bachelor—and raised by Aunt Glad—was that I was well versed in caring for my own things, and busied myself lighting the range to heat up two slugs for the box iron. I finished shaving while they heated.

"I'm leaving. Tell me I'm pretty enough?" Aurélie poked her head into my bedroom, and then her full body, twirling in one of the dresses gifted to her by Gilbert, an elegant pale pink ensemble that set off her coloring well and matched a spray of rosebuds over one ear.

I kissed my fingertips. "Beautiful. And please take care of yourself. I'm struggling to override my instincts to coddle you like a little girl, but I do worry."

"I know, and I do appreciate it. Please remember that I'm not afraid to take care of myself. Even when I'm having a good time." Aurélie hugged me, speaking into my shoulder. "I won't let you down, Fin."

She was out the door before I could tell her that she was the single person alive who never had.

It was raining by the time I arrived at Stéphanie's—which had been why I'd had to pay for the taxi for the entire trip, to my chagrin. This evening was getting more expensive by the hour. But even so, I craned my neck to the melody of Stéphanie's grand piano, accompanied by many voices, burbling with camaraderie and wine, that rang from her open windows. I felt a pang that Victoire wasn't by my side. She operated in this world a thousand times better than I could.

A dark shadow passed the window, silhouetted through the silk curtains. De Gênet, I was certain by the stature. A wave of anxiety crashed upon me, but I set my shoulders and entered the building, refusing to be cowed.

I stood on the threshold when Gilbert's friend—and my very first investor—Édouard Hainault saw me and, with arms wide, cut through the crowd like a hot knife through butter. "Delightful, Viscount Carleton." He pumped my hand.

He, too, wore the jacket without tails, tight fitting and showing off his long, slender form like a well-sewn glove.

Tucking an arm through mine, he led me through the room. Gilbert faced the other direction, head thrown back, laughing.

I took the proffered brandy, against my own strictures. I'd

need it to cope with the brambles germinating in my gut. It was a plentiful crowd, heavy on the feminine side, but with more than a few men, including Gilbert, who was involved in an animated chat with Stéphanie and her red-headed friend Romuald Parry.

Hainault grinned as though we were friends. "I'm so glad to see your face, Finley. My…friend Timothée and I are headed to Capri until April or May. It's nice to have a chance to say goodbye."

"Capri? I've never been." Chitchat was easier than watching Gilbert, who winked at his fiancée. *Since he didn't know I was here yet, did that wink still count for me?*

Édouard gestured to a handsome brunette whose eyes were riveted on us though he was in a conversation with a few others. "You ought to visit. You'd be amazed with how free the people are on some of those islands, especially on Capri. I keep telling Gilbert he ought to take a holiday there. Maybe the two of you? We're always more relaxed when we're free to be ourselves."

The implication of what he meant blossomed in my mind. Hainault knew—or guessed—about my relationship with Gilbert, and was letting me know. Was there a world where Gilbert and I would be free to show our love?

Half-listening to Édouard chatter, I scanned the room. Michel de Gênet met my gaze. He frowned and moved in my direction, stopping when another guest called to him.

As though he understood I'd had a reprieve, Édouard winked at me. "We're only here because we promised Stéphanie we'd come, but her stepfather is not fond of us, and the feeling is mutual. I swore we'd stay another half hour and then we can go home."

We spent five minutes discussing the tower, how it could be

used to further science, and I was regaining my confidence in leaps and bounds. I could do this and hide my concerns from de Gênet. *I could.*

"De Gênet is coming over." Édouard narrowed his eyes at me. "It's you he wants, isn't it? Rumor has it he's promised you a large sum, and all this nonsense over whether some old woman can walk her poodle on the Champs de Mars for its morning shit is threatening that." He clapped my shoulder and then drifted away.

"Carleton." Gilbert's uncle didn't shake my hand. "Can you explain to me what the hell is going on? Gilbert insists I can't—as a gentleman—withdraw my offer, but having my reputation attached to something as absurd as this lawsuit is unacceptable."

Hello to you, too. I took a breath and smiled as naturally as I could. I fumbled for an opening volley and stole Édouard's line about the poodle.

De Gênet glowered for an instant. And then he laughed, thumped my back with his hand hard enough to knock someone less sturdy down. I laughed, too.

"Very good. I'll use that. Perhaps we can embarrass the old lady enough for her to withdraw."

"Eiffel doesn't believe the case will go anywhere. The committee has dragged its heels because of public pressure, but they already voted in favor of construction to commence the digging, so it will happen. This is the final challenge and, with your help, we can overcome it quickly." Free, easy.

"Oui, oui. It might be easier to kill the damned dog."

I cringed at his vehemence.

Peeling my teeth from my dry mouth with my tongue, I took the plunge. "It appears that you're the final decision-maker, de

Gênet." I hoped that would stroke his ego. "You'd be doing us all an enormous favor if you came out as a backer of the project. Publicly, I mean."

His lip curled. "I wondered when you'd appear, hat in hand to beg. I'm listening. Tell me why I should stick my neck out to help your scheme?"

I opened my mouth, but no words came out. As often as I'd been telling falsehoods—this particular lie was too difficult to speak. "Your investment with Eiffel—"

He gave a humorless laugh and drained his snifter. "The money I might make from this tower is minor, so save your breath. If this lawsuit even hints at a humiliation for me, I'll publicly put an end to it. However, Gilbert tells me you're prepared to make a deal. You already know the one thing that will entice me, Carleton."

My eyes searched the room and landed on Gilbert as he met my glance with a slight shiver of surprise, perhaps not yet realizing I was there. He leaned in to whisper to Stéphanie, whose head jerked our way.

"I'd like a guarantee that you'll put your name behind my store in London." His eyes bored into mine. "I wrote to your father when I first met you, asking him to verify that you are his heir and have the right to speak on his behalf."

I was rooted to the spot, mind racing through all of the responses that might have been sent back. De Gênet's sardonic smile deepened. Was this public scene to be my undoing?

I couldn't show a hint of the chaos swirling inside me. I gave the merest hint of a smile. "He's very ill. On his deathbed, so his intentions toward my future will be brought to light very soon."

De Gênet opened his mouth—but my focus was drawn to the

newest guests to arrive: the Paris ballet's étoile Rosette...and Aurélie. Bloody hell.

Stéphanie was aware that Gilbert was pretending to have begun an affair with my cousin—but had the rumor spread? The height of the situation's awkwardness disarmed me. Perhaps I could cut this conversation short and let Aurélie know she must leave before there was a hint of scandal.

Glancing back at de Gênet, his glower alerted me that I'd missed something. "I beg your pardon?"

But de Gênet stared at Aurélie, whose prettiness was only accentuated by the chandelier's light. I held my breath as her eyes met mine across the room. She gave me a tense smile and made her way to my side. "Quelle surprise, I didn't realize we were coming here, but I can take a taxi home if—" She looked at who I was with and caught her breath.

"Who's this, Carleton?" Michel de Gênet slipped around to the other side of Aurélie, blocking the way back to the door. "She looks familiar."

"My cousin, Aurélie Blancmaison. Michel de Gênet."

De Gênet reached for her hand, though she held it down by her side almost rigidly, and kissed it. "One of the tarts from the ballet. Did you really bring your poufiasse to my daughter's party?"

The disgusting slur caused my head to jerk around to de Gênet. That sort of language would have been shocking from anyone, let alone a patron of the downtrodden.

Gilbert appeared, bearing a small plate, his fiancée following behind gesturing to a waiter with a tray of champagne flutes. "Oncle, have a canapé. Stéphanie had them made especially for you."

His timing would have been comical if not for the chaos sparked by Aurélie's arrival. His mouth dropped when he saw her. "Aurélie? What on earth are you doing here?"

De Gênet's deep baritone drowned out anyone else. "Carleton, I'll ask again, did you truly invite your whore to my daughter's—"

Stéphanie inserted her slight body between Aurélie and de Gênet. "I'm not your daughter, Michel, and this is Mademoiselle Blancmaison, I believe. The rising ballerina we've all heard about from her grand debut at the Opéra."

She stroked Aurélie's arm, soothing her. "I've seen you dance, cherie, and you're extraordinary. Sublime. Come and allow me to introduce some people to you, oui?"

Aurélie gave me one last look over her shoulder as she was led away.

"I'm not surprised you seem so comfortable with—what was her name, Gilbert? Blancmaison? No wonder as you spend so many nights at their apartment." Michel de Gênet narrowed his eyes at his nephew. "Or is it because of you, Viscount?"

I gasped. How could he have known?

Gilbert rolled his eyes and laughed. "We're merely friends, Michel. I'm unsure why you need to cast it as anything more."

De Gênet's lips pursed. "I've warned you that I comprehend quite a lot about your friendships, nephew. I also know you often blur the line between friend and lover. You may playact that I'm unaware of what happens in your personal life, but rest assured that you're not the only one carrying out investigations."

Gilbert blanched.

My mouth was dry, and my stomach sank faster than a rowboat with a hole. "It's not what you think. Aurélie is my orphan cousin. I've taken care of her since she was a little girl. My aunt's daughter."

De Gênet stared into the distance, distracted. "Her brother used to work for me until he was murdered, though I'm sure you know about that." He shook his head. "The bastards of Louis the fifteenth were Blancmaisons, he told me. Claimed he was a descendent. Vive la Révolution." He tore his eyes away and scowled at me again. "She's lived with you since she was a child?"

Michel's tone was weighted in accusation.

Not like that. "She's my cousin, Monsieur de Gênet." My cheeks burned. "I take care of her. Like a sister." I raised my chin. "However, she's now launching her career rather spectacularly. She won't need my help very much longer."

He rolled his eyes. "Es-tu une oie blanche? Every one of them is a whore. She has you snookered, eh?" He smacked my cheek lightly, but with a clear dominance that rankled.

The urge to take him down a peg or two surged—to demand whether he used these words when offering to help his charity cases—but this was neither the place nor the time. Everything hung in the balance—Michel's investment, my career. After that was all stitched up, I could tell de Gênet how I really felt about him.

"You look as though you've seen a ghost, Carleton. Or perhaps reaching some conclusions that put your friendship with my nephew in a new light?" De Gênet's chuckle was dry, humorless. "Shall we draw up the contract tonight or tomorrow? For the London branch of Qualité. I'll have my lawyer bring it to you in a few hours. Or perhaps Gilbert will wish to drop it by your apartment later this evening?"

Gilbert straightened his back. "Fin—Carleton can sign the documents in the morning. At your office. You can be sure that he'll be there."

I gritted my teeth and nodded. Now was not the time to argue.

De Gênet held up his hand for Gilbert to be quiet. "You don't want to cross me, Tighe. Je te promets."

A bucket of ice water couldn't have been colder, because it was a promise he meant implicitly. I nodded again, even though he turned from me, and I was clearly dismissed.

"What the hell does he mean about light shed on our friendship?" I channeled all my rage at Michel into my snarl.

Gilbert took a step back, not meeting my gaze. "I really don't have any idea. Can we please discuss this in private? Later?" The cluster of curious partiers surrounding us had grown.

I wasn't having it. "Did he mean Paul?"

He ground his back teeth, furious from the tone of his voice. "I've explained how many times already? Oui—Paul worked for Michel. You know that, so why are you insinuating something sordid?"

De Gênet had clearly implied there was more to Gilbert's relationship with Paul than working camaraderie, but what that might have been was too horrible to contemplate. Nothing made sense except I needed to get out into the air and breathe before I was overwhelmed with the questions swirling in my mind. "I'll fetch Aurélie and take her home. Bon soirée."

I moved to where Stéphanie had locked arms with Aurélie as she promenaded her around the room. I trailed in their wake, feebly, for an introduction or two, glad that Stéphanie wasn't pausing long for conversations.

Finally, it was the three of us. Quietly, Stéphanie said, "Thank you for that, mademoiselle. The gossips won't know what to do with our friendship when word gets out about you and Gilbert, will they? I think we ought to meet for dinner this week and completely set them on their ears."

Aurélie's tight shoulders loosened. "You're too kind."

"I think we ought to head home. It's been a hell of an evening, if you'll excuse me saying so." I tipped my hat to Stéphanie and offered Aurélie my arm. "But I'd prefer not to cross paths with Michel again. Is there another exit?"

Stéphanie tilted her head toward me. "There's a staircase that leads to the kitchen behind me. Why don't you leave that way, and I'll send Mademoiselle Blancmaison in a moment? I do have a few things I'd like to tell her in private."

After Aurélie nodded, I agreed and made my way down a much tighter staircase than the one coming from the entry. Even though there was a party going on upstairs, I was surprised to see such a large gathering of female staff.

Without pausing to think of propriety, I asked, "Do you all work here?" Surely one woman didn't need ten maids.

A woman in black with her hair tied up in a net put one hand on her hip authoritatively. In the other she wielded a wooden spoon. "Sir? What are you doing in my kitchen?"

"I beg your pardon. I wished to slip out unseen, and Mademoiselle Verger told me to come this way." I tipped my head in deference that staff rarely received.

The cook softened. "We've borrowed some of the girls from Monsieur de Gênet for tonight."

"My dear friend's sister Charlotte used to work for Monsieur de

Gênet. Charlotte Barreau. Do any of you know her? She's disappeared, and my friend—" My voice caught thinking about Jody.
"Well, we have no idea where she might have gone."

A few of the women gave pointed looks to one another. "We're
anxious to find her. There's an inheritance. It makes no sense that
she wouldn't tell Jody where she was going. They were very, very
close."

One of the maids opened her mouth and snapped it shut again
after a hard look from the cook.

"I understand you have no reason to trust me. My mother was
a domestique in a large house. My aunts, too." *Please let that add
the edge of familiarity I need.*

"She didn't tell anyone she was leaving. We shared a room."
The woman who spoke glared at the rest. "What? If 'twas me who
disappeared, I'd want you to tell someone looking for me that I
hadn't just up and run away."

"I heard she ran off with the neighbor's groom."

More than one of the women looked surprised at that, and one
said, "Charlotte wasn't sweet on anyone. She'd have said."

"That's enough, Lorraine." The cook frowned. "We don't know
anything, sir. Perhaps you ought to ask the mademoiselle. There's
the door. Sophie, see the gentleman out."

I paused, hoping someone else would pipe up, but either they
knew nothing else, or didn't dare. I did understand. Places were
difficult to come by without a reference, which they might not get
because of my questions. I bid them a good evening and walked
through the side garden to the front door, where Aurélie waited,
shivering under an umbrella. The afternoon's storm clouds had
broken.

241

"Mon Dieu, I had no idea that Monsieur de Gênet would be here, Fin. Please tell me you aren't cross."

"Cross with you? For what?" Had she heard what de Gênet said about her? Hopefully not. Wishing to get away from the building and everyone in it, I pulled her along to the street, glad that there was a taxi waiting. I helped her in and climbed beside her. "I'm not displeased with you. Just confused."

I explained what had happened in the kitchen when I'd asked about Charlotte.

"There's something odd, but what? Stéphanie urged me to come to her if anyone gave me any trouble at the ballet, as though there was something I needed to know, but she didn't explain. She doesn't know me, so what could it be?"

I was as befuddled as she was. Almost. "I think Paul worked for de Gênet, though I don't know how that plays any part, but I agree. There's something I can't put my finger on."

She shivered harder and stared out of the window. I put my hand over hers, hoping to provide some comfort.

"Are you all right? It was as though you'd met him before."

"De Gênet? Non." Her large gray eyes were wet, her forehead wrinkled in grief. "I'm just tired. I ought to have stayed in tonight."

"That makes two of us."

22

We didn't speak any further, and back at our flat, I looked at my bed and realized I was much too restless for sleep. I'd spend all night tossing and turning over signing Michel de Gênet's document that could be my legal undoing.

All at once, I had an overwhelming need to find the comfort of my friends. My true friends, who didn't leave me second-guessing everything I did. The Green Carnation. I walked quickly and hoped the pissing rain would keep the cutpurses at home instead of lurking in alleyways.

It was as though my mind was full of tangled threads like in Aunt Glad's sewing basket after Annabeth would throw down her tedious embroidery tasks—inevitably in tears as she was less suited to such pursuits than even I would have been. To keep her from another scolding, I'd uncoil the snarls and tidy it up before our aunt noticed.

This was the same sort of pursuit, and I ought to be able to be just as successful in unraveling this knot of complications.

What was Gilbert's endgame when it came to my father? Because as much as he insisted that I trust him—and as foolishly as my heart wished to—I simply couldn't fathom why he'd pushed me onto this course of scheming to trade on my father's name. Was he working for the earl? For Michel? For me? Or against some and not the others? If I could figure out what benefit it was to Gilbert, the rest might become clear.

"Monsieur, a sou for a suck? Two for me to pull up my skirts."

Wheeling around, my eyes discerned a figure dressed in black hovering in a doorframe. She was young, even more so than Aurélie, who still seemed like a child in my eyes. Her thin frame was obvious with the wet clothing limp against her. The stone of the building was blacked from soot and smog. The smell of human refuse rose from the privies that weren't part of the sewer system.

How did some men justify being part of this sort of abuse? I shook my head and kept walking. This is what Aurélie would be doing, perhaps, if I hadn't come to Paris. Aurélie wasn't in this situation, and never would be; not if I had life in my body. But this poor girl had no such protector. I turned, dug into my pocket, and found a few sous. "Go eat a meal instead."

Unable to tolerate thanks, I dashed across the street and picked up my pace. I needed to breathe something other than the dank despair surrounding me. Blessedly, I crossed into a new neighborhood that I recognized and headed down the stairs into the Green Carnation a few minutes later.

As usual, the air was thick with smoke, but a violinist screeched a haunting melody on the stage where I was used to seeing Victoire.

Laurent was behind the bar, his shirt tucked in more neatly than usual. The solemnity in his brown eyes let me know at once that Victoire had shared the wretched news about Jody. He came from around the bar and hugged me.

When I finally pulled back, I kept my hands on his shoulders. "How are you managing?"

"The club or ...?"

I shrugged. "Both."

The heaviness of his sigh gave me an inkling. With his head still lowered, he went back behind the bar and poured us each a drink. I'm not sure I ever saw him drink before, to be honest.

He knocked the rim of his glass to mine and downed it in a go. "Victoire's been a help. She's in her dressing room, and I know she'd like to see your mug, even if it's wetter than the rain outside. Maybe you can help her pack?"

Startled, I asked where she was headed. Laurent pursed his lips as if thinking hard. "To find some money to pay the bills for the club. Something about reconciling with her father. Didn't know she had one, tell true."

Jesus wept, that was cataclysmic. I could only imagine one way in which she could do that, and it might kill her, to be honest. I was about to beg her to reconsider, but Laurent wasn't finished.

"I need your help, Fini." All at once, it was as though the life force dripped out of him, and he slouched onto his elbows. "We're not going to be able to keep the doors open for much longer. Jody had the revenues from the cabaret and the apartments in an account. Not much, but now none of the money is accessible since"—he gave me a quick glance—"you know."

Bloody hell. I did know, and hadn't even given that part of it a thought. Jody never felt safe with large amounts of cash and paid a percentage to an agency who collected the rents from the apartments above and then deposited the money into a bank account from which he drafted the cabaret's expenses. No one could get into that account aside from Jody or Charlotte. And without a body to prove his death, it could be years and years before Jody was declared dead, and if Charlotte didn't come back…well…the club wouldn't be able to survive.

Damn it all to hell. Laurent made to pour me a second drink, but I declined.

"Can you think of any place Charlotte might have gone? You had to have known her better than me."

Laurent stared into the distance before looking back at me without a lick of hope in his eyes. "I truly don't. Their mother was dead; they never knew their father. I can't believe that Charlotte would ever willingly leave Jody without a word. Something dreadful must have happened."

I shook my head trying to knock loose some sense. "My friend said that she ran off with a groom." The maids hadn't appeared to agree, so I added, "But there might have been some confusion." Especially since I didn't know if Gilbert had spoken to any of the staff on his own or relied on secondhand information. I didn't believe he would have misled me.

Not that I was currently Gilbert's biggest fan, but he had seemed very clear about that when he'd told me at the ballet.

Laurent opened his mouth and then shut it again, like he held something back. "That's what Vicky said, but it never rang true to either of us. Seems she would have brought round a beau to introduce to Jody, don't you think?"

If Charlotte had been serious about a man, it would have made sense that she'd explain about Jody and the club, but I honestly didn't know her well at all. And I didn't have the energy to think about poor Charlotte Barreau right then. "How long can you keep the club open without new money?"

"Perhaps three or four weeks."

I rubbed the bridge of my nose with my fingertip. "If I can get my hands on anything extra, I'll bring it to you, but I don't think I can. I'm so sorry. Can I help around here? Clean up, or even give you a night off? I don't want to leave you high and dry." Not that I had any idea where I'd squeeze the time from if he accepted.

"I'm keeping my head above water, but thanks. Go and speak to Vicky, won't you? She's not been herself since she told me about Jody, and this new plan has made it that much worse." Laurent pushed a brandy my way, in Victoire's special cut-glass snifter.

The stink of cigarettes and absinthe hung as heavy as the fog outside, and I blinked hard to keep my eyes from watering. I tapped on the door to her dressing room—which doubled as the storage closet.

"Fini, thank God you're here. Please, talk me out of this night-mare, can't you?" Victoire folded me into her arms and pulled me into the tight space at once.

It was claustrophobic between the rickety shelves of bottles—many fewer than the last time I'd poked my nose in. A long mirror with a top corner broken off in a jagged line leaned against the far wall. Another makeshift clothes rack like the one in Jody's flat held a few frocks Victoire wore onstage.

"Laurent said something about you going to your father. But you can't." I kept my arms around her even though it would have been awkward any other time to be in such an intimate position. But if she was as desperate for comfort as I was, we needed the human touch imbedded in such a deep friendship, now gilded in grief.

"I can't go back as myself, non. And I'd hate myself if I go back as—" Her voice broke on a sob, and I shushed her as well as I could. She wiped away a tear crawling down her cheek.

"What about your sisters? Can you ask them for help instead?"

"Catherine promised all of her pin money for the month, but it's hardly enough. Her husband controls all of their funds—even her damned dowry, the connard. And the other girls…well, I died to them the night my father found me in the stables. I can't imagine how Maman could have explained the truth to them without them all fainting into a heap." She wrinkled her nose in the faintest attempt at humor.

"Laurent says you have enough revenue on hand to remain open for a few weeks. Can you put a hold on this plan for a few days? Let me see if I can scrabble together some cash? Perhaps even Charlotte will return, and you can work something out with her?" The words tumbled out, but I had no plan to execute them. There was no cash to be scrabbled.

Again, my mind drifted to Gilbert. Would he consider being a benefactor? The idea of asking him made me want to retch. But the sight of Victoire, defeated, humbled me.

"Do you mean it, cher? Mon Dieu, that would make everything bearable. I can't even imagine actually cutting my hair and having to resuscitate that damned man who I killed that night so Victoire could be free. And scraping for my father—but I have no other choice if you can't help us. Charlotte would have come back by now, surely. She and Jody"—Victoire's voice caught and she had to clear her throat—"were as thick as thieves. Only something awful happening to her would keep her away for this long."

Filling her in with the scant details I'd found out this evening, I found myself agreeing with her. Jody must have been out of his mind with worry, and I'd done next to nothing to help him track her down. I had to put my hand on one of the shelves to keep my balance. Victoire needed me.

"I'll do my best to find that out as well. But promise me that you'll not consider going back to your father until I've exhausted all the other possibilities, won't you?"

Victoire threw her arms around my neck again and sobbed into my shoulder. "Oh, I do promise. Please, please, do everything you can. I don't think I can survive as anyone other than myself."

I promised. What else could I do? I ran the pads of my thumbs under her eyes to clear away smeared paint. "Smile, Vicky. I think I have a way to access some cash. Trust me." Even the echo of Gilbert's familiar phrase made me cringe. "Everything will be sorted. Go out and give us a song, won't you? I'm bone tired and need to sleep, but I want one song to jolly us all up."

She nodded, hope sparking in her eyes, and shooed me away.

My guts gripped with fear, but I did my best not to let it show. I made my way back to the bar and winked at Laurent as though I could fake myself into believing it would all work out.

Victoire emerged and climbed onto her stage. "A song for the hero of the night, Viscount." She strummed her guitar once and began a rather raucous song called "Fleurs and Pensées," which had the crowd engaged by the first refrain. The whiskey pooling in my belly had calmed my nerves enough to make it back home.

I blew Victoire a kiss and clapped Laurent on his shoulder. He covered one of my hands with his and squeezed.

"You look after yourself as well, eh? You're looking peaky."

Wearily, I agreed. "I'll be asleep as soon as my head touches the pillow. I just..." But there really was no need to explain.

"Wait, did your friend find you? I wouldn't give anyone any information, but he seemed amiable enough."

I paused and turned back around. "Friend? Gilbert Duhais?"

"I didn't get his name, sorry. Well-dressed. Handsome. If he comes back, I'll ask." Laurent pointed to the door as though to shoo me out. "Come back soon, but sleep, Fin. Sleep."

It must have been Gilbert—who probably had been Paul's damned lover—and he could bloody well go to hell as far as I was concerned. I almost said something to Laurent, but when I turned back, he was already talking to a patron, and the last thing I needed to do was interrupt any moneymaking for the Green Carnation.

With a final look about, I realized this was the place I'd considered home, as this was where I'd met and made a family with my friends. I'd compromise every last piece of integrity I had to keep it open. Even if it meant groveling to someone who—

I grimaced and pushed the notion away. I could ask Gilbert. For Jody's memory. For Victoire and Laurent. For me. And for all the other miserable bastards out there who weren't embraced by their blood relatives on account of which people attracted them.

23

The streets were empty from the weather. No one who didn't have to be out would be, not on a night like this.

I wished I wasn't, either.

Because I could either focus on my wet feet... or my hopelessly gnarled affairs.

I was due in de Gênet's office in just a few hours to sign the contract to allow Qualité to be built in London—a contract that would perjure me, not to speak of infuriating my father if he ever heard of it.

And there seemed no alternative but to sign. Gilbert wasn't exaggerating when he pointed out I'd likely lose my job if de Gênet pulled his investment from the tower.

I rounded a corner and ran into another body whose head was down, too. Opening my mouth to apologize, I snapped it shut again.

"Wait, Fin. I need to talk to you." Gilbert matched his stride to mine, and I kept my eyes down, watched our feet move in precision like we were marching toward a battle.

"I came to find you. You were right. I should have told you that

I was closer friends with Paul than I admitted to. But we were only friends, nothing more. And now that I know about what he did to Aurélie, it would have made sense if you had—"

"If I had *what?*"

I stopped and waited until he looked me in the eye. "He said you threatened him. Just before he died."

"*Because he fucking frightened her.* I said he needed to leave her alone after he'd already been so damned barbaric. What are you implying?"

He blinked hard, and there was a catch in his voice. "Nothing. I know you. You're a good man, and you would have been well within your rights if you had done more than threaten him."

The wind was knocked from my belly, and my voice dropped a few octaves in shock. "You thought I was the one who slit his fucking throat? I carry a bloody knife because we live in a city full of pickpockets, not because I'm a killer."

"No one ever caught his murderer. It made sense." He bit his bottom lip hard enough to draw blood. "Before I got to know you." He touched my arm, and I stepped back a few paces. "Mon Dieu, I don't mean to offend you. I should have kept my mouth shut."

"You should have, and you did. Now, go away." I shook my head, rain cascading down from the rim of my hat, and continued even faster.

But he kept up with me fine. "I can't. I need to know what I can do to fix this."

It was unfixable.

The bottoms of my trousers were heavy with water, but I

dodged a puddle that ran over the pavement to carry the silty debris of the road away. I crossed the street. "Go home, Gilbert."

"But I want to go home with you, mon vilain."

I stopped and cracked my knuckles. "I'm not your naughty boy. I'm not *your* anything. Just go. Please."

I turned into an alley that provided some coverage from the terraces that flocked the wall so I could slow down before I had apoplexy.

Gilbert was a step behind me. "I've got you in my blood, Fin. I can't be without you. Not now. Maybe not ever."

The walls were grimy with years of mildew and coal. This part of the city hadn't been revamped, though a tarpaulin covering what looked to be a stack of metal barrels hinted that perhaps this neighborhood, too, might end up more pristine. A cat wound itself around my ankle so I almost stumbled. *Ignore him. He doesn't mean it.*

"Please talk to me." His words were clear, round with emotion. "Tell me what I can do to make you believe me."

"I honestly don't have the energy to deal with this conversation on top of everything else. The Carnation doesn't have money to remain open. Victoire is planning to do the unthinkable to beg for some funds from her father. Charlotte went missing, and Jody was bloody murdered. I can't—" My voice broke, and he cupped my face.

"I'll fix it. I know I can't fix everything, and I'm sorrier than I can express, mon beau, but I'll do what I can for the living. I just need you to sign this paper for Michel. It's more important than any of the rest of it. And then you never need to speak to him again."

I fought to breathe. Clenching my hands in fists to keep from touching him, I stepped backward.

"This is the last thing, and I promise, it won't get you into trouble with your father. Not at all. I'll explain it all afterward, but please, just trust me." A drop of rain clung to Gilbert's lashes. It was near impossible not to brush it away

"That isn't even all of it—just the things that are the most horrible. Even if I could understand why you've spun all your fairy stories about my father wanting me to be his heir—" Words caught in my throat, but I forced them out. "I can't watch you marry Stéphanie and pretend you're having an affair with Aurélie." I couldn't. Wouldn't. Not even to keep him.

"Please, you must understand—I must marry Stéphanie; I've sworn to her that I would. As it is, she depends on Michel for everything, which is intolerable for a woman like her. I need to help her rid herself of those shackles."

His body leaned toward me, chest almost touching. "When Michel dies, everything will come to me and my family. But mostly to me. And it was her mother's money that paid for so much of Qualité—it's the only way I can get it back to her. But she knows who I am, knows that it will never be a true marriage. You've seen her with Romu—she's not expecting anything from me other than partnership in this plan. She'd marry him tomorrow if he had any money, but he's a bank clerk, and she only has access to her mother's money if we marry. So, I can't change that, but I'd do anything else you want so I can be in your life. I can't live without you. Please tell me we can be with each other."

That was a true temptation in every sense of the word. In the world as it was, there wasn't a way for us to be open about who we were. Any hint of scandal and the people whom I'd convinced to invest in the tower would withdraw. I'd undoubtedly lose my career. Michel would be merciless in his revenge, I was sure of it. To say nothing of Gilbert's family; the store. His whole life. He would lose all of it.

And my own emotions were too wound up in him to even ask him to be such a fool. I needed to save us both.

Before I could speak, destroy his dreams and—*Jesus wept, my dreams, too*—he slid his hands up the back of my skull, tipping my hat forward. His lips crushed against mine, teased my mouth open and kissed me until I caught fire. Even the dark, soggy night couldn't hold back the flames that engulfed my body. My arms curled around his neck, his hips jutted toward mine with a force that nearly bowled me over.

"I need you," he repeated over and over, and walked me to the wall, pressed my back to it, and slid to his knees and dragged my pants open, exposing me. "Please tell me I can."

All my principles fled, and I nodded, not even daring to breathe. My fingertips scratched at the rough bricks underneath until I found his hair and raked across his skull.

"We shouldn't," I whispered, praying he'd ignore me and let me find the release I'd sell my soul for.

The scent of pipe tobacco assaulted my senses—it was a specific scent I knew: Astley's. The same as my father smoked. Followed by a shout that woke me back up to the filthy alley around me. Gilbert was yanked back, a hideous crack against the pavement.

Yanking up my trousers with one hand, I blocked a punch aimed for my jaw and curled my body around my internal organs to take stock of the situation. A single man smoking a pipe, not particularly big—or intelligent, since we were two against him.

Yet he had the element of surprise, and as Gilbert wasn't on his feet, it only took a few strong kicks to keep him on the ground. I reached for the damned knife in my pocket and held it to his throat.

A trickle of hot blood ran over my hand from where the knife scratched across his skin. He gasped, fluttered in my arms.

And then in a familiar—very British—voice, he snarled, "You don't have the bloody ballocks to slit my throat, Viscount Carleton."

Shocked, I drew in a breath, and my tight hold slackened just enough that bloody Sonny Tolbert was able to twist out of my grasp. He stood just out of reach, face wrinkled in disgust. "De Gênet was right, after all."

Gilbert made a gurgling noise that sliced my heart open. I lunged at Sonny, not caring if the connard died and I was hanged for it. He was quicker and elbowed me in the back after I fell forward, missing him. But this time I was outraged and twisted, holding him from behind around the waist with one arm, the other cinched around his neck.

"What did you mean by that?" I didn't release the scrubby piece of shit, but my attention dropped to Gilbert, curled in the fetal position. "Are you in pain, Gilbert?" Sonny was going to die right there if Gilbert didn't get up, and quickly.

Rolling himself to his knees, Gilbert spat blood. I knew it even if it was too dark to see. Enraged, I used my elbow again to drop Sonny to his knees. "You powerfully underestimated my anger against low-life bigots." I kicked him for good measure and knelt next to Gilbert.

"Can you stand?"

Gilbert lifted his head and nodded. "Catching my breath." He looked into my face, wincing, but he managed to get back to his feet and hovered over Sonny.

"Unnatural inverts," sneered the shit from the ground.

"You never know when to quit." Gilbert kicked his heel into Sonny's temple, but not hard enough to knock him unconscious. "I could kill you right now."

"But you won't, you bloody poof. You don't have it in you, neither of you." Sonny stood, too, shaking his head in pain, but he was calmer than I'd have believed. "What will Michel do when I confirm his suspicions?" He turned faster than he ought to've been able and punched Gilbert in his stomach. "Will he have you killed like your fairy friend with the bar?"

Jody.

Without thinking, my fist thrust again, this time knocking Sonny into whatever was hidden under the tarpaulin. He landed with a heavy expulsion of air, his head lolling to the side.

Sonny was knocked out, giving me a moment to look over Gilbert as well as I could in the damnable rain. How hurt was he? What would I do if he was seriously injured? Hot tears burned the back of my eyes. Damn it, I didn't cry over lovers.

But Gilbert was more than that.

He was everything.

I put my hands under his arms and helped him stagger to his feet. He held steady, crumpled, but not broken. At least, I didn't think so. I dropped to my knees next to Sonny. His pulse was faint. Fucking hell—what would we do about him? What if he turned this around and had us arrested?

Still, the thought of killing him in cold blood—now that he was vulnerable—was unthinkable. Repugnant.

Then Jody's dead body flashed through my mind.

I pushed the stack of barrels hidden under the tarpaulin to hide Sonny's form. If one wounded him further, it wasn't necessarily my fault.

24

I carried Gilbert on my back to the street where I might be able to hail a cab, even in the rain. He couldn't walk. But he could stand, leaning heavily on me. We were in one of those pockets of Parisian slum in between where the beautiful people lived. A sampling of Hell between the Rue de Richelieu and Avenue de l'Opéra. Five-storied buildings crammed together holding a larger population than some entire cities.

A cab pulled aside—possibly due to the fact that our clothes stood out in this neighborhood—but the driver drew back when he saw it was two men with their arms around each other. I held my hand for him to stay put.

"Can you bear to stand alone for a moment?" My whisper was low enough for Gilbert's ears alone.

He could. Thank God, because we were fleeing from a crime scene and needed as much distance as possible between us and Sonny in case some sergent de ville arrived.

Giving my most bland smile, I explained that my friend was too drunk to walk home. The driver looked uncertain. His nose twitched at the smell of imagined beer emanating from Gilbert.

And then I held out the largest coin in my pocket, which did the trick.

"If he heaves, you'll clean it up."

I ignored that and helped Gilbert ease inside, whilst asking for his address, assuming—correctly—that his was closer. I blinked at the upscale address in the seventh arrondissement, but the driver merely looked relieved. I climbed in next to Gilbert and clicked the door shut behind me.

"Are you sure you aren't interested in a life of crime, mon beau? I think you'd adapt quickly." Rain from the window reflected a pattern of tracks down Gilbert's skin. His eyelids were shut, his breathing shallow.

Pressing his hand to my lips, I took that as a sign that he wasn't in any real danger. But a kick to his kidney or a broken rib could be bad enough. I'd waste no time figuring out his condition inside his home.

Regardless of the rain, the seventh was wide awake. The array of umbrellas was like some school of dark fish winding next to the Tuileries gardens, over the Pont Royal to the Rive Gauche. I didn't lose sight of the Seine as we rolled over the Quai Voltaire to the d'Orsay, turning finally to where Gilbert lived on the Rue de l'Université.

I covered my gaping mouth like a damned yokel when we arrived at a fabulous Haussmann building, its sandstone exterior clean despite the city's smog. Around the windows of the first five stories were intricate botanical friezes. The mansard roof over the top floor was still lit up, though most of the others were dark. Servants didn't keep the same hours as their employers, after all.

Gilbert exhaled a small groan, so I asked, "How many flights up? Is there a lift?"

"There is, but I'm on the première."

Any other time, that would have provoked a smile. *Of course Gilbert lived in the most sought after flat.*

"I believe I can make it, though. There's money in my pocket," he whispered, his voice scratchy. "Take it to pay."

Bristling, I ignored him. I might not have as much money as he did—which was an understatement I ignored for the time being—but I was flush enough to pay for a cab.

The driver was pleased enough with the money I gave him that he was willing to help me carry Gilbert up the single flight of stairs. A slim envelope was wedged in between the door and its frame, falling as Gilbert turned the lock. I reached for it and glanced at the name scribbled across the front. It was mine. I inhaled sharply, and then realized it was the papers from de Gênet.

"Shall I wait to take you back?" asked the cabbie, singing a new tune once he saw the door open into Gilbert's palace-like apartment. If I wasn't so anxious, I'd be gaping as well.

Clapping the man on his shoulder with a put-on smile, I said I'd sleep on the couch, but gave an extra tip.

I found the light switch and blinked.

To say Gilbert's life was different from mine was like saying a goldfish was unlike a racehorse.

"Can you stand all right?" I tossed the envelope onto a side table.

"I can. But in the kitchen, there's laudanum. I might need it soon." In the glow of the electric lights, he was much too pale.

In general, I was not a proponent of the stuff. I had seen too many people with addictions to desensitize their suffering. But

Gilbert needed it. Bypassing the dark leather Chesterfield sofas and matching club chairs nestled around a marble fireplace in the salon, I found a tidy kitchen, small but well stocked. Behind the sugar canister sat a green bottle, the stopper so far wedged down it was like it'd never been opened.

After using my teeth to drag the tight rubber out, I found a spoon and hurried back.

"Open your mouth," I said, ready to pour.

"Am I in decent enough shape to open my mouth for you?" He ran a finger across the top of my hand. "You're such a tease, mon vilain. But let me try to move before I take it, hmm? Now that we're here, I'm not sure I'm ready to fall asleep yet."

The knots in my stomach were less tangled. I rubbed the back of my neck. I took stock of him. He had blood dried around his right ear and in the corner of his mouth. A kick there, then. But his jaw wasn't broken.

"Which way is your bedroom?" There were four doors off the hallway, not counting the kitchen.

"I need to clean myself." He scratched his face and saw the blood under his nails and winced. "Frightful, hmm? At the end is a washroom."

Yes. I prayed he wouldn't piss blood—I'd insist on a physician if he did, no matter what he said, because I couldn't allow him to risk himself.

"Let me try on my own. Test it out." The first step was stiff, and I could see his right hip hurt, but he was looser on the second. I exhaled for the first time in a half hour.

Bypassing him, I flicked the light on in the washroom and blinked. White and black tile on the floor and walls, large mirror over a pedestal sink, and holy of holies: a permanently fixed bath-tub connected to water pipes.

Wouldn't Aurélie be jealous—to say nothing of Mademoiselle Jeunesse, whose job it was to bring buckets of water up to our flat.

Gilbert turned the taps, and a small waterfall poured out, as if it was magic.

I held my hand in it, marveling so much I forgot myself. But the water ran down the inside of my sleeve, and I shook it, tickled enough that it woke me up. I turned back to him with a grin, and his eyes were soft. "Help me take my clothes off?"

Even battered he was beautiful. The room was hazy with steam by the time I had him undressed. There was a large purple bruise on Gilbert's right flank, from above his hip bone halfway down his thigh. How dare Sonny bloody Tolbert hurt this man?

He cupped my cheek. "Take off your clothes, Fin." His eyes darted to the bathtub, which might be just wide enough for both of us to stand next to each other. "So I don't slip and fall."

My own clothes were off in record time.

Gilbert held on to my hand and stepped onto the porcelain glazed with a border of black scrollwork, a mix of elegance and masculinity that suited him perfectly. I stepped in behind, pray-ing I wouldn't slip and add to his body's trauma.

There was a thin hose of rubber that fit on the spout on one end with a perforated paddle on the other. He attached it easily, and I gasped again as a spray shot out.

"Help me, mon beau. I can feel there is blood matted in my hair, but I must hold the wall as I'm rather dizzy."

I held the spray over his head, which made short work of the blood I'd missed, hidden by his thick, black hair. It ran in pink rivers down his cheek until it washed clear. There was a hook on a tall copper shaft that held the sprayer, so it rained over us. *Bliss.*

He pulled me closer, so the water hit my face. Bizarre sensation, unlike a bath, or a bucket over my head, or even rain in the summer. The water was much warmer, softer, steadier. I'd stand here all night if Gilbert could remain on his feet.

I curled one arm around his waist—the side without bruises—and stood so close the water pooled in the air pockets between our chests. I'm not sure if my mouth found his, or if his found mine, but a moment later, we were lost in each other. The water beat down on our faces, keeping my eyelids shut.

He sucked my tongue, my lips, nipped at my neck so I had to press against the wall to keep from sliding into oblivion and taking him down with me. The tiles were warm against my skin. I wanted to stretch in the glory of all the sensations, like a cat in a patch of sunshine.

And then he stepped back, and my eyes cracked back open.

"Does it hurt too much?"

Droplets of water trailed down his cheeks, flushed from the heat, or maybe from me. Beautiful, whatever the reason. I could drown in those dark eyes that held steady on mine. Not breaking the connection, he lifted my hand to his mouth, traced his tongue across my knuckles.

His mouth curved into his delicious, lopsided smile. "I knew you had feelings for me, too."

The words and the tenderness and the fucking glorious look in his eyes worked with the hot water to melt the last remnants of ice around my heart, and I nodded.

25

Now that the nightmare was over and I was allowed to think, I squeezed my eyes shut to keep back hot tears. "We need to talk about this. I thought Sonny was going to kill you."

"You saved my life." He blinked, the rims of his eyes reddening, too.

"I wouldn't let you die."

"Mon Dieu, you saved me. What a hero. I didn't think you had that in you."

I held a hand up. "I can't think about what I did. Let's leave it, please." Things would be so much easier if Sonny were dead. Yet I didn't want that on my conscience.

Gilbert searched my face and finally gave a short nod. "I refuse to put any blame on you. What that scoundrel has done, was going to do to us…"

"Gilbert, what did he mean about Michel?"

He wiped his eyes. "I'm a bit woozy. I'm going to get out, but you can stay in here as long as—"

I knew he was not answering on purpose, but he was horribly

pale and probably needed to be out of the slippery shower. "Like hell am I letting you out of my sight." I turned to mess with the taps. "I assume Michel knows about us? Is that why the papers are here? I need you to tell me the truth because it's better for me to be prepared before he blabs about my personal life to Eiffel. I could lose my job and—"

"Non, he's just...suspicious." Gilbert directed me to a small cupboard warmed by a small furnace. It was stocked with fluffy, warm towels, and I dried him off so he wouldn't overexert himself. "Michel never runs his own errands, d'accord? I suppose Sonny left this here a few hours back." Gilbert frowned at the wall. "Perhaps he saw me leave, and followed me?"

"Well, if Sonny manages to get back to Michel, his suspicions will be confirmed. What do you think he'll do?" He looked down while I went to my knees, wiping down each of his legs.

"I don't think Sonny will be able to tell him. You do realize he's probably dead?"

I exhaled. "Good," I answered with vehemence I didn't realize I'd be able to muster. Sonny had admitted to killing Jody. And he'd have killed Gilbert if I hadn't stopped him.

His fingers twisted some of my hair. "You're taking such good care of me, Fin. I don't deserve you at all. If you knew about me, you'd leave."

"What I know is you've helped me. With the investors for the tower, with Aurélie. With Jody." I stood back up and dried my own body, much more quickly and with less attention. My emotions were too much, too heavy. It had been one of the most intense evenings of my life. I put the towel to my face to hide and catch myself.

But he pulled it away. "I'll end things with Stéphanie tomorrow, if you need me to. I can figure out another way to split my inheritance with her."

I wished that was an option, but if it was, I couldn't see how, despite my words in the alley. Gently, I said, "You can't do that. Michel mustn't know about us, not for sure. You do need to keep in his good graces, and God knows he could ruin me."

His lips settled into an obstinate line. "Non. I won't let him hurt you, and I'm tired of him dictating my life. We deserve to be together." He sighed as though knowing his arguments were not plausible and took my hand and led me from the humid steaminess. The cooler air in the hall made it easier to breathe. To think.

"I'm bored to tears going over accounts at Qualité." The excitement in his voice was catchy. "Écoutez, I can work for a newspaper like I always dreamed about, and move in with you and Aurélie."

In his bedroom, an enormous iron bed was heaped with pillows and a white starched duvet. It smelled like spring, even in December. As crisp and clean and beautiful as Gilbert.

"We can't." I wrung my fingers together, not sure how to say what needed to be said. "You know we can't." I wished I was wrong, but I wasn't, and there was no use pretending. "And you'd resent me soon even if it was a possibility—and it isn't."

He pulled down the covers and dropped his towel, gesturing to me with a crooked finger. I rubbed my lips together, scared to even dream of such a thing. Not tonight. Not after that beating.

I swallowed. There was too much at stake to get swept up in the wake of my feelings. "Even if I allowed you to make that sort of sacrifice, I can't risk the tower not being built. Living together would cause such a scandal that it would ruin everything for Eiffel. Too many people are counting on this tower for me to snatch it away for my convenience."

"Are you telling me that we can't be together at all? Because I refuse to accept that, mon beau." There was fire in his eyes.

Could I take the chance? I'd lost my life once before and rebuilt it. It was possible to do, painful as it might be. I'd been searching for him for thirty-one years.

"We'll find a way. Just not yet."

I slid next to him, luxuriating in the quality of the fabric, the heat rising from his steamed skin. Dipping my mouth, I kissed his bruises as delicately as I could until I'd touched each of them, as though I could somehow heal them through sheer willpower, and then I took him into my arms. We lay like that until I drifted to sleep, only waking when I felt him slide back under the covers.

"Are you all right?" I berated myself for dozing off.

"I took the laudanum. Will it make me spill all my secrets?" It was the first time his voice was anything but confident. But it must have been the poppy syrup mixed with the beating that left him so vulnerable.

Soothingly, I said, "If you do, I won't listen, how's that?"

He lowered himself back into my arms. "There are so many things I need to tell you, mon beau. But I'm frightened you'll run away and leave me, and I can't bear it." Gilbert held my hand, ear against my chest, his voice drowsier by the second.

"I promise I'm not leaving." How could I? I had to keep an eye on all those that I loved.

Halfway between sleep and wakefulness, he pressed his lips to my cheek. "You do care for me, don't you?"

I could combust with the intensity of it, and said so.

"Then my plan worked."

And in the cavern of my subconscious I wondered what he meant.

26

A thunderstorm beat sheets of rain against the bedroom, making me dream that I was tossed overboard from a ship, doing my best to get back on. But it was useless, and the waves crashed over me in such succession that I was losing my will to breathe.

"Fin, are you all right?" Gilbert patted my shoulder and rescued me from the horrors of drowning.

Clutching his hand, I opened my eyes. He sat on his side looming over me, eyes wrinkling with concern. "Another nightmare?"

Another?

"You thrash in your sleep a lot, mon beau. But you don't need to. I'm here." He rubbed his hand through his hair, adorably sticking up in the back. He made a circle with his neck, tried to move his shoulder, which was swollen and purple, cringing.

I asked again if he needed a physician, but he waved away my concern. "It would lead to so many questions like you said, hmm?" His hand snaked under the covers but with self-control that was usually dormant around him, I unhooked his fingers.

"We can't for now, and I'm sorry." I sat up and put my feet

firmly on the floor. "Eiffel's holding a meeting this morning about the comtesse's lawsuit. I've got to go into the office."

The tower. And the investments.

I looked at the dainty porcelain clock next to his bed and groaned. I'd missed the meeting.

And then a flood of relief; I had completed Eiffel's task. De Gênet was going to support the tower, which would be a bigger story than the Comtesse de Poix making claims over unknown dangers, so no one would be upset if I waltzed into work late.

Except...*shite*. I sat up, unruffled my own hair. Jesus wept, de Gênet honoring his pledge depended on something I could never distance myself from. I got up, wishing to get home to change, to have time to think clearly.

To not be under Gilbert's spell long enough to be rational.

I explained that to Gilbert again, the crease between his eyes deepening with each statement. "You can't go back home, I won't let you. Not without me. It's not safe until I find out for certain what's happened to Sonny. Ensure that he isn't able to tell tales."

The light of morning brought home to me how difficult this would be on the most basic level. In my professional life, no one ever asked me point blank if I was a pédéraste. A tapette. An invert. All the wretched words society used to strip men like me of our humanity. I was sure there were questions—I was the only unmarried man my age at the firm. I had a decent salary and was told often enough that I was handsome.

But though I'd often skirted the truth, I'd never had to blatantly lie. And any sort of future with Gilbert might make me do that.

He got up and stretched. Even before my heart was engaged, I adored looking at his body. Except those purple bruises haunted me. What if I hadn't had a knife? Would we have ended up like Jody?

A heartbeat later, I was up and had him in my arms, terrified that something might happen to him today when I wasn't there to protect him. But he rolled his eyes.

"You know Sonny only managed because I was occupied, d'accord? Otherwise he'd never have been a match for me. I'm usually quite adept at protecting myself."

How many times had he been in a physical altercation with the man before? I thought back to the bruises and scratches Gilbert had borne multiple times. "What if he's already gone to Michel?"

"Fin, do you truly think my uncle will soil his damned reputation by having me publicized as a pédé?" He rolled his eyes. "Michel can't disinherit me; the law doesn't allow for that, no matter what. And how does he have a way to tie you to a scene in an alley where the upstanding Viscount Carleton has no business being seen? Why would anyone trust Sonny over you and me, or Michel if it came down to it?"

I took a sharp inhale, exhaling much more slowly. Yes, that made some sense, but even the hint of scandal—

Gilbert put his finger to my lips before I even asked the question. "Mon vilain, you aren't—what did you call yourself—a mid-level employee of Eiffel's ironworks. You're now a senior partner, the heir to an earldom, and personal friends with half of Tout-Paris." His eyes went to the side as though struck by inspiration. "Do you know, if Sonny even dares to tell Michel, he'd probably have him...um...taken care of."

I didn't regret anything I'd done to Sonny, but I also didn't wish to think about it. "I'll go home and find new clothes to put on. I just need to clear my head."

His voice rose an octave. "First, I must insist that you sign those documents so that Michel can build his new Qualité in London."

I dropped my head into my hands. "It's criminal. Can't you see? Everything I've done since we met has been morally dubious, but until last night, it skirted illegality."

He pounded a fist in his hand. "Last night was self-defense. Sonny was the one committing a crime, and I won't have you blaming yourself."

I held up my hand to stop him, and continued, as calmly as I could. "If I think rationally, everything I've done in my father's name has been small enough that it's unlikely he'd have me charged and cause a scandal. But this is forgery. It's horrible enough that he *would* have me in the dock. I simply can't."

Gilbert inhaled as though ready to list the litany of reasons why I was incorrect, but exhaled and sat next to me. He took my hand in his and brought my knuckles against his lips. "I know it's difficult to do so after all that's happened, but I must insist. *Your father will never know.* He's bedridden and possibly even dead already. You have my word that you will be his heir. It's all been taken care of."

Ripping my hand away, I stood. I stomped to the balcony, raking through my hair in agitation. "How can you be so damned sure? What piece of the puzzle aren't you telling me?"

He stood, too, walking toward me, arms open, but I turned, unwilling to be lulled back into ignorant tranquility.

"I'll tell you everything, once I've gotten this all cleared up. Once Michel has his store deal finalized. Just trust me, I beg you. I need to get the papers to Michel so he can catch his train. Not following through isn't something he'll forgive either of us for, and believe me that he's a much bigger threat than Sonny."

His bruises were punctuated by the paleness of his blanched skin, and hating myself, I gave in. One last time. I allowed him to lead me to his desk where the papers were waiting and took the ink pen and signed my name.

"Damn it, add Carleton to the end, Fin. It won't work unless you do."

We glared at each other for a full ten seconds before I did his bidding, leaving a splatter next to the surname I was unused to.

"I'm going to take them to Michel at once." His shoulders relaxed as though he'd gotten rid of a tremendous weight, and his entire face lit up. He kissed the papers with a dramatic flourish.

"Are you strong enough to do it? I can take them. I need to know what he'll do to make his show of strength in Eiffel's favor. You ought to be in bed."

"I'm feeling much better, just sore. And frankly, I'm going to nip any threat of Sonny in the bud and tell Michel that the fils de pute attacked me, and he doesn't need to know that you were there at all."

"And you can swear that Michel will come through on the other part—the entire reason I'm doing this?" I needed to placate Eiffel's very real concerns.

"Open the front door and bring the newspaper to me. It will all make sense."

I did so, unrolling it as I walked back in the room. Across the front page was a sketch of Michel de Gênet, and the headline a quote: "Eiffel's tower will herald Paris's entry into the modern era."

Stunned, I looked askance of Gilbert, who smiled benignly. "I sent it in yesterday. Now you see why I must get these papers to Michel at once? He's probably pacing his office like a caged tiger because I did this without telling him."

I had no words.

Gilbert was already dressing, pulling clean clothes out of his enormous closet, moving gingerly. "I told you I'd get everything sorted."

Except my friend was still dead, and his sister was still missing.

I worried my pinky nail in between my teeth, deciding the most politic way to ask. "Was there really no clue left behind of where Charlotte might have run off to?"

Gilbert turned away to straighten his cravat.

"I honestly don't have any idea. But Paris is so large, it's easy for someone to hide if they don't wish to be found." He lifted his bruised mouth to mine. "Kiss me, Fin."

I did what he asked, relieved that he was as mobile as he was after the beating.

"And smile because I'll go to my bank and get some cash for Laurent and Victoire, hmm? It'll be a pleasure to use Michel's money for something he'd hate." He pinched my cheek. "I'm sure your Monsieur Eiffel will have seen the headlines, so you should go and bask in his thanks." Gilbert turned to the mirror over the mantel and ran his fingers through his hair.

"I'll catch up with Eiffel. I've risked everything on this deal with your bloody uncle; I might as well have my glory."

"I promise it will all be fine."

This time it was me who was unable to resist, and I spun him around, crushing our lips together. When I finally let go, his eyes fluttered open, and he ran his tongue over his bottom lip.

"And tonight, you'll explain?"

He nodded. He looked at me for a long moment, and if we weren't both in a rush, we'd be tumbling to the floor.

"There's money in a desk drawer; grab some for your own taxis today. Buy champagne. The best. I'll meet you back here for supper, just the two of us. And I'll make you follow through on that look you just gave me, hmm?"

I did my best to glare. "I don't need your damned—"

Gilbert's hand wrapped around the front doorknob, and he gave me a cheeky grin. "It's all on Michel, Fin. Save your own money for the club, or for Aurélie, or for you to merely enjoy your life. Let's milk Michel as much as we can, for as long as we can."

I nodded, even though his back was turned.

After a moment, I grabbed the newspaper and headed to the kitchen to enjoy reading it while drinking another cup of tea.

27

Now that I'd seen the article quoting de Gênet, I knew that my absence from work wouldn't be a problem. Eiffel would be deliriously happy, and I could take my victory lap. I had to stop agonizing over what I'd done by signing that name, because Gilbert was correct. It was done.

I took another opportunity to bathe in that glorious washroom and borrowed one of Gilbert's laundered shirts. Mine had some splashes of blood—whether Gilbert's or Sonny's I didn't know—and even the idea of putting it against my clean skin was repellent. Gilbert's were a size too small, but it would be unnoticeable under my blazer and tie.

His wardrobe was as neatly organized as I would have imagined. Starched shirts and impeccably tailored blazers, with at least fifteen hatboxes neatly stacked...aside from one sitting on the floor with the lid askew. How many varieties of hat could he have? I bent to lift the orphaned box from the floor, and the unbalanced lid slipped. I attempted to catch it with my hand, and accidentally tipped the contents onto the floor.

There wasn't a hat inside. It was a slew of news clippings and other papers. And a photo.

A card stock photograph, with the date 1867 scrawled across the back. I flipped it over. Two children, wide-eyed and somber, stared back at me: a boy around twelve years of age and his sister. Anyone would know because of how much they looked like each other.

Only Annabeth had a dimple when she smiled.

My chest caved in, and I sat on an upholstered chair, staring. I hadn't seen Annabeth's face since she'd died. I'd left my pictures behind at Aunt Glad's, including this one. But the writing on the back was my own.

How was it here? In Gilbert's apartment?

I must have stared at the picture for five minutes. Annabeth was even prettier than I remembered, and there was nothing that resembled Aurélie when I met her, even though I was sure all this time that there was, because that was the age Aurélie was when I found her.

Tears dripped down my nose, and I rubbed them off with my inner elbow. Every spring, my sister and I were taken to the photography studio, brushed and dressed and forced to stand still until the interminable length of time it took to take the pictures was over and we could breathe again. I'd had a box of them, one for each year until I came to France.

I hadn't posed for a photo since.

And it was only ever the two of us. I was nearly grown before it was clear that our father wanted it, paid for it. I should have known that Aunt Glad had no reason to want them. She despised seeing us on a normal day, didn't need anything extra.

Had my father given it to Gilbert? It would be within the

bounds of reason. Especially if…well…if he had hopes of reconciling with me.

But why wouldn't Gilbert have given it to me? It made no sense, especially after I'd admitted to him that I'd left everything behind in my mad escape from Goole after they pulled up Annabeth's body.

I finally dragged myself out of my stupor and retrieved the scattered pieces from the hatbox. I sat on the edge of the bed, shaking inside.

A small news clipping. In French. *The body of a man estimated between 20 and 30 years of age was found with a slit throat at les Bains de la Samaritaine near Pont Neuf in the 1er arrondissement.* Details on which precinct to take any information leading to an arrest of the perpetrator.

I was surprised a soulless connard like Paul had warranted a half inch in the paper, but he had. And Gilbert had saved it. An unbidden choking noise rattled in my throat. I let the paper drift to the floor and kicked at it with the toe of my shoe, anxious to get it away from me.

There was a larger piece of newsprint, this time in English with a well-rendered sketch that could be me twenty years into the future.

An obituary for my father dated from October 28. Miles Carleton, the Thirteenth Earl of Rawcliffe, was dead. *A month ago.* I read with shaking hands, too numb to even feel anything, not gratitude that he was gone, or any sort of happiness. *Well, I suppose he won't ever have that chance to beg for my forgiveness, after all.*

I wasn't mentioned in the obituary—though I hadn't expected to be, even if half of the British peerage must have been listed as family members. *Couldn't taint the luster of their names by adding his bastard son.*

He was dead and Gilbert had the proof. *He hadn't told me—just asked me to believe him. Why? He could have calmed my nerves fifty times in the past few days by showing me this.*

But he hadn't.

I scanned it again, because perhaps I'd missed some mistake. No. But there was an intriguing line at the bottom, almost as though an afterthought: *Rawcliffe's heir is still unsettled.* In all these months of pretending to be the viscount, it hadn't crossed my mind that there was another heir, but of course there would be. Like the royal family, the Carletons probably had the earldom's succession mapped out for twenty places.

I set it aside, questions—again—about why Gilbert had kept this from me chasing each other through my brain. I walked to the front door of the flat and looked out, wondering if Gilbert might be there and this was some sort of terribly unfunny joke.

I lit a cigarette, staring at the face of my sister, drinking her in and wishing to hell I had a chance to talk to her once more. Because I was utterly lost.

And I was angrier by the minute. What the hell was Gilbert up to?

He'd come to apologize last night. That's what he'd been doing when he searched me out. I hadn't given enough thought to why it could have been so important.

Michel had said…what? That Paul and Gilbert had been friends. With that sly implication, just before Sonny found us. Michel must have sent Sonny. To hurt us, or to scare us?

Jesus wept. Nothing made sense.

I went back to the bedroom and tore through the rest of the contents that had been secreted in the hatbox.

There was a slender leather case with a faded ribbon gummed to the top. I flicked open the clasp and pulled out a note, yellowed along the edges.

Dear Selena,

I suppose I'm being foolish but I'm haunted by worries that something will happen to me. Miles promises that Finny and the new baby will always be looked after, but with all the secrecy, I want to know that no one can ever rob my children of their birthright. Please keep this for safekeeping until the baby is born. We can share a laugh over my foolishness.

Affectionately, your Annie.

Why? How? This was my mother's writing. I'd never seen it before and read it two more times before a tear dripped and blurred the word *secrecy*. I wiped it with the cuff of my shirt. She'd called me Finny. I wish I'd remembered that in the lonely days of my youth.

The note was laid on top of a folded parchment. I smoothed it out. I nearly choked and made a noise from the pit of my soul.

A marriage certificate. *April 1855. Adlingfleet Church. Goole parish, West Riding, Yorkshire. Miles Carleton and Ann Elizabeth Tighe. Witnessed by Peter Montgomery and Selena Tighe.*

My sob startled me.

Paul must have had this, as Selena was his mother, but why hadn't he given it to me when I'd taken him and Aurélie in?

From the hall, a clock chimed that it was nine o'clock. Gilbert wouldn't be back for ages to answer any of my questions. Would he answer them?

Did I even want to know how he could explain any of this, when he'd been hiding so many secrets?

I picked up the paper that had fluttered to the floor and read it again, desperate for some sensible answer.

I wasn't born until July that year, nearly three months after. My world stood on its head, and I dropped the paper again. I pressed my back to the wall and looked at the certificate like it was a viper poised to kill me.

This was a dream. *A nightmare.* I rubbed my hand through my hair to wake up.

There, on the floor, was a paper that said I was the legitimate heir of the Earl of Rawcliffe after all. I would be considered the legal heir, even if my father hadn't claimed me before he died. Not now that I had verification that they were legally married before I was born.

Dear Lord. *He was dead.* Which meant I was the bloody Earl of Rawcliffe. I reread the obituary, focused on the line about there being some question over who the heir was.

It was me. And Gilbert had proof.

There had to be some sort of equation that made all of these disparate pieces make sense. *Please.* I prayed to a higher power that I didn't even believe in.

Because if there was no reasonable explanation, it meant

Gilbert was some kind of monster for keeping this from me. Why would he have done that?

And yet here was a stash of secrets that could have changed my life for the better at any moment since I'd met Gilbert in September.

God in heaven. I rubbed a fingertip over the seal on the marriage certificate. It and the parchment felt real, and the creases and slightly battered condition might be authentic. It didn't look like a forgery, as if I'd know the difference.

If this certificate was real, *I wasn't the illegitimate son, was I?* And Gilbert knew. Knew and didn't tell me. He'd just implied over and over that he knew something that he was unwilling to share. The betrayal would have killed me if I wasn't so numb.

Adding up the pieces, my mother's note to Selena made sense. She'd had a feeling before Annabeth was born that my father would leave us behind like rubbish, and she must have hoped Selena would make sure it didn't happen.

This paper would have changed the course of my entire life. *And Annabeth's.* She'd still be alive if we'd known this. She could have married and had children and been as happy as she deserved.

All of the venom that Aunt Glad—that the entire town of Goole—had toward us for being born in the shame of illegitimacy was *a lie*. I slid down the wall and closed my eyes.

And then I cried like Annabeth died all over again. If there was a chance that this was real, it was inexplicable that they'd do this to us—keep it a secret. We'd only been children. We hadn't made any mistakes except have the wrong parents to be born to. I was on the floor, scraping the parquet with my fingers until they were raw.

Until I was so empty, I'd never feel anything again.

Gilbert had this all along.

He had insisted over and over that I was within my rights to claim Harry's title, but I'd never really believed it was possible. And all the while…? *Harry was the one who'd no legal right to be called my father's heir.* I stood abruptly, back to the wardrobe and the hatbox. Inside was an opened envelope and another photograph, its corner tucked into the edge of the banding. I unstuck it with my fingernail.

It was another professional photograph, the sort that married couples might take on their wedding day.

I'd hoped to never see the face of my arsehole of a cousin again.

Blinking, I shook my head because it also made no sense. Gilbert looked much younger, though it couldn't have been so many years ago. With Paul. They were sitting at a photography studio, side by side, so close their legs touched, Paul's arm draped around Gilbert's. Without thinking, I threw it toward the wall, and it fluttered to the ground. I yanked it back up.

On the reverse side were the words *You own my heart, always. Gilbert.*

Over and over, he'd insisted they'd merely been friends, and I'd so desperately wanted to believe that, I went along with the lie.

Disgust overwhelmed me, and I ran down the hall to the commode. I stood for a few minutes, waiting to expel the bile, but it was no use. There was no getting rid of it.

I splashed water on my face and cleaned my teeth. I put on my overcoat and hat, taking the time to hook the buttons before I fetched the leather case and various pages, slipping them into the coat's voluminous pocket.

Except the picture of Gilbert and Paul. It would be an ice storm in Hell before I ever wished to see either of their faces again.

28

The rush of cold morning air prickled against my skin like daggers. Outside, the world was carrying on as usual. Such an odd feeling when my own would never be the same.

I wrapped my muffler around my neck and began walking without a destination in mind.

Gilbert was in love with Paul. So how did he come to befriend me? What was the motive?

To make me develop some affection for him so he could... what? Have a laugh? Or something much more sinister.

I replayed the words he'd said as he fell asleep last night. *He'd planned it.*

I spent the next hour walking around Paris with a look on my face as though my life had just fallen apart. Because it had.

That morning at Jody's flat—what had Gilbert said? *When revenge is your only thought, I promise that you can figure out how to make it happen.*

Revenge? But for what?

Ordering coffee and eggs, I tried to imagine being the man I'd been yesterday when I went to work. The loss of Jody hadn't healed, but I'd been more hopeful about my future than ever before.

I'd never be that man again.

Inside my overcoat pocket were the assorted papers I'd snatched from the floor. Using my coffee mug to hold them down, I picked through them. A panel from one of the trifold programs given out at the Palais Garnier had a list of the corps de ballet dancers for the 1886 autumn season. Aurélie's name was circled with my name scribbled in pencil in the margin.

That urge to vomit made me break into a sweat, and I patted my forehead with my handkerchief. That's how Gilbert found me? Which meant he must have known who I was. From Paul? I covered my mouth with the hanky, just in case, but the nausea passed.

He was a fiend. Perhaps not in the same magnitude as Paul, though... who knew what horrible things he was capable of?

Revenge.

There was a list with four women's names: Claudine, Louise, Julie. And Charlotte.

Charlotte Barreau? It wasn't an uncommon first name, but there was nothing else to signify what the names meant.

I pulled the envelope from the inside of the case holding my mother's note and the marriage certificate. The heft of the paper brought back memories of school the handful of times I received a letter from my father.

I could have spat. All the time he knew I was legitimate, and he just allowed me to grow up feeling as though I was less than my schoolmates. I ripped the paper in my haste to get the letter out.

Folded into the single page was a bank draft for one thousand five hundred pounds made to me. *Me.* I squinted to ensure I wasn't reading the decimal placement incorrectly, but... it was true. And dated July of this year.

An enormous bloody fortune. Mine. Perhaps I'd not discussed my finances with Gilbert, but he saw where I lived and how much this would have changed everything. There would have been no worries about Aurélie needing a patron. Fucking hell—for this amount, I could easily pay for enough classes that she'd oust her friend Rosette from her perch and my girl could have been the star ballerina. Carefully, I placed the check in my wallet and smoothed the letter flat on the table.

8 July, 1886

Monsieur Duhais-de Génet,

After our conversation, I've had time to reflect. As to your crude attempt at blackmail, let me be clear: I do not believe your claim that you have proof that there was ever a wedding between me and Ann Tighe. However, the ensuing scandal if you were to further harass me to this point would be tedious and cause grief to my mother and my heir. My attempts to ascertain your link to my natural son, Finley Tighe, have proved inconclusive. It was never my intention to cut all ties with Fin, and perhaps my current state of health has made me sentimental in remembrance of his mother. As a token of my good will, I am sending the sum I intended to gift him upon his university graduation. Though I recoil from negotiating with a knave such as yourself, I have a counteroffer. I will agree to back your uncle's store in England if you ensure the following document is legally signed. It is self-explanatory.

—Miles Carleton

Exhaling, I dropped my head into my hands. Oh, Annabeth. If you could have waited two more weeks, this would have been enough money to live on forever. And why hadn't he told her when she went to beg for help? Why had he allowed her to think that she had no choice but to take her own life?

And Gilbert had this. He had sought out my father for... blackmail?

Dear Lord, he must have had access to the marriage certificate and letter from my aunt Selena—via Paul. But what was the endgame in blackmailing my father last summer? At least the sod had paid some money—to keep Gilbert quiet about me, perhaps?

Not that I'd hesitate to cash the check now that it was in my hands and made out to me. I couldn't help Annabeth, but I could fund the Green Carnation until Charlotte reappeared. Or even if she didn't. A silver lining of sorts that might raise my spirits. Eventually.

The document accompanying the letter was even more baffling. Parsing the legalese was a trial, but in essence, Miles Carleton made a deal with Gilbert that if I could be persuaded to promise never to claim any relationship with my father, he'd sign his name as a backer for a branch of Qualité in London. If I didn't comply, he'd press charges of fraud.

A trickle of sweat ran down my temple. Clearly Gilbert wasn't doing any of this for my benefit. I shivered so violently that my coffee nearly tipped over.

My father had said the money was to keep me from using the Carleton name. Gilbert had induced me to call myself Viscount Carleton. He'd insisted it was what my father wished for, when clearly it was the exact opposite of what was laid plain before me. And to be fair, had I been shown these papers when the ruse began, I'd have gladly signed anything to have access to money. I'd kept quiet about our kinship for years now, so it wouldn't have been difficult to continue. Instead, Gilbert had urged me on, setting me up for... disgrace? Humiliation?

Not knowing the marriage certificate existed, my father could have sued me. Perhaps I would even have been arrested. Gilbert had done it on purpose.

Revenge. Fucking hell—had last night been a botched murder? Had Sonny's intent been to kill me—not for Michel, but for Gilbert?

Could Gilbert be so... so... demonic? My life was inside out, down was up, in was out. I could hardly believe what my eyes told me. I had chills and then would break into a sweat. I was coming down with something; surely it was an influenza or virus.

How could he look into my eyes and demand that I trust him? What sort of sick, depraved person does something like that? I didn't even know people's minds worked this way. But each minute we'd spent together was a lie.

Every glance, every kiss, every particle.

Luckily I was seated or I might have fallen in a faint, mind racing. Would my father's estate still take me to court if they found out? What would happen? I'd lose my job, surely, and...

But there was the marriage certificate. Not merely a license to wed, which—though helpful to show probability of a marriage—wouldn't prove that it had happened. No. This was a signed and dated and witnessed document with the date and venue of an actual marriage taking place. I'd never heard of Peter Montgomery, so, theoretically, he could be found and bid to testify, as the rest of the names on the certificate belonged to the dead.

I'd wager it would hold up in court.

And Harry was dead, too. He wasn't able to contradict anything. I scanned the obituary again, the line referring to the state of uncertainty regarding my father's heir.

My mouth settled into a grim smile.

There was no uncertainty about the heir, after all. For whatever reason—and I presumed it was a nefarious one based on the lies I'd been fed—Gilbert had collected evidence that I was legally the next Earl of Rawcliffe.

And my revenge on him would be that I'd use it.

29

After settling my bill, I left the café without touching more than a bite of food. There was too much to do. I decided depositing the money took precedence. This would be the absolute worst day to be accosted by a pickpocket, after all.

The bank manager was skeptical about the sum of my check. I produced the marriage certificate and newspaper sketch of my father and said I'd patiently wait if he wished to wire my father's bank to approve the funds. With a shrug, he turned over the much smaller amount I wished to have in cash.

I took a taxi to Eiffel's city offices. I didn't even wait a minute before he opened his personal door and ushered me in with ebullience. He held the paper with de Gênet's article and shook it with a smile. "Brilliantly done, Viscount. I've already heard from my lawyer that the Comtesse du Poix has withdrawn her objections." His smile dropped, and he patted my arm. "You look quite ill. Is everything all right?"

Unable to be blunt and tell him that my male lover was in fact a monster who'd been trying to ruin my life, I said, "I've received news that my father has died."

Eiffel didn't need to know the news was a month old.

"Please accept my sympathies." His blue eyes narrowed. "I've only just got used to calling you Viscount Carleton. I suppose this means you'll be visiting England?"

And at once, it made sense, though I'd been too rattled to formulate any plans until he said so. I covered my uncertainty with a vague nod.

"Well, as we've—you've—raised the funds we need, and this blasted comtesse is dropping her case against us . . . we'll be breaking ground for our tower within the week. I'd hoped to have you by my side, but of course, you'll be needed in England."

The spark of pride battled with my mood, but it was there, even if dulled.

"We were estranged, but thank you for the sympathy." I could have used it growing up; it was worthless to me now.

"Do you suppose a month will be long enough?" He sighed. "Or would you even wish to come back to work with whatever new duties I suppose you'll have?"

I couldn't imagine what I might be doing in the following hour, let alone the next month or the rest of my life. Would I return to Paris? I couldn't risk seeing Gilbert ever again. I didn't trust myself. I didn't know what I might do to him. I might even end up in jail.

How could I leave Aurélie and Victoire? Start my life over? I couldn't manage. Not again. I couldn't leave Paris, not for good.

The marriage certificate burned in my pocket. An entirely different life than I'd ever imagined lay before me.

Despite any previous held convictions that I'd never take a cent from my father, now that it was possible, I was determined to take every last bloody pound.

What would I do about Aurélie, though? It was a mantra in my head the entire cab ride to the Opéra's rehearsal space. I'd not been inside for a while, but the costumes mistress saw me lingering and—with a very pinched mouth expressing her disapproval—agreed to fetch Aurélie for me.

She appeared in her black practice pinafore and tatty blocked toe shoes. She grabbed my hands in hers with urgency. "What's happened?"

I'd never interrupted her classes before, so it shouldn't have surprised me that she'd know it was an emergency. But where to even begin?

"I've gotten an abundance of extraordinary news," which was one way to put it, "and I'm going to England to sort some of it out."

"England? You said you'd never return." She took a step back, wary.

I glanced at the costumes mistress, who watched with her arms folded across her chest. I lowered my voice so she couldn't over-hear. "My father has died, and I found information that I am his legal heir, after all."

"Are you all right?"

I could scream, but instead I cleared my throat. "Perfectly. But I'm going to ask you to come with me. Begging you, actually."

She touched her hand to her heart, brow wrinkled in confusion. "You know I can't leave, Fin. I'm getting a bigger solo in the next production, and to take time away would leave me back to rot in the corps—if the master of dance even allowed me back at all."

"You could audition for the ballet in London?" I was grasping, because deep down, I knew she'd balk at my dragging her away. "It turns out that I've allowed a despicable person into our lives. I don't feel that I can leave you here alone."

"Mon Dieu. Who?"

"Gilbert."

Aurélie pursed her lips. "Don't be ridiculous." But perhaps she read the truth on my face. She clutched my arm. "What's he done?"

"I've discovered that he was closer friends to Paul than I knew. That makes him dangerous. Please stay out of his way, and swear that you won't tell him where I've gone if he asks."

"I could ask Victoire to stay at the apartment. She can use your room while you're gone." Aurélie swallowed hard. "You'll come back, promise? You're my only family, I can't lose you."

Nodding with reassurance I didn't feel, I insisted I wasn't abandoning her. I pulled out most of the money from my pocket and pressed it into her hands, her mouth dropping. "What is this? What did you do to get this? I can't take so much."

I folded my hands over hers and squeezed. "It's a legacy from my father, in England. There's more, and I need to go and stake my claim to it."

"Did he truly make you his heir?" I'd never seen her gray eyes so wide.

Licking my lips before answering, I shrugged. "I'm not sure he meant to. But it'll change everything, for both of us, and I can't *not* try. I'd never leave you otherwise, you know that?"

Her shoulders loosened. "I do."

"Do me a favor and use the cash to take taxis everywhere unless Rosette offers you a ride, promise? Be careful. I'll send a note once I'm there and have a way for you to contact me. And give money to Victoire so she can pay the bills at the cabaret; can you do that for me?"

"I can." Aurélie blinked hard and threw her arms around me. "I can send a note to Victoire at the cabaret, and she can come tonight."

"I promise that I'm not leaving you, and you promise me that you'll be cautious?"

Aurélie tucked the cash into the tight bodice of her practice gown where it wouldn't drop out. She hugged me once more, darting back to her ballet practice.

The costume mistress came back and glowered. "That was most inconvenient, monsieur. Don't allow it to happen again."

She stomped away, leaving me hollow and exhausted, but at least Aurélie would be safe, and with Victoire.

I didn't have the sense that Gilbert would hurt Aurélie, but it was best to be safe. And she would be. She promised.

30

Through the marvels of modern travel, I was on British soil by nightfall, the trip from Calais to Dover to London uneventful. From King's Cross, I booked an overnight compartment north to Doncaster, and from there, I'd switch to the Lancashire and Yorkshire system and leave off in Goole.

I'd be there by next day's dinner.

I had no idea what I expected when I arrived. It was too difficult to comprehend what I'd discovered in the past twenty-four hours—imagining what could be waiting in the next day was futile.

How was it possible that England smelled different than France? Because it did. Even my voice changed, the broad vowels of my youth replaced my modulated accent I'd honed to perfection over the past years.

The station buzzed with life—slang and accents I'd not heard in the years I was in Paris. I had an hour before the next train and went into the streets. I'd never had a reason to be at home in London, but the aroma of pork pie and jellied eels sold by street vendors hung in the heavy smog. I'd not allowed myself to feel

completely out of place in France, but the familiarity of the com-
motion around me was bracing rather than strange.

I was definitely back in England.

I clutched the bottle of brandy I'd purchased in the dining car
and took it along with a small plate of cheese and bread back to
the two-berth cabin, not caring what odd looks I got as I wandered through the small passageway.

The papers from Gilbert's flat sat on the table by my elbow,
taunting me. I poured with a shaking hand. I hadn't known that
my father's rejection still had the ability to cut me to the bone. But
what did it mean: blackmail? What had Gilbert said, and when?

Nothing made sense, and here I was, gallivanting across Britain in hopes of . . . what, exactly?

I leaned my head against the glass. Hertfordshire. That's where
I was. Flat landscape dotted with sheep. *What was I doing here?*

By now, I was halfway through the bottle and didn't feel as
bleary as I ought to. As I needed to. My wits were razor sharp,
tearing at my heart in a crisscross of anger and denial. There was
no way for me to interpret all of this information Gilbert had
withheld—since July, so a month or more before we even spoke
for the first time—as anything except with malicious intent.

If it wasn't some unknowable game to hurt me, why hadn't Gilbert presented me with the letter from my father's solicitor back in
September? What had been the purpose of me jumping through
hoops to establish myself as Rawcliffe's heir and then positioning
me so I had to sign that document for Michel de Gênet? Nothing
was logical.

And every thread in my mind went back to the picture of Gilbert with Paul. *Paul.* There was no way I could overlook their

297

relationship. Especially the lies Gilbert told so earnestly insisting they were nothing more than shallow acquaintances.

That scribble on the back of the photograph disproved that lie.

For whatever reason, Gilbert's intent was to destroy me. It was clear my father was anxious enough not to hear my name linked with his that he was willing to pay me off—and to back Qualité in London.

Drinking wasn't going to help me solve the riddle, but it might soothe my nerves.

I walked back to the dining car and ordered coffee. I sat and listened to people—people whose lives hadn't been upended and destroyed in the past day. People who remembered how to smile. The clinking of the china was so civilized, and the smooth whirr of the wheels kept my anxious breathing from overtaking me. I sang along in my head, *cha choo, cha choo, cha choo.*

My body ached for sleep, but the coffee ensured I didn't. A headache throbbed behind my eyes, intense, crashing pain. Damned myself with too much to drink. But it was the only thing I could do to try and put blasted Duhais and his betrayal out of my mind.

The swaying of the train lulled me to sleep, and when I woke in Doncaster, I regretted not having slept flat in the berth instead of upright. My neck ached nearly as much as my heart.

I stood on the platform, hoping to catch my bearings. From behind, a woman's hair—jet black curls that shone even in the dimmed light of the station—caught me in the gut. For a half second, I could have believed it was Annabeth.

Doncaster wasn't merely England, *it was Yorkshire.* The patois of accents that sounded like my sister, my aunt...like me before

I'd had it trained away in return for a posher one at school. I always slipped right back into it when Annabeth met me at the train.

She'd always managed to make it to the station at Goole, usually carrying a basket with some small treat, knowing I'd be ravenous after the trip. Aunt Glad never allowed us to eat between meals, not even if I'd missed mine on the train.

Eventually, when I returned after terms at university, I'd have enough money in my pocket to take Annabeth to enjoy tea and a delicacy like her favorite nutmeg custard tart. I cursed myself for ever teasing her for being such a chatterbox. I'd give anything to have her face meet me now.

Could I truly go all the way back to Goole? Or should I turn back? Go anywhere else, lose myself and drink myself into a stupor?

But neither Fin Tighe nor Viscount Carleton did that, and even if I didn't know which I was, I had to keep moving forward. I entered the carriage for the last leg of the rail journey and took my seat, staring over the shrub grass and fields enclosed in stone walls to keep livestock safe as we got lower to sea level.

I walked from the Goole station, alone. With a pang, I realized that hadn't ever happened in my life, and I hurried by Annabeth's favorite tea shop with my eyes averted, unsure how to cope with this fresh rush of sadness.

The Lowther Hotel was thought to be the nicest in town. I stood out front of the black painted wood, tidy and shiny but so provincial to my adult eyes; it shocked me. Annabeth and I had always thought the place was for high-society types. Much too grand for us.

Never again would I allow that feeling to hold me back, whether I was plain Fin Tighe or the Earl of Rawcliffe.

There'd not been cause for me to go inside the hotel. Once, I'd entered the attached pub. I'd humbly handed a note to my uncle Eric who was at the bar, dressed in his Sunday finest, and skittered out quickly.

This time, I pushed past the door made of glass squares, hand-blown and blurry. I wished I could go back and assure my childhood self that there was nothing beyond that door that was too good for me.

The landlord was unfamiliar, not a face I knew from my youth, and I gave my name without thinking.

"Are you kin to our Glad, then?" the hotelier asked, pushing spectacles up the bridge of his nose where they'd slid when he bent to write my name.

"Is she still living?" My aunt wasn't real any longer. She was more like a character from a book. *A dreadful book I never wanted to reread.*

"No, sorry to tell. Died a few years back." He puckered his mouth and gave me a long stare. "You're Annie's boy?"

I'd never thought of myself that way, but nodded. Aunt Glad was dead? She wasn't old—certainly not more than fifty-five. Would I have felt some sense of regret if I wasn't so emotionally numbed by the revelations of the past day?

Probably not.

"Didn't you know?"

"Pardon? Uh, no." I blew out a long breath and put my hands on the counter in some sort of appeal. "We lost contact years ago."

Finger on the key, he pushed it across the till, not even looking at me. "It's nowt to do with me."

I was not interested in thinking about her—not when I needed to remain resolved and manifest the confidence from the marriage certificate in my pocket. "Any idea how I might get to Queen's Chase?"

He turned as though I'd asked where to get my cock sucked on a Sunday after services. "*How?* Didn't the good Lord give you feet?"

I forced myself to be calm. "Oh, aye, but I was asking for a carriage. Can you tell me if anyone's there?"

"Don't keep up with the likes of them." Scratching his chin, he might have smiled. But maybe not. "Missus Hawke, you're needed."

A woman of about my age came through the door behind the till and looked me up and down as scrupulously as Gilbert might have done. Not that I was thinking about him.

"The Earl of Rawcliffe died a few months back, I believe?" I asked.

Mrs. Hawke's mouth turned down for a moment before she patted my hand. "Ah. Now I've placed who you are. You look just like your sister. Your Annabeth was in my form at school. Such a sad thing."

"And who lives in the big house?"

"The dowager countess." She scrunched up her face. "All the others are dead, God rest their souls."

My smile was tight. Perhaps.

Or damn them.

I'd seen the old lady a few times. Annabeth and I were buying something for Aunt Glad at the grocer's once, and her carriage stopped next to us on the street and she got out. She towered over us and made a circuit around us, nose twitching. Not a word, and then she got back in her carriage and drove away.

Annabeth and I had never discussed it.

This time, it would be me with the sour face.

"What of the new earl?"

Again Mrs. Hawke's eyes gazed the room, and she lowered her voice. "My sister delivers their eggs and dairy. And she said there's a lot of goings-on with lawyers and men up from London and even some foreign ones, so I don't rightly know."

The obituary mentioned there was something not settled. No new earl had been installed. It was time for me to decide if I would go back to being pathetic Fin who was frightened to do anything, or if I would become the man I'd been playacting for months. Take my own revenge on my father for claiming the title he so obviously didn't think I was worth.

"Yes, well, I've come back from my home in Paris to settle things. As far as you know, the dowager countess is receiving visitors?"

She nodded, smile bright. "Aye, love, I can call a carriage for you if you'd like?"

"I would. Perhaps give me ten minutes to drop off my things and refresh myself?"

"It might take as long as a half hour. I'll send up a pot of tea, shall I?"

I gave her my winningest smile and a wink. "Ta." When was

the last time I used that? Yorkshire sucked me back into who I was before I left, and I struggled against it. I wasn't that boy.

I followed her up to my room to tidy myself.

The lodgings were more elegant than expected for Goole, though this wasn't a side of the town that I'd ever had cause to become familiar with. Aunt Glad and Eric lived in smaller row homes off the main thoroughfare, and I'd been away at school for most of my life.

My delivered pot of tea was perfection, and I let it soothe me as much as it could. I still hadn't crafted a plan on how to handle my visit to Rawcliffe's—*my*—estate, but hoped I'd figure it out before I arrived.

A carriage waited at the curb of the hotel. I watched out the windows as we left town; the rooftop of my childhood home was somewhere in the distance. I was relieved I'd never have a reason to venture back. It was no place for an earl, after all. My father had made it clear when he'd visited on Christmas mornings.

Oh, I was going to do this. The months playacting Viscount Carleton had seasoned me. *You might not have wished for me to find out about your secrets, Gilbert, but you've just done me a million-pound favor.*

31

By half past three, I was on my way up the drive to the house I'd never been good enough to visit, let alone live in, dizzy with amazement over what I was daring.

I'd run the last time I came this direction. I'd vowed never to return when I left it.

But this was entirely different.

An edge of hysteria tinged my racing thoughts. Queen's Chase was utterly enormous, made more so as it was set apart in its own great, green park. I was so used to the cramped apartments in Paris that this was shocking. Even the grands boulevards were flocked with compacted homes, nothing like this.

The entire neighborhood surrounding the alley where Sonny attacked me and Gilbert could fit inside the grounds.

The high wall of the house's front façade was gray stone fitted with faux gothic windows. Tucked on one side was the entrance above a curved set of stairs. I blinked at the wooden door built like a medieval portcullis.

Did I dare? Would my grandmother fight me about my rights, or would she have me escorted out? Like last time I was here.

I gritted my teeth. I wasn't twenty-two any longer, damn it. I wasn't a terrified young man searching for a rope to keep my head above water. And this time, I'd have the law on my side, wouldn't I? A wave of nausea rolled over me.

How would Rawcliffe's mother react?

She wouldn't have me escorted out. If she told me to leave, I'd do it. And I'd return with solicitors, just as Harry probably would have done after being raised in such grandeur. I'd been familiarizing myself with his role for months now. Perfected it. I could pull this off.

Then I was up the steps, ringing the bell.

Was it only yesterday morning I was in Gilbert's flat?

If the butler was surprised that anyone had dared to face the rain on a weekday afternoon, he didn't show it. This inadvertently gave me some more courage, and I lifted my chin higher.

It took all my willpower not to gaze around the wood-paneled hall like a yokel. But it was difficult not to. A winding banister led to an upper level that was hidden except for two halls radiating from either side. The hall was full of hot-house blooms. Amaryllis. They'd been Annabeth's favorites.

He took my hat and coat and led me to a well-appointed parlor. A green marble fireplace was the size of our kitchenette in Paris. Carvings on the wood-paneled ceiling proclaimed this family had been on the side of the Lancastrians during the War of the Roses; it was a field of red.

Scattered around the room were gilt-framed portraits of long-dead Carletons. I examined a man on a horse; high-collar and fashionably mussed hair indicated turn of the last century. There was something about the shape of the nose that could mark us related.

"That's my late husband's father, Henry." There was no hint of northern burr in the voice that shook me.

I whirled around. The dowager countess—my grandmother. She was shorter than in my memory, but just as imposing. An echo of a smile was on her thin face. She was dressed in black, for her son, presumably. It set off her white hair well.

"I'm Finley Tighe." I inhaled through my nose, chest out, stood a little taller. "Your grandson."

Still dark eyebrows raised ever so slightly. "Yes, I've been expecting you."

Expecting me? The answer was surprising. I rubbed my lips together. They were chapped from the cold.

"My condolences about your son." It was the prettiest I could say it without snarling.

Something in her eyes flickered. Interest, perhaps. "I'm sure not."

She looked me up and down to see if I passed muster. For once, I did. I did the same to her.

Plunging in, I said, "I arrived in England this morning. Were you aware that your son married my mother? Before I was born? It was legal, which means that—" My hand shook as I withdrew the certificate from my interior pocket, but she gave a slight shake.

"It's not necessary. I've seen it already." She reached out to gently touch my arm, but I pulled back. "Your lawyer brought it to my attention a few weeks back."

My lawyer? What the hell? I rubbed the back of my neck.

She sat and indicated I should, too, in a chair close to her own. I sat where I damn well pleased, a bit farther away. No Carleton would bully me. Not anymore.

"He was charming. Very French. He said you'd do your best to come as soon as possible. Was Paris too busy to leave it so long?" Plucking at the lace doily on the arm of her chair, she was polite, but I saw her heartbeat in her throat, racing like mine.

My head tilted, eyes narrowed. What was she on about? But she knew I was in Paris, which was more than I knew about what was happening here. I lifted my shoulder in a non-answer.

Familiar blue eyes lifted and reminded me of Annabeth. I looked away.

"Gilbert with two surnames. Both began with a D, I believe, and the second something like a flower. Genitan? De Gênet, that was it—like the Norman Plantagenets. He said that you'd be in touch."

Gilbert was here. Here. Maybe even sat in this seat. For half a second, I squeezed my eyes shut to keep the sadness at bay. He'd lied and called himself my lawyer to spy on me. The kick in the gut almost made me bend forward and clutch my abdomen in real pain.

"I suppose he brought you up to speed?" This time the smile peeked out for a second before she frowned. "It's been the source of much contention with my husband's distant cousin or nephew or whatever he is. His lawyers claim that yours was poorly trained."

They'd be right.

"He—that's Warnwood, the hopeful heir—demanded to have the certificate verified himself, but our family solicitors checked the Archbishop of York's offices. My son did, indeed, purchase a special license to marry your mother, and it matched the parish registry. They validated it before I returned it to your lawyer, so I commanded Warnwood to stop using the title until I saw you for myself." There was a glint in her eye that was unreadable, even if I wasn't so befuddled.

And now that I was here? I daren't ask, because presumably I oughtn't to feel nervous that it was unsettled. I tightened my grip on the arm of my chair, and she caught the action, softened her face a fraction.

Grasping for control, I said, "It's difficult for me to forgive past slights."

Having the grace to blush, she crossed and recrossed her ankles. "Has your employer raised enough capital for his tower? Even in Yorkshire the news is full of the controversy."

At least I knew the answer to that. "He hasn't, though it's close. We hope to break ground any day now."

"Fascinating. I long to hear more, if you'll tell me. I suppose we'd best get to know one another." She stood and gestured for me to follow. "Where are your bags? You intend to stay, don't you, now that Queen's Chase is yours?"

Mine?

Mine.

I could have fallen to the floor in relief. This was happening—without me even needing to make a scene.

"I'll stay in the hotel." I wasn't sure I could bear another hour of this stilted awkwardness.

"Surely not. I've had your rooms readied for two months now." Her finger looped the strand of pearls at her neck, and she toyed with them. "I'll move to the dower house. It was prepared for me at the same time I fixed things for you, but without you here, I didn't see the need to leave." Her shoulders sagged. "I did spend a few nights there in October when Monsieur de Gênet indicated that you were on your way, but you never came…" Her voice trailed off.

October? Gilbert had been here as recently as that? After we'd made love the first time? No. *Fucked.* After we'd fucked. I gritted my back teeth so hard it hurt.

"Can I admit that I'm relieved not to have to manage Warnwood? In fact, I'm *delighted* to send him the official notification, now that I've laid eyes on you, and know for sure that you're alive and undoubtedly not an imposter with those looks. Will you go back to Paris, or have you sorted things there?" There was a hint of hope in her voice, almost that she wished me to stay.

It would be difficult to leave behind the Green Carnation and Victoire and Laurent, but I'd pay the bills for the cabaret to stay open. Knowing they were able to keep it would have to be enough. But it was the loss of my cousin that I couldn't reconcile. I'd find a way to bring Aurélie here. Or to London. She could audition for the ballet at Covent Garden and have the career she deserved. I could rent her a luxury flat, and if she ever wanted to go back to Paris, she could go as a star.

But as for me, if there was a chance I'd run into Gilbert Duhais, I'd stay put in England.

"No, that part of my life is finished." *Fini.*

32

My grandmother allowed me to roam the house without her, only noting when dinner would be served. As a child, I'd only been brought in twice through the kitchen, as though Annabeth and I were too lowly to come through the front doors. Not now. I had no compunction opening every room and surveying what was now mine. It was a balm to my nerves, to say the least.

My things had been brought over from the hotel, and I was shown into a suite of rooms that was not only ten times nicer than my flat in Paris, it was at least twice as large.

But not nearly as comfortable as Gilbert's place.

Calmer now, I shaved and dressed in my evening jacket, the black. Lady Rawcliffe didn't seem the sort to appreciate a man in blue.

The old lady waited for me in a wood-paneled room. She asked what I liked to drink and fixed it herself. It was a much better label than I drank at the Green Carnation. Smooth. Easy to drink.

"Did you enjoy your tour of the house?" she asked, her voice as bright as her eyes.

"I did." Balancing manners with a distinct lack of warmth was difficult. This woman had never been my ally before, and I wasn't sure that I'd accept her obvious friendliness now that my circumstances had so radically changed. I had no idea what to even call her.

It was extensive, though, this new house of mine. *Mine.* What would Gilbert think about all of the trappings? He'd been here, hadn't he?

A large portrait above the fireplace stopped me in my tracks. Annabeth smiled down at me to the dimple in her right cheek. Not the little girl from the photo, but as she looked just before she died.

I moved closer. When had this been painted? And why? So macabre.

"That was me when I married your grandfather. You mightn't believe it to look at me today, but I was nearly as beautiful as your sister back in my day."

Wheeling around, I looked her full in the face, and yes, she did have the same dimple still, now that she smiled.

My resentment spewed out. "You stopped and looked at my sister and me on the street once, do you recall?"

She twisted her hands in front of her abdomen, eyes downcast. "I needed to see for myself if the stories were true."

"And what did you think when you saw us?" My voice tightened. I turned away, not wanting her to see the hurt on my face.

"I saw two grandchildren who ought to have been in the schoolroom upstairs." Simple words and stark delivery.

"We would have been pleased for you to rescue us."

Her voice was low, kind. "She's buried on the property. You left before that happened, didn't you?"

I cocked my head to the side, blinking. "Pardon?"

She toyed with her rings. "When I heard—well, she wasn't allowed to be—"

I almost choked on the words. "Annabeth's here?" I'd always assumed she'd been put into a pauper's grave.

She touched my sleeve. "I'll show you tomorrow when it's light. I sit with her, wondering what would've happened if my son had married..." She twisted her necklace. "But I suppose he did."

A deep frown marred the papery skin of her forehead. "Do you feel happier knowing that they were married? Does it help ease anything?"

I hadn't sorted any of that but other than the relief that I hadn't ruined everyone and everything I held dear, the resentment that it could be true, and that Annabeth and I suffered for a lie was too much to keep inside. "There's no easing my sister's death."

"Miles didn't even mention it on his deathbed, when you'd think he'd have finally found the courage to admit what a ghastly thing he'd done before meeting his Maker. We would have reconciled with the truth, had he told us. After so many years, it seems incredible that it ever mattered who Annie was before they married, but I'm very ashamed to admit that it would have rocked the family at the time." She took a deep breath through her nose. "But your lawyer found the marriage certificate, and it's sorted for you now. I wish I could do more."

Neither of us could do anything about how our shared relation handled his affairs, and, frankly, I needed a few hours to stop the distress. I decided to make it easy on myself and offered her my arm. She looked at it for a full few seconds, like she might refuse. But when she lifted her eyes, they were shiny with emotion.

I blinked and looked away before I believed her.

She patted my sleeve. "I've never been taken in to dinner by a more handsome man. And I've never seen an evening jacket like that; it's so elegant, so French."

The dining room was big enough for a small army, but she had our seats next to each other, explaining her hearing wasn't as good as it used to be. I couldn't have said what we ate, though it all tasted fine. But as the meal continued, my shoulders loosened, and I even found myself smiling once or twice. Perhaps it was a show to put me at ease so I didn't fuss, as Aurélie would say.

"What's happened to make you so sad, Finley? That was my father's name, did you know? He went by Finny."

Like my mother had referred to me. *Finny*. Almost like *Fini*. I blew out my breath and frowned at my plate. I was named after some long-dead grandfather. Proof, perhaps, that at least for a single, sentimental moment, my father claimed me as part of his family line.

I sat back, twirled the crystal goblet in my fingers. "No, I didn't know. I know absolutely nothing whatsoever about your family or your husband's family. I know little enough about my mother's people. No one ever bothered to tell us, and now they've all died. Except Aurélie, my cousin in Paris. My aunt's daughter. Selena Tighe. She was unable to find any decent work in town thanks to what happened with my mother, so she ran off."

"Your lawyer said that Selena had the marriage certificate. Her story was that she challenged Miles to do better for you and Annabeth, and he refused. Chased her off with solicitors and claims of fraud. But it pleases me that she had a daughter. A cousin for you."

Ah. That's a story I believed was probably true. Bless Selena for caring so much for Annabeth and me. But had the false accusation against his mother given Paul the idea to commit some sort of extortion of me?

Eleanor watched my face with interest. "Thank goodness that you have someone to love. I can see it in your face. Aurélie, that's a lovely name. She should come and visit."

"She's a ballet dancer."

My stare challenged her to say something dismissive. Instead, she kept her face a mask of politeness. "How extraordinary. She must be very talented." She asked if I wished for another glass of wine and gestured for the footman to refill my glass when I said yes.

It gave me a moment to regain my composure.

"Would you like me to tell you any family stories? Is there anything you wish to know?"

I hated myself because I did. At least a small amount. Maybe I could capture that sense of belonging that had eluded me my entire life. That sense that Gilbert had given me for a few hours. The happiest in my life.

I respected her more for keeping her eyes locked on mine. "If I could go back in time, I would, my dear. I imagine this is overwhelming."

Pushing my chair back, I had to fight to keep the fresh blaze of my anger in check. She'd zeroed in on it too closely. "My life's been less than easy, Lady Rawcliffe. I've learned to handle situations as they arise."

"You're a survivor, Fin—may I call you that?" Her luminous

skin turned pink. "Your lawyer referred to you that way, and I suppose that's how I've thought of you."

Gilbert didn't deserve to be here with me tonight, at this table. But the echo of his presence was suffocating. I could hear the French inflection on the i. *Fin.* Never Finley, but Fin, like a friend. I missed it enough that I had to blink at the heat behind my eyes.

Forcing myself back to Yorkshire, I inclined my head. She could call me whatever she wanted, as I didn't plan to see much of her.

"Surviving is more difficult than many people believe, and it appears as though you've thrived. Certainly looks as though you have made a success out of yourself with no help from those of us that knew better." She frowned and let out a deep sigh.

Something about the way she didn't hide that she'd been wrong made me like her a little more. Just a drop. And she didn't linger on the emotional side of it, which was my undoing. That was a skill I'd never developed.

"Monsieur de Gênet told me that you've been gathering investors for this tower for the world's fair. Would you tell me? I have some money of my own that isn't entailed to the estate, and, to be bluntly vulgar, *now yours*, but is it something that you believe in? I admit to reading whatever I could about the venture since I found out about your life in Paris. It's terribly exciting." The way her eyes lit up made my chest ache over how much she looked like Annabeth.

And likewise, it was a comfort to me. Not that I could ever confuse them, but to see something so familiar after so many years. Well, I had no words.

I spent the next hour outlining all of the various scenarios with Eiffel's tower. She asked intelligent questions—more so than any of the men who'd written me checks in Paris. Nothing about the venture was too small, too inconsequential for her to want to understand.

We stayed put even after the footman cleared the table, until she yawned and I realized with shock we'd spent the entire evening talking, and I forgot to hate her.

33

The following morning, I woke late, the exhaustion from the traveling catching up with me. At first, my heart thudded with panic, as if I were tardy for something. But I wasn't. What would I do to occupy myself all day here? I'd go mad without some task.

As I made my way downstairs, the footman handed me a folded note on thick stationery.

> *Fin,*
>
> *I'm in my greenhouse. Please come and find me if you wish for company. Otherwise, you deserve a few hours to acclimate without me breathing down your neck. My husband always told me I push too hard. I only wish you to believe how welcome you are.*
>
> *Eleanor.*

There. She'd solved my worry about how to address her. Grandmother was too awkward after so many years. But her name meant we could be friends of a sort. Perhaps.

Enough food to feed ten people waited on the sideboard. I helped myself to much of it, bypassing the kidneys with a shudder. After that morning Victoire had come to tell us about Jody's death, I doubted I'd ever be able to eat them again.

I resolved that I wouldn't think of Gilbert today. And it would get easier. It would.

But though I wasn't a believer in any way, I did wish to visit my sister's grave. Through the lead glass windows of an ornate greenhouse, I saw Eleanor brandish flower shears. I knocked on the window, and she met me with a smile, a basket of pink and white amaryllises over her arm. A squeeze of my hand. "I cut these for her. They're her favorites, aren't they?"

The way she spoke as if Annabeth were alive made chills race up my spine. But I took a handful of the flowers and followed a path paved with slate that twisted through a grove of trees to some architectural folly someone with too much money had built to look like a crumbling church.

A wrought iron bench sat close to a marker, flat against the ground. Annabeth Tighe. 30 May 1857–17 April 1878.

Ay, hold it true, whate'er befall, and feel it, when we sorrow most. 'Tis better to have loved and lost, than to have never loved at all.

Did I agree? I'd be much better off today if I'd never met Gilbert, for example.

I laid the flowers on top and sat. Where would we be now if Annabeth had waited to speak to me before choosing to end her life? Why hadn't she known that I would have helped? I'd have taken her away. It would have been easy enough to pretend she was a widow. And I was so close to finishing my courses. Nothing held me in Goole or in Yorkshire.

Why hadn't she known that?

Could I have done more to make her trust me, or to feel loved? That gutted me still. The idea that Annabeth believed I wouldn't have helped her.

I patted my pocket for a handkerchief, but tears didn't fall. Instead, my pulse quickened, and I fought to breathe. I had to loosen my tie. She did know better. She had to've. Had to. I pounded my hand in my fist, wanted to yell and scream and kick something. Break something.

"Fin? May I sit?"

I gestured to Eleanor.

"You're unhappy."

Jesus wept, I was. Furious. Why had my sister been so foolish as to think she had no reason to stay alive?

"She left you all alone, didn't she?" Eleanor put her hand on my arm. I shook her off, unable to hear her calm voice through my haze of mounting rage.

Forcing breath through my nose so as not to crumble into my anxiety, I gave one short nod.

She had, damn it. All alone.

"You would've helped Annabeth. I don't even know you, and I can tell you would've. You're such a kind soul, so easy to love. No small wonder your cousin in Paris cares so deeply for you."

I raised my eyes to her, ready to snap. I wasn't. I was impossible to love. I'd been shown it over and over again.

Eleanor lifted her chin. "Everyone who was supposed to love

you and take care of you was derelict in their duty. Annabeth was your only real family, wasn't she? And she left you."

God damn, how she could she talk so calmly, so precisely, when my heart and my head pitched like they were in the middle of gale-force winds?

I balled the handkerchief up and had to walk away. I made it a few yards and leaned against a tree, burying my face in my arms. Over and over the words shouted in my head. I'd failed her.

But Eleanor didn't walk away so I could grieve in peace. She touched my back. I growled for her to leave.

"I don't think I will. You have so much misery inside you. And I'm one of the causes. That lovely young woman isn't buried there because you failed her, but because *I did*. And my son did. And my husband."

Had I said the words out loud? "You did, but—"

"No. There isn't any but. Everyone insisted that you adored Annabeth. She knew it. But it wasn't enough, and sometimes that's the way it is. You couldn't have done anything else for her. After a life of hurting and not being loved by her family except you, she couldn't take any more pain."

I turned, ready to yell that she was wrong. I clutched the rough tree bark under my fingers, was swallowed up by the emptiness.

"It wasn't your fault," she said again, this time with anger of her own. She strode closer, gritting her teeth. Then she poked my arm with her finger. "You've allowed this to destroy your life. Because of mistakes that other people made." She thrust her finger into my arm again. "If you're going to be angry, be angry at me." Her voice was raised as loud as mine.

Again, the tempest roared up from the deep cavern of my soul, and I yelled back at her. "I am. I'm so bloody furious that if your son were here, I'd kill him with my own fucking hands." I panted. Flailed my arms.

She pressed her lips together so hard they turned white. But she said nothing in her defense. There was none.

"We were children. And nothing. We got nothing, *nothing* from any of you." I took a step closer, but she didn't flinch, didn't budge. And I saw the shine in her eyes that she understood how wrong it was. And it made me ready to listen to her, maybe.

She exhaled. "You didn't." She pulled a lace-edged hanky from her sleeve and dabbed her eyes. "My husband never spoke about either of you, and neither did Miles. It was easier to pretend that you didn't exist. Otherwise, I'd have had to acknowledge that I raised a man so callous that he'd refuse to care for his own children, and that was too painful."

Eleanor made fists. "I was a bloody coward, Fin. And for years now, I've said if there was anything on earth I could do to make up for it, I would. I don't expect you to forgive me. I've sat here every day for eight years and apologized to this patch of dirt. And that's my burden, not yours. You oughtn't have one. You were the only one to love Annabeth. You must forgive her, dear boy. And forgive yourself."

She turned and left, her head still high.

Her words were etched into my soul. Forgive. Outrageous. I wasn't angry with Annabeth.

Oh, but I was. Furious. Seething for years for her leaving me, for not trusting me.

321

For giving up even if there was a way we could have solved it.

And forgive myself? Chills ran down my head like a cold shower of rain.

A cold breeze blew through the copse, and I lifted my collar. An echo on the wind that sounded like her voice. Absolution. Forgiveness. I shivered.

Was that what Annabeth would want?

Dammit. It was.

But what would be left of me if I let her go?

Gilbert said it. I was dull. Unremarkable. Unmemorable.

What would I have left if I let go of my sadness and anger? Who would I be? I'd go back to the young man who left no lasting impression, whom no one wished to spend time with.

For a while, I believed I was enough for someone to love, that I was a whole man. Gilbert's fucking plan had worked.

It was a lie.

The voice whispered again. Leave the past down at the bottom of the Ouse.

But the future... well, that was a new story. One that I didn't have an ending for yet.

34

Somehow, the days came and went, and I still lived at the end of them. Gilbert Duhais wouldn't destroy me, not completely. But he occupied my mind.

I'd sent Aurélie a letter again begging her to leave Paris and enclosed a voucher for passage to England anytime she might need it. And another check, promising to provide whatever she might need in the future. I didn't wish for her to believe I'd run out on her. I wanted her to know she had a home if she needed one. She would always have a place with me.

The money I sent to Laurent to keep the Green Carnation open was the first taste of actual pleasure I'd felt in ages. The doors could remain open for at least a year, and I'd send more when it was necessary.

Eiffel, though, was a more difficult letter to compose. I gave a brief accounting of my taking stewardship of Queen's Chase and asked what I might do to help. Eleanor had made one or two suggestions of having visitors around—even a small party to introduce me as the new earl. I begged off, too drained from the recent events to imagine faking my way through an evening of polite chitchat.

One more week. I'd move past all the shocks by then, surely. I might even find some pleasure in inviting some of those pompous twits I'd gone to school with who couldn't be bothered to respond to my letters about the tower last summer. Jot a note to Lemworth Bryant, who must have heard about my change in social position by now.

He'd be the one scurrying for favor, wouldn't he?

Eleanor was thoughtful enough to have the Parisian papers sent up from London. They were nearly a week behind, having to make their way to Yorkshire from France, but I scoured them for any hint that Michel de Gênet had refuted the glowing article Gilbert wrote in his name. There was nothing to indicate a problem. Eiffel was in a good position without any further help from me as it appeared that the tower would be built, and the ground had been broken on the Champs de Mars a few days after my arrival in England.

Upon learning that, I chose to take a break from my former life and learn to accept the reality of my new one, and pretend my time in Paris had been a dream.

Still, I was restless and unable to settle myself on anything productive. Eleanor insisted that I would come up with a routine that suited me, but I'd never been idle for more than a handful of hours at a time, and even that was a rarity. I took to sleeping late, and trying to read, but my sorrow seemed to know no bounds.

Eleanor waited in the hall when I finally emerged from my room a fortnight after my arrival, twirling a ring around her finger. "Fin, I hate to tell you this. You're so unsettled already, and I'm sure it's a coincidence, but I read something—" She forced a smile that didn't reach her eyes. "I never wish you to think I held back something from you."

The hair on the back of my neck rose, and I followed her, faster paced than usual. On the desk in my new study was one of the French newspapers I hadn't seen, folded, not on the correct seam. Her hand trembled slightly when she held it out for me.

"De Gênet must not be an uncommon name, perhaps...? But your cousin's name is so pretty and unusual, it jumped out at me. I pray I'm mistaken."

I glanced over the headline.

DEPARTMENT STORE HEIR
ARRESTED FOR MURDER.

Weak-kneed, I sat, pushed my hair back with one hand.

> Gilbert Duhais has been taken into custody for the murder of his uncle Michel de Gênet, owner of Qualité, Paris's largest clothier. Duhais was heir to his uncle's fortune, which police believe is one of the motives.

No.
No.
Gilbert? My Gilbert? It couldn't be. He wouldn't. His uncle?

> Duhais, 28, was found with the murder weapon in his hand at the apartment of his paramour, Opéra Ballet dancer Aurélie Blancmaison, following what witnesses

say was a charged quarrel over Mademoiselle Blancmaison's affection.

"You mentioned she's a ballerina. I'm so concerned that this might be about her, and I know that you'll need to do something, if so."

"Hush," I begged, holding my hand up, unable to process what I read. It couldn't be true. A mistake. Some dreadful joke.

> Both Blancmaison and Duhais claim that it was self-defense, but the police prefecture claims this was a premeditated murder, which could result in his execution or at least imprisonment in a penal colony. Monsieur Duhais was found with a train ticket to the coast in his pocket. As of yet, Mademoiselle Blancmaison hasn't been arrested, but sources close to the police imply that she was a collaborator.

Self-defense? Had Aurélie been attacked? Someone scooped out my insides and left me hollow. Slumped over, ribs caving in. Gilbert, arrested? And Aurélie his collaborator?

Was Aurélie all right? Bloody hell, de Gênet...? What was Michel doing at our apartment?

My mind went to the beastly language de Gênet had used about Aurélie at Stéphanie's party. He'd been vicious. But most of the men who attended the ballet were chauvinists who thought the same about dancers. Aurélie wouldn't stand a chance in a courtroom insisting she wasn't truly part of the patronage system at the ballet, especially as she'd been "anonymously" gifted classes.

I rustled the paper, looking for a continuation of the story. But this was the only hint.

"Fin, is it your Aurélie? And was that your lawyer, too?"

I shook my head, hard, hoping to dislodge the fog and make sense out of what I read. I struggled to insert Aurélie into a situation in which she'd have to deal with Michel de Gênet. I went to the window and pulled back the draperies. Aurélie? How hurt had she been? It was unbearable, the not knowing, the not having a way to find out her well-being.

And fucking hell, what had happened to make Gilbert kill his uncle? Or anyone? He'd certainly never have attacked Aurélie. Not even my loathing for him could mask that truth. Me, perhaps, but never Aurélie.

He would have protected her, though. How many times had Gilbert insisted that I keep Aurélie away from de Gênet? Why? Because it was obvious now that there were many things I didn't know about his uncle.

Horrid, wretched, violent things.

And yet there was no way I could reconcile Gilbert being the villain in any scenario with Aurélie.

"I must leave for Paris at once. I have to know how Aurélie is. I must see for myself that she's safe. Help her out of this monstrous accusation."

I strode to the grand staircase to my bedroom, Eleanor on my heels, continuing to talk as though I could pay attention to her.

"I can be ready to go with you in three quarters of an hour, if you'll allow me. I know it's difficult to believe, but I'll do anything within my power to support you and your cousin. Please remember how much you have at your disposal now that you're the Earl of Rawcliffe."

And she meant it. I touched my hand to hers. Her ability to blindly believe that not only was Aurélie innocent, but that I could manage to do anything to help her meant more than I could say. "Thank you, but it's easier if I do this on my own."

Her still-dark brows moved together. "Faster, you mean. Yes. Write down your Paris address, and this afternoon I'll have the lawyers set up an account you can draw from while you're there. Please. I won't fail you this time."

I scratched out the address and handed it to her, squeezing her fingers. Her eyes held mine, and then she pressed her palm to my cheek. "I'll call for the carriage." She paused at the door. "You must love her very much."

Dear God, of course I did. The notion of Aurélie suffering horrified me. It took me back to my terror when I couldn't find Annabeth.

But it wasn't only her, as much as I wanted to believe that it was.

Gilbert was in danger, too, and no matter what happened, if he'd rescued Aurélie in my place, I couldn't let him die for it without lifting a finger, could I?

35

When I disembarked in Paris the following afternoon, I bought all of the dailies, saw Aurélie and Gilbert's names splashed across the front pages, and tried to make sense of the drama.

With my heart thudding, I scanned the first. The second. And the third, which I balled up and threw against the pavement.

The case was made that Aurélie was nothing but a glorified prostitute, someone lower than the gutter flower they called her. They concluded that she'd turned to de Gênet as the wealthiest of her prospects, and Gilbert couldn't handle the rejection, so he beat her up before killing his uncle.

"Fucking lies." I said it aloud to no one in particular, and my voice was hollow.

If the man with the slit throat hadn't been Michel de Gênet, it's likely the juge d'instruction—the magistrate in charge of the investigation who decided whether it merited a trial—would have figured it was self-defense, and it would've been over.

But he was Michel de Gênet, one of the wealthiest men in Paris, a man who ran charities for the debris of Paris—the women whom no one else gave a toss about. He was a certifiable saint to most everyone who'd heard his name.

As his heir, Gilbert was under much more scrutiny, and honestly: this was the sort of dynamite the public craved like the Romans adored their gladiatorial arenas.

It had all the makings of an international tabloid affair. The handsome young heir, the ballet dancer whose star rose due to illicit benefactors, the millionaire famous for being an upstanding pillar of society. Hero to the downtrodden.

Because of the sensationalism and the court's concern over jury contamination, there was a rush to have the trial conducted and finished before the end of the assize's session next week. The papers had already concluded Gilbert was guilty, and many openly called for his execution. It was surreal, but I couldn't dig into my feelings, because Gilbert's wasn't the only death the opinion writers were calling for. They were hungry for Aurélie's, too.

According to all of the papers, Aurélie was disreputable in every way. She was a ballet dancer searching for the wealthiest abonnés, who paid for her extra classes. She'd been promoted from the corps de ballet with the only possible explanation being that she'd relied on patronage from any number of abonnés.

The sickening reality of the gross imbalances of power between the abonnés and the dancers—most of whom were recruited from the poorest arrondissements in Paris—wasn't touched upon. Fucking hell, it was ghastly. My shame over blithely allowing my cousin to have been put in this situation . . . well, it was galling.

In a few of the seedier tabloids, the journalists went further. This wasn't the first instance Aurélie had relied on men to get what she wanted. She'd lived with a man for years as his pet plaything. I trembled reading the first paper that included my name...and my employer. Bloody hell. Had Eiffel seen it, and worse, would it doom his tower after all the work we'd all put into making it a reality? I didn't even want to think about Eiffel believing such heinous things about me.

Obviously, I had to find Aurélie, but had no idea where. But I did know where to find Eiffel. I needed to explain. I checked my pocket watch. If I hurried, I'd possibly catch Eiffel in his office before he left for the evening. I took a cab and offered extra if he could get me there quicker.

When I got to the door, my heart throbbed in my throat. I lifted my chin and reminded myself that I owed this man an explanation.

His secretary raised her brows when she saw me and left me lingering in the lobby for a few minutes as she spoke with Eiffel behind the closed door to his office. She didn't make eye contact when she gestured for me to go in.

"Damn you, Tighe. Damn you." Eiffel stood and moved toward me with his hands balled into fists. I steeled myself for a blow, but instead, his shoulders sagged. "What have you got to say for yourself?" He picked up one of the newspapers on his desk—the one in which I'd seen my name linked with his.

"Monsieur, none of what they said about me or my cousin Mademoiselle Blancmaison is correct. It isn't like that, I swear."

"A ballet dancer, mon Dieu, and here I was, sorry for you that you were so brokenhearted you wouldn't even look at another woman."

I ground my teeth and sat, even though he hadn't offered me a chair, because I wasn't leaving until I made him understand that Aurélie wasn't anything like she was being portrayed.

"If you're losing investors, I can provide any funds that you need. I've tied up loose ends in England and have access to my inheritance. I beg your pardon that both of our names have been attached to this... Well, it must be a pack of lies because Aurélie would never, and honestly, neither would Gilbert Duhais. There's clearly a misunderstanding, and if I weren't so eager to make amends with you, I'd already be working on how to sort it out."

Eiffel leaned back on the edge of his desk and cocked his head. "We broke ground last week. A private investor already made the same pledge as you, thankfully, so I was able to move forward without de Gênet's involvement. My bank has already returned the money to your old friend Duhais, because there is no way I can be tied to this scandal. I'm not a violent man, but I might have called you out if you had destroyed my tower."

I continued to mumble apologies, and Eiffel crossed his arms over his chest, sighed.

"Tell me how you're so sure your cousin is innocent? She's a dancer, for heaven's sake, man. Which is simply an extraordinary notion. I never pictured you living with a ballet dancer." His look was piercing. "What do you believe happened between her and de Gênet if you claim they aren't lovers?"

I could hardly explain how I knew that Gilbert and Aurélie weren't sleeping together. Not without exposing myself. I ran my tongue over my lips, which were terribly dry. "Aurélie only met de Gênet one time that I know of, and he was terribly rude. Called her names. My cousin is dedicated to her craft. She doesn't wish for a patron, at all, and would never wish for his attention."

"Hmm." Eiffel. He exhaled deeply and went around to a bar cart in the corner of the room. He poured himself a brandy and then one for me even though he didn't ask. Then he handed it to me and nodded for me to drink. He sat down in the other club chair next to mine rather than behind his desk.

"Santé. It's interesting that you say so, and it rings true. Do you remember me saying I hadn't had much luck with de Gênet? I don't indulge in gossip, but that doesn't mean I never hear it." His lips twitched. "I will not mention any names, and I will deny anything if you quote me, but a woman I know very well was accosted by de Gênet a few years back, when I was working on the roof of Qualité. I confronted him, and he called the woman a liar. And a few other choice pejoratives. The man, frankly, is a connard, and I was surprised he was willing to pledge anything to the tower."

Something about his story tickled a memory. "Pardon my insolence, but can you tell me how he attacked this woman? The story feels familiar."

He sighed. "As it should—though a cad is a cad, and unfortunately, so many men think they can paw at a woman below them socially and get away with it. But, without being very explicit, he grabbed her and kissed her. He called her revolting names when she broke free from his grasp. She had a number of bruises."

Oh, God. Eiffel was right—this sort of story wasn't uncommon, and it was exactly what had happened to Aurélie at the ballet. "Then I hope you can believe me that my cousin was a victim in this instance. I haven't spoken to her since I've been back in the country, but I know it to the depth of my soul."

"The woman I know was quite rattled. I thought about choking the bastard myself, so I have sympathy for your friend Duhais."

Gilbert was the last person I wished to think about, and I felt a sense of urgency to check on Aurélie. I stood to leave, and Eiffel drew to his feet as well.

"I'm sorry for your cousin, Tighe. I am. But you do understand that our working relationship is finished. I can't have any sort of opprobrium attached to my name, nor to my tower."

"No, I understand. I appreciate you believing what I said about my cousin. I will repair her reputation."

Gustave Eiffel opened the door for me. "Admirable goal, though I can't see how you can change that. I'm surprised you aren't more concerned for your friend Duhais. I'd assume that as he was found holding the murder weapon, there's a possibility of the death sentence?"

My mouth dried. I swallowed the last of my brandy. "Hopefully, he can afford a clever enough lawyer to escape that fate." It was the only thing I could manage to say. I didn't have the emotional resources to cope with that possibility.

"And your cousin? I'm honestly surprised she hasn't also been arrested yet. You do realize it's only a matter of time?"

I was at a loss and fumbled for my hat. "You're right, and I must do anything I can to protect her." I shook Eiffel's hand and stumbled into the newly dark, cold evening.

Would I find Aurélie at our flat? Surely the ballet company wouldn't allow her to continue to dance with the defamation of her character hanging over her? On one hand, her presence onstage would surely sell tickets. But this story was too salacious, and the open discussion of patronage couldn't be helpful for the compagnie.

I took a taxi back to our flat, and Mademoiselle Jeunesse pounced nearly as soon as I walked through the vestibule. "Monsieur, a word."

Something in my face must have let her know I was no longer uncomfortable talking to her. She fidgeted, her voice shrill. "After this scandal, you must vacate the apartment. Immediately."

"From what I've read in the papers, mademoiselle, it appears as though you're helping to drive the narrative about this libelous gossip about my cousin. My situation has recently undergone a radical transformation, and I have the wherewithal—and the bank account—to take you to court if you continue to fan the flames."

She took a step back, hand touching her collarbone. I pulled a few bills from my pocket and handed them to her. "This will cover the length of my notice, and I will maintain the flat until I am finished with it. Bonne nuit, mademoiselle."

Never had the carpeting outside my flat looked so worn and sad. Well, we'd be out of here as soon as I found a new place for Aurélie. I fished for the key and knocked.

But the flat was empty. A few splatters of blood on the wall of the salon and a small pool that soaked through the carpet were all that was there to tell the tale of what might have happened between Aurélie, Gilbert, and Michel de Gênet.

Jesus wept.

I sidestepped the monstrosity, aching to do what I could to console Aurélie as quickly as possible. There was a note on the console next to the door.

Fin,

I don't know if you'll be back, but if you do—I'm at Stéphanie Verger's apartment until I figure out what to do next. Please.

Please. Dear Lord, the single word held a mountain of anguish, and even though I was tired enough to fall over where I stood, I immediately set off. So many questions ricocheted around my head. Why Stéphanie, and even more concerning: was Aurélie safe with Gilbert's fiancée?

How had any of this come to happen in the first place?

A half hour later, I was welcomed into the drawing room of Stéphanie's flat. The maid hurried down a hallway and left me bombarded with flashes of the previous times I'd been here. The last visit had been wretched enough with the slurs that dripped from Michel de Gênet about Aurélie. Though the first time, the night I'd brought Victoire and cemented my complicity to use my father's name, was hardly cheerful, either.

"Fin, oh mon Dieu, you've come, you've come." Aurélie barreled into the room and threw herself into my arms. Had she always been this frail?

The blotched and red face of my cousin nearly broke me. "My God, Aurélie. I'm so sorry."

She blinked some tears away, and after she loosened her grip, Stéphanie herded us over to a settee. Sitting half on me, half on the seat, Aurélie wouldn't let go of my hand. "You're truly here, Fin? Did you hear these wicked rumors about me? They've destroyed my life." Her sobs began anew. "I've been let go by the compagnie. They refused to listen to reason."

Aurélie's entire life was ballet. I couldn't imagine her not having the opportunity to be onstage again. But right now, I was more worried that she'd lose more than her career.

My eyes met Stéphanie's. "It's simply horrifying all the way around, Lord Carleton—"

"Fin. Please, just call me Fin. There's no time for anything superficial at the moment."

"You're correct. I'm relieved you've come back to Paris. Aurélie needs you, and I've been trying to—" Her dark eyes welled, and she dabbed at them with her handkerchief. She flashed a grim smile. "I'm convinced that Gilbert is going to be executed." Her lashes drooped.

"It's all my fault, Fin. How can you bear to look at me? I've done this." I'd never heard Aurélie so fatalistic, not even when she was an abused little girl.

"Hush. I don't know what happened, but I do know that there is no way you can be to blame. I lay that squarely at Michel's feet." I gave her hand a squeeze.

What had happened that would make Aurélie believe this was her fault? It couldn't just be that she'd been attacked.

Stéphanie pulled her hat off and took pins out. A tumble of black curls fell to her shoulders, and she didn't look much older than Aurélie. "This is as good a time as any to explain everything. Fin loves you, Aurélie. Tell him, so he can help determine the best course of action."

My cousin bit her lip so hard I worried she'd draw blood. But she nodded and took a deep breath.

"A few years ago, Paul began to come by when you were at work. To my school, to the apartment. Sometimes he'd be on the 'bus waiting for me."

I nodded, on the edge of my seat. She'd told me this before, when it was happening. I'd told him to leave her alone.

She read my mind. "More often than I said. He was a madman, Fin. He needed money to leave Paris because someone wanted him dead." She shrugged. I imagined that Paul had fingers in many dangerous pies. That was the type of person he was.

"He threatened me. Said he'd drag me to one of the bathhouses because there was someone who wished to meet me... That's where he worked as a pimp." She shivered so hard she lost her breath.

Like a splash of cold water, I woke up. Focused. That's where he'd been murdered.

"You told him you were going to Nice, didn't you? He knew I was alone." Aurélie scraped her front teeth over her bottom lip. It was chapped and raw, presumably from doing the same thing over and over for days.

"Yes." It was hard to force the word out. I'd inadvertently alerted him she was alone. Unprotected.

Her face dropped into her hands, and her shoulders shook in long, heavy sobs. "I said I would, but then he needed to forget I was ever his sister after. I'd meet him the next day. I was sick, Fin. I sat up all night plotting how I could make him stop this. I wanted to dance, and not sell myself."

Fucking hell. She'd never told me. I pulled my hanky from my jacket and handed it to her. She blew her nose loudly and caught her breath.

"I didn't wait for him to fetch me, sent a note that I'd meet him

there, *on my honor*. As if he knew what the word even meant."
Her terror was so visceral, I felt it, too, a malevolent presence in
the exquisite drawing room that I wished to vanquish. Stéphanie
reached a hand out and grabbed Aurélie's other, for courage.

"You always made me carry a knife. And he never expected it,
not from me, you know? But I'd never allow him to do that to me,
never again." Eyes flashed fire, and I nodded.

No. She couldn't. Paul had already stolen too much from her.

"I wrapped a shawl over my hair and most of my face so no one
would recognize me. He was awful, Fin, contemptuous that I'd
come, like he hadn't threatened me." Aurélie put her feet back on
the carpet, as though she was going to stand. Her hands moved as
though she was reliving the moment.

"He'd booked a private bath, where I was to meet this man.
We walked down the hall, and it was mostly dark. I can't bear
the smell of ammonia. That's what it was like down there. I could
barely keep from gagging. No one was around besides me and
Paul. I kicked the back of one of his knees. He dropped, and I
pulled his head backward and used every bit of anger I'd held on
to for years and slit his throat."

For a second, she dared me to judge her, and then she crumbled. I held out my arms to show her that I didn't, not in the way
she might fear. "I did it so I could live my own damned life."

Yes. And she had. It wasn't only me taking care of her basic
needs; I'd taught her to take care of herself, too. I was amazed.
Gratified, and impressed. She'd taken care of herself. All this time
I worried she was unable to, and she was stronger than I'd ever
been.

"My God, Aurélie—I'm so proud of you. That was more brave

than I've ever been in my entire damned life." I pressed my temple to hers. "You were strong and courageous. He was a bloody miscreant." Depraved. Violent. Twisted and despicable. And she'd killed him. I tried to embrace her, but she pulled back.

Her smile was watery, eyes red-rimmed. "But someone saw, after all. I didn't know until a few months ago when he came to let me know that if I didn't wish to be arrested, I'd better do what he said."

A shiver raced down my spine, made worse from the flash of fury on Stéphanie's face across from us.

Aurélie searched for the words. "It was Michel de Gênet. He was following Paul that day, because of Gilbert, you know? Looking back, it's the only explanation."

"Michel?" My voice still worked. How could my voice still work?

Stéphanie touched my arm. "Michel was suspicious about Paul's relationship to Gilbert. A month or two back, Sonny told Gilbert that he'd been put on alert to follow them and report back to Michel."

That old pain of disgust writhed in my abdomen. "So, Michel knew about Paul and Gilbert?"

"Oui, and he told Sonny to get rid of Paul. But I did it first. Michel did nothing to me then. I'd done him a favor, I suppose." Aurélie rubbed her cheek on her shoulder. "But when he saw me again at the ballet the night I debuted with the corps de ballet, he told me he knew what I had done, Fin, and then he attacked me. I was so scared, and I kicked him and raced out from behind the curtain. And you were there, and you looked so proud, and I was so ashamed that you'd never feel the same about me if I told what I did to Paul."

I'd been a naïve fool the evening of Aurélie's first performance. I believed de Gênet's good press. "You could have told me."

"I told the master of the stage what he'd done, and he said I was a fool not to form a liaison with him." Her short, sharp laugh was particularly lacking in humor. "And besides, what would you have done, if I'd come clean to you? If you'd spoken to him, he would have ruined your career. We'd have lost our apartment. And if you didn't, you would have insisted I quit the ballet. Why should that pig have that much power over our lives because he was a fils de pute?"

Dear Lord, she was correct, though I hated to admit it. I squeezed her hand and urged her to continue.

"Then when Gilbert arrived at the apartment building a few days after, I was sure he was there to threaten me, but he didn't, and I was so confused. And Gilbert continued to be nice. De Gênet didn't come back to the Opéra for a while, and I stopped being frightened. I had a reprieve, and I was too relieved to question it." She drew a ragged breath, and I hated the need to urge her on.

"I wish you would have said something. Anything. So I'd have known that this was such a threat."

Stéphanie shook her head, aggravated. "Fin, Lord Carlton, pardon me, but this isn't Aurélie's fault for not telling you. Nor is it your fault for not knowing. Too often we blame the victims, but I won't allow it. She's correct, you would have locked her down."

"You would have said it wasn't safe for me to dance, and I couldn't give that up, not for anything. And besides, I thought, if it came down to it, I could just do what he wanted. Get it over with."

That was an appalling thing, but I refused to linger on it.

Aurélie wasn't finished. "It seems unbelievable, but I can take the things that scare me, the things I went through as a child, and bury them away where they can't frighten me. And that's what I did with that horrible man. But then he appeared in the cloakroom again. The night Jody died, and I was finally going to confess everything to you so you could help me, but obviously, there were too many other things happening that weekend, and I couldn't add to your burdens." She twisted her skirt in her hand so hard it seemed she'd rip it.

Her hands moved in a dance of...not contrition. Self-defense. As if she needed to defend her actions to me. I was gutted. "When I came to Stéphanie's party with Rosette, and Michel called me all of those evil names, well, Stéphanie saw something was wrong. I told her everything. She said I needed to stay as far away from him as I could, that he liked to hurt women, and she was doing her best to prove it so he'd be jailed."

My girl walked to one of the long windows and pulled back the drapes. "Tell Fin about your maman, Stéphanie. How you've known all along that he was a monster."

"My mother was married to Michel for less than a year when she first saw his temper. He was erratic, and would be cruel when there were quarrels. Unfortunately, all of the money she brought to the marriage was legally his, though she was doing her damnedest to find a loophole to get some of it back. She was going to tell him the day she died. They'd been riding—alone—and she was thrown from her horse." Stéphanie's tone made it clear she didn't believe it was an accident. She stood and pulled a decanter of red wine from the sideboard, pouring three glasses.

From where I sat, she struggled to pull herself back together. Her mouth was compressed and grim when she handed me my wineglass. "I said at the inquest that I believed it was incompetently handled." She'd questioned why her mother suffered two black eyes and had blood under her nails that matched three scratches under Michel's left eye. "The judge was a friend of Michel's." Stéphanie squared her shoulders, as unshakable as a fortress. I shivered. How could she look so calm? This was her mother's possible murder she was talking about. "That was the day I decided I'd ruin him, if it was the last thing I did."

"Bloody hell, why on earth did you stay in contact with him if you believed he murdered your mother?"

"Money. I had none. I depended on Michel for my apartment, for my clothing allowance, for my bank account. It's been agonizing to behave civilly to him. But Gilbert and I decided that we'd marry so I'd have equal access to Michel's fortune. By rights, I ought to be at the very least a shareholder. We planned for me to take charge of the new store in London after we took care of Michel, and then, after a few years, Gilbert and I would divorce. Split the money, and go on with our lives."

It sounded ominous, and if it were anyone else besides Gilbert Duhais, I'd feel some sympathy. "Take care of Michel, how, exactly?"

"Prison, most likely with his clout. But anyone else who'd abused so many women would face the guillotine." Stéphanie's face was grim. "If I walked away, there'd be no one to help his victims."

"A-a-abused so many women? What women?"

Aurélie swiveled and sat next to me again with a flounce. "Fin, the man was a fiend. He hurt so many of his staff, and Stéphanie was helping them escape, if she could."

Escape? My face must have betrayed my confusion.

"Two women who worked for Michel went missing, and no one knew what might have happened. Except I knew what he'd done to Maman and worried that it would be even easier for him to have women taken care of if they weren't in the public eye. I allowed the housekeeper at Michel's to know that I recognized their precarious position. If she caught wind of someone being mistreated, she'd send them to me." Stéphanie chewed the inside of her cheek and stared into her wineglass. "Your friend's sister—Charlotte, oui?—I...well, I spoke with her before she disappeared. Said I'd write her a reference, loan her funds to get away, but she was adamant that Michel couldn't get away with hurting anyone ever again. I warned her not to confront him, but there was nothing I could do. Then she was gone. And when Gilbert told me that you were asking for her, I wasn't sure if I could trust you."

Charlotte. Poor, brave Charlotte. And Jody. Jody might still be alive had he learned the mystery of his sister's absence. "Why didn't you say something? My friend died looking for answers about her."

"Would he have let it go if he knew? I've been asking myself that, and honestly, I don't think he would have abandoned his need to punish Michel. And I needed to carry out my plan. You see, I was arrogant. I thought that as long as I got the girls away and safe, they would testify against Michel when the time was right, and he'd at least be sent to prison."

Agitated, I rose and strode across the room, back and forth.

"How many bloody women needed to be hurt before you did that, Mademoiselle Verger?"

She lifted her chin. "You ought to ask the metropolitan gendarmerie, Fin, because I accompanied each of the women to report Michel's offenses, and even after six visits, they still never took it seriously."

"S-s-six women?"

"Not including your Charlotte." Stéphanie ground her back teeth, her fury clearly written on her face.

"So, these six women are all willing to repeat their stories in court?"

Aurélie walked over and linked her arm in mine. "They are, and there are three more downstairs. Stéphanie allows them to live and work here until they can find new jobs. But do you think any of that will matter to a jury made of men who probably also don't care about working-class women?"

That's why she had so many maids in her kitchen. Any lingering doubt that she was a decent human evaporated. Everything I'd heard this evening sickened me, and yet—hadn't I understood the world was unfairly balanced against women? Perhaps on one level, but not as deeply as the women who had to take precautions every day to maintain their security.

"But that day with Michel at your apartment, Aurélie. Explain what happened, or shall I?"

"Stéphanie told me to come to her if I needed help, and she'd help. And I thought I could manage. But now Gilbert's in jail, and I'm so scared about what will happen to him. Can you forgive me?"

I put my hands on her shoulders, looked into her eyes. "There's nothing to forgive, Aurélie. Not from me." I didn't wish to think about how Gilbert fit into this equation, but there was no alternative. "But I'm listening."

"I haven't confessed the worst bit. Don't interrupt or I'll never be able to. I had the night off from practice—it was the understudies' turn. I didn't bother to latch the door, like you always said." Pressing her fingertips to her temples, she screwed her eyes tight. "There was a knock, and I—" She choked on a sob. "Fin, you'll be so cross with me, but I assumed it was Mademoiselle Jeunesse coming to fuss about something, and I opened without looking."

My chest got tight, so tight I could only get air in with my mouth open. Ragged and sharp.

"And it was de Gênet?"

Nodding, she crawled closer to me, pressing her shoulder into my armpit and curling her knees underneath her. "That fucking sadist came in. He pushed past me."

Her voice stumbled. "He told me that you'd abandoned me when you returned to England. That it was obvious I meant nothing to you. And I could smell the liquor on his breath. His eyes were wild. So frightening. He called me a tease. A saloppe. He said I deserved to be punished."

Inhaling through her nostrils, she stopped, as if she had replayed it in her mind, and it was too painful to share. I stroked her arm with my thumb, back and forth; in the same rhythm she always rubbed fabric against her cheek.

"You're none of those things, Aurélie. You're a talented young woman who happens to be beautiful. If a man is affected by you, it isn't because you made it happen. You are who you are." I made my tone as soothing as possible.

"He wanted to kill me. And he would have. I tried to get away, and I'm fast. I can kick hard, but it made him angrier, and he yanked me by my hair." The words tumbled out of her mouth without taking a breath, each wound described in such detail I wanted to beg her to stop telling me, but she had to say it, to get it out.

How she'd survived I wasn't sure. But he hadn't managed to rape her.

Rubbing a closed fist over one eye did nothing to slow the tracks of tears. "I had my knife, next to the bed. I've slept with it since…you know…?"

Oh, my throat closed tighter with every word, understanding where her story veered. I fought to keep the knowing from my face. I nodded. "Since I gave you one when you lived with me, when Paul left. Yes."

When she needed a symbol to remind herself she wasn't completely vulnerable.

"I was able to bring it closer to me with my fingertips when he…was…"

I gave her a short nod; she didn't need to explain.

"Then I got it in my hand even though it was so sweaty. I didn't slice across because I was in the wrong position, but I thrust it so hard into"—Aurélie tapped the hollow of her throat—"*here*. And he gurgled and let go so he could touch his neck, and maybe I ought to have just run, that's what I keep telling myself, but I didn't. I went behind him and sliced all the way across. *All the way*, when I should have just left."

Pulling her back into my arms, I rubbed her back as though she was small again. As soothing as I could. Inside, I quaked.

347

That second cut was the difference between striking for survival and murder. Utterly unfair—especially in a situation like hers.

Aurélie sniffed into the handkerchief I handed her. "You'd think I'd faint or cry, but non. I watched him die, and *I smiled*, Fin."

She inhaled, stared off into nothing, exhaling with slumped shoulders. "When I was sure he was dead, I snapped out of my rage and understood what trouble I was in, what was going to happen to me. And it was so *wrong*, because I didn't ask him to do that, but everyone thinks I'm a whore just because I dance, and I'm not. I'm not." The pitched shrillness of her voice at the end set my blood cold, and I grasped for something—anything—I could do to provide comfort.

Her voice dropped to a whisper. "Stéphanie had told me to come to her. And I remembered Gibby helped with Jody, and I thought he could help me, too. I washed myself—my hands, oh Fin! They were..." She shuddered but soon steadied herself. "I cleaned as well as I could, and changed into my plainest dress and shoes. I wore a scarf over my head, and I climbed down the fire escape as soon as it turned dark."

And what had I been doing at that same time when I ought to have been here, with her? Idly reading some book on family history, or walking through the garden? Counting the money in my new bank account?

"Stéphanie sent for Gibby, and when I told him, he said he'd take care of everything, that he wasn't angry, just that he would fix it."

Aurélie buried her face in her hands, shoulders shaking so

hard I thought I might have to intervene before it blew into full-fledged hysteria. "I crept back up the fire escape and waited for him to knock at the front door, like nothing was unusual. He promised he'd find a way to get rid of the body. But when he came and knocked to be allowed in, Mademoiselle Jeunesse followed him. She lectured him about propriety—I heard her through the door, as though she knew him well enough to talk like that. She finally left, and I brought him in, but Mademoiselle Jeunesse returned some time later after fetching a gendarme to make him leave." Aurélie wept too hard to continue, so Stéphanie took the story up.

"It seems that there was no time to remove Michel's body."

It all unfolded in my mind like I was watching it onstage.

"Gilbert insisted it was him, Fin. When they arrived, he said he'd come in and saw I was being attacked and slit his uncle's throat. But no one believed it was to protect me. They kept asking, why would he do that… *for me?* Insisted that Gilbert must have been hoping to murder his uncle and this was the best way to do it." Her nose and eyes were red, and she twisted a lock of hair so hard she would cut the circulation off in her finger.

"Without you, I wouldn't even be alive, Fin. You've given me so much, and now, because of me, Gilbert's going to be sent to a penal colony or executed. I went to the jail and begged him to tell them it was a lie, but he said that he had enough money to get away with it, but I wouldn't. They'd think I was a greedy gutter flower. And he had to save me, for your sake. Because you'd never forgive yourself if something happened to your other sister." She looked at me, expecting me to disagree.

My other sister.

My voice cracked with the need to make her know it. "He's right. You are my family, Aurélie. The only one I have."

Gilbert was correct about all of it. Aurélie would've been executed already for killing Michel de Gênet. And I couldn't bear to lose her, no matter who else I lost. I loved her as much as I loved Annabeth. Aurélie had kept me alive in those years of misery.

All this time, I was under the impression that I'd rescued her. *But I was wrong.*

She'd saved me. She'd given me someone to live for, to belong to.

Sadly, Gilbert overestimated his own powers of persuasion.

And he might die for the mistake.

36

I'd asked Aurélie if she wished to leave with me, but though there was some sort of dilemma in her eyes, she chose to remain at Stéphanie's.

I couldn't really blame her; I had no desire to go back to the flat, either. I decided that I'd fetch my luggage and ensconce myself in a hotel since I could afford it. After telling Aurélie I'd return the following day to check on her, Stéphanie followed me to the door. There was a sense that she needed to tell me something in private.

"Sonny's body was found two weeks ago."

Her blunt words took me back to my final evening in Paris, though I'd done my best to keep any happier memories of traitorous Gilbert at bay. "What does that have to do with me?"

Stéphanie tapped her foot impatiently. "Gilbert is my closest friend. He told me, and it's a problem. Not because he's dead—he was a complete shit, just like Michel. But he can't be arrested. He would have corroborated the maids' testimony if there'd been a chance of his facing life in prison, and he could have pinned it on Michel instead of himself."

I shook my head, befuddled. "I'm not following."

"Who do you think got rid of the bodies of the missing domes-tiques?"

Charlotte had been dispatched by bloody Sonny Tolbert? I exhaled sharply as though I was delivered a punch square in my solar plexus.

Gilbert had had Jody's body removed from his apartment.

"What about Charlotte's brother? How involved was Gilbert"— I snarled his damned name—"in the *tidying up* for Michel?"

Stéphanie readjusted her stance. "Gilbert only had a guess about Sonny because we tried to work out how Michel could have gotten rid of the women. He wouldn't have dirtied his hands with the *tidying up*, as you call it." She looked away, pursing lips to the side as if debating. "It was a calculated risk that Gilbert took, asking Sonny to help with your friend's body, and Sonny didn't even act as though it was a difficult task. I'm so sorry about Jody's death. We guessed that either Michel ordered it after Jody hounded Michel, or Sonny took it on himself to get rid of Jody because he wouldn't let his sister's disappearance go."

Jody wouldn't *ever* have let Charlotte's disappearance drop. Not even if he'd known the risk was to incur de Gênet's wrath. I gave myself a moment to let all of this sink in and enjoyed a flash of satisfaction that Sonny was dead, in no small thanks to me.

"Gilbert knew all along that it was Sonny who killed my best friend, and said nothing to me? Nothing?"

"Shh, lower your voice. Non. He didn't tell you because he assumed you'd do something as reckless as your friend and also end up killed. At the very least, you'd have said something that would alert Sonny that you knew Jody from the cabaret, which would have likely also given Sonny the means to blackmail you. And Gilbert couldn't bear Sonny having any power over your life."

Scoffing, I rolled my eyes. "Gilbert despises me. He tried to set me up for God knows what sort of punishment by persuading me to dine out on my father's name. He's as much of a connard as Sonny or Michel."

Stéphanie looked pained. "That's not true, or at least, it wasn't as soon as he got to know you, but I can understand why you don't believe me." She sighed. "I urge you to visit Gilbert at the prison. Listen to what he has to say, because it's simply not my place to tell you some things."

"I never want to see that baratineur again."

She opened her mouth and closed it again, like she wrestled with herself. And then she said, "You might not have the chance, if you don't do it before he goes to trial. The papers have already tried and convicted him, and honestly, I think he'll be lucky to survive and just be sent to a penal colony."

I fussed with putting my overcoat back on, not trusting myself with a response about Gilbert. "Right now, my only concern is keeping Aurélie from being arrested, too. From what I've read, the public is questioning why she hasn't been. I'm going to find the best lawyer in the city. Thank God I've inherited enough to pay for it."

Stéphanie smoothed the collar of my coat, the small lines around her mouth deeper than they ought to have been. "That's wise, though I hope it won't be necessary. Gilbert has sacrificed himself, so let's pray that will satisfy the mob."

"Pardon me, Stéphanie, but I can't think of him like a hero. Not with what I know about his lies."

She opened the front door. "I do understand that your feelings are hurt, but I wish you'd allow him to explain now, while he's still able to. Will you forgive yourself if you could have heard his defense before you lose your chance?"

I refused to answer and excused myself.

December in Paris can be miserable, and that evening was true to form. I wandered toward the Champ de Mars to look over the foundation for Eiffel's tower. It was not ours any longer, though I still had a proprietary interest. Iron pilings were under tied-down tarpaulins next to where the earth was overturned for the four legs of the structure.

It wouldn't be happening if it hadn't been for me and all the money I raised.

Or if Gilbert hadn't introduced me to so many investors.

No. I wouldn't give him an ounce of credit. As I pulled my collar around my ears as a barrier from the biting wind, I wondered if it was cold in his prison cell.

Not that I would find out, because even knowing all he'd given up to protect Aurélie, I despised him.

Damn it. I hailed a taxi to retrieve my things at the flat.

Mademoiselle Jeunesse dared to come out when I dragged my valise down the steps. Without a word, she handed me an onionskin envelope with the telltale markings of a telegram. She scampered back into her own home and loudly drew the chain over the lock.

I leaned against the brass mailboxes and felt a sense of terror that this would only be further calamitous news.

Dear Fin,

The house is lonely now, even though you've been gone hardly two days. I believe I might visit Paris in the spring so I can see you, unless you need me sooner. I'd rather not lose you again, though I'll wait for an invitation before delivering myself on your doorstep.

Dearest, please know that whatever the outcome of this situation with your cousin and your friend, I'll be there for you, as I know you must care for them both so deeply. Please, watch out for yourself. There are some crimes not even your respectable dowager countess can protect you from.

You will always remain my beloved grandson. Nothing you do will ever change that.

Yours, Eleanor

Postscript—I've always wished to visit Paris and could never convince anyone to take me. I believe I am now old enough to come on my own. Please don't forget my invitation. April or May would suit me perfectly.

She must have paid a fortune for such a long message, and the idea that she did it merely to cheer me up had me fumbling for the handkerchief I'd inadvertently left behind with Aurélie. I used the cuff of my sleeve in its stead and wiped my eyes.

She was wrong, though. I didn't care about Gilbert. Only Aurélie.

Except that wasn't true.

And I had no idea what I could do about it.

37

Even in a luxurious suite at one of the city's best hotels, my sleep was restless. Anxious. Full of nightmares that lingered even when the gray dawn broke through the velvet draperies.

I must do what I can—not only to make sure that Aurélie isn't punished for protecting herself—but to make sure that Gilbert doesn't die for taking the blame.

She'd never forgive herself, and I knew well enough how guilt could haunt one's life.

Sluggishly, I shrugged on one of my tweed blazers from Qualité. I wish I'd never run into that scoundrel Gilbert, but I had, and he'd been correct when he told me weeks earlier at the ballet: we were knotted together in some way I was unable to cut away.

Unable to eat, I walked most of the way through the winding neighborhoods of the Rive Gauche to the fourteenth arrondissement's most notorious building, La Santé, the formidable stone fortress of a prison where Gilbert was being held until his trial the following week.

The structure was as gloomy and dismal as could be expected.

God help me, I'd prefer nearly anything to avoid meeting with Gilbert. I despised him, but I didn't wish him to die or to be sent to rot off the coast of Guiana in South America. And it was also best to hear his version of events before meeting with prospective lawyers for Aurélie.

At the front gate, I stopped short and had to control the urge to run away like a child. A guillotine. Smaller than I'd imagined as a student reading about the horrors of the revolution. The blade was washed—blessedly—and not shiny, but the metallic clink of my imagination sent chills racing up my spine.

No. I didn't wish Gilbert to die.

It took fifteen minutes to convince no less than three employees to search out the warden in charge to speak with me. I relied on my English accent to confuse the man who needed to believe that I was part of Gilbert's defense team, but not so much that he sent me away in disgust.

Throwing up his arms, he finally barked for one of the jailers to take me to an interrogation room. Through the close administrative hallway, there were rumbles of noise from the cells that lay behind solid steel doors. It was brightly lit with kerosene that burned my nose.

"Wait here," the jailer said in staccato French, assuming incorrectly that I was ignorant of the language. The room was small, though not as small as the cells were, most likely. Three chairs were spread around a heavy metal table bolted to the concrete floor. An upside-down U made of iron protruded from the middle of the table.

I thanked him in English, and he didn't react, so I repeated my gratitude in embarrassingly broken French as I sat down.

And then I waited.

It was close to an hour before the key in the door was turned, and it creaked open. A guard behind Gilbert pushed him through. Bloody hell, he looked awful. Pathetic. Manacles attached to his wrists were secured to the bolt through the table.

His eyes widened when he saw me before dropping his gaze to the floor. A hint of color suffused his cheeks.

"I never imagined seeing you with a beard, Duhais. It suits you." I continued in English, in the hope that I was right and the guard wasn't conversant.

Those beautiful dark eyes simmered with some emotion I couldn't translate. "My valet thought it would be the perfect touch to set off my new uniform. So pleased you appreciate the effort."

The guard spoke in French—to Gilbert—that he'd be just outside. He shut the door and opened a small window so he could watch us.

I don't know what I thought I'd feel when I saw Gilbert again, but it wasn't this. This wishing I could kiss him and throw a punch to his chin in equal measure. To be fair, he looked as though he shared the same warring emotions.

"What you've done for Aurélie is tremendous." It was going to be difficult to maintain a lack of emotion in my voice, but I couldn't alert the guard that I was there for anything other than a purely professional reason.

"My uncle was a piece of filth."

I picked at a piece of lint on my thigh. "He was much worse than that. He killed Charlotte. And Jody. And you bloody well knew and didn't say anything."

Gilbert's jaw worked hard. "I suspected about Charlotte only. I had no idea that he'd hurt Jody. Or have Sonny do it. Not until it was too late."

"You didn't even have a thought to Jody's safety when he confronted you at le Chien Volage? Or when he said he was going to have words with Michel?"

One of the manacles pulled his arm down when he attempted to reach out toward me. Thank God, as we didn't need any sort of histrionic display. "I sincerely didn't. I knew he'd chased some of the poor domestiques off, and Stéphanie believed that he and Sonny murdered the women, but until I asked Sonny to help me remove Jody's body, I couldn't be sure. And then the worst had already happened."

I stood and paced the room, unable to look at Gilbert. "Why did you lie to me? About my father wishing to be back in my life."

"Fin, I apologize. For all of it. If there was anything I could take back, I would." There was a tremor in his earnestness. I glanced at him, and his body leaned in my direction, beseeching. "All of it besides getting to know you. I'll face that damned executioner outside ten times over to pay for the good fortune of having had you in my life, at least for a short time."

"Spare me the melodrama, because I don't wish to lose my breakfast. You set me up. I read that letter from my father. The very last thing he wished for was to have me in his life. And yet, you convinced me that he not only felt regret for everything in my childhood, he wanted to make me his God-damned heir."

"Congratulations. Here you are. *His God-damned heir.*"

360

My voice betrayed me. "Why?" It was loud enough that the guard turned and glared.

"Sit, please. I know I have no right to ask you to hear me out, but please. Sit."

Straightening my tie, and catching my emotions back up, I sat, straight-backed, and looked him full on. I steeled myself for whatever cruelty he would unleash.

"I've done some terrible things, Fin. And made even worse choices. I know that now. But I was a fool. I met your cousin Paul when I was twenty. Michel's son had recently died, and he insisted I move from Amiens to Paris so he could train me up as his successor. Paul had been working for him. Odd jobs. I was naïve. Thrilled to have come into such good fortune, and Paul was kind to me when Michel was anything but kind." There was a hard edge to his words and he couldn't meet my eyes. "I had no idea about any of the horrors Paul had done to Aurélie. Didn't know he had a sister for ages. He could be very charming, and I was wet behind the ears."

He ran his tongue over parched lips and winced at some internal thought. "Do you know, I never understood why I wasn't mad for any girls, until one day, he touched my face. Brushed back some hair from my eyes. I couldn't stop thinking about it. About him."

I jabbed my thumbs into my forearms to distract me from a fleeting dart of pain. "Do you sincerely believe I have any desire to hear how you fell in love with that despicable—"

"Non. But I didn't. Not really." He made a sad noise. "Oh, I no longer know what I felt for him because now I know who he really was, and I'm disgusted. But you don't wish to hear of my regret, even though I need you to know I have it. He moved into my flat. I can see now, finally, that he used me. He got to pocket his salary while I took care of everything else. He reported on me to Michel—nothing to put himself in harm's way, of course, but small things that didn't make sense until much later. I always thought it was Sonny who was the snitch until that night at le Chien Volage."

His forehead wrinkled in grief. "Paul told me a different story about Aurélie. He said that you were selling her. All of the horrific things that he did, he blamed on you. I was appalled. Horrified. And he was a damned good actor—even made himself cry over it. Said he was terrified you'd hurt him if he tried to intervene."

I dug my fingertips into my thighs until it hurt, trying not to picture what Gilbert was telling me, but I could imagine the scene all too well.

"Mon beau—"

"Don't you dare call me that."

Gilbert clamped his lips together, hard. "I beg your pardon. Non, I don't deserve to call you anything." He choked back a sad sort of moan in his throat. "When Paul's body was discovered, I naturally assumed it had been you. I didn't know anything about you except what he'd told me, so how would I know better?"

"So you stalked me and tried to blackmail my father?" I wasn't about to allow him to manipulate me into a sense of guilt or sadness.

362

"I'd be more ashamed if it didn't ultimately work out so beautifully for you, but non—that wasn't my intention. Paul's mother had the marriage certificate. There was some story about her life being ruined when she told your father about it. She fled to France, and I suppose Paul thought he'd figure out a way to use it against you."

The annoyance made me snort. "Or at least keep me from ever being acknowledged as his legitimate heir."

I needed to get out of this stuffy room devoid of anything positive before I screamed and was led out in my own manacles. I moved to the door to escape all the anger welling up inside of me.

"Wait, please. Fin, I realized quite early on that you were a decent man. The most decent man I ever met, in fact. What you do for Aurélie—well, I'm in awe."

My hand dropped from the knob, but I didn't turn to Gilbert.

"The night you told me about what Paul did to her as a child—I went home and panicked. How could I have had feelings for such a disgusting, monstrous person? I'd been so very wrong about everything, and there'd be consequences because of my ignorance and malice. My God, I'd even put the ad in the newspaper to make it look like he was searching for you. I'd already done so much hoping that you'd provoke your father into suing you for libel. But I also had the proof that everything you said was true. I just had no idea how to tell you, and I kept putting it off. Your father was sick—close to death—when I met him in London last summer. And because Harry had died...well, I hoped that if I just kept going, it might turn out in the end. And it did."

I wheeled around on my heel and slammed my palm on the table in front of him. "You continued to lie for your own convenience. There were so many instances you could have come clean. Allowed me to make the decisions about what I was willing to give up to take care of Aurélie. If I'd had that check, she would have been safe, but instead, she was pawed over by the abonnés—"

"That's why I paid for her classes, anonymously. It was the least I could do for her, and once I realized that you were the man you are, I said I would continue to pay for her lessons. When your father died, I went to England to your grandmother and showed her the marriage certificate to ensure that you would be recognized as the heir, but it wasn't enough—because I wasn't sure how to break it to you that none of it was a lie."

Gilbert curled one arm onto the table and hid his face. "The last night we were together, I was so anxious to tell you, but my feelings were so strong, and all I kept telling myself was that you'd never forgive me."

"I won't."

He raised his head, and his cheeks were damp. "I know."

We stared at each other for a long moment, my chest huffing with anger and . . . sadness. It was almost unbearable. "I still don't understand why you needed me to sign papers for Michel."

Nodding slowly, he eased himself back to sitting upright. "Michel found out about us. Probably from Sonny. He wanted you dead."

My hand reached to my empty chair for balance. "Dead?"

"As though I'd keep in line if he did something so vile. So I gambled and showed him the marriage certificate. A British earl couldn't simply disappear into the gutters of Paris without someone noticing, and he knew it. Especially if you were in a contracted agreement with him. I hoped that if he was legally dependent on you to get his London branch of Qualité built, he'd have to leave you alone. At least long enough for Stéphanie to finally have enough of a case against Michel for the police to have to do something to restrain him."

There was so much to digest, and I could hardly grab on to the enormity of the schemes Gilbert had been running.

Gilbert had tracked me down to ruin me. And then he contrived to save my life. All of my muscles were limp as though I'd been run through a clothes mangle.

"I know what happened at my apartment with Aurélie. I just don't understand why because..." *you're likely to die for it.*

"Aurélie is a brave woman, and she never deserved any of the horrible things that have happened to her at the hands of brutes like Michel. And Paul."

No woman did. No *person* did.

I heaved a sigh and busied myself with putting my hat on just so, so Gilbert wouldn't see that I was...well...moved.

"Thank you." It was low and gruff, but he must have heard it. I knocked for the warden to let me out. He peeked through the small window on the door and nodded.

"Fin, I'm sorry. Truly. But I hope you'll realize one day why I've made this decision, even if it results in my meeting with Madame la Guillotine out front."

The warden was followed by a second jailer, who waited for me to leave before unlocking Gilbert's chains. I gave him one last look and asked, "Why?" before I could stop myself.

He flashed a smile that held an echo of the cheeky one I'd adored. "I hope that you'll understand that this will prove to you once and for all that even though I started out behaving abominably, I'm in love with you. I'm so sorry for the trouble I've caused. Maybe someday, you'll forgive me for being such a fool."

38

'm not sure exactly what I did for the hour following my conversation with Gilbert. After hurrying past the guillotine—which was somehow even more menacing than it had been before I'd been inside the prison—I simply wandered. There'd been a sprinkling of sleet all day, which mixed with the coal dust, leaving everything coated in a dismal sludge.

Even if I understood—to a small degree—what Gilbert had been hoping to achieve, I couldn't forgive him for the ill will. It was too deep a cut.

Everything turned out for the best, in the long run. For me, at least. Aurélie was stranded without her career. Jody and Charlotte were dead. Gilbert waited for the whims of the jury to decide his fate.

And, if I could believe him: he loved me.

Blowing into my hands in an attempt to warm them drove me to find a boulangerie for a pastry and a warm cup of coffee. The closest was next to a tobacco shop, with the newspapers hawked by a young boy wearing few enough clothes to send me shivering. I grabbed a copy of each, tucking them under my arm, and gave him some extra change so he could buy himself a drink to try to keep the chill off.

Petit Rat Shares the Blame

I choked on a sip of drink and hastily wiped my mouth.

> Aurélie Blancmaison was a willing partner in crime when one of her lovers conspired to murder the other. Gilbert Duhais prepares his defense, but when will the dishonored ballerina share his punishment?

Unable to eat, I scalded my tongue with another swallow of coffee and headed back into the cold morning. Stéphanie had given me the address of Gilbert's lawyer, and I made my way there to see if there was a way to cobble together a decent defense based on the testimony of the maids who'd escaped from Michel de Gênet's clutches.

The lawyer was coming out from his office just as I walked into his waiting room. Exuding not a drip of confidence, the lawyer rubbed the small of his back, as if it ached. "Can I help you?"

I stuck out my hand. "I'm Finley Tighe. The man Aurélie—"

He changed his stance, looked over his spectacles. "Yes, yes. I know. But you were in England? That's why we haven't contacted you."

"I was, but now I'm here, and I wish to take the stand in Duhais's defense."

The man was slight, made smaller by his voluminous robes. But an intelligence in his eyes gave me a moment of hope for

Gilbert's future. He pursed his lips before speaking. "Frankly, I'm unsure how you could help—unless you have a decent reason for my client to have spent so many nights at your flat with Mademoiselle Blancmaison."

"Gilbert didn't tell you?"

The man folded his arms over his chest. "It's like speaking to a brick wall. He won't consider explaining, even if it saves his skin."

My eyes darted around the room.

"Shall we speak in private?"

Nodding, I followed him into his own office and shut the door. I settled into a leather chair that was cracked on one arm. Idly, I rubbed the slit. It was like a knife wound.

"Monsieur Duhais was found holding the murder weapon, and had a train ticket to the coast in his pocket. It stinks of premeditation. The fact that witnesses testify he spent multiple evenings with Mademoiselle Blancmaison gives clear indication that they were having an affair. The prosecutor has checked with the ballet, and he also paid for her private lessons." He shut his eyes and removed his spectacles, rubbing the bridge of his nose before replacing them. "I'm not a very sophisticated man, but even I know that is how these affairs with ballet dancers are handled by the abonnés. Unless you can give me a sturdy reason why Monsieur Duhais's uncle was at your apartment—besides the most obvious one, that he was also romantically entangled with your cousin—I'm not sure I can see a way out of this." He stood, as if dismissing me.

It was too unfair. I kept firm in my chair. "Pardon, but Michel de Gênet was a monster. He attempted to rape my cousin Aurélie Blancmaison and was killed to keep that from happening. If she's called as a witness, she'll explain."

"Monsieur, you realize that the prosecution will tear her apart in cross-examination? I read her account to the police, and it was full of holes. She changed her story more than twice. The safest thing for both her and my client is to pray she isn't called as a witness, because I don't want her making this worse for my client. And it's likely she'll be escorted off the stand in police custody."

Flummoxed, I persisted, anger pitching my voice an octave higher. "Aurélie is the victim. She was scared of de Gênet. And that reprehensible connard was responsible for God knows how many deaths, how many crimes—"

"You must excuse me, Lord Rawcliffe, is it? But do you know the reputation of my own client? Because I'm doing all I can to keep from having that knowledge introduced, praying that jury doesn't know what working for Michel de Gênet entailed for Duhais. There's a delicate balance I must maintain—if we destroy de Gênet's reputation entirely, it makes Duhais look even guiltier for being the henchman, d'accord? Allowing you to get on the stand and ramble about these crimes would very likely be the signature on his death warrant. Bon journée."

Fucking hell. Was he correct? Would my testimony make things worse? "Have you spoken with the police about all the maids who de Gênet brutalized? And Duhais's fiancée—her mother might have been killed by—"

"The domestiques were paid off by Mademoiselle Verger. The truthfulness of their testimony will be called into doubt based on that, at least in a courtroom where they'd be subject to cross-examination. Very likely it would have the adverse effect of indicting Mademoiselle Verger into the plot, as well."

I winced inwardly.

The lawyer sighed. "I'll do my best to reduce the sentence to life imprisonment, but I'm afraid that he's been tried and found guilty through the press, and frankly, even saving his life might be beyond my capabilities. I'm sorry, Lord Rawcliffe, but I have to be in court in a half an hour."

There had to be an equation to save Gilbert's life and keep Aurélie from being arrested, too. God help me, I'd figure it out.

Hopefully, in time.

Back on the street, I realized I was at a loss. I thought about knocking at the Green Carnation for Victoire or Laurent to pour me a stiff drink. Or seven.

The news coverage about Gilbert's guilt had been horribly one-sided, indeed. And they *were* hot to crucify Aurélie as well. The newspapers had been crafting opinion on everything in my life for months.

If so many loud voices hadn't been adamantly against Eiffel's tower, he'd have kept his government funding. Gilbert wouldn't have had a reason to ensnare me in his revenge fantasy. Michel might have had his attention captured by another poor girl.

At least he was dead, the tosser.

I turned onto l'Avenue de l'Opéra, where I'd spotted Gilbert for the first time. I wished I could go back and erase that night and—

God, but I didn't wish to forget Gilbert Duhais.

I'm in love with you.

I gasped with realization. Fucking hell. I was in love with him, too.

My eyes went hot, and my skin buzzed uncomfortably. I couldn't allow him to take the blame to save Aurélie and accept an excruciating sentence. Likely death, if I could believe the signs around me. She'd never forgive herself, and I . . . well, I'd never get over the loss of Gilbert.

A wagon crossed the road in front of me, emblazoned with *L'Expression* in gold lettering. It was one of the newspapers that had shredded Eiffel and Gilbert. I watched it pull up to the pavement. The driver jumped out and tied the horse's bridle to a hitching post before ducking into a nearby storefront.

The name of the paper was scrolled across the window. I followed the wagon driver in, not sure if I was going to blast the editor for destroying so many parts of my life.

Or offer myself up as an alternative sacrifice.

"Can I help you?" A chap wearing a green eyeshade gave me an odd look.

"I demand to speak to someone about the ghastly reporting being done about Aurélie Blancmaison."

He snorted. "And you are?"

"The Earl of Rawcliffe." Oh, it felt good to throw down that title.

"You're the cuckold or what, exactly?" He picked up a pad of paper and gave me an expectant look.

I wasn't there to give the reporter a story, damn it.

"You've got the details entirely wrong. She's my cousin and—"

"Lord Rawcliffe, I've lived and breathed this story for the past five days. I know exactly who you are." He glanced at a clock on the wall and pulled off the headpiece that shaded his eyes from the horrible lighting in his office. "But I'll tell you what. Why don't you and I have a chat, and maybe you can tell Mademoiselle Blancmaison's side of the story? The readers are eager for more information, and no one is willing to give it to us."

I straightened my tie to give myself a moment. Because what if I could change the discourse? Did I dare? I asked his name. "Well, Monsieur Piguet, I'd be happy to. I assume you've already checked with the metropolitan police to interview the maids that Michel de Gênet assaulted? Perhaps looked at the inquest records detailing the inconsistencies in Madame de Gênet's unfortunate riding accident? I was told her solicitors filed for her divorce the day before she died."

Olivier Piguet stopped in his tracks. "I beg your pardon?"

"No? Well, there are six living victims I can help you secure interviews with, as well as give you the names of the unfortunate women de Gênet killed. My cousin wasn't having an affair with anyone. She was the victim of a predatory monster."

Piguet pursed his lips and stared into the distance. Hopefully, he was already drafting a new narrative about the case in his mind.

I kept pressing. "Gilbert Duhais checked in on Mademoiselle Blancmaison before he left to visit me in England, and found my cousin being attacked by his uncle. Michel de Gênet assaulted her twice at the ballet. You can check with the master of dance. She lodged several complaints."

Piguet scratched the words into his notebook, his tongue sticking out of the corner of his mouth. "I can follow up on that." He ran his hand through thick, ashy hair, and an intelligent smile spread across his face. "I'll be damned. So assuming all of this is true—why was Gilbert Duhais spending all those nights at your apartment?" He flicked through the pad in his hand. "According to a Berthe Jeunesse he was there quite often."

Three months ago, Fin Tighe would have run scared when

faced with this question. The fourteenth Earl of Rawcliffe just took a deep breath and smiled. "This is going to be on this evening's front page? I want a guarantee."

He held out his hand for a shake.

"Monsieur Duhais was there to spend the nights with me."

The young journalist blinked a few times. "You're pulling my leg."

I just smiled and shook my head. "Monsieur Piguet, as soon as you print this in your paper, I will become an outlaw in the country of my birth. I can never return to the estate I just inherited because I'd be thrown into prison to serve hard labor for being a homosexual. You have my word of honor that I'm not lying."

Piguet swallowed, hard. "Then why on earth are you telling me this?"

Outside, the horn on an omnibus honked, like a warning. But I knew the risk I was taking.

I never wanted to return to England anyway.

"Because I'm in love with Gilbert Duhais, and if telling the world means that he has a chance to live his life with me and helps to clear my cousin's reputation, then I'll take that gamble."

EPILOGUE

May 1889
Paris

The masses of rhododendrons flanking the walkway were fragrant, and Eleanor stopped to breathe in their scent. A small crowd piled up behind us as we paused on the path toward the massive iron structure.

"Will you go up to the top?" I'd do it again, if she wanted to. I'd been up dozens of times, but I never tired of it.

"Not today. It's magical enough from here." She tucked her arm into mine and smiled. Annabeth's smile. I hadn't lost it forever.

"I'm quite overwhelmed with our tower, Fin." She gestured to the teeming crowd, overflowing to see the sights of l'Exposition Universelle.

She wasn't the only one. Despite all the worries, the tower was a sensational success. Millions of people would be coming in between now and August, and then—hopefully—millions more over the next twenty years. Nearly twelve thousand a day in the past two weeks alone to see what Eleanor and I both referred to as "our tower." I was giddy.

Because Eleanor was Eiffel's foreign investor, bless her.

On a notepad, I scratched out my share of the profit from the tickets each night before I went to bed, pinching myself because it was still so unreal, and I might die with a smile on my face, after all.

Checking my pocket watch, I teased her not to blink. I counted down under my breath until hundreds of opal glass lights all over the tower switched on. It was otherworldly. A triumph of modern man. She gasped along with the thousands of other people around us.

Including me, and I'd seen this spectacle every night for a week. I couldn't keep away for anything.

It matched the joy in my heart. Electric and mystical. Quintessentially Parisian.

Eleanor hid her yawn behind her fan. "All right, my dear boy, I admit I'm tired from the journey. Can we come back tomorrow to see the exhibits? I simply must watch that American cowboy."

Chuckling, I agreed. "And you shall." Buffalo Bill drew huge crowds. But I could afford an expensive seat. *A whole damn stadium of them.*

As we made our way out of the maze of tourists, I spotted a familiar figure clinging to the shadows. He, too, had come to see the tower lit up. Would he speak to me? I had to try.

Moving toward him, I removed my hat respectfully. "Monsieur Eiffel, I congratulate you on your triumph."

His lips twisted into a smile. He held out his hand for a shake. "Dowager Countess Rawcliffe and Lord Rawcliffe, what a pleasure to see you here. It's our triumph. It couldn't have been managed without your rounding up so many investors, as well as your own vital investment."

My already happy mood soared higher than the highest point of the tower.

"No, sir. This tower was going to be built; it was conceived just as we yearned for some symbol in this modern world. To usher in the future and all the possibilities we have yet to discover. The world needs your tower. Paris needs it. And look at how we've all come together, basking in its glory." I lifted my arms, overcome by the magic of science and technology. I remembered what he'd said that day in his office. "It is like you said, *the laws of natural forces always conform to the secret laws of harmony.*"

And wasn't it true?

After all, Gilbert was destined to be in my life, one way or another. The magnetic pull we had couldn't be denied. It would have happened somehow, someway, even if I'd never found my cousins Paul and Aurélie.

Eiffel gave me another hearty shake and then kissed Eleanor's hand before we drifted off, leaving him to stare at his masterpiece.

I gave one last glance at Eiffel's Tower over my shoulder, as if I couldn't see it from nearly every vantage point in the city.

I'd been part of its creation.

We walked a quarter mile before the street was clear enough to call a cab back to the luxurious apartment I still adored. It wasn't far from the Champs de Mars, but it was too much for Eleanor to walk.

As we walked up the single flight to the premier étage, Eleanor said, "This is frightfully pretty. Are there any more for sale in the building?" She ran her gloved hand along the ornate chair rail. "Now that Queen's Chase isn't my home, I'm thinking about moving to Paris. I always found Yorkshire dull."

After letting the world know who I truly was, I wasn't about to get into a fight to keep a house I didn't want to live in. Eleanor and I decided to invite that wretched cousin Warnwood to move in. He was happy to do so. Luckily for me, it had been enough of a scandal when I'd telegraphed my truth to the world. Petitioning Parliament to have the title stripped from me was something dear cousin Warnwood decided would taint the family name even more than I'd done. He contented himself as Viscount Carleton with an exceedingly generous allowance and the understanding that there'd never be an heir to usurp him.

"I'll be sure to ask Stéphanie this evening and let you know."

Stéphanie was making money hand over fist as a real estate mogul. She relished the freedom to make her own fortune on top of what she got from the grand magasin. I assumed we'd see her that evening.

The portrait of Eleanor as a bride hung over the mantel. I'd had it shipped here first thing. I could imagine it was Annabeth, and seeing her every day made her loss a smidgen more bearable.

"Back at last? I worried you might have to meet me at the club. Who wants a glass of champagne?" Gilbert finished knotting his tie and raised an eyebrow.

He came to my side and pressed his mouth to my cheek. I breathed deeply and slipped my hand around his waist, whispered that I loved him. Because I couldn't stop myself. I needed to know that whatever happened, he'd realize how important he was. *Vital*.

I uncorked a bottle he'd chilled all afternoon and refused to laugh at the sultry expression on his pouty lips at the explosion. *Who exactly was the naughty one?*

"Are you sure you don't want to come?" I asked Eleanor, who pooh-poohed the question with a wave of her hand and then another yawn for punctuation.

"I couldn't stay awake another hour for a million pounds." She rose and set her glass down. "Tell our dear Aurélie I'll be there tomorrow, after I restore my energy." She gave us each a kiss. "I'm very excited to hear that chanteuse of ours, Fin."

Eleanor grinned with Annabeth's dimple. "I might even ask that gun-slinging celebrity Annie Oakley to teach me to do the quick-draw." She made a gun with her fingers and shot us both, blowing the imaginary smoke away with a wink before making her way to her bedroom.

Gilbert took a florist's box off the bookcase and presented it, open. Side-by-side white carnations with the edges dyed a bright kelly green.

With a brush across my lips, he pinned mine to my lapel. "Did you think tonight would ever arrive?"

My head shook oh so slowly. "Feels like I've waited my whole life." Hands slid up the back of his skull, his silky hair ruffling under my fingers. I brought his mouth to mine.

Dear Lord, I love this man. I loved the way every kiss still was as exciting as the first. Or better.

I pinned his green carnation on, too.

It was a fine night for a walk, the sky a strange glow from the tower that we hadn't gotten used to yet. Our hands grazed, and I pressed my fingers in between his. We were well known in the neighborhood—after our relationship was splashed across the newspapers it's not like we had reason to be secretive. People might have been disapproving, but at least they'd believed that Gilbert was a hero for rescuing Aurélie from his uncle's violence.

It was a compromise I'd make over and over again just to have saved them both.

We were cognizant that the dark streets were dangerous and were more cautious than we used to be. Yet we didn't hide. We just kept our eyes open. The world might never be safe for the likes of us. But we weren't going to swallow up who we were in fear of what the darkness held.

No Sonny Tolberts would catch us unawares again. No one had concerned themselves further over his disappearance. Like poor Jody and Charlotte. Too many dead in a city the size of Paris to care if another poor person slipped away.

Still, I'd set up a charity for young ballet dancers to receive training based on talent rather than their desperation to take up with any abonnés. Aurélie and Stéphanie were so vigilant in maintaining the foundation's integrity that we planned to expand to more women that autumn.

Gilbert and I arrived on foot twenty minutes later. A less busy section of the Boulevard des Italiens, but still fashionable. The bottom of a Haussmann building, white walls done in the Greek revival style. Columns and plaster statues of gods. Over the top? *That was the point.* If we weren't going to stay in the shadows, we might as well invite everyone else to our party.

Eccentric we might be judged, but we were rich. Between Qualité—the fifty percent Gilbert had left over after giving Stéphanie the half he'd promised as well as control over the store in Paris and the one being built in London—and all of the investments that Eleanor had made in my name, we'd never have to struggle. Not even if the cabaret was a failure.

But it wouldn't be. Not any time soon.

We both stopped and looked up at the blinking lights that spelled out *Triomphe* in red, white, and blue.

We shared a grin. Gilbert put his arm around my hips and hugged me. We'd won. Maybe not everything, because there was so much we'd lost. But we'd shone light under a lot of closed doors. And perhaps they could open, and little by little we could change the world.

The majordomo stood with shoulders back as we cut in front of the line winding down the block and tipped our hats. The sight of Victoire and Laurent in the foyer made it easier to breathe. We shared kisses, murmuring Jody's name. He was with us in spirit. I was sure of it.

At a series of rounded red-leather booths that flanked the large dance floor and stage sat Édouard Hainault and his lover Timothée. They greeted us in the Continental way and made room.

"Lord Rawcliffe and Lord Qualité." Édouard lifted his glass and inclined his head. "To your victoire continuing, my loves." He knew I was back to plain Fin Tighe in the day-to-day life, but he loved to tease.

"All the effort I made to secure him that damn title, and he nearly lost it on a gamble," said Gilbert, taking a drink after raising his eyebrow. It sounded like a joke, and no one besides us needed to know the whole story.

And, in any case, it was the sort of gamble I'd make any day for the same result.

Stéphanie Verger came by in a fuchsia gown with just enough

sparkle to make everyone else's look gaudy. Her arm was wrapped around that ginger-haired Romu she'd eloped with a week after Gilbert's trial had concluded. He'd become almost as dear a friend as she was. They pressed into the booth with us, laughing as loudly as everyone else.

Nine thirty and we signaled for the doors to be opened, and greeted the crowd like guests we'd invited to a private party. A steady stream of glittering people came in, bubbling in riotous happiness overflowing like a bottle of champagne, bottles of which popped all around us like the fireworks to celebrate the tower.

The band struck up the number that signaled the show was about to begin. Multicolored lights clicked on around the stage, and we strolled back to the booth where Victoire had eccentric artist James McNeill Whistler enraptured with tall tales.

Seated on the red leather, Annie Oakley refilled her glass and threw her head back, laughing. I asked her about shooting lessons for Eleanor, which made her laugh harder. She promised to give her fifteen minutes after her show to learn how to hit a target in rapid succession.

Olivier Piguet sent over yet another bottle of champagne. I beckoned for him to sit with us, and he did so with a grin.

"She's utterly nervous to make her stage debut," he said, eyes not leaving the stage.

Gilbert waved away his concern like so much smoke. He and Piguet had become dear friends, and not only because Piguet published various articles Gilbert wrote for the newspaper. "No need to be. She'll be glorious. And besides, she's already been triumphant on the stage. This time, it'll be a piece of pie."

"A piece of cake," I said with a laugh. And she would. Aurélie was meant to be a star.

Her husband agreed. After conducting his own interview of Aurélie and a deep dive into the corruption in the way young dancers were treated, he'd shown enough sensitivity that she'd fallen for him before his career had taken off. It was a delight to watch them grow deeper and deeper in love.

When the curtains drew back and Aurélie took to the stage in a remarkably fashionable red gown, I knew we'd be successful.

Classically trained she might be, but my girl could kick her legs higher than any of them. And sing—who'd have ever thought that? She was beautiful. Always had been, but a little bit of age became her. And so did marriage.

After her song, Aurélie came to our table. She sat on my lap and threw her arms around my neck. She included Gilbert in her hug, and he rubbed her arm.

Her breath was ragged, and she choked on her words. "I can never thank you enough, you fellows. You've all three saved my life."

"No need for thanks, ma belle. That's what families do for each other." Gilbert was always a sentimentalist. Especially about Aurélie.

I snorted. "The real kind of family, you mean. Blood often doesn't count for shite." All three of us knew that well enough.

Aurélie stood and offered her husband a saucy smile. "Mon amour?"

Olivier never had to be asked to dance twice.

Winding my arm around Gilbert's waist, I pulled him closer

so I could smell the ocean-scented cologne on his skin. I could afford it now, too, but it always smelled better on him.

Together, we were a force of nature—not unnaturalle in any way. And together, we harmonized, shared our song with the rest of Paris, with everyone who needed to know they weren't alone, battling forces stronger than themselves.

"Will you dance with me?" I asked, allowing every ounce of happiness to show. "For now?"

Because later, I wanted much more than a dance.

And since we'd made harmony from all of our secrets, I was sure we would.

He cut his eyes to the crowd and then back to me, the lopsided grin lighting up his face as bright as Eiffel's monument that dominated the skyline. We slipped into the chaotic revelry that would put us on the map as sure as the damned tower ever would.

"Toujours, mon vilain."

Always.

I'd bloody well hold him to it.

Fin

ACKNOWLEDGMENTS

Authors can be greedy creatures, monopolizing conversations to dissect plot twists, analyzing the psychology of characters, and rambling on about the finesse of creating the perfect absinthe louche (sorry about that, Em). This book wouldn't exist without the support of so many people, and I'm overwhelmed with the kindness I received.

First, I'm especially grateful to my amazing agent, Caitlin Blasdell, for seeing the potential in this book and being such a fabulous champion!

Enormous thanks to my brilliant editor, Kirsiah Depp, who helped me polish this book way beyond what I hoped it could be—you've been gorgeously supportive and thoughtful. Thanks to the team at Grand Central/Hachette who did so much behind the scenes: Sarah Congdon, who designed the cover, Leena Oropez, Lauren Sum, and Anjuli Johnson. Being a debut author is stressful, and I'm so grateful that everything has been seamless on your end. All your efforts are very much appreciated!

Thank you to my children, Aidan, Emma, Maisie, and Scarlett, who have lovingly tolerated me rabbiting on about "The Paris Book" for the past five years. You've been utter champs.

The book wouldn't have come together without the hand-holding from my critique partner and dear friend Felicia Grossman, who read each chapter as it was drafted (and then again ad nauseam while still managing to add heartfelt inline comments on the ten millionth read). You're a true heroine, darling! Sincere blessings to Deana Birch, who inspired the twist of Aurélie rescuing herself—it was a plot changer and so damned clever. It's time to meet up for drinks in Paris again—soon. And to Rumi Georgieva for providing me with the perfect muse for Fin.

Tremendous thanks to Laura Deck, who offered an open door to her wonderful lake house for R&R and editing. And unconditional friendship that helped more than I can describe. Thanks, too, to Dave Deck, who tolerated me arriving with overnight bags more often than he probably imagined. Wine and pimento cheese are on me next time.

Thank you to Rose Sutherland for all the love and Parisian food advice, and to Maryann Marlowe for the enthusiasm and writerly information. Thanks to Michael Parkyn, Marina Scott, Rachel Berros, Nathan Jones, and Lindsay Burroughs for the friendship and all the support and love!

A special shout-out to my former colleagues and forever friends: James Thompson, Mike Hanley, Mariza Vehab, Marybeth Johnson, Dave Duncan, Dick Anthony, Steve Nigro (my favorite "4 ½"), and Keith Claassen. I wouldn't be in one piece without y'all. Thanks to Craig Seal for the multiple reads and Jill Seal for the cheerleading. Oh, and I can't forget the Happy Hours you listened to the plot twists of the other drama.

ACKNOWLEDGMENTS

You, too, Carri Davis, love you!

Jessica Kovalcik for the last-minute heroism photography; this would have been a fun thing to know about all those years ago at Rocknxs.

A bittersweet thank you to Kerri Goffredi. I miss you every day.

Bill, even though it's awkward to include your ex-husband in the acknowledgments. Yet here we are. Cheers, buddy.

Finally, thank you to my parents, Christine and Mike Marshall, for everything, to my beautiful sister, Melanie Trainer, and to my beloved grandmother, Margaret Stainton Hickman, who inspired so much of this story.

READING GROUP GUIDE

DISCUSSION QUESTIONS

1. Gilbert speaks highly of the French aristocracy in his conversations with Fin and even invites him to a party one night. What role does money play in their affair?

2. Does Fin show more appreciation for his French inherited identity or his English background? Why do you think that is the case?

3. Do you think Fin feels accepted in France? When does he feel comfortable with his identity, and with whom?

4. Gustave Eiffel, similar to his tower, is a commanding figure in Fin's life. How does Eiffel's construction of his

tower aid Fin's contentment or dissatisfaction with high French culture?

5. Throughout the book, Fin constantly caters to Aurélie's needs. Why does Fin feel a constant need to take care of her?

6. Fin has a distant relationship with his family and only contemplates his familial love after Gilbert inquires more about it. How do you think Fin's lack of family care impacts his romantic confusions?

7. What role do women play throughout the story? How do characters like Aurélie, Victoire, and Stéphanie supplement Fin and Gilbert's romantic affair?

8. Toward the end of the book, Fin discovers that he wasn't born out of wedlock. How does this discovery change his view of his family?

9. Why does Gilbert feel a need to accomplish everything his uncle asks him to do? Is Gilbert compensating for something else?

10. How does Aurélie change throughout the book? Does the ending represent her independent growth, or did she require the help of other characters, such as Fin?

AUTHOR Q & A

Q. What inspired you to write this book? Did other books or forms of media inspire you to write this love story?

A. As a child, I was enraptured by ballet dancing. I read everything in my community and school libraries that I could get my hands on. Noel Streatfield's *Ballet Shoes* was battered and dog-eared (and I threw some Easter eggs in for any other fans!). When I was teaching history, I enjoyed finding snippets of interest for my students to connect to actual people in the times we were learning about, rather than just the big power players. I came across an article about how the dancers in the Paris Opéra were trained like courtesans of a sort, and that all the beautiful pictures I'd loved by Degas were showcasing this exploitative system. I knew I'd be writing a book with that woven in.

One of my grandmothers was a World War II "war bride" who visited her large family in Goole, Yorkshire, each summer. Sometimes, she took my sister and me along, and we'd stay for multiple weeks. I spent much of my time strolling around, exploring. My aunt Pauline Stainton introduced me to a family mystery:

my grandmother's grandparent (great-grandparent?) claimed to have been the child of the unmarried "housekeeper" (we've all watched *Downton Abbey*, so my guess is someone lower in the staff pecking order) and a son of the house. Twelve-year-old me was entranced with the romance of that. Adult me and my son were abandoned by his father and realized that was hardly a story with any romance.

I was exploring perceptions of my sexuality when I drafted this novel, and as a closeted teacher in the South, it just felt easier to take a step away and have Fin and Gilbert be queer men rather than women. It was less likely to raise eyebrows and tie this directly to my experience. Plus, it's clear that men in the 1880s had some power advantages over women, and I wanted to feel free to explore the what-ifs of revenge and faking identities without being hamstrung by the realities of the inequalities of men and women through my main character. However, while writing, I realized I was exploring the various roles of women in France of the 1880s, and using Fin's lens as he wakes up to his own privilege in the face of the unequal treatment of the women in his life, even as he's grappling with the unfairness of his own position. My eyes opened at the same time and got me to be more honest about myself.

Q. Why did you choose to make many of the characters members of the French and British aristocracy? Would their experiences have been different if they were of a different socioeconomic class?

A. To me, the power—or lack thereof—and status aren't necessarily the same for different characters working inside the same system. For example, Fin absolutely had more advantages than his cousin Paul by having a powerful father. He was well educated, fed, and clothed, and had the security of knowing he had a place to sleep at night. Paul is undeniably a villain, but not because he's poor. Aurélie also makes decisions that society deems immoral based on her lack of power inside the system, but in context, we agree with her choices.

Victoire had been raised as an aristocrat of sorts—she's the only character who was in that situation from birth—but it didn't provide any security for her once she was cast out by her father. Michel de Gênet was raised in an intact lower-middle-class family, but "pulled himself up by his bootstraps" in a way that many see as the pinnacle of success. Yet, he's still a monster. Stéphanie came from a monied family, and lost all of it when her mother married. However, she still has some privileges because of her position in society.

My intent was for the characters to be judged on their actions and reactions to situations outside of their control, rather than their status at birth.

Q. **What were the differences between being queer in France and being queer in Britain in the mid-1800s? Why was it important for you to explore queer identity during this time period?**

A. In some ways, it was vastly different, even if society at large might have felt the same contempt for LGBTQIA+ individuals. Under the Napoleonic Code, private sexual acts between men were basically ignored *legally*. Social conventions were not so lax.

It was a "don't ask, don't tell" situation where queer men needed to be on their guard as they could be fined for obvious interactions between themselves, would almost definitely be shunned by many in society if they were caught. But things began to change to the point that queer men from the rest of Europe and America considered Paris a haven.

In 1885, Great Britain passed what became known colloquially as the Labouchere Amendment that widened the older laws criminalizing provable sodomy to include any acts of "gross indecency," which could be a simple wink at another man across a pub. The amendment changed the standing laws from the penalty of hanging to (considered much more lenient) up to two years in prison working hard labor. That charge could be a death sentence. Oscar Wilde, for example, died a few years after completing his grueling time in prison.

It was important to me because I'm fascinated with the idea that people are similar over time and place. Members of the queer community didn't spring up in the recent past after a hiatus since the Roman era. And we know bans on morality don't make people in a society follow the rules imposed on them. I believe it's clear that there was forward momentum in individual rights in the context of sexual expression that was quashed again in the 1930s. I had no idea until I started researching, so I wanted to explore and share what I found.

Q. How did you come up with such a varied cast of characters (from Aurélie the ballet dancer, to Fin the engineer, to Victoire the cabaret dancer)? Where did you pull your inspiration from?

A. I tend to do a lot of character work before starting to draft. I want to know why people make the choices they make and what their secret dreams are. The things that get them out of bed in the morning when life gets really tough.

So many of my friends are queer, and I wanted to represent many facets of that community rather than a stereotype, because everyone is an individual, with varied reasons for their decisions.

Maybe my own struggles with math (unless we're talking about figuring discounts, where I am a pro) prompted me to create Fin as an engineer. But honestly, I feel that he grew up without any sure footing, and the finiteness of math gave him something that wasn't going to change on him.

Victoire is my hero and is an ode to the many trans men and women I've loved in my life. Aurélie was living what I always thought was my dream life—until I realized that there were so many darker aspects to the life of a ballerina in that time and place.

Q. Why did you choose to center your story around the construction of the Eiffel Tower?

A. Would you believe that was the last piece of the plot puzzle? Fin was an engineer looking for a job, and the controversy behind the tower's construction was absolutely news to me when I was researching. I kept asking everyone who had the misfortune of casually inquiring about my writing if they had any idea that the French really didn't want the thing to be built, and it was universal ignorance in my corner of the world. It was a delight to delve into the idea that one of the most iconic landmarks on earth almost didn't come to pass because the consensus was that it was a terrible eyesore.

I'd never been someone who dreamed of seeing the Eiffel Tower in person…until I wrote this book. When I finally got to Paris and stood underneath it, I felt so proprietorial. I had the opportunity to take my three daughters there last fall, and they were as enchanted as I was. It's simply a lovely piece of architecture, and I'm so happy to have put my own stamp on its history.

Q. How much research did you have to conduct for this book? Were there certain topics that were harder to find comprehensive research on?

A. In general, I am a research fiend. And I love nonfiction. I can spend days watching documentaries on things that most people can't manage ten minutes of. I love reading (and highlighting) books that might turn over one little nugget about a topic. I never know what might trigger a plot twist or character trait.

My French is not fabulous, even though I took it for years. Luckily, I can read it better than speak it, which was helpful because so much of the information I needed specifically about the tower was in French. And even then, I didn't find much that was about the investment scheme Gustave Eiffel came up with. I'm hoping that if I made any egregious mistakes, people will remember this was a work of fiction!

Q. What is one thing you wish for readers to know about you?

A. I struggle with ADHD and severe anxiety. I muddle through as best as I can, and try to use the hyper focus aspects of ADHD when I'm writing and researching. But really, I want people to know that I'm human, and likely made some blunders when writing this, but they came from a place of love, compassion, and goodwill.

I've lived through a lot of difficult situations, so I do my best to reserve judging people for slip-ups. Also, this makes me chuckle—maybe it's me in a nutshell. I had a co-worker once verbally attack me for being too nice. She said she was tired of my "Pollyanna Bulls***." I was crushed. A few months later, she said that, okay, she was taking back the BS part. I really was Pollyanna-ish, but it was sincere.

Q. When you're not writing, how do you like to spend your time?

A. I get fixated on research when I'm plotting a new book. I spend months discovering my characters and think of all the ways I can torment them. When I'm not doing that, I get on crafting kicks (I love re-creating things I saw in a store but can't afford), enjoy repurposing furniture, singing off-key in the car at the top of my voice, and cooking. I can't bake worth a damn, but I simply love cooking for dinner parties. I really enjoy spending time with friends and then recharging my batteries because all the fun just wore me out. And large bodies of water. I don't swim really well, so I don't need to get in the water, but just looking at it calms my soul.

MASKS

Most people have compartments that they divvy up their lives: work, relationships, parenting, school friends. I always guessed that the more overlap of the niches, the more comfortable the life of those lucky individuals. But some of us have ever-increasing slices of life that never seem to join up like a neat Venn diagram. It's exhausting. Trying to remember how much information I've shared with different people in different spheres in my life hasn't been because I enjoy being secretive, but rather because I'm concerned with the rejection my vulnerability might receive if I'm completely straightforward.

On the surface, it might not make sense that I've written a book about a young, queer engineer—especially the engineering bit. I'm worthless at math. But, like Fin, I've lived my life in a fragile balance of cubbyholes. It made sense to me, as a historical fiction author, to create a character whose entire life experience has been a contortion act of masking his true emotions in order to keep those around him comfortable.

Fin lives in a world of gray from his upbringing in a poor household to his ritzy boarding school experiences, where he is neither an entitled peer nor quite a working-class servant's child. He has all of his physical needs met, but his emotional life is wholly inadequate aside from the loving relationship he has with his sister. When he relocates to France and explores his sexuality, he is again left in the space in-between. Unlike Victoire, who bravely lives her life in her identity, and Jody, who's comfortable enough in his skin to open a queer cabaret, Fin keeps his emotional world very separate from everything else, hiding fundamental pieces of his personhood from nearly everyone in order to be accepted.

I totally understand that feeling.

When I first encountered the term *bisexual* in the late eighties/early nineties, it was usually the punch line of a joke. The idea that it could mean me was too frightening to face because I still thought in terms of the binaries of needing to declare my allegiance to *this* or *that* when—like Fin—I'm someone who lives my life in the gray areas of *both*.

I had a dear friend in high school who jumped "out of the closet" with gusto and became a celebrity in local drag venues. I was his (he still identifies as male) trusty sidekick and found increasing comfort in the safety of queer nightclubs. There was no sense of "typical" or "normal" that I had to achieve to find acceptance. I could dance and flirt with men and women and dig into what made me *me*. I lived my early twenties life in the progressive/alternative/goth club scene, which didn't force me to choose a role. I had short-short hair but dressed like a vamp. Dated guys in eyeliner and skirts. I still wore a mask, but the sense of theatrics made it exciting rather than expected. And I could also change it anytime I wanted without upsetting anyone.

Years later, when I circled back to my lifelong dream of novel-writing, I stumbled across an article discussing the patronage system of the Paris Opéra Ballet. It happened to have been in place at the same time there was a sexual revolution of sorts in Paris and Berlin, when clubs catering to queer and queer-friendly clientele sprang up like mushrooms. The period of western European history from the late Victorian era through the Great Depression was vibrant with explorations of sexuality and self-expression. The nebulous legality of homosexuality was being tested nightly in cosmopolitan venues.

I dug into researching all I could of the artistic lifestyle of the underbelly of Belle Époch Paris. W. C. Morrow's *Bohemian Paris of To-day* [sic] was invaluable in painting pictures of the glorious licentiousness of unencumbered young men and women of the creative world. *Absinthe: History in a Bottle* by Barnaby Conrad III painted the ravages of addiction to the common hallucinogen. Absinthe was so cheap and readily available that its use became rampant—so much so that it eventually was the only alcohol to be banned by multiple countries. A deep dive into the artwork of Edgar Degas featuring ballerinas and abonnés was much darker than the pretty dancers I'd seen as a child. How could all of this be in such plain sight, and yet mostly unexplored in modern popular culture?

At first, I tried to write the book from Aurélie's point of view. I was obsessed with ballet for most of my life, and it made sense that she would be my protagonist. Writing women characters in contemporary fiction—to say nothing of former times—comes with a deep exploration of gender roles and how society views womanhood. Right up my alley. But when fleshing out her story, I'd based her cousin Fin's lineage on a piece of family mythology of a housekeeper great-grandmother and the grandly titled father of her illegitimate child. Fin kept speaking to me louder. Yelled, even. Perhaps it was because he wore so many masks that I could easily identify with him, and the parallels of the come-as-you-are openness of the LGBTQIA+ community of my own young adulthood felt starkly obvious.

I chose to write about a character who understands he has the privilege of his white, male identity, but who also would suffer greatly if he makes a wrong decision that would leave him open to persecution. Perhaps I subconsciously wished for the courage to vicariously live through what happens to someone increasingly anxious about exposure who finally must choose to throw all his cards on the table and live with the outcome, no matter what it might be.

Fin—like me—had one foot inside the door of the freedom of the Green Carnation cabaret and he just needed a push (or a swift kick in the rear) to allow himself the opportunity to live his whole life as *himself* rather than a man he hoped would be easier for everyone in the periphery of his life.

Nearly a hundred and fifty years later, it's still a struggle to embrace the enormity of allowing your greater community to see your true self. I wholeheartedly thank the real life Fins and Gilberts for paving the way. I'm in even more awe of the Victoires and Laurents who faced even more prejudice due to identity and race. And I weep for the Jodys who are still brutalized and murdered just for existing.

As a high school teacher, I mentored the Gay/Straight Alliance club and was continuously proud of the students who refused to hide themselves away to satisfy the bigots. I wish there had been something like that when I was their age, because perhaps I would have been kinder to myself for not fitting into a clear role. I'm sure there were questions about my sexuality, but though I supported the students and was open about writing queer novels, I didn't expose my identity. And that was my choice, I suppose. No one should be forced to out themselves. Now I feel as though I let them down.

If a privileged woman like me was too frightened to be honest to the people in my personal life, how can I expect younger people—more vulnerable and at much higher risk—to understand that they don't have to hide themselves away behind masks and pretend to be something they are not? Over the past few years, I've finally been brave enough to take off my own mask and let many people know who I am.

But for the rest of you, just in case you hadn't guessed it yet: I'm here, and I'm queer.

ABOUT THE AUTHOR

Maureen Marshall is a former history teacher, whose passion is wandering through the old parts of European cities. She has lived in Scotland, France, Sweden, and most of the mid-Atlantic states where people can catch blue crabs.

YOUR
BOOK
CLUB
RESOURCE

VISIT
GCPClubCar.com

to sign up for the **GCP Club Car** newsletter,
featuring exclusive promotions, info on other
Club Car titles, and more.

GRAND
CENTRAL

FOREVER

TWELVE

LEGACY
LIT

balance